Red Light

Praise for *Red Light*

"The characters and sense of place are intensely real, and the complexities of the relationships resonate with authenticity."—*Pittsburgh Tribune Review*

"Parker's latest sizzles along, an infectious blend of atmosphere, action, and passion."—*Publishers Weekly*

"An admirably constructed police procedural that's also an unsparing examination of a gallant woman's search for a moral code worth the commitment."—*Philadelphia Inquirer*

"Parker's book is far more moving than thrillers have to be."—*Los Angeles Times*

"T. Jefferson Parker is among the best of the new breed of crime novelists."—*American Way*

"What makes his novels memorable are always the complex characters. An excellent thriller."—*Booklist*

"*Red Light* is a police procedural that is in a league with Ridley Pearson and Michael Connelly—which is as good as the genre gets. Parker does a fine job with investigative detail and has crafted well-drawn and memorable side characters."—*Flint* (MI) *Journal*

Red Light

T. JEFFERSON PARKER

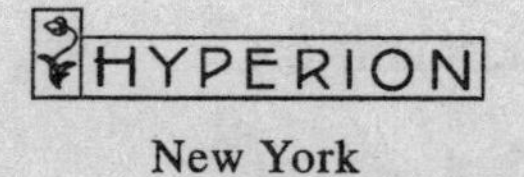

New York

Printed in the United States of America. For information address: Hyperion, 77 West 66th Street, New York, New York 10023-6298.

ISBN 0-7868-8975-6

FIRST MASS MARKET EDITION

10 9 8 7 6 5 4 3 2 1

For Paul and Jenny

Red Light

Prologue

You might not have liked Aubrey Whittaker. She acted superior. She walked as if she were the most beautiful woman on Earth, which she wasn't. She didn't say very much. She was tall but wore heels anyway, and if she finally did say something, you felt like a driver getting a ticket. Her eyes were blue and infinitely disappointed in you. She was nineteen.

She let him come to her place again that night, something that had only happened once before. Strictly against policy. But he was different than the rest, different in ways that mattered. In her life she had learned to read men, who were as easy to understand as street signs: Caution, Yield, Stop. But did you ever really know one?

Aubrey had chosen a small black dress, hose with a seam up the back, heels with ankle straps and a string of pearls. No wig, just her regular hair, which was blond and cut short, sticking up like a boy's. The lipstick was apple red.

She made him dinner. She could only cook one thing well, so she cooked it. And a salad, rolls from the bakery, a pot of the good French roast coffee he liked, a dessert. Flowers in a squat round crystal vase that had cost a lot of money.

They sat across from each other at the small table. Aubrey gave D.C. the seat with the view of the Pacific. "D.C." was the abbreviation for Dark Cloud, the nickname she'd invented to capture his pessimism about human nature. It was an ironic nickname, too, because D.C. wasn't dark to look at, but light, with a broad, tanned face, a neat mustache, sharp eyes and a chunk of heavy blond hair that fell over his forehead like a schoolboy's. He was quick to smile, although it was usually a nervous smile. He was taller than her by a good three inches and strong as a horse, she could tell. He told stupid jokes.

She told him he could hang his gun on the chair, but he left it holstered tight against his left side, farther around his back than in the movies, the handle pointing out. Whatever, she thought. The idea of safety pleased her, made her feel compliant in a genuine way. Aubrey Whittaker rarely allowed herself a genuine feeling, couldn't always tell them from the ones she portrayed.

They talked. His eyes rarely strayed from her face, and they were always eager to get back. Hungry eyes. When dinner was over he sat there a moment, wiping the silverware with his napkin. He was fastidious. Then he left, at exactly the time he'd told her he'd leave. Off to see a man about a dog, he said. Another little joke of theirs.

At the door she put her arms around him and hugged him lightly, setting her chin against the top of his shoulder, leaning her head against his ear for just a moment. She could feel the tension coming off him like heat off a highway. She thought that the kind of guy she wanted would be a lot like D.C. Then she straightened and smiled and shut the door behind him. It was only ten minutes after ten.

She flipped on the kitchen TV to an evangelist, put the dishes in the sink and ran water over them. She watched a car roll out of the parking area below, brake lights at the speed bump. It might have been D.C.'s big, serious four-door or it might not have been.

Aubrey felt warm inside, like all her blood had heated up a couple of degrees, like she was just out of a hot bath or had just drank a big glass of red wine. She shook her head and smile lines appeared at the edges of her apple-red lips. It's just unbelievable, girl, she thought, what you've done with your life. Nineteen going on a hundred. You finally find a guy you can halfway stand, he trembles when you touch him through his clothes and you let him drive away.

Oh that you would kiss me, with the kisses of your mouth!

Song in the Bible.

I sucked you off in a theater.

Song on the radio.

Has everything changed, or nothing?

She rinsed the dishes, dried her hands and worked in some lotion. The fragrance was of lavender. Through the window she saw the black ocean and the pale sand and the white rush where the water broadened onto the beach then receded.

In the middle of the living room Aubrey stood and looked out at the water and the night. Thinking of the different shades of black, she pried off her high heels, then got down on all fours. Balance. She could smell the lavender. From there she was eye level to the arm of the black leather sofa.

Tentatively she placed her left hand out. Tentatively she raised her right knee and slid it forward. Then the hard part, the transfer of weight to her other hand and the moment of peril as the left knee came up to support her.

She wavered just a little, but when her left leg settled beneath her she was okay and very focused because she had to repeat the whole complex procedure again. Her doctor friend, the shrink, had advised her to do this. She had never learned. She had walked at eleven months.

Her doctor friend had said that for an adult to develop fully, to form certain concepts, especially mathematical ones, she needed to know how to crawl.

Then she heard the knock at the door. A flash of embarrassment went through her as she realized what she was: a six-foot woman in a short black dress crawling across her living room through the scent of lavender.

She sprung up and walked over. "Who's there?"

"Just me again, Aubrey—"

It was a little hard to hear, with all the cars roaring by on Coast Highway.

"—Your Dark Cloud."

She flipped the outside light switch and looked through the peephole. The bug bulb must have finally burned out because all she saw was one corner of the apartment building across the alley laced with Christmas lights, and the tiny headlights out on Coast Highway, miniaturized in a fish-eye lens clouded with moisture. She hadn't replaced that bulb in months.

When she opened the door she was smiling because she half expected his return, because she knew he was in her control now. And because she was happy.

Then her smile died from the inside out and she formed her last thought: *No.*

Chapter One

"Out of the way, please. Sheriff's investigator. Come on now. *Out.*"

Merci Rayborn ducked under the ribbon and continued down the walk. Her heart was beating fast and her senses were jacked up high, registering all at once the cars hissing along Coast Highway to her left, waves breaking on the other side of the building, the citizens murmuring behind her, the moon hanging low over the eastern hills, the smell of ocean and exhaust, the night air cool against her cheeks, the walkway slats bending under her duty boots. She figured a place like this, oceanfront in San Clemente, would run you two grand a month and you still got termites in your walkway and spiderwebs high in the porch corners.

Or maybe you got worse.

Two patrolmen were talking to two paramedics, all four of whom nodded and stepped aside. Merci stopped short of the entryway alcove to 23 Wave Street and looked at the door. It was open about two inches. It was painted a flat Cape Cod gray. The red splatter a foot above the doorknob looked wet in the overhead light, a yellow-tinted bulb so as not to draw insects.

"Sergeant, the neighbor heard a disturbance, suspected something was wrong. He saw the presumed blood. He called us at ten forty-five. We got here at ten fifty-five. We knocked, identified ourselves, no response. The door was ajar. I proceeded inside, found the body where it is right now, notified my partner. Together we searched the apartment for any other possible victims. Negative. And for a perpetrator. Negative again. I checked for vitals, and found the victim deceased. Then we called it in, sealed it off."

"What else did you do inside?"

"Nothing. I closed the door to the same approximate position I found it in. Not using the knob."

"Did you touch any of the light switches?"

"Yes. I forgot that. Forgot to tell you that."

"This outdoor light, was it on when you got here?"

"Bug light, affirmative."

"Was the door ajar when the neighbor first came down?"

"That was his statement."

"See if he'll let us set up shop in his place. If he says no, do it anyway."

"Yes."

"Start an Order of Entry Log, fill it in and fasten it to

this wall somehow. Nobody gets in but the coroners and Zamorra. Nobody."

"Yes, Sergeant."

The paramedics were leaning against the walkway railing but stood up straight when Merci turned to them. They were young and handsome and looked to Merci like TV actors.

"We went in, examined her and came back out," one offered. "We didn't defib or try CPR. She was cold, blood already draining down, extremities in early rigor. I turned on the lights just inside the door there, then turned them off. Looks like gunshot."

Merci looked at her watch: 11:40, Tuesday, December 11. She gloved up, then toed open the door with her boot.

Muted light shone from inside. Merci saw a kitchen, a small TV screen flickering, a dining-room table with flowers, a sliding glass door beyond the table. But what drew her attention lay just inside the arc of the door she now held open with one elbow: a young woman in a black dress, arms thrown casually back like someone deep in sleep, her face peaceful and unmarked and inclined slightly toward the sliding glass door behind her. Her chest and stomach were still wet with blood, which looked black in the weak light. The blackness had progressed onto the pale carpet on both sides of her.

Merci knelt down and placed two of her right fingers on the woman's jugular vein. She believed that she owed hope to the dead, even if the dead were beyond it.

She pulled a little flashlight from her pocket and found the hole in the dress, below the left breast but close to center, straight over the heart. She looked for another but found none.

The neighbor said nothing about hearing a gunshot. Merci retraced her steps to the front door and pushed it closed with her boot. The paramedics who looked like actors watched her, a fade-out.

She stood between the body and the dining room. No signs of forced entry or struggle, so far. She noted that the table had been set for two. A pair of seductive high heels stood near the couch, facing her, like a ghost was standing in them, watching. The apartment was still, the slider closed against the cool December night. Good for scent. She closed her eyes. Salt air. Baked fowl. Coffee. Goddamn rubber gloves, of course. A whiff of burned gunpowder? Leather. Maybe a trace of perfume, or the flowers on the table—gardenia, rose, lavender? And, of course, the obscenity of spilled blood—intimate, meaty, shameful.

She listened to the waves. To the traffic. To the little kitchen TV turned low: an evangelist bleating for money. To the clunk of someone on the old walkway. To her heart, fast and heavy in her chest. Merci felt most alive when working for the dead. She'd always loved an underdog.

In the bedroom she found a purse with a wallet. There was a thick pinch of hundreds in the wallet, some twenties, several credit cards and a driver's license. Aubrey Whittaker. Nineteen.

The woman was a girl and the girl was only a little over half her own age. The year Aubrey Whittaker was born, Merci was a junior in high school. The year Aubrey Whittaker was murdered, Merci was an Orange County Sheriff Department sergeant, Homicide Detail, age 36. A single mother. A once proud woman recovering from a broken heart, and from what police psychologists like to call critical incident stress. She'd painted up her exterior, but inside she was still a wreck.

Aubrey's slaughtered youth made Merci sad and angry, but many things about her career made her feel that way. She looked out the bedroom window toward Coast Highway. The building next door already had its Christmas lights up, a neat outline of tiny white bulbs blinking at random. On the big dresser across from the bed Merci found a jewelry box filled with expensive-looking rings and necklaces. Under the lamp there was a greeting card propped up, this one with a soft-focus photograph of a tree on a hillside. She bent and read it without touching it.

In the muted blue sky were the words: *In God's World* . . . The quip was completed inside: *There's a special place for Friendship.* It was signed: *Sincerely, Your D. C.*

She could hear the footsteps on the walkway, louder now. She listened as they came toward the door and stopped. Voices.

She went to the door and looked through the peephole. She saw Paul Zamorra in the elliptical foreground, and the two Coroner's Autopsy Team techs behind him. When she opened the door her partner met her with his joyless black eyes, then stepped inside. The techs followed him.

They all looked at Aubrey Whittaker. Zamorra walked to her side, knelt down and looked at her some more. He brought gloves from the pocket of his sport coat, worked them on. "Get to it, guys," he said. "We've got about twenty minutes before the hordes thunder in."

• • •

The hordes thundered in: three More patrol units bearing six deputies; the paramedic supervisors; the Coroner's Investigation Team; the rest of the Coroner's Autopsy Team; the county pathologist; the crime-scene scientists; the crime-scene technicians; the criminalists; the assistant district attorney and two of his investigators, all trudging down the wooden walkway to Aubrey Whittaker's place under the drone of two Sheriff Department choppers that circled overhead and beamed unhopeful shafts of light into the city below.

The police reporters came next.

And, as always, concerned citizens multiplied as the minutes wore on, drawn from the darkness by the flashing lights of the prowl cars.

Close neighbors compared notes on the apparently deceased girl who came and went from 23 Wave Street at late hours: very attractive, well dressed, very tall, quiet. There was firm disagreement on what color, style or length of hair she had.

Outsiders gathered what they could, speculated. Most everyone was bundled up in something, arms around themselves or each other, blowing on their hands, puffs of breath coming out when they spoke. Surfers in hooded Mexican ponchos leaned against their little trucks drinking tall beers, slurring their vowels.

• • •

Merci Rayborn at first admitted only five people into number 23. Two were the best crime-scene people she'd ever worked with—Criminalist Lynda Coiner and Crime-Scene Investigator Evan O'Brien. They were standing near the door when she finally opened it, knowing she'd need them first.

Then, the assistant DA and his man. The People. They were the ones she'd bring her case to, the ones for whom she was really gathering evidence. It didn't hurt that they were smart, quiet and knew the drill. Last, the coroner's investigator, mainly for the body temp, which would help them with time of death, and the body cavities, which can leak evidentiary fluids into the transport bags, complicating the job of the lab pathologists.

And everyone else, thought Merci, can stay the hell out for half an hour. Let my people work.

While they worked, Merci and Zamorra toured the apartment. It was an upscale interior in a downscale building: good carpet, leather furniture, recessed lighting aimed to dramatize good prints of Kahlo and O'Keeffe, Hockney and Basquiat. Over the expansive black leather sofa in the living room hung a painting she'd never seen before. It was ghostly but vibrant at the same time, a little too crime-lab for an ocean-view room, in her opinion. It was a Rembrandt of someone raising somebody else from the dead.

Good luck, she thought. She had tried it herself, twice.

Zamorra spoke occasionally into a tiny tape recorder. Merci, as always, wrote her observations into a small notebook with a blue cover.

She wrote: *Aubrey Whittaker, what did you do?*

But between the contents of Aubrey's closet—provocative clothes and lots of them—and the contents of a leather-bound calendar in her purse—a blizzard of dates with a blizzard of people listed only by initials, coded notes in the margins, phone numbers all over it—Merci came to suspect that Aubrey's profession was one of the oldest. The 240-count box of condoms Zamorra found beside a pair of thigh-high leather boots in the bottom of the closet seemed to confirm it.

Nineteen and a real pro.

The bed was neatly made. There was a Bible open on the stand beside it. A crucifix hung on one of the bedroom walls. And the damned evangelist on TV.

Zamorra stared at Merci. It hurt. Zamorra's newlywed bride had been diagnosed with a brain tumor just two months ago; since that day his sharp face, once sly and charming, had taken on an expression of increasingly resigned menace. She was worried about him but didn't think she knew him well enough to question or intrude. Good fences made good neighbors and Zamorra's fence seemed excellent: He said almost nothing about anything. She was going to talk to a doctor about him.

"I saw her yesterday," Zamorra said.

Merci felt her heart rise, settle. "Yesterday. Where?"

"Some of the vices were huddling with her at Pedro's. I took it she was a call girl they were going to chum with. I sat at the counter, got a number four and didn't ask."

"Who in vice?"

"Kathy Hulet and your tall blond friend."

"Mike?"

"Yeah. Mike McNally."

"I'll be damned."

"We all are."

"It's a matter of timing. Let's go see the neighbor."

On her way out of number 23 Merci asked Lynda Coiner if they'd found any brass.

"None yet," she said. "But if it's here, we will."

• • •

The neighbor was Alexander Coates. He lived downstairs, three units over, in number 2. He wore baggy black nylon pants with elastic at the ankles, a scoop-neck T-shirt and a red silk robe. Athletic shoes, new. Short gray hair in a widow's peak, neat gray beard, wide gray eyes. He asked them to sit. In the fireplace, gas flames huffed over ceramic logs. Wooden letters on the mantel spelled NOEL. Merci smelled a familiar green aroma, masked by a floral spray.

"I'm devastated by this," he said. "Aubrey was such a sweet girl. So young and good and . . . oh, I guess you could say mixed-up."

"Let's start with what you saw and heard," Merci suggested.

Coates looked at Zamorra. "Can I get you coffee, cocoa, anything?"

"No."

Coates exhaled, looked into the fire, began. He was home alone tonight. Around eight-thirty he had heard footsteps on the wooden walkway above. He heard a knock upstairs—Aubrey Whittaker's place, number 23. A moment later he heard the door shut. Nothing of consequence, then, until a little after ten o'clock, when he heard Aubrey Whittaker's door shut again, and footsteps going back down the upper walkway in the direction from which they had come earlier.

"How could you tell her door from number twenty-four or twenty-two?" asked Merci.

"From living here eighteen years. I've listened to lots of people come and go. You know."

Yes, she did know. Because she could imagine Alexander Coates. You've waited for lots of dates, she thought.

You've waited and listened to their footsteps and wondered how they'd turn out. You can tell a lot about a man by the way he walks.

"All right. Next."

"Next, at approximately ten-fifteen, I heard footsteps coming down the walkway again, in the same direction. I heard them stop at Aubrey's. I heard the door open. Then, immediately after the door opened, or almost immediately, I heard a loud thump, like something heavy hitting the floor. Then the door closed. Not a slam, but . . . forcefully. Nothing for a minute or two. Then, thumping on the floor again. It was like the first thump, but continuous, like moving furniture or a fight or a struggle of some kind. It lasted for maybe a minute. Then quiet again. Then footsteps going back down the walkway toward the stairs."

"Did you look?" asked Merci.

"No. I was in the bath."

"Did you hear a gunshot, a car backfiring?"

"Nothing like that."

"Did you think of calling the police?" asked Zamorra.

Coates looked at Zamorra with his wide gray eyes, then back into the fire. "No. None of the noises I heard were alarming. None were loud or seemed to indicate trouble. They were just noises. My policy, Detectives, my personal belief on such matters is that privacy should be honored. Unless disaster is . . . well, you know, happening right in front of you."

"But when you got out of the bath, you decided to go to her door?"

"Correct. When I got there—this would have been around ten forty-five, I saw her door was open."

Coates sat forward, set his elbows on his knees, rested his head in his hands. "I thought it was blood on the door. The door was open maybe . . . six inches. I did not touch it or look past it. I literally raced back to my home and dialed nine-one-one immediately. I didn't know what to do with myself. I went back upstairs and looked at the door again. I said her name, foolishly perhaps. I came back down here. I paced the floor for what seemed like hours. The young officers arrived at exactly ten fifty-six."

Merci watched Alexander Coates weep into his hands. Experience had taught her to keep a witness talking and thinking instead of crying. Tears cleanse the memory as well as the eyes.

"You did all right, Mr. Coates."

"Did I really?"

"Absolutely. Now, when you went up to number twenty-three the first time, was Aubrey Whittaker's porch light on or off?"

The sniffling stopped. "On."

"And the second time?"

"On as well."

"Did you hear cars coming or going from the parking lot during this time?"

"Yes. But there's the Coast Highway traffic, so the sounds get mixed up. I can't really help you there. You learn not to hear cars, after eighteen years on Coast Highway."

Half an hour later they were almost finished with Alexander Coates. He said that Aubrey Whittaker rarely had visitors that he noticed. He said that he and Aubrey sometimes talked in the laundry room by the office, because neither worked days, so they washed their clothes in the slow hours. She had gorgeous sad eyes and a sharp sense of humor. She never mentioned irate boyfriends, stalking ex-husbands or enemies of any kind. She was not, in his opinion, hard or mean-spirited. However, in his opinion, she was alone and on a journey, searching for something in her life she had not found yet. It was Coates's impression that Aubrey was an escort of some kind. She drove a dark red, late-model Cadillac.

Merci nodded at this summation, again wondering her way into Alexander Coates. Years ago, a wise old mentor had told her that putting herself in another's shoes would make her a better detective and a better person. She had absolutely no knack for it, and she didn't believe him then. She'd never seen a reason to try to understand people she didn't like in the first place, which was almost everyone. But the old guy, Hess, had been right: In the two years, three months and twenty-two days he'd been dead, Merci had worked hard at this, and she'd learned a few things she might not have learned otherwise.

Such as, if you spent eighteen years in the same apartment, listening to your neighbors and their lovers come and go, you got good at it.

"Mr. Coates, those two arrivals you heard upstairs, they were the footsteps of men, correct?"

"Yes." A confessional glance and nod.

"The same man, or two different ones?"

"Oh, different men, certainly. I was going to tell you that if you didn't ask."

"How sure are you of that?"

"Well, if you hear two voices, you know there are two people. Same with footsteps."

"What else about them, by the sound of them?"

Zamorra aimed a look her way but said nothing.

Coates settled his bottom into his chair, readying himself for his presentation. Eighteen years of anecdotal data, Merci thought, about to find its way into a thesis.

"The first? Heavy, but not overweight. Not in a hurry. He was light on his feet, but you can't fool the boards. Pounds are pounds. Young and probably athletic. And familiar. Familiar with the area. He was wearing hard-soled shoes or boots. Not cowboy boots, they have an entirely different sound. I pictured a young businessman coming home from work, happy to be home, eager to see his wife or his lover. When he left he was . . . reluctant. He wished he wasn't leaving, but he had to."

Zamorra was staring at the floor, his pen in his hand.

Coates looked at Zamorra with concern, made an internal decision, turned his attention back to Merci.

"The second? A much lighter man. He was young also, light on his feet, quick. Soft shoes. In somewhat of a hurry. I couldn't tell if he was familiar with the area or not. He left much more slowly than he came. He sounded . . . unsteady. Uncertain. I think I remember him pausing, about halfway down. I may have imagined that. I can't swear to it. I pictured him as a young man eager to see someone. Eager to get there, get what he wanted, then eager to leave. You know, an impatient young buck on his way to the next thing. When he paused, I saw him realizing he'd forgotten something. But he didn't go back."

Coates sighed and looked into the fire.

Zamorra abruptly shut off his tape recorder, cast his black eyes on Merci, then the man. "How much pot did you smoke in the bathtub?"

Merci had smelled it very faintly, too, when she had first sat down. It hadn't seemed relevant, yet.

Coates's face took on an expression of blank defiance. "One half of one joint."

"Strong stuff or cheap stuff?" Zamorra asked.

"Very strong."

"There're other people to talk to," said Zamorra. He stood and walked out.

Merci finished her notes. The door slammed.

"That man is unbelievably angry," said Coates.

"Believe it. Thank you."

Back on the upstairs walkway, Merci stood aside for the coroner's people to wheel Aubrey Whittaker past. She thought that Aubrey Whittaker would most likely have been wheeling around in her red Cadillac if she hadn't answered the door for the wrong guy. She looked out to the sparse 2 A.M. traffic on Coast Highway. Zamorra was already interviewing another neighbor.

Inside she was greeted by the green eyes and wide smile of Evan O'Brien. The CSI held up a small paper bag. Merci took it and looked in at a cartridge casing that had rolled into the bag's corner.

"The forty-five caliber Colt," said O'Brien. "Load of choice for many in law enforcement."

Merci Rayborn looked at the CSI with a hostility that could overtake her in a heartbeat. Jokes about her profession were never funny.

"Hey, Sergeant, don't rain on me for some of the best physical evidence you can ask for. Lynda found it."

"Raped?"

"Apparently not. And no signs of forced entry. Looks like some kind of scuffle or something in the kitchen."

"How many shots?"

"Probably just one. There's a hole up in the corner of the slider. Your bullet is out there in the ocean somewhere."

"Find it."

"Yes, Sergeant."

Chapter Two

Merci met Mike for breakfast at seven in the courthouse cafeteria. She'd had three hours of sleep and now seemed to have feathers between her brain and her thoughts. Tim, Jr., had awakened when she went into his room. She had held him until he fell back asleep. He was just a year and a half old now, her little man, her reason for everything.

Starved as usual in the mornings, she got the big-eater's plate. Mike set down his tray of yogurt, fruit and coffee with envy. He had a file under one arm, and he handed it to Merci.

"Copy of Whittaker's jacket," he said. "Thought I'd save you some time."

She scanned the top sheet: one drunk driving conviction two years prior; one arrest for pot, pleaded down to a misdemeanor for her attending a drug diversion program; one pending charge of solicitation for prostitution—to be dropped for her cooperation in a vice-squad investigation of outcall sex-for-hire.

"We'd finally talked Aubrey Whittaker into helping us go after the outcall service," he said unhappily.

Mike had a pleasant face and a serious disposition. It seemed to have gotten more serious during the last few months. But he'd been there for her, off and on, for over a year now. She liked him and trusted him, and he let her keep a little distance between them, a little padding. Marriage: no, not now. Cohabitation: no. Innermost feelings and secret confessions: not yet. The future: later. The insulation seemed to be part of her character. Mike understood this, even if she didn't at times.

"That was just two days ago," said Mike.

"Which outcall?"

"The Epicure."

"Is that the Italian prince?"

"He's a YACS thug."

YACS was a new term in law enforcement, a new threat to the innocent. It stood for Yugoslavian-Albanian-Croatian-Serbian, who—in spite of littering the aisles of history with each others' dead—were lumped together for ethnic reasons. They'd mostly stayed East Coast, but Southern California was getting its share.

"I thought the YACS were supermarket robbers, truck hijackers," said Merci.

"Well, this one peddles flesh and calls himself an Italian prince."

Mike peeled his banana without desire, bit into it. She thought this was emblematic of him: His whole life was a should instead of a want. That was part of what made him Mike, what made him good. Sometimes, actually noble. Two hundred and twenty pounds of muscle, a boy's smile and blue eyes clear as a desert sky, for whatever that was worth. Worth quite a lot, sometimes. Other times she thought it was vanity.

"Priors?"

"Stateside he's got pimping, pandering and some assaults. Women, of course. Back in YACSville, who knows?"

"I hope you get him."

Mike shook his head slowly. "She . . . Aubrey Whittaker, tried to stand up for the guy at first. Said if we wanted a bust just bust her. Wouldn't admit that he was taking almost the whole outcall fee, which he was. Wouldn't admit she was encouraged to keep her 'clients' satisfied, whatever that took. Wouldn't admit that she was working for tips, which she was. He's a pig, selling nineteen-year-olds to rich old farts and high-tech nerds with million-dollar companies and no morals. You do that to a girl, you're stealing her soul. I'll get him. And you'll nail the shit who killed her."

Mike wore a silver cross around his neck. Merci could see the chain behind the open collar of his blue dress shirt, a glint within a shadow. He'd started wearing it a few months back, when he joined the church. Merci had only gone twice: She would not attend any church where worshipers were forced to stand and greet their neighbors.

"Good luck on the next-of-kin search," said Mike. "She went to court to change her name, wouldn't tell me what the real one was."

"Where'd she grow up?"

"Wouldn't come clean with me. Oregon, Seattle, Texas or Ohio, depending on who she was talking to. Iowa is what she told me."

"And on to California, to start over."

"I think it's sad. What do you have?"

She ran down what she knew. She and Zamorra would do a walk-through later today, as the early lab work was done. That was when they could really put things together. But for now—one shooter who might have used a silenced weapon; possibly someone Aubrey had known well enough to open her door to; no rape or robbery. Motive—none as yet. Witnesses—one who heard noises. Suspects—none. Unless you wanted to include the johns in her black book, of which there were many.

Mike listened, his eyes moving left and right. When something was bothering him his eyes got restless and wouldn't land.

"It doesn't make sense," he said. "A wad of money in her purse, no rape, nothing taken? Why kill her? To hear what a silenced automatic sounds like?"

"I can't add it up either, Mike."

"She was . . . well, nineteen."

"I think she knew him. Lynda said the place was crawling with prints, like any domicile. It's just a matter of running some of them through CAL-ID and AFIS, see what pops."

"Is the black book coded?"

She shook her head. "Half-assed, maybe. Plenty of initials and names to go on."

"Some of them get elaborate on their codes. It's more to do with denying the john's individuality than for security."

"Not her, from the looks of it."

"Then you might have the key. That and the brass, if you get a suspect and a gun."

Mike opened the yogurt, looked at the inside of the foil lid. He had long blond eyelashes and when he relaxed and stared at something he looked innocent and bewildered. Sometimes she wanted to hold him close, like she held Tim, Jr. There was something gentle in Mike—she saw it most often when he worked his dogs. Mike ran the bloodhounds for the department. He had told her straight out that he was a dog person, not a people one. He'd been trying hard to change that, for reasons that didn't seem entirely his own.

"Merci, I'd like to ask Brighton to let me work the murder with you."

Brighton was the sheriff; and working the case with her was out of the question.

"No," she said.

"But we've got a big overlap with the outcall op we're running. I can help. Believe me."

"Then help, Mike, but I don't want anyone assigned to this except me. It's mine and Paul's."

"Hell's bells, Merci, you could think about it for more than two seconds."

"Why? I don't have to."

Through her fatigue and growing anger, Merci saw Mike's face fall with his disappointment. He looked like Tim, Jr., when he first understood the bottle was empty: crushed in a new way, time after time.

"Mike, look. I'll share what I have with you. I'll keep you in the loop. But I don't need a vice sergeant in the brew right now. I've got all the help I need."

" 'A vice sergeant in the brew.' "

"Right."

"Is that like a fly in the ointment?"

"No, Mike. It is not."

"Are we still on for the movies tonight?"

"I'm already worn out. Rain check?"

"It isn't raining."

He stood and lifted his tray all in one motion. She watched him dump the food into the trash can, rack the tray and walk out.

• • •

Melvin Glandis, assistant sheriff, stood over her desk with a stack of tattered files under one arm. He was a big triangle of a man, wide shoulders, narrow hips, short legs, small feet. He was rumored to be an accomplished ballroom dancer. His face was pink and good-humored. It was eight that morning.

"Here's your Christmas present. Solve it by New Year's Eve, you get a smoked ham."

"Leave the file. Keep the ham."

Glandis dropped it to the desktop. "Patti Bailey, shot and dumped, nineteen sixty-nine. Add it to your dead hooker list. Maybe you'll have better luck with it than we did."

She knew what the file was. At the end of every year, Sheriff Brighton randomly assigned an unsolved murder to each of the investigators in Homicide Detail. It was a way of cleaning house, and every once in a while they got results.

These results were trumpeted to the press and public, positive PR for the department, as when a deputy saved a life or helped a woman give birth because she couldn't make it to the hospital in time. It helped citizens to believe that even forty-year-old cases weren't just being closed and forgotten. The detectives either loved or hated the unsolveds, depending on whether they wanted overtime or not.

Merci thought that they were primarily a waste of time, overtime included. If the dicks of yore couldn't button down their own cases, how could anyone else?

"You look tired," said Glandis.

"So do you."

"Up all night with the hooker?"

"More or less."

"A silencer. Jesus."

Merci had long ago lost her amazement at the speed of gossip within her department. The air inside the county buildings was stiff with it.

Glandis shrugged. "Let me know if I can help. I was first-year robbery-arson back then, but I remember some things."

"Thanks, Mel. How are we on the body-parts boy?"

Most of an eight-year-old boy had been found dismembered and decapitated, his parts wrapped in plastic trash bags and buried in his neighborhood. No arrests or suspects yet. The case was taking fist-sized bites out of Rayborn's soul. Wheeler and Teague got it, good investigators, but Merci wished it was hers. It wasn't personal but it was personal.

"We found a kiddie raper living one street over, ex–mental patient. They haven't located him yet."

Merci shook her head and thought about her own son meeting such an end. A dark, svelte violence in her shifted and stared out past its coils.

"How's Junior Tim?"

"Totally great in every way."

"I'd expect that, coming from you."

He knocked twice on her desktop with his big knuckles, pivoted in shiny black shoes and turned to Zamorra's unoccupied desk. He slapped down another unsolved file, then moved on.

• • •

She made her usual nine o'clock call home. Her father told her that Tim, Jr., had gotten up regular time, wolfed his breakfast and was now hurling blocks around his room. Merci heard shrieks of delight in the background. The words *body parts in plastic bags* shot through her mind and she banished them with force.

"Kid's got an arm for a one-and-a-half-year-old," said Clark.

Arm in plastic. Banished again.

"Take his temperature when he settles down, I—"

"Already did, dear. Ninety-eight point six."

"After lunch—"

"I will."

She missed him. By his absence she could feel his shape: a large, round, warm part of her. Missing. Gone. Elsewhere. But there was no way she could be there all the time, even if she wanted to. There was work to do. Work held her little family together. And it held her together, too. It always had.

"We're going to take the trike out later if it warms up. Then hit the market. We'll be here when you get home."

Clark had moved in with her two years ago, after her mother's death. Merci had watched him crawl toward his private abyss, then crawl back away from it. Tim, Jr., had a lot to do with that turnaround. Her father was great with him. She thought of them as The Men.

"I miss my Men."

" 'Bye honey. We miss you. Don't work too hard."

• • •

Noon came but Paul Zamorra didn't. No call. No message. No word. She'd only worked with him for three months, and this was the first time he'd done anything so unprofessional and disrespectful.

Merci called his home at one, got the machine. The hospital, she thought. She found the number Zamorra had given her for his wife's room at UCI Medical Center, but decided not to call. She felt powerless over medical conditions, and she was afraid of what she felt no power over.

She ran a background on Alexander Coates: clean.

She checked the number of unsolved prostitute murders in the last two years: three.

She talked to a phone company security manager about getting an incoming number list for Aubrey Whittaker. She wanted it fast, no warrant, no subpoena, no bullshit, please. He said he'd call her back.

She looked through Aubrey Whittaker's leather-covered calendar/address book and considered some of the names she found there. Some were first and last, most just first initials and last names. Some even had what appeared to be credit-card numbers. Christ, she thought, charge a nooner to the credit card and when your wife pays the bills tell her it must have been the mobile car detail. Mobile sex detail.

Plenty of the names had no numbers attached. Private customers, Merci thought, no YACS middleman eating up the profit? She thought she recognized two of them and she called a friend at the Orange County *Journal* who could run a print search on them. She promised him a first tip in return, if any of them turned into a story. She threw in twenty more just for good measure, guys with names that sounded important, guys who would bend easy if she leaned on them.

On the day she was murdered, Aubrey Whittaker had a date with "Dr." at 3:45 P.M. and "din" with "DC," 8:30 P.M. The day before she'd had four dates on the calendar.

Sunday mornings, to Merci's astonishment, were marked by 8:30 A.M. entries that appeared to relate to sermons, and Aubrey's opinion of them.

Putting Christ First—Ken H., good but at times unrealistic.

Not terribly likely, Merci thought: They must mean something else.

Six phone calls later Merci found out that the Reverend Ken Holly presided over Newport Maranatha Church, and had indeed delivered a sermon of that title three weeks earlier.

Yes, he knew Aubrey. No, he didn't know she was murdered. He sounded somber.

He knew little of Aubrey, except that she had joined his congregation a few weeks ago. She was well-dressed, private, apparently unattached. She'd joined the Christian Singles. He wasn't sure what she did for a living.

He asked Merci to keep the name of his church out of the newspapers, if it was in her power. She said it was and she would. He agreed to meet with her any time, or to gather up the names and addresses of some of the Christian Singles who had known Aubrey. Merci thanked him and asked him to have them ready by this time tomorrow.

She went to the restroom, washed her hands and wondered what it must be like to do what Aubrey did for a living. In the mirror she saw someone not cut out for such work, a dark-haired, big-boned woman with an unforgiving and guileless expression on her face. The face had some tenderness in it if you looked hard. Mostly it just looked eager to nail you.

She watched the coroner's team take photographs and X rays of Aubrey Whittaker's body. There were no bullet or lead fragments left inside, so far as Merci could see. Near the center of Aubrey's right ventricle was a small dark disturbance in the pale muscle: probably the bullet hole, said the deputy coroner.

Merci was surprised by the entry wound. The tear was jagged but small, but the edges of the flesh had been lifted up and burned. The skin in a half-inch radius around the break was scorched black. Surrounding the dark circle was another half inch of reddened flesh. Outside of that began the undisturbed perfection of Aubrey Whittaker's young body.

"The gun muzzle was right up next to her dress," said the deputy. "The silk was burned. And the skin."

The exit wound was twice the size but showed little discoloration. A small flap had been torn in the skin. It was nine centimeters higher than the entry wound. Merci visualized the apartment and the angle of the shot, and her mind's eye followed a line from Aubrey Whittaker's heart to the upper part of the sliding glass door, where the CSIs had found the hole.

"Looks like straight in and out," said the deputy coroner. "Didn't hit a bone, or at least didn't hit much of one. I'd say the ammo was hard-tipped. With a softer nose, it would have flattened more by the time it came out."

The full medical autopsy was scheduled for late that afternoon.

Merci hovered over Evan O'Brien's shoulder in the crime lab, watching him get the fingerprint cards ready for CAL-ID and AFIS. Two distinct sets already, one of them belonging to the decedent. O'Brien was the most effective fingerprint tech Merci'd ever known. His knowledge of comparison points was matched by his knowledge of the labyrinthine state system, which he'd helped digitize during his tenure with CAL-ID up in Sacramento.

She watched Lynda Coiner get the .45-caliber Colt casing ready for the Federal DrugFire registry, on the chance that the same weapon had been used in a narcotics-related crime. This didn't smell like drugs to Merci, but it was worth a try.

Merci helped one of the lab techs develop and dry the last of the crime-scene photos, which she would need for the walk-through. One set for her, one for Zamorra. Thank God for her college photography courses. As she stood in the twilight of the darkroom with the blow dryer roaring she watched Aubrey Whittaker's body take shape on the photographic paper, appearing slowly and steadily, as if conjured by a medium.

Aubrey Whittaker, she thought: servicer of men, sermon critic, home entertainer, Christian Single. Change your name, leave your home, begin again.

Who are you?

She burned two copies of the Responding Deputy Report, the lab data and the CSI sheets.

She didn't read any of it because she wanted to learn it fresh, right there where it happened, when she was there with just her partner. A crime scene was always different in daylight.

She spent a few minutes down in the impound yard, talking with Ike Sumich, a young tech that she considered to be a real up-and-comer. Like Evan, Ike was one of her people. Merci liked the idea of tribes. She was forming one, collecting members because they could help her and because she liked them.

Sometimes she would look at them and imagine what they'd look like thirty years from now.

Sumich looked good in her future-vision, but he had a gut he'd need to get to the gym to avoid.

Ike had helped her out in the case that almost got her killed a couple of years ago. She had no pending business with him; she just wanted to check in, let him know he had a friend in Homicide.

When Zamorra finally came into the detective pen it was almost 3 P.M. He was freshly shaven and his hair was still wet from a shower, but his eyes looked empty and red.

"Are we ready for the walk-through?" he asked.

"We're ready."

"I'll drive."

Chapter Three

Merci unlocked the door and pushed it open, calling on her memory. "Coates heard the noises and made the call at ten forty-five. Deputies Burns and Sungaila arrived ten minutes later. This porch light was on and the door was ajar about four inches. All three of them saw the blood."

She gently swung the door inward again and watched it come back toward her. It once more stopped four inches short of the frame. Standing in the shade of the building, she shivered once in the cold December air. She found the CSI sheets, scanned down the typewritten copy.

"CSIs examined the porch for shoe prints, but between the old paint and all the foot traffic, they couldn't find anything useful. That, from Lynda Coiner. If we believe Alexander Coates, Aubrey's first visitor wore hard-soled shoes or boots, her second wore soft ones. What do you make of Coates's ear-work, Paul?"

"Sixty-forty. Sixty he's right."

"I gave him better than that. I think we should consider two men. Were they working together is the question. Working on what is the next question."

Zamorra said nothing. He faced the door with a bloodshot stare. He pointed to a small, crescent-shaped cut in the gray door paint. It was deep enough to reveal wood, just to the right of the blood spray, heart-high.

He looked at his copy. "O'Brien says that was where the casing bounced off, on its way to the dinner table. Coiner found the brass inside the flower vase. That was good work."

"She had the bounce to go from."

Zamorra slowly shook his head. "He shot her from right here. Didn't even come through the door. She opened it and zip, all she wrote."

There was something mechanical in his voice, Merci thought, something distanced: He's still in the hospital with his wife.

They stepped inside. The front door swung almost shut again. Bright afternoon light shot through the sliding glass door and the windows. The day was clear and cool and the sun was already low out over the ocean. Merci felt the heat coming through the glass. She noted the bullet hole in the upper left corner of the slider, the one she hadn't noticed the night before.

Nobody's perfect, she thought, but she expected herself to be. What was it Hess had said? Forgive yourself, Merci. You've got another fifty years to spend with you.

Duly noted.

The CSIs had outlined the body in dark chalk before removing it. Merci looked from the case file to her partner.

"I don't get this. Coiner and O'Brien say she was dragged three feet into the dining room. That, from the blood smear on the carpet."

"So he could shut the door behind him," said Zamorra. "Her feet were in the way."

"But why, Paul? What did he do in here? He didn't use her sexually, at least not that we know of. He didn't take anything we know of. He left cash, credit cards, some good prescription drugs in the medicine chest. He took a big risk coming in. He wasted time. Why?"

"Maybe he took her picture, got himself off, then hit the road."

Merci recalled the recent unsolved murders of prostitutes: two found in motels at different ends of the county, one dumped on Harbor Boulevard, down by the car dealerships. All three were streetwalkers. One strangled, one bludgeoned, one shot in the head.

"No semen."

"Maybe he used a rubber. She had plenty."

Merci thought about this but couldn't make it fit. The whole thing seemed so efficient, so cold, so sexless. There was no evidence he'd even touched her, other than to drag her out of the way of the door.

They stood at opposite ends of the dining-room table. Merci noted the place mats, the matching cloth napkins beside them, the short crystal vase in which Lynda Coiner had found the casing. There was a nearly empty glass of water at one place, and a nearly full cup of coffee at the other. She could see the oblong smudge of lipstick near the rim of the water glass. Both were laden with black fingerprint dust. Merci could see where the tape had been lifted off the tumbler. She got down to a good angle for light and saw fingerprint dust on the glass table, too. Prints galore.

She went into the kitchen, saw the still-crusted baking pan on the counter, and the flatware, salad bowls and plates in the sink. There was a wing and a thigh in the pan. No booze glasses, no booze bottles. Standing in front of the sink you could see the ocean out a window to the right.

"Okay, Paul. So she makes dinner for someone. Her calendar said D.C. Let's say it's the eight-thirty arrival that Coates heard—a big man, light on his feet, familiar with his surroundings. He knocks and she answers. No loud words. No loud music. No sounds of struggle or gunshot or anything else. They eat their salad and chicken. No alcohol. At ten-ten he leaves. All's quiet for five minutes. We know this because Alexander Coates is in his bathtub with his trusty stopwatch."

Zamorra had moved into the living room. He stood in the sunlight looking down at Aubrey Whittaker's high heeled shoes. His voice sounded flat, abstracted. "Then Man Friend Number Two climbs the stairs and comes down the walkway. He's a smaller guy, wearing soft shoes. He doesn't knock but she opens the door anyway."

Merci leafed through the CSI reports to see if the doorbell had been dusted. Evan had worked it and found nothing. She said so.

"Maybe he wiped it," said Zamorra. "Maybe he knocked quietly. Maybe Coates belched, splashed, yawned—just didn't hear."

Merci considered. "She hears the knock or the ring, goes to the door and opens it. But not before she turns on the porch light and looks through the peephole. This is important. She must have recognized him. If she didn't, why did she open up? She's a call girl. She's seen a lot of things. It isn't her nature to trust. But she opens the door."

"She knew him," said Zamorra. "She thought she did. If we cancel out Coates's assumptions based on sound, we're looking at the same guy. The simplest explanation. The dinner guest, D.C. That's why Coates didn't hear the knock. It was soft, because he'd just left. He knew she'd assume it was him again. A soft knock, she comes to the door and says who is it, and he says it's just me, Man Friend Number One. I forgot my jacket. My cell phone. My glasses."

Merci came into the dining room and looked at the chalk outline. "So he came to dinner knowing he was going to kill her."

"Absolutely. That's why he left and came back."

"To get the gun. Because he couldn't carry the gun in without her seeing it."

"That's what I get, Merci. And not just a gun, but a gun

with a noise suppressor. We got four neighbors who were home last night, and nobody heard a shot. Nothing like a shot. You know what a racket a forty-five would make here. A covered porch and entryway, the door half open. It had to be silenced."

Merci thought he was right: The shooter came here to shoot. Then she tried to take it the other way: Man Friend comes to dinner and leaves mad, by the time he gets to his car he's furious, gets the gun and goes back up. Working girls get killed by furious johns all the time. But she couldn't get any logic out of that one. She didn't think Aubrey Whittaker was working that night. Call girls don't make dinner for their clients. The bed was made up. And nobody carried a silenced .45 auto unless they planned to use it. Soon.

"All right," she said. She hadn't worked with Zamorra long enough to know how he reasoned, so she wanted to take things slow, get them right from the start. "Take our path back to the first fork, though. What if there were two guys?"

"Then it's connected or unconnected."

"Connected is a lot of coming and going, a lot of personnel on the job."

"Lots of secrets to keep," said Zamorra. "I like one guy, period, no matter what Alexander Coates heard."

Merci was leaning that way, too. "That could explain why he came in after he shot her."

"Exactly. To clean his prints off of everything he touched at dinner."

"And something else, now that I think of it."

Zamorra looked at her.

"He wanted the brass. A semi-auto ejects to the shooter's right. He would follow her in as she fell, look to his right for the shell. He couldn't have heard the case hit the door because the gun just went off. Even a silenced auto is going to make a noise. He wouldn't have noticed the nick in the paint. That was our luck. He didn't find his casing immediately, so he pulled the girl out of the way, shut the door and looked again. But he still struck out, because he was looking in the wrong part of the apartment. Even if he'd thought of a ricochet, what are the chances of him looking into the flower vase? It was all the way to his left."

Zamorra was nodding. "The trouble with that is, it works for Man Friend Number Two, also. If he's connected with Man Friend Number One, then he cleans the place and looks for his brass. If he's not connected, he likes all the fingerprints Man Friend Number One must have left, but he still wants his casing."

"How does he know what his partner touched?"

"He goes with the obvious."

Merci followed this one as far as she could. One path, many forks, one fork at a time. "Nobody plans a murder but leaves his fingerprints on the silverware. If we find a load of good prints, that means two guys, not working together. Two sets of footsteps. Two guys. Just like Coates said."

Zamorra looked down at the body outline like he'd never seen it before. He cocked his head like one of Mike's bloodhounds. Uncocked it, kept staring.

"What."

"I'm pulling out walls, putting in windows."

She said nothing. She figured it was like Hess seeing things that weren't there.

"You know," he said, "just trying to get past my own bad ideas."

"I know about that."

"Two guys. Just like Coates said," he repeated her words verbatim. Something in the tone told her he was lending credence to their earwitness for the first time.

Stoned or not.

"But why?" he asked. "Why kill her?"

"I've been thinking about that ever since I saw the money in her wallet. In fact, I wondered if that might be part of the answer."

"You lost me."

"He's aware of us. He left the money to make us wonder."

"That's far-fetched." Zamorra looked at her uncomfortably, then away.

She felt the rage blast through her, clear and clean as the winter sun coming through the slider.

She didn't say it, but what she was thinking was: I got my partner killed because I thought a psychopath was too stupid to come after me. Far-fetched. Bastard used my gun on Hess. Almost got myself killed, too, and sometimes I still want to trade places with him.

With his back still toward her Zamorra shook his head, then said something she didn't hear.

She tried to keep the anger from her voice, something she was never much good at. "Say it again, Paul. I'm a big girl. We can't work together if we can't talk."

"I said you were right," he said gently. "Nothing seems far-fetched from a guy who just shot a girl in the heart."

She could see him in profile against the window, looking at her from the side of his bloodshot eye.

"Sorry," said Merci.

"Accepted. I am, too."

"I'm sorrier."

"No, I'm much, much sorrier."

She was relieved he actually got her joke. She smiled to herself and sighed. "Sometimes I think I got problems, until I look at the cases I work."

"Me, too. Then I look at Janine."

Janine was his wife.

• • •

They stood between the kitchen and the dining room, Merci reading her notes on the Coates interview. "This bothers me," she said. "Some kind of struggle here, according to Coates. First a thump, then another, but a sustained one. He said it was a minute or two later. I figure the first thump was Aubrey hitting the floor. If a struggle ensued, who the hell was it between?"

"Coates said it was like furniture being moved."

The cabinet under the sink was open, the door handle screws were half torn out of the wood. The second drawer was all the way out, the runners were bent so bad it wouldn't close.

Merci knelt, looked at the damage. "Lots of strength, to pull screws and bend metal. But Aubrey's peacefully laid to rest twelve feet away, two minutes earlier, if we believe Coates. No visible bruises or abrasions, nothing under her fingernails, nothing on the body that points to a fight. So who's our killer fighting with in here, his conscience?"

"There's our two Man Friends again."

"The Man Friends weren't here at the same time, if Coates is right."

Zamorra looked at her long, then shrugged. "What he says doesn't fit the evidence. The thing is, you get loaded and your time-space judgment goes straight to hell. You think twenty minutes is going by while you have meaningful thoughts. Really, five seconds went by while you tripped out."

Merci considered the distance from body to kitchen. "Even if Coates was off, even if the struggle happened right after the first thump, it wasn't Aubrey in a struggle. Shot in the heart and fighting for her life, she doesn't lose one drop of blood on the kitchen floor?"

"Where's that leave us? Someone else up here when Man Friend Number One left?"

"It's possible."

"A third guy. Wasn't invited to dinner. Nobody heard him come or go. Hid in the bedroom? Jumped out to rescue her when she got shot?"

Merci was listening but didn't answer. She was flipping through to the CSI report, looking for reference to a good shoe print that Lynda Coiner found on the kitchen floor. There were three prints left by the same shoe, with a back-slanting series of treads that looked to be shaped like big commas. The tails tapered toward the heel. The heel had a central circle with spokes leading outward to the edge.

O'Brien had photographed it in reflected light, then lifted a big print using fingerprint dust and a sheet of white paper. They could match an impression if the detectives could come up with a suspect shoe. It looked to be a size twelve, probably not a dress shoe due to the pronounced tread pattern. And very likely a soft sole and not a hard one because of the clarity of the print left on the hardwood floor.

Zamorra was on the same page. "This shoe print," he said. "It doesn't fit with what Coates said either. The big guy, the size twelve, was supposed to be a hard-soled shoe or boot. Mr. Snappy-Dressed Businessman coming home to his family. I think our earwitness was a little too stoned to keep things straight."

"He liked her," Merci said. "He's trying to help her by helping us."

"If he wants to help us he could just admit he's a little foggy on some of this. You know, a half-assed witness is worse than none at all sometimes."

Merci just shook her head. "I know that. But I want to know what happened here. I mean I really want to know."

Zamorra knelt and looked at the loose handle of the still-open sink cabinet, then to the drawer that was pulled out and stranded on its bent runners.

"I do too," he said, almost like it surprised him.

Merci wondered what it must be like to investigate a murder while your wife was dying. There was a time when she had believed she could use her will to keep people from dying, but now she didn't. Zamorra didn't seem like the kind of guy who'd believe in that. It was naive.

What she came up with was that Paul must want to run away sometimes, to make his own hurt stop. When Merci was in her greatest pain—after Hess and her mom died, after a monster named Colesceau had almost killed her, right after Tim, Jr., was born—she pictured a small house on a Mexican beach, with bright purple bougainvillea potted on the deck and herself sitting there in the shade.

She imagined that beach house in Mexico now, then

she was back in Aubrey Whittaker's kitchen. What did Aubrey Whittaker picture, when the paying guys were doing their thing? A house with a beach? Eternal fire?

"The fingerprints," Paul said, like he'd come to a conclusion. "And her little black book. There's going to be a straight line in there, somewhere. And it's going to point right at this creep."

Chapter Four

Merci sat with Tim on her lap and let Clark clear the dishes. The old house was cold this December, and she could feel the draft on her ankles through her socks. Past the windows she could see, in the bright beams of the yard lights, the big patio with the baby's trike and the barbecue, the cats on the wall and the orange trees beyond. The lot was surrounded by the grove and the grove was surrounded by housing tracts you couldn't see until you walked right up to them. She'd rented the house for its privacy, and because it was cheap.

Tim had on a knit cap, half against the cold and half because he looked cute in it. It reminded her of Hess, Tim's father, because he'd worn a hat the last couple of times she had seen him. Tim, Jr., looked like Hess. It was hard to think of him without thinking of all that had gone wrong.

She banished Hess from her thoughts, trying to be gentle about it.

"Poker night," said Clark. She knew it was poker night because her father was washing the dishes fast, eager to make his eight o'clock game. It was Clark and his old retired friends from the Sheriff Department. Every Wednesday.

"Win lots," she said absently. Her mind was on the work of the day, no matter how hard she tried to forget it. "Hey, we homicidals got our Christmas bonus today."

"Your very own unsolved?"

"Mine's from nineteen sixty-nine. A woman named Patti Bailey. I brought it home for pleasure reading tonight."

Clark was scrubbing away at a saucepan. He was a tall, lean man with nice gray hair and glasses. She watched him scrub. Merci wondered at what year a man entered the age of sharpened elbows. Hess had sharp elbows, even though he had been built heavy and her father was built slender. Clark looked back over his shoulder at her.

"Buy a novel if you want pleasure."

"You remember it?"

"Barely. I was just starting burg-theft in sixty-nine. I think Rymers and Thornton got that one."

"They still around?"

"Thornton's up in Arrowhead, I think. Rymers died."

"How?"

Clark turned again. When he smiled the lines in his face changed direction and he looked sweet and wise. "Stroke."

Merci said nothing. Her dad was always telling her to

leave her work at work. To leave alone the things she couldn't change. To understand that not every death in the world was a homicide she needed to solve. To get a life—a contemporary phrase he'd started using, which hugely irritated Merci.

He also wanted her to marry Mike McNally, have another baby, be stepmom to Mike's boy, Danny, be a mom instead of a mom cop. To Clark, being a cop was just a job, a concept that Merci had never understood.

To her it was a life. When she looked at her parents Merci couldn't see where she'd gotten her single-mindedness and her drive. God knew how Tim, Jr., would end up, if things like that could just barrel right into your soul.

• • •

While Tim pulled the ears and chewed the nose of a stuffed panda, Merci read the Patti Bailey file. The body was found in an orange grove culvert near the corner of Myford and Fourth, in unincorporated Orange County. Gunshot. The year was 1969.

The panda flew across the bedroom. Tim waddled in hot pursuit.

Myford and Fourth, thought Merci. Odd. It was just a couple of miles from here. Now it was called Myford and Irvine Boulevard. She wondered if Brighton had shuffled the deck to give her something close to home, then wondered why he'd bother.

The dicks were Rymers and Thornton, just as her father

had remembered. A kid had found the body in the ditch; his dad called the sheriffs. The responding deputy was one Todd Smith.

Merci looked at her son. He was gouging at the panda's eyes now, grunting happily.

Patti Bailey was a plain looking woman. Twenty-three, petite, lank brown hair pulled behind her ears. She had heavy eyelids and a crooked smile in her mug shot. Merci thought it took a lot of guts to smile for a mug, or maybe a lot of alcohol or dope. Her impression of the year 1969 was that everybody was loaded and disrespectful to authority. She was only four at the time, so it was just speculation.

Bailey had been arrested three times for prostitution, tried and convicted once. She'd dodged marijuana and barbiturates charges—both dismissed, same judge. Two tumbles for possession of heroin: eighteen months in all.

While Tim throttled and cooed at his panda, Merci read through Todd Smith's report. Bailey was found by the kid on the evening of August 5. Smith got there at 6:30 P.M. and found the woman facedown on the slope of the culvert. All she had on was a bra and a pair of shorts.

The medical autopsy found no conclusive signs of rape. No sign of struggle. There was THC in her system, nembutal and .08 blood alcohol. She'd eaten peaches and chocolate chip cookies less than an hour before she died. She'd been dead about twenty-four hours before the kid found her.

Merci looked quickly through the crime-scene and autopsy photos. The autopsy had been performed in a funeral home because the county had had no facilities of its own back then. The photos struck her as most homicide photos did: The victims looked so disrespected, so brutally dismissed. What could you have done to earn such contempt? She'd been shot from behind and up close. The bullet entry was a clean black hole and the exit tore open a crudely triangular flap at the bottom. Went through her heart—right atrium. The M.E. said maybe a .38 or maybe a .357 Magnum, which was the same diameter but considerably faster. Any number of more exotic calibers could have made the same hole.

Merci cringed when she looked at the bullet-path study, in which the deceased Patti Bailey lay on her side with a long dowel pushed through the middle of her torso. She looked like something spiked for a barbecue.

Merci turned over the pictures and sighed.

Tim now had his toddler's hair comb and was styling the fur on the panda's head. More like hitting it with the comb. He was talking to his customer, a series of bright syllables and occasional words that formed his sincere and expressive babble. He was smiling. From this angle, he looked like her.

Go into cosmetology, she thought, open a salon and make people pretty.

It struck her as strange that while she would trade little on Earth for her job, she wanted none of it for her own son. Maybe Tim will see it like Dad does, she thought: It's all just a way to pay the bills. Be a banker, a sales guy, a lawyer. Take pictures of mountains or models. Play ball. Why see all this?

Because people die every day who aren't supposed to, and the assholes who do it shouldn't go free.

There it was. Inelegant but true.

It looked to her like Rymers and Thornton had done what they could. No murder weapon. No witnesses. Not much evidence collected: some partial shoe prints in the soft soil of the orange grove and a short list of drug-suppliers and johns who might or might not have had a reason to kill Patti Bailey.

The case stayed active for two years, open for eight more, then it was filed in the unsolved cabinet. Until now.

Merry Christmas.

• • •

Mike McNally called right after Tim went to bed, as he did almost every night.

"I'm really sorry about today," he said.

"It's okay."

"Look, we're going to get another girl to help on the outcall owner. But I know where to find him, and you should, too."

Merci wrote down the name and the home and business addresses: Goren Moladan, Newport Beach and Dana Point.

"He's got the assaults on the girls," said Mike. "But he

did his time and his probation, so he's clean right now. I don't think he knows we're going inside on him."

"We'll do what we can to keep it that way."

"You guys must have gotten prints all over the place in there. Aubrey Whittaker's place, I mean."

"She made dinner for someone that night."

Mike said nothing for a moment. "Well, something's going to pop then. You think it was the shooter?"

"That's the percentage."

"Domiciles are full of latents though. I mean, a lot of people come and go."

"Yeah. Coiner says it was crawling with loops and whorls."

Mike was quiet again for a beat. She could hear his bloodhounds, Dolly, Molly and Polly, barking in their run.

"Merci, I'm really sorry for jumping in your face today. I was just disappointed. We agreed to set Wednesdays aside for movies with the kids. You know, with the old men at poker night. I was just counting on seeing you. I know you're tired."

"It's really okay. It just surprises me when you get so absolutely pissed off so quick. You remind me of me."

The joke fell flat. Mike tended not to get jokes other than his own, which were often dumb. He'd lay them on you like a six-year-old handing you a toad. *This horse sits down at a bar, the bartender looks at him and asks, why the long face?* And so forth.

She could hear him breathing. Then she heard the old

furnace kick on in the basement, the shudder of the ducts and the hiss of warm air through the floor vent. One of the cats slunk in, then out.

"Merci, have you thought about what we talked about?"

Her heart sank. "Sure."

"And?"

She tried to compose herself. "I'm still not ready, Mike. It doesn't feel right. It feels too soon."

"We can make it whenever you want. Wait a year. It's got to be right for both of us. What's important is we start planning. Otherwise it'll never happen. The years, man, they just keep speeding up."

"Let's wait."

Another silence. There seemed to be an endless river of them lately. She felt punished.

The dogs were still yapping in the background. She could imagine Mike's face drawn in disappointment, his blond forelock hanging disconsolately down, his eyes blue and wide.

"Because of what happened with Hess?"

"Yes, exactly."

"It's not me?"

"I love you, Mike. I respect you. It's not you."

"You put off a good thing long enough, maybe it just goes away. It says that right in the Bible. 'Hope deferred is a sadness to the heart.' "

She felt her anger and guilt collide. Careful now. "I don't want you to be sad."

"I meant your heart, too."

"I know. It's coming along, Mike. Things are going to be okay."

"I'll stick with you."

"I need that."

"You've got it. Stick with me, too."

"I will."

Another pause. "See you tomorrow, girl. Danny and the bloodhounds love you, too."

"Good night, Mike."

• • •

No sooner had she hung up than Gary Brice from the Orange County *Journal* called. Brice covered the crime beat. She trusted him as much as she could trust any reporter—he had never printed something she had asked him to hold back. He'd always trade a favor for a favor.

Sometimes he reminded her of herself, except that the uglier something got, the funnier Brice thought it was. She understood his bleak view of things but didn't see how he turned it to humor.

Maybe it had something to do with the way memories are stored, which is what Dr. Joan Cash told her about her own critical incident stress. Cash said that Merci's memories of the murder of her partner and lover, and her subsequent shooting of the predator Colesceau were "dysfunctional" memories. Dr. Cash wanted to fix them with Eye Movement Desensitization and Reprocessing (EMDR), a new technique with which she had had some success.

But Merci thought of her memories as fully functional, their function being to torment her with guilt. Over what she should have done. Could have done. Might have done. She had analyzed the entire sequence of those last days a thousand times, stopping the action for hours to vet every millisecond, every decision, every misjudgment.

Yes, she believed she had found some things she could have done better. . . .

Then there were the nightmares, terrifying and shameful, far beyond any words she could use to describe them for Cash or anybody else. They left her short of breath, stewing in the gamy scent of her own fear and sweat, trembling in hard, regretful silence.

She wondered briefly if Brice's way might be better: convert all to dark comedy, add a giggle, sleep tight.

No. Not everything in life was amusing. Unless you were talking to certain psychopaths.

"Got some interesting men on your wish list," Brice said.

"Shoot."

"What's it all about?"

"You'll have to tell me."

"I think it's Aubrey Whittaker's little black book. She was a prostitute, I know that."

"Can't confirm or deny that one, Gary. Give me something good."

"Okay. There's the owner of Del Viggio Construction—they're big in north county. There's an assistant pastor at Newport Maranatha Church. There's the defensive line coach at a local junior college. There's an Irvine millionaire who owns a bio-tech pharmaceutical company—they're working on an herbal, low-cost version of Viagra for women. There's a pro basketball player who's got a second home in Laguna Beach. Some married, some with families, some with neither."

She was more than a little surprised. "All that with twenty names. I should have given you fifty. In fact, I think I might."

"High-line girl," said Brice. "What amazes me is these guys'll give an outcall service a real name and a good credit-card number."

She wouldn't comment on that, although it amazed her, too.

She took down the names as he matched them to their occupations and marital status.

Then she gave him twenty more, all of which she'd copied from Aubrey Whittaker's address book. Some of the names had corresponding credit-card numbers, some were without. Merci wondered if Aubrey's private clients might be her big boys, her regulars, the ones who might be lucky and rich enough to get a home-cooked dinner.

Preposterous. Call girls just don't cook for clients.

Merci looked over at Tim, who was using a large orange pipe wrench to clean the panda's mouth.

"Is that all?" asked Brice, a touch of mock irritation in his voice.

"Yes."

"I've got another question for you then."

"Shoot."

"Would you go on a date with me next Friday night?"

"No. How old are you?"

"Twenty-six."

"I got you by ten."

"You're the most beautiful homicide cop I've ever seen. I like your wise-ass personality, too. Something easy. I'll meet you for a drink, we'll see one of those action movies, then go drink more and talk about it. When you can't resist me anymore, you can do whatever you want with me, then discard me."

"Thanks for the names. I need the others tomorrow."

"How about just coffee then?"

"How about just names?"

"I guess you're tight with the bloodhound man."

"Pretty tight."

"You'll regret this," said Brice, in a theatrical tone.

"I'll learn to live with it."

"You can learn to live with warts, too."

"No warts. No date. But thanks for asking anyway. I'm very slightly flattered."

"An age thing," he said. "Cool."

She hung up and wondered at men. There was Mike who saw no humor in anything. There was Gary who saw no seriousness in anything.

And there was Tim, Jr., asleep on his blanket in the corner with one hand on his orange pipe wrench and the other on his panda.

Chapter Five

"Mr. Moladan will see you now."

Merci glared at the receptionist on her way past. The woman was blond, young, unreasonably beautiful. She smelled like free sample day at Macy's. Merci noted that Paul Zamorra looked at her and got a smile back.

They'd agreed to lean a little on Moladan even though he wasn't a suspect. Yet. But if a john had killed Aubrey, it might have been one of Epicure's, not one of her own. Moladan would have his name. Merci volunteered to do the leaning because it would come naturally to her: She thought pimps and panderers who beat up their girls were even more disgusting than the spineless clowns who leased their bodies.

The office building was in Dana Point, overlooking the harbor. Epicure Services was in suite 12, upstairs. Behind the receptionist's desk was a hallway that led past two small offices. Each office had two women in it, and all four of them had phones to their ears and pens in their hands.

At the end of the hall were fake wood double doors meant to look impressive. Holding one open was a powerful looking, middle-aged man with dark curly hair, a big mustache and a big smile.

"I am Goren," he said. "Please come in and be seated."

Zamorra sat and Merci stood. Merci watched Moladan move behind his desk and sit down with his back to the gray December sky. He was wearing a tight black polo shirt, jeans and cowboy boots. He moved lightly for a thick man in boots.

There were framed travel posters of Italy on the walls. A signed photograph of the Italian soccer team for 1997. A string of black-and-white shots of race cars going down a track. The featured car in each was an Alfa Romeo.

Moladan pushed aside a computer monitor. "Police usually like coffee," he said.

"I don't," said Merci.

Zamorra shook his head no.

"Then how can I help you?"

He smiled in a practiced way, teeth showing behind the mustache, but his eyes were hard and alert. His accent was thick but his diction was good.

"Tell me about Aubrey Whittaker," said Merci.

"Aubrey, she is one of my contractors."

He pronounced her name *Obrey*.

"One of your girls."

"I do not use that term. No. Women, perhaps. Never girls."

"She's nineteen."

"Yes, an adult American woman. Something has happened?"

"The cards your receptionist gave you said Homicide Detail. What do you think?"

"Then I think yes."

"You've got a bright future."

Moladan sighed and sat back. Merci watched him hard. He crossed his thick arms over his thick chest. He had a vertical scar on the left side of his forehead.

She stared straight at him and said nothing.

He said, "What am I to do, read your minds?"

"She was murdered Tuesday night. Surprised?"

In a first interview Merci liked to crowd the facts and the questions, get the guy answering with his emotions.

"I am . . . I am absolutely surprised, yes."

Merci nodded and pulled out her notebook. Zamorra set his tape recorder on the desk.

"This helps us keep things straight. You don't mind, do you?"

"Why . . . no. Not at all. I will join you."

Moladan produced a black mini recorder, turned it on and set it on the desk.

"You make a lot of tapes, Mr. Moladan?"

"When detectives accuse me of murder, I tape."

"If we were accusing you of murder you'd be downtown right now. In fact, that's where we're going if you don't turn that thing off and put it back."

She could see the anger in his eyes. Without the smile, his face looked worn and hard.

Moladan clicked off the recorder, then set it back in his desk drawer.

"We know she worked for you," Merci said. "We know she was visited Tuesday night by someone she knew and trusted. We know he was a big man, thick and strong. We know he was a man with some manners and some means—not a transient, not a burglar, not a psycho. And we know from two of the neighbors that this man spoke with an Eastern European accent. We put all that together and guess what—we thought of you."

"I did not see her Tuesday night. I was at home. In the lounge. Listening to the band."

"What, you've got your own lounge musicians at home?"

"Where I live, I mean to say. I live at the Lido Bay Club in Newport Beach."

Moladan was proud of his address. Merci knew it as a rich man's hangout in Newport. Yachts, booze and fun. Nixon hid there when the Watergate heat was on. The decades had seen it go from young and glamorous to aged. Now it had Goren Moladan. It struck Merci as the perfect place for a guy in his line of work because it was full of rich old men.

"Selling girls must pay you pretty good."

"I sell companionship. Of the highest morals and quality. It is expensive. I make an honest profit."

"How expensive?"

"One thousand for the consultation, introduction and first hour, and two hundred per hour after this. These are minimums. There are travel and overnight premiums. There are increased premiums for exotic activities or destinations. It is written into the agreement that no escort is to be touched or spoken to in a suggestive manner. It is written into the agreement that she is to be treated according to her wishes at all times. It is understood by my clients that fine dining, fine wine and liquors, fine automobiles are expected by my escorts. They may accept or reject any offer whatsoever, from alcohol to body contact beyond arm-in-arm walking."

"Quaint," said Merci. "How do you find such gentlemen?"

"They are screened carefully."

"By the airheads on the phones out there?"

"The women place advertising and they interview potential clients and escorts. There is much preliminary work to be done."

"How many girls do you have?"

"Many women. All ages, all cultures, all personalities. But no girls, I'm sorry."

"What I asked was how many."

"On call to me at any time, approximately eighty."

Merci thought about this. Eighty Aubreys out there,

plying the night in their big quiet cars. Tending to the lonely rich of Orange County. Dispatched by one Goren Moladan, Italianate pimp and entrepreneur.

"So you were in the Lido Bay Club lounge Tuesday night. What hours, exactly?"

"Nine o'clock until two. The employees and my companions there will prove me innocent. I will give you names and numbers."

"I'll get those myself. What I need from you are the names and numbers of all your clients who used Aubrey Whittaker."

"Oh, Sergeant Rayborn. This I cannot do. The heart of my business is confidentiality. Without it I am nothing."

He sat back and raised his hands like a man fresh out of options.

"Without confidentiality, Sergeant Ray—"

"Even with it you're still nothing. Nothing but a fake Italian pimp with a lot of rich johns."

"This is absolutely not true. I am Serbian, and proud of it. From now on, Sergeant, I will require my attorney. You have taken this conversation beyond civilized limits."

"Listen carefully to me, meatball. We know about you and del Viggio. We know about you and Assistant Pastor Spartas. We know about you and Collins, the defensive line coach at the J.C. We know about you and the drug whiz making cheap Viagra tea for the ladies, you and the slam dunker from Laguna."

"Fucka you. Fuck you police."

Moladan was up in an instant.

Zamorra was, too. His sport coat slid off him and onto the seat of his chair, though Merci never really saw his hands move.

Moladan glared at her, then at Zamorra. Something there brought him up short, got him thinking.

"Sit down, loser," Merci said. "And don't spit on that nice shirt. The little guy on the horse will have to be dry-cleaned."

Moladan slammed his body back into the chair. His face was red and his dark eyes had turned brighter with anger.

Zamorra was sitting again, coat folded across his lap.

Merci leaned forward. "This is what you're going to do. You're going to call up Aubrey's guys on the computer and print them out on the printer. When I interview them I'll say I got their names from Aubrey's little black book. I'll keep my newspaper and television friends out of here, when they want to know what the victim did for a living. I won't whisper Epicure Services in anyone's ear. You'll lose Aubrey's business for a few weeks, because her guys might become a little shy. But then, she's dead, so you've lost her business anyway. When her friends get hungry again, you'll have someone else tall, young and eager for all the hot crap their money can buy. Right?"

Moladan looked at Zamorra again, then back to Merci.

"Things can be looked at in this way."

"Philosophize later, creep. Print now."

Chapter Six

James Gilliam, Director of Forensic Services, had left an emphatic message on the While-You-Were-Out pad on Merci Rayborn's desk: *See me immediately, bring Zamorra.* He had left the same message on her voice and E-mail.

Gilliam, excitable as a stone, had something hot.

Zamorra apparently got the same message. On their way down to the lab he told Merci that he might have to leave the powwow early. Janine was undergoing a procedure the next morning and he needed to arrange some things. He'd have time after to hit the Bay Club and check Moladan's story.

"I hope it goes well," Merci said. Lame, she thought. But Zamorra was vague about everything so you had to be vague right back. It was only through the constant department buzz that Merci had learned Janine's diagnosis: brain tumor. Zamorra had never actually said those words to her.

"It's an experiment," he said.

She waited for elaboration and got none. The word "experiment" sent a little shiver up her spine. This was the most forthcoming her partner had ever been, so there was no use pressing it.

"Let me know, Paul, if there's anything I can do."

"There isn't."

She wanted to tell him about Hess and Hess's cancer, how he had been beating it even though the stats had said it would kill him. Back then—two years, three months and twenty-four days ago—she had believed that her hope and will could change things. Now she didn't. But she believed you needed to hope and will anyway, just in case. Although just in case wasn't going to do Paul or Janine Zamorra any good at all right now.

They took the stairway down. She listened to the sound of Paul's hard-soled brogues on the steps, comparing the noise to the cushioned *thump* of her duty boots. She wore the boots with almost everything except a skirt because they were stable and comfortable and looked badass. Three pair. Man Friend Number Two could have been wearing duty boots, she thought.

The December wind whipped up through the stairwell and she felt the cold air on her face. The naked black sycamores by the courthouse shivered. Merci buttoned up her windbreaker and jammed her hands in the side pockets.

"I liked the way you handled Moladan back there," she said. Something to cheer Paul up, get his mind off things.

"Whatever look you had on your face when he went rabid, it worked."

"I was thinking about Janine."

What do you say to that? She imagined what Moladan must have seen in Paul: a dark, slender, hate-faced man who'd just slipped off his coat to more easily draw down or thrash the living shit out of him. Zamorra had transferred in from Santa Ana P.D. a few years back. Santa Ana was a tough city. He had arrived with an aura of danger about him—rumors about punching out homeboys three at a time, something about the Golden Gloves gym up in Westminster, about a temper you didn't want to see. His dad was a junior state something-or-other weight champ.

When Merci first met Paul she thought his quiet manners and physical stillness were some kind of shtick. After a while it came to seem authentic. He was just quiet and didn't move around a lot and if that made people uncomfortable, it was fine with her. When he opened doors for women he made it look cool. So when Sheriff Brighton asked her what she thought of partnering up with Zamorra she said okay. He was dark and solitary, but that was better than being a macho windbag like some cops tended to be. In the three months she'd been working with him, Merci felt as if she knew Paul Zamorra only a tiny bit better than when she'd first met him. She knew he had nice trim suits but not many of them.

The mystery was good, though, because she believed most people were more interesting with their secrets intact.

"Nice call on the Eastern European accent," said Paul. "It had him thinking."

• • •

Gilliam let them into his office and shut the door. This was new. Usually he walked them through the lab, showed them hair and fiber samples under the scopes; the print cards on an overhead projector; the bullets and casings; the sketches for bullet-path reconstruction; the tape lifts for gunshot residue; the dummies and samples for bullet impact reconstruction; the knives and blunt instruments; and the autopsied body if they wanted to see it. Gilliam wanted them to see everything.

He sat behind his desk in a fresh white lab coat. He had a closed file in front of him and a doleful expression on his face.

"Thanks for coming," he said. "I'll go through the early lab stuff and the medical autopsy right here in the office. After that, we've got a problem to discuss. I think it's a problem."

Merci said nothing. She'd never seen Gilliam so glum. He had always avoided meeting her eyes with his own because he thought she was attractive, something that had taken her five years to understand. She didn't know what to do about that, except to ignore the problem and respect the man. She could live with secrets; words were what threw her.

"Fine," said Zamorra.

"Let's start with the body," said the director.

Aubrey Whittaker had died of massive coronary failure due to gunshot. The bullet had entered and exited the right ventricle, making a 1½ centimeter entry tear and a 1¾ centimeter exit passage. Missed the ribs, the sternum, missed the vertebrae. Death was almost instantaneous, judging from the lack of edema at the entry and exit wounds and the low level of blood histamines. The projectile shock was prodigious, Gilliam said: The impact was great enough to burst capillaries in her eyes. From the tearing of the dress, the blast destruction of flesh and the tattooing of unburned powder around the entry wound, Gilliam said it was either a Zone 1 or a Zone 2 gunshot—contact or near contact with the body. She had eaten within two hours of expiration: chicken, a mixed green salad with pine nuts and tomato. No alcohol. No drugs. No evidence of recent sexual activity, forced or otherwise. No evidence of strangulation, blunt force trauma, maiming or torture. No signs of struggle.

"We found four very light abrasions, one almost directly over each shoulder cap, one in the middle of each lower armpit. Ante or post mortem—we can't say. They were very difficult to see until we hit them with ultraviolet."

Merci tried to picture the scene, then wrote in her blue notebook: *drag marks.*

"Now, for the guns and ammo," said Gilliam. He opened his file to read from the criminalist's report. "You can check with Dave Sweetzer for follow-up, but here's the gist of his findings."

The shell casing found by Lynda Coiner was a .45-caliber Colt; centerfire, of course. This information came from the headstamp on it. The cycling toolmarks indicated an extractor and ejector, thus a semiautomatic.

"Dave makes a big note here for you guys," said Gilliam, "that the casing wasn't new. It had been fired before and reloaded at least once. Keep that in mind when you make your case for the DA."

"We're thinking sound suppressor," said Paul.

"So is Dave. There wasn't enough powder tattooing to match the tearing of the skin or the silk. The sooting isn't enough, either. And the bullet wiping—that's the ring of material around the hole where he looks for the lubricants—that wasn't pronounced as it should have been in a contact shot. He suggests that two or three extra inches of a baffle would account for all that. Not to mention that nobody in an apartment house heard a forty-five go off. Of course, a forty-five caliber Colt is a good candidate for a sound suppressor. It's subsonic by a couple hundred feet per second, so there's no sonic crack to deal with. The bullet hole in the plate glass is consistent with a forty-five bullet. From the exit wound and the straight flight path Dave's thinking a hard, jacketed round."

Merci made a note of this as Gilliam continued.

"Of course, we can't prove a bullet from that casing was the round that killed the woman. We can't prove a bullet from that casing went through the plate-glass door. We can't prove the bullet that killed the woman ever *went* through the plate glass. We've got no bullet. From what I understand, it's somewhere out in the ocean."

She hadn't seriously considered it at first, but now she wondered how you could retrieve such a thing. The dive team? If she could get a bullet-path projection, maybe. How deep was the water a half a mile or more out, where the bullet would finally hit?

She cursed herself for not being able to dredge up a bullet in the vast gray Pacific.

Gilliam looked at Merci with absolutely the oddest expression she'd ever seen from him, then back down at the criminalist's report. Did he really think she should have come up with that bullet? *What the fuck is going on here?*

"No fingerprints or conspicuous anomalies on the brass," Gilliam said. "So, let's get on with the other physical evidence, shall we?"

They had analyzed carpet fibers found on the kitchen floor that didn't originate from Aubrey Whittaker's apartment or her car: beige in color, a polyester/nylon blend. Gilliam said they appeared to be of an ordinary commercial type used by a number of carpet manufacturers. Such a carpet would be relatively inexpensive and relatively common. Gilliam could be more specific later, when they'd had time to compare samples more exhaustively.

Merci made a note, but common beige carpet was about as helpful as a witness who saw two arms, two legs and a head.

They had analyzed animal hairs: two from the kitchen

floor, two from the dining-room table, one from a kitchen counter. Gilliam said they couldn't tell goat hair from poodle hair in any absolute biological way, it was simply a matter of what looked right. His guess was dog, horse or cow. Two were black; two were light brown; two were white. Each was between 1 and 2 centimeters in length.

"Bring me an animal and we'll take it from there."

Merci made a note to check if Aubrey had liked to ride, and to find out if any of her acquaintances were around horses, cattle or dogs.

Gilliam flipped a page in his file, then looked at Merci again. "We got some fibers off of the woman's dress after we unzipped her, before we took the photos and X rays. They're a black wool and Orlon mix, definitely not from her dress. Possibly a sweater or outergarment of some kind, possibly a scarf or muffler, maybe even a cap or gloves. If they don't match up with something she owns, then we can look to the suspect. The fibers range from two to three centimeters long."

Merci wrote: *whole closet, check dry cleaners.*

"The shoeprint from the kitchen is a good one," Gilliam said. "Not real heavy, but clean. You can see the sole pattern, the nicks on the heel. Size eleven or twelve. The woman was a female size ten, by the way. We can put a guy inside her place, on that floor, if we can get the shoe. We ran it past our manufacturer's catalogues but nothing's come up yet. The problem is, sole patterns change all the time, but shoes can last for years. Decades, if they're not worn much. And they're manufactured everywhere from here to China and back. We might never find it."

Gilliam said the sole pattern and print shape pointed to a work boot or outdoorsman's shoe of some kind, a shoe made for traction and longevity.

Then he leaned back, took a deep breath and sighed. "On to the fingerprints?"

"Is that where our problem is, James?" asked Merci.

He considered. "Depends on how you look at it."

"Then let's look at it."

Gilliam fingered the file, closed it, then began.

The lab had sent the fingerprint cards through the normal channels: AFIS, a federal registry; CAL-ID, which was state. Prints—as the detectives probably knew—were pulled from the apartment surfaces, the doorknobs and light-switch plates, the dining-room tabletop, etc. More specifically, they were also pulled from the dinner flatware left on the table and the food containers and cookware that hadn't been rinsed or washed.

"We eliminated all the victim's prints before we sent the cards through," said Gilliam. "That's one of the reasons it took a while to get to the registries. In fact, we've still got some prints we haven't sent through yet. It takes time to view each one by eye and compare it to the sets we took off the girl."

Gilliam looked at each of them then nodded, as if he were answering a question. Neither Merci nor her partner had said a thing.

"Look," he said. "We got two, maybe three different people whose prints were in that place. Two of them might actually be the same person—they're partial, unclear, iffy. Not enough to take to the registries. But the other one left his sign all over. Flatware, tabletop, doorknob, coffee cup. And, well . . . CAL-ID's got him. They've got all of us in law enforcement, living and deceased. They're Mike McNally's."

Merci felt feel her heart beating under the windbreaker.

"Coiner knows," said Gilliam. "But I've got to go to Brighton with it. Soon."

Zamorra looked at Merci.

She looked back, then to the director. "Let me talk to him first."

Chapter Seven

Spahn, the vice captain, told her that Mike had called in sick. He looked surprised she didn't know. All the sworn people in the department knew they were more or less together, and most of them, like Spahn, assumed more. The younger deputies treated them as an item—respectfully. The oldsters had begun asking about wedding bells. To Merci it was all a flagrant violation of her privacy but there was nothing she could do about it.

"I'm sure he's at home," said the captain, helpfully.

She drove to his place out in Modjeska Canyon. The afternoon had gone dark and windy, with enormous cumulus rotating in from the northwest. She thought they were like God glowering at you, getting ready to teach you something. The storm was supposed to hit by midnight. She drove fast with her 9mm on the seat beside her, left hand on the wheel straight up, the other free for the shortwave or the phone.

Mike's was a small home on a big lot, plenty of room

for kennels in the back, neighbors not too close. The canyon was named after the opera star who had built a summerhouse there in the early 1900s. The house was set back off a dirt road, surrounded by tremendous oaks that cast the lot in eternal shade. The place was still heated with a woodstove in the fireplace. It was quaint to look at but even colder than her house, and never seemed to get any sunlight. She'd never liked it.

Mike had moved to this dark home about three months back, corresponding to his darker prevailing moods. Corresponding to joining his church. Corresponding to more direct talk of marriage and more evasion on her part. He said he felt empty. He said he wanted to feel the spirit of God in him. He said he wanted security in his life with a woman, with her.

Merci respected his confessed darkness and emptiness, though she wondered at their causes. He'd never lost a loved one to death. His parents and siblings were all alive and kicking. He hadn't gotten a partner killed. He had never been made a fool of by a psychopath. Career on track: healthy, nice looking, plenty of friends.

She had a hard time believing in things that were shapeless rather than specific, emotional rather than tactile. She believed that things made feelings: Tim, Jr. = Happiness; Too Much Scotch = hangover; Bad Judgment = dysfunctional memory and nightmares. Sometimes she wondered if Mike was looking for things he wasn't ready to find.

She parked by the woodpile and noted the fresh cord of

eucalyptus stacked under the eaves, a plastic tarp roped over the top. His van with the built-in dog crates was up beside the house. The bloodhounds were already barking when she got out. Smoke rose from the chimney until the breeze tore it against the branches of the oaks.

When he answered the door she could tell Mike was drunk. She'd seen him drunk maybe three times in her life, so there was no mistaking it. He was a lousy drinker.

"Thought it might be you," he said.

"Three martini lunch?"

"Bottle of Scotch some jerk gave me for my birthday. Hits you hard. Come in."

She stepped in to familiar sights. The braided rug on a hardwood floor scarred by dog nails. Non-matching green couches at right angles, big enough to sleep on. Steamer trunks used for coffee tables, littered with magazines and coffee cups and some of Danny's toys. Danny's king snake in a glass tank by a window. The oak and glass case filled with long guns against one wall of knotty pine. And the framed reproductions featured in all the outdoors magazines Mike subscribed to—dogs, birds, trout.

"I guess you talked to Gilliam," said Mike.

"Yep."

"Want to tell me what he found?"

"I want you to."

"I figured you would. You want some of this shit?" He waved a tumbler at her.

"No. Talk to me, Mike."

They sat on different couches, a traditional sign of contention between them. Merci preferred it that way, but Mike, unless he was pissed off, liked being close. She noted the hairs on the couch fabric, just like the ones Gilliam had described—bloodhound hair.

He leaned forward on the couch and set his glass on a trunk. "I was there Tuesday night. Got there around eight-thirty, left around ten-fifteen. At that time, *incidentally,* she was still alive."

Merci heard the dogs still yapping back in the run, some jays cawing out in the oaks.

"Start at the beginning."

He sighed, swept up his glass, took a gulp and looked at her. "It was strictly business."

"Whose?"

He glared at her. Beneath the boyish forelock of blond hair his eyes looked small and viperine. "Don't read shit into this that isn't there."

"I'm just listening."

He drank again. "I wanted to get some things straight on the Epicure Services sting. There were a couple of things we needed to agree on, get in place. We were going to wire her for a meet with Moladan."

"You take in your piece for dinner?"

He nodded. Merci knew Mike carried a .45 automatic. It was the gun the old-timers liked, known for its alleged stopping and knockdown power. Most of the younger guys used hot 9mm or .357-Magnum loads, known for *their* alleged stopping and knockdown power. The difference was about three hundred feet per second, which meant you could silence a .45 auto, whereas with the others you got a sonic crack that no silencer could suppress. Mike, low-tech and fond of the past, had opted for the bigger, slower load.

"Where did you carry it?"

"Usual place."

"What did she say?"

"Hang it on the chair, but I didn't."

"What did you talk about?"

"How to wear a wire, how to act a part, how to nail Goren Moladan, what do you think?"

"Who's D. C.?"

He blushed. Even in the dim lamplight of the mountain house she could see it.

He shook his hair off his face. "Me."

"Meaning what?"

"Just a nickname. Aubrey had a real lively sense of humor."

Merci let the silence work on him. She felt hollow and betrayed, and she felt the beginnings of fury.

"Dark Cloud," he said finally. "Because I'm always serious and never smile."

"You sent her that card. About friendship."

"That's what it was all about, Merci. *Friendship.*"

Mike took another drink. Then he rattled the ice and got up. He had the drunk's deliberate motion through space, the aura of numb assurance. She glanced to the little table set up near the kitchen, with the phone and answering machine and notepad on it. Mike hung his holster on the chair there, except when his son, Danny, was around—every other weekend—and when he went to bed at night. Then it was over a coat hook on the back of his bathroom door. It was on the chair now.

He sat down, his refilled glass held overcautiously out in front of him.

"Let me tell you what I saw in her, *Merci.* What I saw in her was someone young and full of potential and life. I saw a complete waste of a human being, doing what she did. That was my opinion of her and she knew it. From the first time I saw her. And she, well, she knew I was right. I was doing everything I could do, within reason, to get her out of that world. She wanted a friend. She wanted a man who wasn't just paying up and getting off. She wanted a father and a brother. A friend. And that's what I was trying to be."

"How?"

He huffed through his nose, stared at her. "How do you think? I took her to church with me a couple of times. We'd pray and talk about options, other things she could do. We'd do everyday stuff. We walked on the beach. We went to a park. We'd just . . . *be.* That isn't too much to comprehend, is it? Two people who are just content to *be*?"

Merci felt as if her skin were on fire. It was actually getting hard to see well. When she got mad her vision constricted and lost color, it was like looking at things through the barrel of a shotgun.

"Not hard at all. What was in it for you, Mike?"

"What do you mean, *in it*?"

"I can't get any clearer than that."

He drank, and set down the glass. "I liked her. I respected her, uh, predicament. She was a sweet person, with a good sense of humor, and she'd been screwed over by everybody she'd ever been close to, starting with her own parents. She hadn't seen them in three years. I felt like her . . . protector. Like a guy who could give her a fresh start on things. And what that did for me, *Merci,* was it made me feel good about me. Because I didn't want anything back from her. I wasn't taking. I was just giving decency and respect to her. Just common everyday kindness. It made me feel . . . good. And needed. I think she needed me."

"Was she in love with you?"

He looked away, at the fire, out the window, then down. "I think she was starting to feel that way. When I saw all the trouble she'd gone to for dinner, I realized that. Not before."

"Were you in love with her?"

"Absolutely fucking *not.* Haven't you heard anything I've said?"

"I never heard you say you didn't love her."

"Don't play word games with me. You're better at it and it's a shit thing to pull."

"I asked if you were in love with her."

"And I said not. Which part of that sentence is so confusing?"

She could feel his anger overcoming her own, nullifying it like a backfire. She said nothing for a beat, hoping he'd cool off. But she could see from the color of his face and the nervousness of his eyes that he wasn't.

"I'm in love with *you*," he said. She'd never heard those words spoken with such venom.

"Oh Jesus, Mike," she said quietly. Then she stood and walked over to the fireplace. She could feel the heat. The old hardwood creaked under her boots. A gust of wind whistled through the oaks outside and she heard the plastic tarp slapping against the firewood. She walked over to the gun case, the telephone table, the window facing south.

She'd never had her job and her heart so mixed up in the same thing like this. Pulling different ways. With Hess there hadn't been discord, just disagreement. The heat near the stove and Mike's anger made her feel claustrophobic and faint. The hollowness inside of her had been replaced by a dry fire.

Was she just an incredibly selfish bitch who made her men either dead or miserable?

"There's a lot of you in this," said Mike.

"Please explain that statement."

"You never . . . you never offer me anything."

She looked at him. He was talking into the glass.

"You don't touch. You don't kiss. You don't talk. You don't plan. You don't dream. You don't make me feel necessary or even present. You don't do anything."

"No. No, that's right."

"So what am *I* supposed to do?"

"Fall in love with someone else."

"I told you *I wasn't in love with her!* Don't you get it?"

She finally did get it. It had just taken a few minutes to see it. Mike was right. Mike was telling the truth. Part of the truth, anyway.

"You were falling in love with her. And you were unhappy and afraid of what it would lead to."

He'd turned on the couch to see her, something imploring and flagrantly juvenile in his face now. He stood, wobbly.

"I never once touched her with that in mind. I shook her hand. I hugged her when I left that night."

Strange how her heart felt then, like it had been wrapped in an iron blanket and dropped off the edge of a ship. She walked over and faced him.

"But what, Mike? You never, you never and you never. But then what? What's the last sentence?"

"I never did anything toward her like that. I behaved just like you do."

"But."

"But I enjoyed her company."

"Enjoyed it."

"I enjoyed it a lot. I . . . I *craved* it. What she looked like and how she moved and how she talked and what she said. What she smelled like. I wanted to be there. In the same room with her. She made me feel like doing all the things I wanted to do with you. But I had those feelings completely, one hundred percent under control."

"Did you, Mike?"

"Absolutely. And you're a fool if you don't believe that."

"You kill her?"

He tilted heavily around the couch, stumbled, caught her arm and threw her across the room. She knocked into the wall but kept her balance, hands thwacking backward against the pine.

"Yeah," he said. "I bought a silencer. I had dinner with her then iced her. Arrest me."

She glanced again toward the telephone table and he saw her do it.

"You know I'm kidding," he said. "Right?"

"I'll think about it. I'm going to go now."

His voice was rising now, panic and shame and who knew what else.

"Merci, I'm really awful damned sorry for what I just did. That isn't me. You know that isn't me. You know, right? You know?"

"I know. Stay where you are."

She stared at him as she walked across the room to the front door.

Mike stayed, planted where he was, like he was surprised, like he just now realized what he'd done. There were big tears running down his red face and his mouth was turned down like a Greek mask.

"I'm so fucking sorry, Merci. I love you so much. Don't go. Don't you go away, too."

She trotted to the car because to run was to admit fear. She got the keys in one hand and rode the butt of her H&K with the other. She looked into the backseat before getting in. Then she hit the door lock and started up the big V-8. She saw Mike appear in the doorway, then a fan of dirt falling in the rearview as the Impala dug its rear tires and roared off the lot.

• • •

She stopped at a market in Orange to get a sandwich and the day's newspapers. Her hands were still trembling as she slid the quarters into the machines. Her heart was beating fast and flighty inside and it felt like it wasn't in gear. A bad taste in her mouth. A bum asked her for money and she wanted to pistol-whip him.

She called headquarters for Zamorra, she had to talk to him, but he was still at the hospital.

She got back in the car, drove to the far corner of a near-empty parking lot and cried. She gave herself exactly one minute, shed her tears, then tamped them down with a deep, shuddering breath.

Sneaking bastard, she thought. He doesn't have the balls to kill anybody.

And now she had a murder confession from him. A drunken, sarcastic one, but a murder confession just the same. You could use something like that to obtain a warrant for search. You could use something like that as evidence in a court of law.

Or you could just assume it was spoken in anger, meant to convey its opposite.

She knew he hadn't killed Aubrey Whittaker, though he'd probably done just about everything else to her.

Merci got out of the car, walked around it a few times, got back in. She dug out her appointment book and checked the rest of the day. In spite of the fact that her lover had probably betrayed her with a prostitute, then confessed the murder to her, she did have some good things to look forward to.

Such as a two o'clock appointment to see psychiatrist Dr. Sid Botts—whose name she'd triangulated from Aubrey Whittaker's address book, the calendar and a little common sense—the second-to-last person to see Aubrey Whittaker alive.

And a three-thirty with Newport Maranatha Church Christian Singles leader Reverend Lance Spartas, one of the two johns who'd come up positive on the federal firearms check. He owned a Smith .45-caliber automatic, purchased ninety days ago.

And a five o'clock with Bob del Viggio, builder of housing tracts, political donor, client of Aubrey Whittaker.

Plus a turkey-on-rye still untouched on the seat.

Get it together, woman.

She called the hospital but Zamorra had just left.

Aubrey Whittaker's murder made it to the front page of the local section in the *Times, Register* and *Journal.* So far, none of the reporters had found out anything she hadn't. All three described Aubrey as a "professional escort." Nobody mentioned Epicure Services.

She folded up the papers and tossed them in the backseat and looked out the windshield to the blackening sky.

Chapter Eight

Botts was a round, disheveled man with a wispy Freudian goatee and rosy cheeks. His reading glasses hung from a cord around his neck. His white shirt looked neither clean nor pressed, and his corduroy jacket was drawn tight around the stomach but rose unsatisfied from his shoulders. His handshake was warm. Merci felt an impulse to find the nearest couch, plop down, spill it all about Mike McNally.

The building was in Santa Ana, the other end of town from headquarters. Merci stepped from the receptionist-free waiting room into the consultation room: a couch and armchair, a desk with a banker's lamp on it, four shelves filled with books, two more lamps and two windows with blinds drawn against the dark day.

"I read the paper today," he said. "I was very saddened. Even though you had told me about her when you called."

"Thanks for meeting."

Botts sat behind his desk and Merci chose the couch. He watched her take out the blue notebook. "Like I said on the phone, I can't betray Aubrey's privacy here. I can only talk in very general terms about her. But if I can help you find who did it, then I'm willing. It seems the humane thing to do."

"I'll level with you, Doctor. Aubrey Whittaker was a prostitute. I assume you know that."

"Yes."

"We don't have a suspect yet. I've got a copy of her little black book, plenty of names and dates. Too many. Just the existence of that book could provide motive for murder. I need to narrow down, zero in."

"What do you want to know?"

"If she was seeing someone. Someone outside the trade."

Botts cleared his throat, then spoke gently. "Yes, she was. She never told me his name or occupation. But she'd met someone recently—approximately one month ago—and she seemed to have hopes for a relationship with him. She was rather . . . excited about him. She said they met at church. I don't know which one. She was always attending new ones, hoping to find one she really liked. That was Aubrey, in microcosm, very much looking for something she could be happy with. Trying different things, like the wigs she wore. All of them blond, interestingly."

Merci couldn't decide if this was interesting or not. She made a note: *all blond for Botts, but closet had other colors.*

"What was wrong with the other churches?"

"Too shallow. Too personal. Too prying. Too social and not religious enough. Aubrey wanted a God that was fair, but stern. She wanted to be punished, then saved. She thought she deserved both."

Merci considered the contradictions in Aubrey Whittaker: sell the body and search the soul; God of forgiveness and God of wrath.

"What else, about the church guy?"

Botts leaned onto his elbows. His jacket rode higher. "Tall. Strong. Handsome. Polite. Honest. Unmarried. She said he was unlike any man she'd ever met."

"Where does he live?"

"She never said."

"A member of the church?"

"That is very possible."

Merci thought. "Was she in love with him?"

"I think so, yes."

"Was she afraid for her life?"

"No. I do not believe she thought she was in any kind of mortal danger."

"How did you diagnose her?"

Botts cleared his throat again. "Depression."

"What did you prescribe?"

"Nothing. We talked about medications, the plusses and minuses. She chose not to take that course."

"Was that the right decision?"

"I believe so. After our first hour, I told her she had very deep unresolved emotions toward her father. She laughed at the obviousness of this. I did not. I won't go into that history with you. But I will say there was good reason for her feelings. She was obviously not psychotic or delusional. I sensed in her tendencies toward grandeur and perhaps paranoia, tendencies toward depression. She was self-flagellating, self-critical. It was clear to me that large areas of feeling were left unexpressed and unexamined. Anger, specifically. She had closed off some things, in self-protection. But, in my opinion, for her age, she was clear-seeing, self-aware and mentally vigorous. I didn't think she needed medication. She needed *meditation*. Time to think things through. And a new job, preferably in a different part of the world. Anywhere but here or in Oregon, which was where she grew up. Portland."

Merci thought. In her notebook she wrote: *Oregon to Botts, Iowa to Mike.*

"What was she like, Doctor? In lay terms?"

He smiled. "Irreverent. Alert. Caustic at times. Self-deprecating. Self-critical. Quick to laugh, quick to castigate. She was very sentimental about certain things. Horses—although she'd only ridden a few times. Good men—even though she'd never met one, until this new fellow. It was apparent to me that she took great stock in an ideal world, one from which she felt excluded. She reserved her most punishing and negative feelings for men in general, and for herself."

"What did Aubrey Whittaker think of herself?"

Botts sighed. "Mostly she detested herself, Sergeant. At other times, there was pity."

Merci thought about this. About the way a life can get bent a little, and later the bend takes you around in circles. Like the steering linkage on your car. Trouble was, you got going fast enough and the bend would take you right off the road and into a truck. A truck with a silencer.

"She ever talk about her boss?"

"Never."

"Goren Moladan?"

"No."

"She was working outside the agency, from what I can tell. That can be fatal, in the wrong circumstances."

"It seems today like everything can be. Driving on the freeway, answering the door."

Merci often took statements like that as professional affronts, but she let this one go. "Dr. Botts, was she paying for these sessions herself?"

"Yes."

"Last question for now, Doctor. In the time you treated her, how many men did she have real hopes for? Like this last one, this guy she supposedly met at church?"

Botts shook his head slowly, with visible sadness. "Just him."

• • •

Lance Spartas, assistant pastor of Newport Maranatha Church, had insisted on meeting Merci away from his work. She smelled a guilty conscience in this, easy enough when you find a guy's credit-card number in a prostitute's black book.

He was tall, dark-haired and handsome, with a smile that looked like he had just been caught at something and knew you'd forgive him. Thirtyish. Sharp clothes, big watch, snappy haircut. A squirrel, she thought, the kind of guy she'd like to dunk in a toilet.

They sat in the bar of a pricey little steak house on Coast Highway. A wall-to-wall aquarium behind the bar looked otherworldly to her: bright spirits easing through rock and bubbles. The bar was almost empty.

"Thanks for meeting off-campus," said Spartas. He sounded anxious.

"I understand."

"I really didn't know her well. She only came to the chapel once that I know of. She came to my group, Christian Singles, after worship. This was, oh, six, eight weeks ago. I never saw her after that."

Guilty conscience, Merci thought again: eager to help, eager to please, eager to lie.

The barmaid came by and gave Spartas a smile. She called him Lance. He called her Sherry. He asked how she was and when she was going to come to worship with them.

"Saturday nights are a killer," Sherry said, jamming a stack of bills into a plastic holder atop a round tray. She got a soft drink for Spartas, a cup of coffee for Merci, then swung into the lounge, tray up, athletic shoes squeaking.

"Ever go to Aubrey's place?"

"Well, no. I have no idea where she lived."

"Ever see her off-campus?"

He shook his head but said nothing, lips tightened around his straw. He glanced at her, then looked at the aquarium.

"Did she come to church alone?"

"Uh-huh. After worship she showed up at the Singles. We're the twenty to thirty age group. She introduced herself, said she was a marketing consultant based in Orange County, just moved from Fort Worth. Grew up there. Said she liked to ride—horses, you know, liked to roller skate, liked to visit galleries. She said she was twenty-three years old, but she looked younger to me. The paper said nineteen. I didn't think she was that young. The part about being an escort surprised me."

"Did it?"

"Absolutely."

When he looked at her, briefly, she saw the guilt brimming up into his eyes. He couldn't fool his own mother, she thought. She made a note of Aubrey Whittaker's third home state.

"What did you think of her?"

Spartas breathed deeply, stirring his drink. "She was a little aloof. Kind of arrogant. Like the Christian Singles were beneath her somehow. She seemed very sophisticated. She had a sharp tongue. Tall. Nice figure and face. Beautiful dark hair."

Merci noted that Aubrey was a brunette for Spartas. "What did she want from the group?"

Spartas nodded. "I wondered, too. What we all want, I guess. Fellowship. Friendship. Maybe somebody to fall in love with. But I don't know. She didn't seem particularly interested in our activities, in any of our members. Of course, she was only with us once. Like she was shopping."

"Then what, you called her?"

She could feel him wince. He wiped his mouth with his napkin.

"No."

He looked at her.

"Yeah. Yes."

"You want to tell me about that?"

"I wanted to know if she'd join us on a ski weekend up in Big Bear. She said no."

"Then you asked to see her."

The wince again, a psychic shudder she could feel but not quite see. "Yes."

"And when she explained the deal, you whipped out your credit card."

A big exhale from Spartas. He looked at her with a mixture of panic and shame.

"Where did you go?"

"Four Seasons."

"October fifteenth, Monday night."

"I guess."

"Don't."

"Yes, correct."

"How much?"

"A thousand for . . . her. The room was three-fifty. Wine and cheese another fifty."

"How long were you with her?"

He shook his head. It seemed to have retreated down between his shoulders. "Five minutes."

When the barmaid strolled up and asked how they were doing Lance mustered the smile that said he'd been caught at something. The part about forgiving him was gone. "Everything's fine, Sherry. Thanks."

Merci watched her head to the waitress station at the other end of the bar.

"Was it a good five minutes?"

"Come on," he said quietly. "Yeah, sure. It was fine."

Merci sipped the coffee, felt the waves of discomfort rising outward from Lance Spartas.

"You do it again?"

"No. Just that. It was . . . well, what's it matter, but that was the first and only time with, you know, for money." He turned to her then. "This isn't getting back to the church, is it? That's my whole life, down the drain. The whole thing."

"You lie to me and it will."

"I've been one hundred percent honest with you."

"Good."

"All I've *done* is worry since the second you called."

He wiped his forehead with the damp bar napkin, staring at the fish.

"When she left the hotel that night, were you angry?"

Spartas considered. He shook his head. "No. I wondered at what I'd just done. How it could have happened. Angry at myself, yeah. That. Not at her."

"So that forty-five you bought three months ago never came to mind?"

He turned to her again, thin lips parted, eyes wide. "It's under my bed. I swear to God. I'll show it to you if you want. It's still in the box. It's never been fired."

Merci said nothing for a minute, let the accusation hover. Spartas squirmed on his stool.

She leaned up close. "Maybe it didn't quite go like you said it did. Maybe it went an hour and five minutes and things just wouldn't line up for you. Maybe she made a crack about it. Maybe she did more than that. A woman can hurt a guy that way. Maybe after what she did, she *deserved* to get iced. Maybe that made you so furious you followed her out fourteen hundred bucks poorer, trailed the snotty nineteen-year-old home. Thought about it, went back a few weeks later and evened things out."

"Swear to my God I didn't."

"You kill her?"

"No!"

"Want to?"

"No. Nothing like that. No."

"What about the gun?"

"I got it for home protection," he said. "There was an armed robbery down the street last summer. The guy who lived there scared them off with a gun. So I got one, too."

Lance Spartas struck Merci as the kind of schmuck who'd shoot his neighbor or himself before he managed to clock a bad guy. The hapless citizen was as dangerous as a creep sometimes. Like a Sunday driver.

"Then where were you Tuesday night?"

Spartas smiled like a man just pardoned. "Christian Singles potluck, thank God! I can prove that if I have to. Seven until midnight."

She looked at him. He wasn't her kind of guy, but he was okay—decent looking, clean, more or less the overgrown boy most men seemed to be. "Why her, Spartas? If that was your first time paying for it?"

He looked at Merci, then down into his drink. His face had flushed pink.

"She was the most beautiful woman I'd ever seen in my life. She was just absolutely beautiful. When she said I could own her for a thousand dollars and a good bottle of wine, I took it."

"Own her."

"That's what she said."

"She proposed?"

"Well, yeah. I thought she was a marketing consultant, whatever that is. I didn't realize she was a professional until I had the credit card out. By then, it didn't matter. Man, I wish I could just go back and have it all to not do over again. I feel like I've been touched by Satan."

"You feel anything for her, or just yourself?"

He gave her an odd look then, something she couldn't read. His voice was a whisper. "I feel like if her soul goes to hell, I had something to do with it. Like I should have done something to help her."

She studied him hard. Beyond the selfishness and fear and guilt was a decent man. Or at least a decent boy. With a bad conscience and a sheen of sweat on his face.

Merci slid off the stool, dropped a couple of bucks on the bar.

"Thanks. Lance, keep the gun in the box and the dong in your pants. You don't know what you're doing with either of them."

• • •

Bob del Viggio greeted her at his job site with a handshake and an appraising eye. He had a crafty smile, broad shoulders, black curly hair. Mid-forties, she guessed, heavy and strong, a big solid ass he seemed proud of. Chinos, a blue work shirt, construction boots.

He led her into an on-site trailer, threw out his super and motioned for Merci to sit in front of a table littered with blueprints and ashtrays. He poured coffee into a foam cup; Merci declined. She could see the big blades outside, stalled by the rain, brown water standing on the building pads.

She got right to the point—del Viggio's recent credit-card charge by Epicure.

"Yeah, that was me," he said.

"Who was the girl?"

"She called herself Gayla. You know, it's all first names. All made up. I recognized her in the paper. Aubrey something, it said. That sounds made up, too."

"Tell me about it."

"Not much to tell. I went through Epicure, the girl met me down at the Ritz. Two hours later she left. Pretty much by the book."

Del Viggio appraised Merci from the other side of the makeshift desk. He sipped the coffee, looked out a dusty window, then back to her.

"I donated big to Brighton's campaign last time. Part of his Gold Circle Club."

"Who cares?"

He shrugged, big shoulders tightening the fabric of his work shirt. His forearms were thick and tanned. "Brighton, hopefully."

"If you think a few thousand bucks to a campaign chest lets you do whatever you want, you've got another thing coming."

"That's not what I meant. What I meant was, I'm a law-respecting guy, I try to play by the rules, I try to help out good people. And he's one of them—that's all."

"So much for the rules when you called Epicure for a girl."

He nodded. "Yeah. Look, Sergeant, I shouldn't have done that. I got caught. You can wreck my marriage, my family, a big part of my business. I'm asking you not to. Don't, because I didn't hurt her. I sure didn't kill her Tuesday night, assuming that's why you're here. I . . . I did what I did, tipped her way too much and off she went. I bought a whore. I didn't kill her. I can account for my whereabouts."

Del Viggio held her gaze across the desk.

"First time with her?"

"Yeah."

"But not with Epicure."

"No."

"How many?"

"Twenty, thirty."

"Before Epicure?"

"Yeah, others. I'm that way."

"Married and all. Two children, high-school age."

He nodded, leaned to his left.

"Show me their pictures and I'll arrest you right now."

He leaned back. "I'm asking you to let it slide, Sergeant. I don't deserve it. But I'm asking anyway. I'll do anything I can to help you. You can name it. But don't wreck me."

His plea seemed genuine, though Merci detected nothing desperate in it. Del Viggio was a man used to accommodation.

"It's . . ." His voice trailed off.

"It's what? A tragedy? A shame? Terrible what happened?"

"It's the way I am," he said. "I don't like it. I don't respect it. But I can't change it."

"You own a sidearm?"

"I've got a Smith revolver under the bed. A trap gun I never use."

Merci studied him for a long moment. "Tuesday night," she said finally.

Del Viggio sighed and shook his head. "Cindy. Talk to Goren Moladan."

"Why not Gayla?"

"Unavailable."

On her way back to headquarters she stopped by Seashell Cleaners and picked up Aubrey's clothes: four dresses, two suits, three pairs of jeans, two sweaters.

The clerk looked at her with uncertainty but said nothing besides "Sixty-two fifty, please."

Chapter Nine

Brighton held open the door to his office, shut it when she was in.

"Listen to that," he said.

She heard the rain roaring down outside. It took quite a storm to announce itself through the thick county building walls. The windows were vertical slits and through them Merci could see the water pouring down. Six hours early, she noted, according to the news.

"Sit, please," the sheriff said. He sprawled back into the chair behind his desk and locked his fingers behind his head. Brighton was a big man. Merci thought he looked like a farmer: ruddy complexion, veinous hands, pale and sun-beaten eyes. He was getting near the end of his career and talking to the press about retirement again.

He'd talked about it near the end of last year, too, and the year before that. The reporters always wanted to know who the next sheriff would be. The editorials were a little stronger this year, she had noted. The papers thought maybe it was time for Brighton to endorse the young blood he would leave behind.

Merci had always hoped that the young blood would include hers. A chance to move up. There would be a big shuffle—some up, some down, some sideways, some out. It had always been her personal plan to run the Homicide Detail by the time she was forty, run the Crimes Against Persons Section by fifty, be elected sheriff by fifty-eight. Fourteen years ago, when she'd first been sworn and hatched her timetable, it had seemed possible if unlikely.

But things change. Tim Hess, her old partner, had been killed in the line of duty by a murderer called the Purse Snatcher. Merci had dispatched that monster, and she'd gotten decorated for it. But the sworn men and women of the department knew the truth: Hess had saved her ass in the eleventh hour, and it was her gun that had been used to kill him. You didn't run Homicide Detail—let alone the whole Sheriff Department—unless you had the respect of your people. Even now, at times, two plus years and a thousand prayers of forgiveness later, Merci Rayborn still wasn't sure if she respected herself.

But Merci now had something that seemed far more important than running the Crimes Against Persons Section by fifty: She had her son. He was beautiful and bright and precious and possessed an infinity of potential. It was her job to let it happen for him. She could never have predicted such a change in herself, and she'd had little time to prepare for such a change. She'd made love to Hess just once, back when she'd believed in the power of her own will, thinking it might save his life. Instead, they had created one.

"I heard about Mike and the girl," said Brighton.

"Sir, I apologize if I got in Gilliam's way. I wanted to talk to Mike first. See if there was some simple—"

"No, not that," he said, waving a hand. "That's fine. I called you in here because I was thinking more along the lines of what in hell happened."

"I believe that he was developing feelings for her."

Merci heard her own voice as if it were someone else's. It sounded strange to her: automatic, prepared. *Developing feelings. Christ.* Like she was Wally the Weasel in Public Information, doing a press briefing.

"Whittaker was one of the Epicure girls vice was working," she continued. "Mike recruited her. She invited him for dinner. He went. Later that night she was murdered."

She compared her mechanical voice to the sinking, humiliating anger in her heart, and she understood what she was doing.

Brighton understood it, too. "You don't have to do PR for the stupid sonofabitch."

"No. Thank you, sir." She felt the anger draining out of her, the disappointment pouring in to replace it. She felt like a complete sucker, a dupe, a punching bag. Brighton had always been in favor of Mike and Merci together. He'd mentioned it. He'd approved. That had meant a lot within the department.

He watched her like a farmer watching wheat. "Look, I'm going to have to let this slide around here. Mike had the sweets for a whore, went to her house. That accounts for his fingerprints all over the damned place. Okay. These things happen. In vice, these things happen more than they should. My official line is a slap on the wrist for McNally, but really no big deal. You're going to have to deal with your end of it, Merci. I can't stand up and bark just because Mike acted stupid. I'm sorry."

"I know, sir. I didn't expect anything like that."

"When things cool off, a month or so, I'll move him out of vice. He seems to understand the feelings of dogs quite well."

Brighton smiled and Merci joined him. He told her he had Gilliam and Coiner under penalty of death if this got out to the press. Same with her. She smiled bitterly and looked away.

"What's it look like so far? The Whittaker thing?"

"Someone she knew. He knocked. She had a peephole. The porch light was on. She knew him, or thought she could trust him. One shot in the heart with a silenced forty-five, the second she opened the door. After he shot her, he was inside for at least ten minutes. He left wads of cash in her purse. Didn't take a thing we know of yet. It's strange, sir. Clean and cold, like a contract killing. Up close and personal, like a love thing gone bad. I've got a list of johns and a call-out sheet coming from the phone company. We've got plenty to work with. There's motivation all over the place, if she was thinking blackmail."

Brighton considered. "Any prints besides hers and McNally's?"

She told him about the latents not good enough to send through AFIS or CAL-ID. She told him they hoped for a DrugFire hit on the brass casing. She told him about the hair and fiber and shoeprint, if they could eliminate Aubrey's own clothes and those, possibly, of Mike McNally.

Brighton listened passively. He wasn't a guy who filled up silences. "And how's Miss Patti Bailey?"

"I've barely scratched it, sir."

"I don't expect you to kill yourself on it," he said. "I give those out to clean the files. If we solve one, fine."

"I understand."

"Bailey was a prostitute, too," he said. "I'm sure you figured out that much by now. I remember she was mixed in with the narcotics suppliers back then. You know, that was nineteen sixty-nine. Supposed to be free love and cheap highs and bell-bottoms. A lot of it was. But the speed racket guys weren't giving it away. Neither were the heroin sellers. And we had lots of professional girls out on Harbor Boulevard, servicing the guys who weren't getting it for free. Lots of conventioneers. Tourists."

"Like now."

"Exactly." Brighton swiveled in his chair and looked out one of the vertical windows. "That was a long time ago. I was forty years old that year. A captain. Two years later, they asked me to be the sheriff. Thirty years of that. It seems like about fifteen minutes."

"You've done well, sir."

He swung back, a dry smile in place. "Time to think about stepping aside."

"You've said that every year, sir. For the last few, anyway."

He smiled but his eyes narrowed. "That's the perception?"

"Just mine," Merci said quietly. Even at thirty-six, her talent for saying the wrong thing was undiminished.

"I appreciate your candor, Sergeant. Give me some more of it now: How would you feel about Nelson Neal as sheriff?"

Watch it now, she thought. "Fine. Not inspirational."

Brighton nodded. "Craig Braga?"

"Yes."

"Mel Glandis?"

"Same as Nelson."

"How about Vince Abelera, over in the Marshal's Department? He wants it. He's got some rank-and-file P.D. support, a good face for the cameras."

Merci had heard Abelera's spiel on the TV news: If he

was sheriff, he'd trim the fat and hire more deputies, he'd franchise some of the inmate population into private "jails," the public would become his "customers," law enforcement was a "marketplace." He said the Sheriff Department should be run like any corporation. He was handsome, dressed well and had good teeth.

"I think he's telling people what they want to hear. Everybody wants to save money. Everybody wants more cops."

Brighton nodded again. His eyes were small and bright in his craggy face.

"You still have your eyes on the Crimes Against Persons Section?"

"It seems years away."

"And someone's got to be running Homicide Detail when Peralt retires. That's early next year."

"I'd love to get my hands on it. But you need the respect. I'm thirty-six and I'm a woman. I'm a mom. There was Hess. I'd need . . . extra respect."

Brighton listened, cocked his head to the rain, then looked back at her. "You have mine. Sorry about your boyfriend."

"I'd rather you didn't call him that."

"Noted. I'm sorry the dumb prick didn't exhibit better sense with this girl. We're all going to suffer for his antics now."

"I do appreciate your saying that."

"It'll blow over. Unless it leaks all over the department and the reporters get it." Brighton seemed to consider this possibility, then he blinked and shook away the vision. "Look, tomorrow's Friday. You could use a day away from here. Do what you can with the Bailey case. But Rayborn—don't kill yourself over this one. Nineteen sixty-nine was a bad year then, and it's a bad year still. Bring me the guy who shot Miss Whittaker. That's who I want."

"You'll have him, sir. I promise that."

• • •

Zamorra was at his desk when Merci walked back into the pen. His face looked tired but his eyes were oddly hopeful.

"Moladan checks out at the Bay Club," he said. "Pond scum sticks together."

"McNally went to dinner that night. Friends. They'd become the best of friends."

Zamorra looked at her, shaking his head. There was lipstick on the collar of his white shirt.

"How is she?" asked Merci.

"Tomorrow's the day. Tomorrow morning, at six."

"I'll say a prayer then, Paul."

"There's a chance it could work."

The prayer or the "experiment," Merci wondered. Whatever that was. If Paul wasn't going to talk, she wasn't going to pry.

She sat down and glanced at the list of johns that Moladan had given them. More names for Gary Brice to run, she thought. She looked for a note from Coiner or O'Brien, hoping they'd lucked out with AFIS or CAL-ID on one of the latents. It would be nice to know somebody else had been to Aubrey Whittaker's home, other than her own alleged boyfriend. Boyfriend. She'd always hated the word. Ex-boyfriend sounded even more preposterous. What in hell was he? Ex-*something*. At any rate, no note.

"I'm going to make another pass through Whittaker's place," she said. "Check the closets and dry cleaning against the fibers Gilliam found."

"I'm in."

Merci was happy for that. For one thing, she thought partners came up with more than singles. Two pair of eyes, two minds, all that. Two guns, if it went that way.

But more, she hated the idea of being alone, especially in a place that wasn't hers. She had felt this way ever since the Purse Snatcher had fooled her. In the end, she'd taken his life, and he'd taken her courage. She could always feel the fear inside, humming along her nerves, a simmering anxiety that could rise to panic in a couple of beats of her heart. The panic brought coldness to her bones, weight to her muscles, a haze to her vision. It made her feel slow and helpless.

It was tripped by things that would have embarrassed her if she'd told anyone about them—dark rooms, elevators, parking structures. Cars at night or early morning.

Baths. Using the bathroom. Bathroom fans that whirred on when you hit the light switch. Showers. The walk from her bedroom to Tim's room late at night. The walk back. The ocean. Trees without leaves.

Anything she did alone, or anything she looked at that made her feel alone.

She had plenty of antidotes: security lights in the yards; double-checking the car before getting in; a gun hidden safely in every room; one .32 backup strapped to her ankle and another under the seat of both the Impala and her own Trans Am; nightly courtesy patrols of her area by Sheriff Department deputies; an expensive alarm system installed in her old orange grove house; more hours on the range with the nine jumping in her hands, again and again and again.

Having her father move in was partially an antidote.

Seeing Mike had been partially an antidote.

Socializing after work once a month on Thursdays was an antidote.

None of them worked. It was still there inside, ready to flare up, like a gastric virus picked up on some exotic vacation. Much worse than that, actually. More like a freezing river that would take you with it, shut you down, sweep you under forever where it was too cold and dark even to breathe.

She called Roy Thornton up in Arrowhead. Personnel had dug up the number for her. He said he'd talk tomorrow if she wanted to, gave her directions, told her to bring her snow chains. They already gotten two feet, much more to come.

He also asked her to bring the old file to help refresh him, to jar the memories "out of this tired old gourd."

Then she called her father to say she'd be home late.

"SUDS Club?"

"Yeah."

The Sheriff's Unsocial Deputies Society—named by Evan O'Brien, who had an eye for a good acronym—met on the second Thursday of each month, 7 P.M. at Cancun Restaurant.

"Keep Tim warm and dry," she said. "I miss you guys."

"We miss you. It's chaos out there on the freeways. Be careful."

Chapter Ten

The rain heaved down and made freeway lakes in the low spots, cars planed off the asphalt or into each other. Merci couldn't see dick out the windshield even with the wipers pegged and the defroster on full blast. All just water and red lights and the roar of rain on sheet metal three inches from her head. It took over an hour from the sheriff building to Aubrey Whittaker's apartment in San Clemente. Zamorra left headquarters after Merci did but got there first.

He was already inside, standing in the living room, still wearing his black overcoat, watching the storm roil the Pacific. She saw a pink shiver of lightning branch into the dark water. She flipped on some lights, Aubrey's dry cleaning hooked in one of her hands, hangers digging into her fingers.

"Okay," she said. "A black wool and Orlon mix garment, possibly a sweater, knit cap, gloves or muffler."

"I'll take the kitchen," he said. "It's been bothering me."

So be it. She hit the bedroom lights, placed the dry cleaning on the bed, slid open the mirrored closet door, then hung the clean clothes at one end. Starting at the other end, she began taking out hangers three or four at a time, laying them on the bed.

Merci, not a good judge of the cost of clothing, estimated several thousands of dollars on the first twenty hangers—dresses by designers of whom she was only vaguely aware. A smart red leather outfit with gold buckles on the straps still had a price tag attached: $1700.

The most Merci had ever paid for a dress was $335 a little over two years ago. It was long, black and simple, worn just once.

The smell of perfume wafted up as she lifted the hangers. After the dresses came the skirts, then the blouses, then the more casual tops. On the other side of the closet were coats and jackets, pants, some frankly provocative leather and vinyl items. Merci wasn't sure how they were put on. She wanted to be able to imagine herself in such a thing, but couldn't.

You don't touch. You don't kiss. You don't dream.

A scared, sexless cow, she thought: There're worse things to be, aren't there? Maybe she *would* be heading up the Homicide Detail by age forty.

She had an urge to try on some of Aubrey Whittaker's clothes, just to see how they looked. The red leather getup would be the one. She ranked this among the top ten most stupid ideas she'd had in her life. Banished it. Banished it again.

The sweaters were folded and stacked on the left side of the top shelf. Black cashmere, black cotton, black angora. No black wool. On the right-hand part of the shelf she found some knit caps and berets, two pairs of knit gloves and three mufflers. Lots of wool there, but only the gloves were black, and no Orlon in the mix according to the labels.

She checked the dry cleaning next. Nothing that matched what the lab had found.

Then she searched the laundry basket in the corner: lots of underwear and clothes but no wool. She noted the shoes and boots, the sandals and slippers, the 240-count box of condoms beside the leather thigh-highs. What a thing to do for a living, thought Merci. She figured that Aubrey Whittaker had probably spent more time in sexual intercourse in one year than she herself would in her whole life. She felt bad about this, in indefinite ways.

You don't plan. You don't dream. You don't do anything.

The dresser on the opposite side of the room contained more underwear than Merci thought one woman would ever own. You name it, Aubrey had it. But the socks were cotton or cotton/Lycra. The athletic clothes were more of the same.

Underneath the Lycra shorts in the top drawer she found a stack of opened mail. It looked like mostly greeting cards. She sat in the chair in the corner and turned on the reading lamp next to it. She checked for return addresses on the colored envelopes, none. She checked the postmarks—Santa Ana. They were addressed by hand in small, neat print that immediately sent her heart into a quick acceleration. She put them in chronological order and started with the earliest.

Blue envelope, matching blue card with a bird on it.
Hang in there. Rough times, but worth it.
—A Supporter

Green envelope, matching green card with whale on it.
Sometimes it's hardest to do what's right.
—A Supporter

Red envelope, matching red card with a pine tree on it.
The heart heals best in the broken places.
—A Supporter and Fan

They were all in Sergeant Mike McNally's neat printing. She should know.

Her own card would read:

My trembling heart says fuck you, you two-timing asshole, eat shit and die.
—Merci Rayborn

White envelope, matching white card with a cactus on it.

Proud of what you did today. Thanks.

—MM

Yellow envelope, matching yellow card with a bumblebee on it.

I can't express how highly I think of you.

—Not So Secret Admirer

"I could vomit," she said to no one. She heard a cabinet shut out in the kitchen, Paul trying to figure the struggle between a live man and a dead woman lying ten feet away.

She put back the cards and found another collection in the same drawer, under the workout T-shirts.

The envelopes were legal size, plain white. Same postmark, no return address. They were addressed by computer or a good typewriter, she couldn't tell which.

The writing inside was typewritten or computer-generated, too. Double-spaced, a common-looking font.

November 11

Dear Aubrey,

Just wanted you to know you did the right thing. Moladan needs to go and you need to help me get him. It might not feel like it now, but you're doing the RIGHT thing. When we've taken care of him, it's going to help us take care of YOU.

Take Care,

Mike

November 17

Dear Aubrey,

Funny to write a fan letter to someone I hardly know. It's got to be a first. I don't mean to harp on things, but I wanted you to know how PROUD I am of you and what you're doing. Every once in a while when I'm around a person I get a strong feeling that there's some kind of blessing in store for them. I feel they're going to get out of their trouble, rise and fly, become the great person they were destined to become. I see that in YOU. I'm thankful to have some small part in it. It's a pleasure just to watch. I'll help you think of a plan when this is all over. I want very badly for you to be free of the chains that hold you. I want to see you FLY up into the sun and disappear into its light.

All Best,

Mike

Merci shook her head and dropped the first two letters to the floor.

November 28

Dear Aubrey,

Had a nice Thanksgiving dinner and I said the prayer before the meal. I thanked God for all the blessings in this world, for this life around us, for the bounty and the goodness. I thanked God for people like YOU. I hoped you were doing something that would bring you nearer God. I wished you could have been with us. Though I've got no idea what my fiancee would think of that! Some things are hard to explain! I'm just fantasizing now, but I hold you in my thoughts.

True Best,

Mike

Dec. 3

Dear Aubrey,

You're right, I am a dark cloud and if you want to call me D.C. that's fine with me. At least you see what's inside me. Sometimes I think I'm a dark cloud trying to be a sunny day, but you know, all the stuff I see all day makes me serious and then I get gloomy and then I get sad. There's actually a lively HEART in here somewhere, though I don't feel it all the time. Anyway, just was thinking about you and wanted to communicate. I hope you don't find these cards and letters to be a nuisance.

Sometimes when I write to you I feel like I'm writing to someone I've never seen or met, someone I never will see or meet, some ideal kind of woman you have in your head but never really see. It's strange, what emotions do to the way you feel. Your bones and blood feel different inside. Like your body is running on a different kind of fuel. I've never been good at expressing myself but it's easy for me to write to you. Easy to just say what's on my mind. Like I said before, when I see you I see a person who's going to FLY someday. Someday soon. It's nice to see you starting to do it. Nice to see Aubrey Whittaker growing into who she can be. I'll do everything I can to help you.

Your Pal,
D.C.

Dec. 5
Dear Aubrey,

I have to say that what you talked about yesterday disturbed me QUITE a lot. It's one thing to joke a little about my fiancee and what she should or shouldn't be doing for me, but that crack about exposing "my relationship with a prostitute" to the people I work with sent a bad shiver down my spine. I HOPE you were just joking. You've got a sharp tongue and a fine mind, young lady, so I'm going to give you the benefit of the doubt. But some places you have to go carefully. I'm proud of my relationship with you—because I'm proud of you—but there are so many ways it could be misconstrued by my co-workers, not to mention my fiancee. Anyway, I don't mean to OVERREACT to what you said. I just want you to know that I hold all of my relationships—ours, all of them—sacred. Don't mess with that.

Always Your Friend,
D.C.

Merci read the letter again. She thought: I don't mean to get overly SUSPICIOUS, but I wonder if this WHORE was talking about blackmail.

Dec. 8
Dear Aubrey,

I'm really sorry for blowing up on the phone, but when you talked about "payment for what I'd been getting" I just saw red. I thought what I was "getting" was being offered free of charge. I've treasured every minute of it! You can't charge people money for EVERYTHING, you know. And please, don't even joke about my fiancee, or the people I work with, anymore. Those areas are off-limits for some things. If I've been taking advantage of you in some way, I'll be the first to "make a payment" to make it right, but I honestly don't see that I have. What have I taken? What could I owe? You know, we need to talk. Will call soon. I do honestly miss you in ways I've never missed anybody. I really AM looking forward to dinner at your place.

Your Admirer,
Mike

You missed her and you were afraid of her and she was yanking your chain. And three nights later, thought Merci, just after the dinner she made for you, she was dead.

Merci felt like taking a scalding shower with oven cleaner and a wire brush. It was like all of Mike's earnestness and naïveté and colossal stupidity had turned to tar and she'd been dipped in it.

Means, motive and opportunity, she thought. The three textbook requisites for homicide, and Mike had them all.

She collected the letters and put them back. In the same drawer, close to the back, she found an unlabeled VHS tape. She actually shuddered, thinking what you'd get on a private video belonging to Aubrey Whittaker.

She took it and went to find her partner.

He was sitting cross-legged on the kitchen floor, facing

the still-open drawers and cabinet. No overcoat now. His elbows were on his knees and his face rested on his fists and he didn't move when she came in. There was a little dustball directly in front of him.

"Why the lower two drawers?" he asked quietly. "Why the cabinet under the sink? There's a struggle of some kind in the kitchen, between who and who we don't know yet, but the stuff on the counter is fine. The upper drawers aren't open. The toaster and spice rack and utensils weren't disturbed. The counter TV wasn't knocked down. The notes and cartoons stuck to the refrigerator with magnets weren't knocked off. But the wood screws on the cabinet handle were wrenched out. The metal runner on the drawer was bent too bad to close. There was some real strength there. Something fierce between them."

She went with the obvious. "They hit the floor fast, and that's where they fought."

He shrugged. "I told myself that. I just couldn't picture it. Two grown humans. Not children. Not snakes."

Merci tried to picture the scene, but it wouldn't form for her, either. Hess had taught her to picture things. She could do it, but she couldn't do it well, yet.

The obvious again: "CSIs must have dusted the living shit out of it."

"They got the handle, the drawers—zip. Wiped clean."

"No, I mean *everything*. Everything lower than the top of the cabinet. Two people fight like that, how's the winner going to remember everything he touched? That's good paint. The floor's got a good finish. The appliances are perfect. They'll hold prints."

Zamorra was nodding. He looked back at her, then down at the dust ball on the floor in front of him.

"That, they didn't do. Coiner and O'Brien were thorough, not exhaustive. I didn't see anything in the file about the drawers that weren't open, the bottom of the refrigerator, the trash compactor, the dishwasher, the floor. Look at all the good surfaces in here that weren't tried."

She did. Some were dusted. Some were tagged where the prints had been lifted. Some were not.

"Even the best CSIs miss things," she said. She'd requested Coiner and O'Brien because they were the best the department had. Her people. She would trust them with her life.

"It's not a criticism," he said. "This little ball of dust here, it's what I got out of the corners, from under the reefer and the compactor and the dishwasher. I'm going to cut Gilliam loose on it. Just eyeballing, I can see a couple of clothing fibers that don't look like the others. Months old, probably. But if there was a struggle in here, something came loose. It's worth a try."

Zamorra stood, then bent over and used his pen to slide the dust ball into a plastic bag. He looked at it, then at Merci.

"It's absolutely amazing to me how much faith we humans can put into long shots. I guess it's just hope. Hope to the max, stretched out as far as you can stretch it. 'Til it's as big around as a hair."

"Then we try to walk on it. Across the Grand Canyon or something."

"Yeah, and back again. What did you find in the bedroom?"

She held up the tape. "Let's see."

• • •

Merci plugged the tape into the VCR atop the big TV in the living room and sat down on one of the black leather sofas. Zamorra sat on the other. The screen filled with gray static then popped into living color.

Aubrey Whittaker walking on a beach in the evening. A man's voice establishing time, date and location.

Aubrey Whittaker in-line skating in a park. The same voice narrating again.

Aubrey Whittaker sitting roughly where Paul was, talking about the first time she rode a horse. The same guy, laughing at a comment.

Most of the shots were in close and on her face. Merci was surprised by how beautiful she was. Her skin was fair and her lips were red and her body was effortlessly graceful and her eyes looked like something you'd see in a magazine. The camera must have been on full zoom. Close, closer, then blurred when it got too close.

"Now, why are we doing this again?" Aubrey asked the camera.

"So you can see how lovely you are," answered the guy, *"when you're just being you."*

"And I'm supposed to watch this thing every time I feel like blowing my brains out?"

"Every time."

Laughter.

End of feature presentation. Gray infinity.

Neither said anything for a long moment. Merci looked out at the black sky and the black water, heard the rain still falling hard, saw one tiny light on one tiny vessel flickering south to north far out on the sea.

"That's McNally's voice, right?" he asked.

"Yes."

What Zamorra said next surprised her.

"What she has is a big growth in her brain matter. Nobody knows why she got it. Or how long it's been there. Glioblastoma. It's the size of a lemon. It's a level four tumor, which means it's growing fast. This kind of tumor is one hundred percent fatal. They've told us how long she'll live. Fourteen months if it's treated by surgery, chemotherapy and radiation. Six if not. You add the eight months, but they can be eight months of hell."

Merci watched him watch the storm.

"But they've got this new experimental thing. A new protocol, they call it. It's a combination of radioactive seeds and chemicals they put down into the thing. It's supposed to kill it. They know exactly how much damage each seed can do, and they plant them so they won't ruin the good brain cells. That's our hope. Hope again, but this time it's stretched out to the size of a radioactive, chemical-laced pellet. And you know what I think?"

"Tell me."

"I think it's going to work. And you know something else?"

"Go."

"She does, too."

Merci watched the tiny boat light disappear. She felt an incommensurate grief over this, like the storm had not just swept away one light but had extinguished light itself. She told herself that if the light showed up again it would mean Janine Zamorra was going to get a miracle. Half a minute later, there it was.

"So do I."

"Thank you. I'll be gone all day tomorrow. Maybe the next."

"I know. I'll pray. Can I visit?"

"Let's see how it goes."

Merci got up, rewound and ejected the videotape. Her legs felt heavy now, like she'd been in the gym for hours. She thought of Tim, Jr., and couldn't remember ever missing him so much or wanting to see him so badly. Tim. Dad. The Men. A smile and some laughter, a glass of wine. Then to bed while this whole miserable shitstorm blew itself out.

But no, tonight was her social night, the monthly get-together that she herself had instigated in order to build a loyal army around her—or was it just to break the aloneness she felt at times? An obligation was an obligation.

Zamorra's voice had an edge. "Mike's got problems."

"They seem to be getting worse every minute. He told me today he killed her. He also told me he didn't."

"Which is it?"

"He didn't kill her. It's not something Mike McNally has in him."

Zamorra looked at her. His eyes were sharp and unforgiving. "Maybe you don't really know what he's got in him."

"I realize that."

"Maybe I should talk to him."

"Not yet."

"Maybe we should just fire a round through his gun and see what the lab says."

"I thought of that, too."

"Let me talk to him. I'll get the gun. It's not a problem."

She hadn't thought it through, and she didn't have time to think it through right here, so she said what she thought was right. Hoped was right. Hope, now stretched out to the diameter of an opinion.

"No. Not yet. I will if we need to. He couldn't kill her, Paul. I know that."

"People get fooled all the time. Look at Aubrey."

Chapter Eleven

She ran through the Cancun parking lot with a newspaper over her head but her shoulders and hair were wet by the time she got inside. She found her group in the back, seated in the usual big booth beneath the fronds of the mock *palapa.*

Sheriff's Unsocial Deputies Society was Merci's gig all the way. She invited who she wanted, excluded others, served as hostess and MC, made sure the tab got paid and the waitress got tipped. It was a wholly self-serving venture, she admitted, a way of *networking*—a word she'd long mistrusted.

She understood enough of office politics to know you had to play in order to get ahead, so SUDS was her hand-picked team, the people who would rule the department someday: Merci's People.

Her two hard rules for admittance were only that she like them and they like her, and they had to be good at their jobs. Beyond that, anything went. At first it was Ike Sumich, Lynda Coiner and a young deputy named Joe Casik. Then Evan O'Brien and one of the young burg-theft detectives—Ed Mendez. Kathy Hulet from vice was a welcome addition, though she was a draw for some unwelcome male deputies who learned about the SUDS from the unending department gossip. Merci didn't want a singles club, which is why she'd not included Mike. After a couple of meetings she had to add some oldsters, guys like Gilliam from the lab, Stu Waggoner over in Fraud and Ray Dunbar. Merci had actually had a few deputies ask if they could come. She'd let two out of three feel welcome, the other not.

On a night like this, with her nerves rankled over Mike McNally's overtures to a high-line whore, Merci wished she could just go home to The Men. But if you started something you had to finish it, this was clearly evident.

Merci slid into the booth next to Kathy Hulet. Attendance was light: Joe Casik, Evan O'Brien, Lynda Coiner.

Tonight's topic seemed to be nature versus the new Orange County toll roads, which cut through thirty-something miles of unpeopled south county hills. Motorists had killed two mountain lions, a dozen deer, eight wildcats and countless rabbits and squirrels. Casik, an environmentalist, hiker, birdwatcher and photographer, was haranguing about the fate of a toll roads agency plan to include "wildlife corridors" under the road, to aid in the movement of deer and big cats.

"The *idea* was okay," he was saying, as Merci nodded to the waitress for her usual Scotch and water. "But the trouble is, the deer are scared of the damned things. The corridors are just tunnels under a highway, with thousands of cars roaring up on top. So the bureaucrats try to lure the deer into the tunnels with something good to eat. Alfalfa. But they've got no idea that alfalfa is toxic to deer, so the deer that the cars don't hit are being poisoned in the wildlife corridors. We're growing some fat vultures, is all we're doing. I see 'em everywhere on my hikes."

"Venison is delicious," said O'Brien. "They could give the deer meat to the poor. Issue them passes to prowl the corridors. Free forks and knives."

"Napkins, too," said Coiner. "And they still charge three dollars and sixty cents to drive that thing out to Green River."

Casik pointed out that nature had scored two human lives to balance the sheets: a late-night single-car colliding into a light stanchion because the driver was trying to miss something in the road—most likely a deer.

"Too bad, though," said Coiner. "It was an old lady and her granddaughter."

"They have deer sensors you can put on your car," said Evan. "They let you know when . . ."

Merci tuned out. The bar music was loud and the lights

were low and these faces—faces she usually liked seeing—just made her feel alien and irrelevant. She wished Hess was here. She wished The Men were here.

Hulet touched Merci's arm while Casik and O'Brien talked about fire ants and killer bees. "You all right?"

"Clobbered. Long day."

Yeah, and you get those Africanized bees after you and it's all she wrote . . .

Hulet was a long-legged brunette who couldn't disguise her good looks and never tried to. She was Vice Detail's best john-bait, and she'd gotten herself into some hairy situations and never lost her cool. She played second base on the deputies' slow-pitch softball team.

"You look it," she said. "Go home, get some rest."

"I'm going to, soon."

"What's with Mike?"

Got a brother in Texas who's got fire ants, they bite him and his hand swells up for three days . . .

"I got no idea," said Merci, though in fact she did.

"God, he's been weird lately—stressed out and tired all the time. Looks like he's been awake for a week. Gone sometimes when he ought to be at work. Says he's been in church. Whatever. But this Whittaker thing really got to him. I've never seen him so . . . guilty. You know, for letting it happen. I mean, she was his girl and she was going to wear a wire for Moladan, and the next thing we know somebody's capped her right in her own apartment. But

Mike was weirding out before that, so it's not just the Whittaker thing."

Plus the fire ants eat a lot of bird eggs, just wiped out the quail in west Texas, where my brother lives . . .

"I know," said Merci. "Believe me, I know. He's been leaning heavy on me this last month, too. Real touchy, real raw."

"Well, he's in love with you, so that's all that is."

"I guess."

"You look thrilled."

Collect a bunch for a fire ant farm, send it to my nephew up in Seattle . . .

"Kathy, I wish I lived on a tropical island sometimes. Me and Tim and a thousand paperback novels. Rum and pineapple juice."

"Obedient servant boys with tight brown buns?"

"They come when you ring a bell."

Tight brown buns? What the hell are you two talking about over there?

"Try Club Med. I'll go with you."

"Hey, I might take you up on that."

So Merci stuck it out for an hour, the voices and faces blending and blurring as she sipped her Scotch.

No, Glandis doesn't have the balls to challenge Brighton for office. That'd be like a pit bull biting his master.

Glandis just plays dumb.

Good actor, then. You ever met his wife? Looks like

Cruella DeVille. But look, Glandis needs Brighton's backing. Nobody's going to be the next sheriff unless Brighton endorses. He's the machine.

Either way, Brighton's gotta step down before too long, I mean he's what, seventy, seventy-one?

Seventy-two. Glandis isn't any youngster. There's Vince Abelera in the marshal's office, he seems okay. But I'll be dipped in red ape shit if we get a marshal as sheriff. We need some young blood running this show. Some of our own blood.

"Merci, why don't you just announce you're running for sheriff?" This from Joe Casik.

"I'm not old and wrinkly enough yet."

"I'll support you."

"Me, too," said O'Brien. "The rank and file of SUDS will weigh in behind you."

"You guys," said Merci, standing. "I'm sorry, but I'm definitely not running for sheriff, and I'm definitely over this one. I've got an early interview tomorrow—way up in Arrowhead."

"Bring your chains," said Casik.

"I'm planning on it. Sorry I'm such a dud tonight. 'Night, kiddies."

" 'Night, Mom."

" 'Night, Mom. Love to Timmy."

Merci trotted through the rain to her Impala, checked the backseat with her penlight, swung open the door and checked the backseat again. She sat rubbing her hands together and flogged the pedal to get the engine warm.

She took Irvine Boulevard back to Tustin, back to her house in the orange grove. She slowed at Myford and looked at the tract houses. Rain came down in sheets, flooded the gutters, swamped up over the sidewalks.

Myford and Fourth, she thought: Patti Bailey with her heart blown out, dumped on the side of the culvert. Back then it was nothing but groves. Now it's nothing but rain.

Chapter Twelve

White brilliance. Even her good sunglasses couldn't beat the blinding sunlight reflected off the snow. Merci felt the chains on her tires crushing the road ice, felt the cold on her face through the windows. Second gear and the big Chevy still wanted to slide.

She hated snow, always had, but she couldn't believe how white it was, how perfectly, flawlessly white. The drifts beside the road looked ten feet high. Then the mountainsides—blankets of white, perforated by pines. And the trees themselves, heavy with snow and stunned by sunshine, stood motionless, like they were afraid to move.

Roy Thornton's place was past the village, off a little road that dipped into darkness then rose again into the world of purest optics.

When she stepped inside she smelled coffee, bacon and burning wood. Thornton was tall and heavy, plenty of gray hair, a shy smile. His eyes seemed small and a little sad, shaded by diagonal folds of skin, but they twinkled when he looked straight at her. He said to call him Roy. He introduced his wife, Sally, who was making breakfast in front of a window looking out on Lake Arrowhead.

Thornton got two cups of coffee and led Merci back to the den. Merci got the couch. Thornton took a beat-up old lounger. Merci set the file on the coffee table in front of him, got out her blue notebook and a pen. The windows had curtains tied back for the view.

"How's Orange County?"

"Crowded."

"Most densely populated county in the state now."

"I read that recently."

"Lots to do."

"The murder rate's dropped in half over the last two years. We can't explain it, other than lots of jobs and excellent police work."

Thornton smiled. "It's nice to have citizens too busy making money to commit crimes. Still lots of gang stuff?"

"Too much."

"We didn't have that when I was there. Hardly any."

Merci drank her coffee, looked at the trout mounted on the wall. There was a TV in one corner, one of the old RCAs with wooden legs and cabinet, cloth and wood stripping over the speakers. On top of it was an arrangement of plastic greenery with a small nativity scene in the middle.

"Sally and I went down for Tim's funeral."

"Yes."

"Good guy. Worked hard. One of the few guys I knew who lived for his job but wasn't an asshole. I liked him."

"I did, too."

Thornton's small sad eyes studied her, revealing nothing. Merci had to fight herself to keep from wondering what he knew, what he'd heard. The answer was: It didn't matter.

"Patti Bailey," he said, leaning forward, picking up the file. He set it on his lap and leafed through. "We never got a break. We did the groundwork, interviewed family and friends, some of her customers—nothing. There were some good angles. Drugs, bikers, her clientele. Maybe too many good angles. Lots of motive in a crowd like that. And she talked a lot. Seemed to be in the middle of a thousand little intrigues. You know, biker mentality—who gets the speed market this side of the Ortega Highway, who gets the other side. And every grimy Hessian was trying to make every other grimy Hessian's girl. I remember two or three guys thinking Patti was all his. Mexican heroin. Some pot. Mostly speed and downers. She got herself into the transport side, made some money. Ambitious, you could say. Thought for herself. How well she thought is another question."

"You get as far as a decent suspect?"

"No. Couple of the bikers made sense—the ones that thought she belonged to them. But we couldn't make anything stick. We looked at a couple of johns, guys with ties to Leary's Brotherhood down in Laguna, but nothing popped. Those guys didn't care about her enough to kill her. They were loaded, free-love guys, plying her with dope. She was one of hundreds. We got some shoe impressions out of the orange grove near the body, but the soil was so loose they didn't help much. Estimated a size nine, if I remember right. Guy took her clothes apparently. Nobody saw anything. She'd been dead for a day before we got to her. Large caliber handgun, likely."

Merci looked down at her notes: *sus*—then a zero with a null slash through it.

"What did your gut say, Roy?"

"Yeah, guts. Well, two things. First of all, I don't think she was killed there. I think she was moved. We couldn't prove that—no drag marks, no witnesses. Hard to say how much blood soaked into the ground, or didn't. We dug in the right places but couldn't find any lead. I think the body was moved. What's that tell you? Means he killed somewhere incriminating, somewhere harder to clean up. But still somewhere he could get the body out without being seen. A car, maybe."

"Did she turn her tricks nearby?"

"She used a couple of different motels up in Santa Ana. Her address was a hotel called the De Anza, up Fourth Street. Old place, downstairs was a restaurant. There was some prostitution going on there, but Bailey wasn't using it for business. Mostly enlisted men from the Tustin air base or Pendleton. We didn't find much in her room. That wasn't where he killed her."

"You were thinking john then."

Thornton frowned and shook his head. "Yeah, at first. But it was careful, too. What struck me about the murder scene wasn't what we *got,* but what we didn't get—no prints, no bullet lead or brass, no tire tracks we could work with. We got some nice wide broom marks on the road shoulder. We could see where he'd kicked the footprints when he left the grove. Pretty clean work, for such an ugly homicide."

Merci thought, wrote: pains to cover tracks—calm and efficient. "Premeditated?" she said.

"I still ask myself that question. You take a hooker and a gunshot wound and you don't get premeditated out of it, ninety-nine percent of the time. But you factor in moving the body, sweeping up most of the prints, you get another dimension. What I thought at first was a pissed-off john who didn't have the money, or couldn't get it up, she wouldn't do what he wanted. Then I thought it had to be one of her biker Romeos, who thought she belonged to him. Then I wondered about the drug connections. And still, I still think those aren't it. I think those aren't it because I worked them and got zip."

"Why'd he take the clothes?"

"I figured blood or semen. Nothing else made sense."

"Some kind of predator then?"

Thornton shook his head and leaned back. "No. Just guts again, but to me it was too neat. And it didn't match up with anything else we had. You figure if a guy's bent that way he's going to do it again."

He was quiet then. Merci looked at the snow outside, at pendants of ice hanging in the shade of the northern eaves. She could sense that Thornton wanted to say something. It was the same silent notification that suspects gave under interrogations sometimes, when you knew they were about to lay it all on you.

"What?" she asked quietly.

Thornton sighed. "That was a tough year, sixty-nine. Sheriff Bill Owen just up and resigned all of a sudden. He said it was health reasons but he was healthy as a horse and we all knew it. We had a supervisor—the big guy, Ralph Meeks—resign over a payola scandal. Remember him? Most powerful guy in county politics, run out for taking bribes. We had an old Mexican farmer—Jesse Acuna—beat half to death, claimed it was racist cops trying to rid the county of minorities. Cesar Chavez, ACLU, got in on that; and, of course, the press loved the story. Had a *New York Times* reporter here for that one. Did a whole series on what a rich, white, racist county it was. And we had a bunch of deputies who were John Birchers, they were going into neighborhoods and starting up volunteer police departments—organizing these right-wing groups to keep law and order in the land. Some people said they were vigilantes, some said they were old-fashioned patriots. Me, I think I'd go with the vigilantes. People liked to believe the Birchers beat up that farmer, but I don't think anything was ever proved. Vietnam just kept dragging on. The whole county was overflowing with dope—grass by the ton up from Michoacan and Oaxaca, LSD pouring out of the Brotherhood in Laguna, barbs and uppers plentiful and cheap. You know, high-school student body presidents caught with kilo bricks in their lockers. And all the parents in their flat-tops and bouffants, pissed off, voting hard-line Republican, guzzling their Scotch. But their kids with hair to their butts, quoting Marx, burning the flag, stoned on their dope. Everybody hated everybody else. Everybody got a divorce. My own kid joined some no-good religious cult and went to Guatemala for a year. We still hardly talk. Horrible time. The Black Panthers and the Black Muslims. Everybody waiting for the next Watts. Every week, the body count from the war getting higher. Nixon promising to win it. Young men coming home in boxes by the hundreds, like the government was sending them over so they could *get* killed, thin the opposition. Goddamned Manson and his clan—that was the week right after Bailey. All the horrible music. I felt like . . . well . . . we had law, but no order."

Thornton stopped, gazed out the window. Merci thought about that time, 1969, but didn't come up with much because she had been four. She vaguely remembered lots of hair, peace signs, psychedelia. Lots of heat coming off the TV screen: the war, Nixon and his twenty-four hour five o'clock shadow, Kissinger and his bloodhound eyes. She had loved *Mod Squad* and *Mission Impossible.* Didn't understand most of Rowan and Martin, though her parents laughed all the way through it. Merci remembered her mother wearing short skirts that showed off her legs, Clark with his regulation flattop and thin ties. She remembered some political meetings they went to—films on the Latvia, Lithuania and Estonia tragedies, the Congo tragedy, the Cuba tragedy, communists inside the United Nations.

Sally Thornton brought in two TV trays and popped them open. Merci's had a depiction of a Fourth of July picnic on it, with flags and watermelon and a three-legged race going on. The breakfast was huge and fattening, just the way Merci liked it. She'd turn it to muscle in the gym.

"And Patti Bailey?" she asked, when Sally was gone.

He looked at her and shrugged. "Nobody cared. It didn't make much of a splash in the papers. Sheriff Owen never pulled out the stops like he used to on big murders. No reward organized, no extra dicks assigned. Just a routine case."

To her mind, Merci had never had a routine case. She took each of them personally, which a cop wasn't supposed to do. Not so much the victims, more the perps. She took them very personally. She wanted to make sure they got a fair trial, then the needle, or thrown in a dungeon forever. It was a bad quality to have and she knew it. Hatred was a dirty fuel, but it was a fuel that burned hot and long.

Thornton sat forward. "I like it up here. Clean air, fish

in the lake. The country's different now. Everybody out for himself, trying to make the most money. All the commercials are guys and dolls in business suits. The questions are all smaller. They don't matter as much. Whatever makes good TV. Lots of law. Lots of order."

Merci thought about this. "Tuesday night a woman got murdered. I'm going to find the creep who did it. To me, the questions that matter are still the same. That's why I do what I do."

Thornton smiled. Merci saw nothing condescending or humoring in it.

"That's right. Now you got this Whittaker woman. I hope she doesn't turn into your Patti Bailey. Hope you're not sitting on your porch someday, fat and retired like me, and some sharp young cop wants to know why you didn't solve it."

"No offense was meant here, Roy."

"Offense? I hope you find out the truth, young lady. I hope you kick ass and take names. I'd be offended if you didn't."

"I will."

"Look. I made a call. Bailey was tight with a sister and we kept in touch. She had some interesting things to say, most of it too late to help us. She'll talk to you. She's down the mountain, in Riverside. Here."

Thornton slipped a sheet of paper into the file, handed it back to her.

"The phone's in the kitchen."

• • •

Merci followed a CHP escort back down the mountain, first or second gear most of the way, through the ferocious brightness of late morning. She had coffee at a truck stop, read the papers, watched the big rigs rumble in and out, checked through her blue notebook.

She wrote: *Nobody cared . . . let it slide . . . you let it slide when it's going your way . . . whose way is unsolved? Who benefits?*

She called both home and office to retrieve messages. Mike had called her at home before she left for Arrowhead, but she'd turned the recorder down when she heard his voice. The upshot was that Mike was sorrier and more ashamed than he could express to her. He left a message on her work machine, then two more at home. He sounded like he was about to cry. Listening to them, Merci felt pity and fury vying inside her. But beneath these predictable emotions, she felt something even worse. She felt her respect for Mike sliding away in huge masses, like earthslides after weeks of rain.

She made me feel like doing all the things I wanted to do with you. But I had them totally, one hundred percent under control.

Then how did you make such a mess of things, she wondered.

Evan O'Brien, the CSI, had left one message on her work machine: He wanted to talk. Important.

• • •

Cheryl Davis was Patti Bailey's twin sister. She was fifty-five years old, brown and brown, pretty face and pretty heavy.

"The problem with the cops," said Cheryl, "was they didn't realize Patti had changed."

Merci asked how.

"She wasn't riding with the Hessians anymore. That was the year before. She wasn't hanging with the drug people in Laguna because all they'd pay with was dope. She didn't want dope—she wanted money. That's why the detectives never got very far. They were asking the wrong people. She was in with a different clientele when she was killed."

"Who?"

"Higher class. Businessmen. Politicians."

Merci considered. "That's quite a change."

"Patti was ambitious. She was . . . Sergeant Rayborn, Patti was an absolute bullshitter, but sometimes the things she said were true. And she told me she was servicing powerful men. The elite, the movers and shakers. It made her feel important. No, she didn't give me names. She wasn't loose . . . that way. I wouldn't have recognized them anyway, because I was living down in Key West then. That's a whole other story, but we wrote back and forth a lot. She liked to write. So did I."

Cheryl Davis sighed quietly and looked down at her hands. She was wearing a big knit sweater against the cold.

The house was a tract home off of Tyler; built, Merci guessed, about the time Cheryl's sister was shot. Builders didn't bother much with insulation back then. There were three cardboard boxes overflowing with Christmas decorations in the corner of the living room. Nothing up yet, Merci noted.

"What was frustrating for me," Cheryl said, "was I might have helped. I had the letters. By the time I realized the police had interviewed the old crowd, it was a year later. I gave the detectives copies of them, but to be honest, I think they were onto other things by then. Her letters were always grandiose, and kind of vague anyway. Just like she was."

Merci looked at the woman. "I'm sorry about what happened. I feel bad for you."

Hess would have liked that, she thought: feeling what someone was feeling, or at least trying to.

Cheryl Davis wiped a tear with a tissue that had been balled in the pocket of her sweater. Prepared, thought Merci.

"Give me something," Merci said. "Anything I can run with."

"Okay."

Cheryl got up and went out. A few minutes later she came back with an old-fashioned briefcase, the ones with the expandable sides and multiple dividers that would just get fatter the more you put in it. A big handle. It was worn.

"Oh," said the woman, catching Merci's eyes. "This was Dad's. I put all the stuff in here about the investigation.

Thought it might bring me luck, you know. Anyway, you can borrow it."

"Thank you."

Cheryl Davis unlocked the flap and pulled it open. Then she shut it again and locked it. "No. I just can't go there again. Not now. Please take it."

She set the case in front of Merci and remained standing. So Merci did, too. Interview over.

"I'll give you something else. I gave it to Rymers and his partner but never heard anything more about it. Patti wrote me in one of those letters that's in there, she said she knew who beat up a farmer named Jesse Acuna. I guess he was a real family man, lots of kids and grandchildren, lots of friends. Did good things for people. It was a big mystery, who'd do such a thing to him. I didn't recognize his name back then, but I guess it was big news in Orange County—somebody beating up a farmer who'd never committed a crime in his life. He almost died. Anyway, Patti says in there she knew who did it. Said she had it 'documented.' That's the word she used. I'm not sure what she meant by that."

"How'd she find out?"

"I think he was, you know, one of her customers."

Merci put Thornton's and Cheryl Davis's statements together and shook them up. "Was Patti servicing cops?"

"She never said that, no."

Merci wondered if the highway between the Hessians and the power brokers might have been cleared and paved by the law. There had to be connective tissue. Anything could happen. Just look at Mike.

"I'll return this," said Merci, hefting the case. It was heavy.

"I hope it helps you." Cheryl Davis was dabbing her cheek again as she walked Merci to her door. "You know what Patti was, Sergeant?"

"Tell me."

"She was bright and funny and cute. So loyal. She and I couldn't have taken more . . . different paths. But she loved me the whole way. No matter how far down she got. You know what one of her best features was, her prettiest parts? Her neck. It was slender and graceful, just beautiful. She'd wear necklaces just to show it off. I'll never forget this string of faux pearls she wore to the prom in high school. So . . . elegant and so . . . humble. And for someone to do what he did is a sin. It's not just a crime, it's a sin."

"It's the ugliest sin there is, Ms. Davis."

Chapter Thirteen

Colin Byrne, reference desk assistant for the UC Irvine Library, had everything ready for Merci when she got there. It was almost three o'clock. Byrne, whom she had talked to on the phone only an hour earlier, had set her up with a private study room in the archives section of the building.

He was a lanky blond with innocent blue eyes and a necktie with pictures of hounds on it. His trousers were held up by suspenders with designs of magnifying glasses on them.

"You caught me in my Doyle gear," he said when she noticed the magnifiers. "Glad I'm not wearing the bullet-hole tie. That's the hard-boiled look."

"Not real bullet holes, I hope."

"No. But it's nice to meet a real detective. I'd never ask, but I wonder if you're working the case of the murdered escort, down in San Clemente."

"I'd never answer, but no, it's something else I'm after."

He smiled. "You name it, you got it. *Anything.*"

He rolled out the chair for her, then tutored her through the search features on the computer. She could search by topic or specific name for any period of time from 1887—when the county's first newspaper went into regular publication—to the present. All county papers were contained in the program: the smallest and most temporary weeklies, college and junior college student papers, members' newsletters of yacht clubs, professional journals, the three major dailies that now circulated in Orange County. Even some of the corporate newsletters.

"We're missing three months of the old Huntington Beach *Watch,*" said Byrne, "because they lost their archival copies in a fire. Same with some early copies of the Newport *Ensign,* but that was flood. Other than that, it's all here. You'll be amazed how fast you can get around the last century of newspapers with this computer. It's usually best to go big-to-small. Let me know if you get stuck."

"Patti Bailey" got her seventy-two hits in eight publications, most of them in the Los Angeles *Times* and the Santa Ana *Register.*

Reading through the stories from the bigger papers, she didn't find anything she hadn't already learned from the case file. The *Times* printed a polite request for greater police action on the case, on the one-year anniversary of her death.

The Tustin *News* had a feature story on the boy who had discovered the body. He'd been looking for lizards in the grove, thought Bailey was asleep when he first spotted her. They ran a picture of him pointing at the side of the culvert.

They also had a police blotter notice of Bailey's arrest on drug charges almost a year before her death. It was only one line, mixed in with the car stereo rip-offs and drunken driving arrests: *Patti Bailey, 22, of Santa Ana, was arrested by Orange County Sheriffs on suspicion of possession of barbiturates after being pulled over on 17th St. for erratic driving Wednesday night . . .*

After the murder they also ran a two-part investigative piece about prostitution out of the De Anza Hotel, which was up on Fourth Street, just out of the Tustin city limits. The article said that Patti Bailey was "known as a tenant," but was rarely seen at the De Anza. The reporter wrote:

> It is easy to picture this happy-go-lucky 23-year-old among the inebriated celebrants in the De Anza Lounge on a rowdy Friday night. Here, the scent of illicit activity mixes with the perfume of tequila. Beautiful women come and go, with eyes that are at once inviting and challenging.

The accompanying photo spread showed the De Anza on a "fabled" night. The three pictures were from the newspaper's photo file, taken at a New Year's Eve party eight months before the murder: a hacienda-style room with a fountain and potted plants, a long bar staffed by Latin men in bow ties, plenty of drunk-looking men and young women in miniskirts. It was a big room with exposed ceiling timbers, a wrought-iron chandelier draped with paper streamers, the background fading to black around crowded tables of men and women.

The hotel owner denied knowing of anything illegal transpiring on his property, so most of the information came from the prostitutes themselves. "Patti had very high-class friends," said "Blossom." "She came here mostly to eat and drink." The reporter confirmed that Bailey was a permanent resident of room number 245. He was not permitted to see it.

The article went on to quote some enlisted men, regulars at the De Anza, who said they came for the atmosphere and cheap margaritas.

High class, all right, Merci thought.

Santa Ana Police Chief Ed Simpson called the place a "trouble spot," and said they could enforce the law there but they couldn't shut it down. City hall would have to do that.

One week after Bailey's death, it did.

A Tustin News editorial that ran four months after Bailey's murder contained an interesting nugget.

> Rumors of prostitution at the De Anza Hotel circulated widely long before it was shut down by the

City of Santa Ana. Rumors of law-enforcement personnel frequenting the hotel circulated for almost as long. The News can only hope that there was no connection between the longevity of a house of sin and its alleged popularity with some elements within the law. Where police are involved in crime, no citizen can be safe. Perhaps the murder of Patti Bailey helped to illustrate this tragic truth.

Merci rolled back in the wheeled chair, stretched her legs. What was wrong in '69? she thought. Cops beating up farmers, cops hanging with whores?

She went back to the New Year's Eve photo of the De Anza and enlarged it to full-screen, half expecting to find someone she recognized at one of the tables.

No luck.

She hit the print command to make copies of it all.

• • •

The name Jesse Acuna got 238 newspaper hits in 1969, 135 the year after, and an even 50 the year after that. Last year, he'd still been referred to 16 times in the local press. He was ninety-five years old, living in San Juan Capistrano down in the southern part of the county.

Merci remembered hearing about him in elementary school.

She scanned the articles that came out immediately after the beating.

Acuna was found unconscious and bleeding by his grandson, Charlie, at sunrise on the Fourth of July. Jesse Acuna had just come from the chicken coop, collecting eggs as he'd done every morning for as long as anyone could remember. He was sixty-four. His grandson was seven.

Intensive care for a week. Hospital for a month. Left eye destroyed. Slurred speech for the rest of his life. Ninety stitches in his scalp and face. Eight teeth knocked out. Two fingers crushed beyond meaningful repair.

It pissed off Merci Rayborn immediately and immensely, what had happened to this old man. To the boy, too. Merci wondered how the Fourth of July picnic pictured on Sally Thornton's TV trays stacked up against the Fourth of July surprise that Jesse Acuna and his grandson got.

Two of the baseball bats used on Acuna were found at the scene. Footprints in the barnyard, tire tracks on the dirt road. Charlie saw three men get into the getaway truck—a light-colored pickup, no camper, big tires, went fast. Big men, he said, masks on. Charlie was scared mute for three days before he could even speak.

The farm was a hundred acres of rolling hills down in the south part of Orange County.

Merci scanned through, filling in, connecting the story with her memory of it: no arrests, no suspects.

Five weeks after the beating, Acuna's story hit both the *Times* and the *Register*. He said that his one hundred acre orange grove—owned by his family since the early

1800s—was located between two valuable parcels of land. The parcels were worth millions if the land was subdivided, developed and sold. But the parcels were worth "many, many millions more" if they could be connected by a major road through the hills that separated them. That land was his.

He'd refused to sell it or grant a road easement through it, in spite of offers that were a hundred times what he'd make in a good year on his oranges.

He'd been sued by two cities and the county itself, trying to stretch their powers of eminent domain—and he'd won all three suits in court.

He'd had his land annexed by one city, which condemned the buildings for code violations committed at a time before codes; then seen his land annexed by another city that said he could stay right where he was.

Then came the threats. First by some small-time real-estate hustlers who thought hired muscle and a fire in the machine shed would scare him off. Another who suggested Acuna's children—he had eleven—might come to harm on their way home from school someday. He'd had his brood driven to and from school by a couple of able-bodied farmhands for nearly two years.

He'd had his trees poisoned with herbicide right before harvest; he'd had his wells poisoned right before Christmas; he'd had gunmen shoot out the windows of his home while he slept with his wife of thirty years, Teresa.

Acuna said that none of that had really frightened him.

It strengthened his resolve to stay. He said that farming was in his blood for generations, all the way back to the *ranchos* and before that. He said that oranges were all he knew; they had fed his parents and his children and his grandchildren and he saw no reason why they couldn't feed *their* children and grandchildren. Everybody ate. Everybody worked. His oranges were good.

None of it frightened him until one hot spring morning that year, when two men drove up in a white Mercedes-Benz and told him they had a terrific offer for his land. He offered them fresh juice, which they drank in the shade of the courtyard. He listened carefully to their offer. Acuna said it was extravagantly large, but he was forced to say no for the usual reasons. He wouldn't disclose the figure to reporters, because it was "private." They told him there would be trouble if he didn't accept. He asked what kind. They wouldn't say. But Acuna told the papers that he could tell from their faces that they meant what they said, and he knew when they left that some calamity would soon befall him.

Two months later, it did.

When he could talk again, Acuna told reporters he had no intention of selling his farm: It would have been like selling his heart.

Six months after Acuna had been beaten, the headlines were considerably smaller, the articles much farther back in the papers.

The county re-annexed a large piece of south county

ground when a fledgling city defaulted on services payments. Acuna's farm was part of it. The county then rezoned the whole one hundred acres R-1, residential. Acuna was shortly presented with deadlines for sewer construction and hookup. He was ordered to pay residential rates for municipal water, electricity and natural gas—an increase of roughly 500 percent. The land received a new tax assessment and Acuna got a staggering property tax increase—close to 700 percent. Farm subsidies and agricultural tax breaks no longer applied. He was ordered to pave all his roads, then apply for a conditional-use permit under the "existing, nonconforming" clause. Acuna did, and his petition was immediately denied by the County Board of Supervisors on January 14, 1970.

After doing the math and thinking it over, Jesse Acuna finally sold the land and everything on it to Orange Coast Capital for 4.2 million dollars.

Merci found nothing about cops being blamed for the beating until the following year, when the anniversary articles all came out.

Acuna, speaking from his new home in San Juan Capistrano, told the local newspaper that he believed the men who came to make an offer and threaten him that day last spring had been "the police." He thought this because he was sixty-four years old at the time, a Mexican farmer in a world of white Republicans, and he knew cops. He knew what they looked like, how they acted and how they walked and talked, how they thought.

In answering the reporter's six million dollar question, Acuna admitted that he'd never seen those men before or since the Fourth of July, 1969. His attackers wore masks. The article carefully noted that Acuna had no evidence to substantiate his attackers as police, just his own observations and opinions about the men who had driven a white Mercedes-Benz into his life one hot spring morning and shared a pitcher of orange juice with him in the courtyard.

The reporter had gone back through the original police interviews and found not one instance in which Acuna had speculated that his attackers were policemen.

At this, Acuna shrugged and "stared off at his small garden with his one good remaining eye."

Merci thought: I might not tell the police if I *thought* my attackers were policemen, either.

Merci continued forward, noting the way the rumor grew, until the ACLU was calling for internal investigations and the Los Angeles *Times* was treating Acuna's opinion as if it was in all likelihood true. The county's other large daily—the Santa Ana *Register*—was far less convinced. Their editorials said that Acuna's story wasn't substantiated, and they'd take it seriously if it ever was.

The *Register* subtly insinuated that Jesse Acuna might have suffered brain damage in the beating, thus coloring his recollection of faces and events.

The *Times* said that if Acuna's story was born of brain damage from the beating, then law enforcement should be *eager* to remove the cloud of suspicion from over its own head.

The then-small Orange County *Journal* weighed in with a call for justice for men and women of all races and colors, enthusiastically ignoring the cop accusation altogether.

Cesar Chavez appeared, neither endorsing nor rejecting Acuna's story, but using the unrest as a focal point for promoting the United Farm Workers Union. His talks on the Fullerton and UC Irvine campuses drew thousands.

Merci remembered a rally she went to around that time. A much smaller rally. Mom and Dad took her. It was outside, in the parking lot of a new church. It was very hot—summer or early fall. The rally was to give the police a vote of confidence, and it was sponsored by the local membership of the John Birch Society. There were picket signs and buttons with pictures of a man's face and the word *LIAR*. She could remember the bumper stickers that were given out: *Support Your Local Police.*

The thing that made it all stick in her mind wasn't any of that, but the tremendous wind that blew that day, out of the desert toward the sea, so strong that picket signs were torn from their sticks and blew around like leaves. Her mother got furious when she discovered Merci with some other kids atop the fellowship hall hurling signs that would fly flat as boomerangs fifty yards then bank up abruptly when they hit the gusts then skip out over the new tracts of houses and pinwheel corner-by-corner across the sky like it was hard.

Jesse Acuna signs, she thought. She'd never realized that until now.

At any rate, the ACLU and the *Times* lost. The Federal Ninth Circuit Court heard arguments, then declined to order Orange County police or Sheriff Departments to supply personnel photographs of employees so Acuna could search for the men who'd threatened him.

By then it was nearly two years after the beating, and the article of the circuit court's decision was one small column in the *Register*'s "Local Notes" section, and on page B-22 of the *Times*.

History had closed another of its small, colorful, but not hugely significant chapters.

The headline of that day's *Journal* was:

BUGLIOSI ARGUES ACCUSED
MANSON FOLLOWERS "DERANGED"

Shortly after that, Merci discovered, two police forces and the Sheriff Department had voluntarily supplied photographs for the farmer to examine, but Acuna didn't find his men.

• • •

She rolled her chair back, stood, walked to a window and stared out at the clear, windy day. The storm was gone and the sky was a pale, foreign blue. It looked wrong, like it had blown in from somewhere. Iceland?

The trees in the quad outside the library were stripped from the wind and black from the rain. Yellow leaves on the concrete. She wondered why college campuses always had so many flyers everywhere—ranks of white and yellow and pink sheets with phone-number strips cut into the bottoms, plastered to the railings and kiosks, soaked and torn by the storm.

She'd enjoyed her years at Fullerton. Psych major, emphasis in criminal justice. Plenty of imbeciles in psych, she'd found, a catchall for do-gooders with low ambitions and petite IQs. But she got to read a lot of good books. And spend a lot of time alone. Or with Ben, her kind-of boyfriend. Ben could chugalug two twenty-four ounce Fosters in a row without throwing up. Joined the Forest Service, never called, never wrote. Good days, really, and just a few thousand years ago.

She kept looking out the window, then covered one eye. The colors were still good, but the distance went to hell. No perspective.

Might be hard for Acuna to find his torturers with just one eye, she thought.

Even with two.

But she wouldn't have put much stock in Acuna's theory, even if he'd had three good eyes.

Why cops? Back in '69, it was always the cops. The cops were pigs. All those cartoons with the hogs tucked into tight little uniforms, beating with their big billy clubs and blasting away with their enormous revolvers. Cops were the first scapegoat for every violent, whining victim, right? You got struck by lightning, bitten by a snake, had a bad dream, you could always blame it on the big, bad pigs.

So Jesse Acuna didn't like cops, that was fine. Merci wasn't in love with every one of them, either. It didn't mean they beat him over half to death with baseball bats when he came out of his chicken coop July 4.

He said it because he believed it. They printed it because he said it and it made good copy. It fit the political sway of the day. And it was probably just bullshit.

But Patti Bailey knew the truth, or claimed she did. One of her johns let it slip. And Patti Bailey was living in a hotel rumored to be a cops-and-girls playground.

She went back, printed it all out, thanked Sir Arthur and asked a favor of him. She wanted to draw a line between Bailey, Acuna and the cops.

"Crooked cops in Orange County, circa nineteen sixty-nine," she said. "I want to know all about them."

He gave her a sly smile. "Give me a day, Sergeant."

Chapter Fourteen

It was almost six when she got back to headquarters, Friday night coming on, most of the plainclothes already gone for the weekend but the uniforms of the night shift looking brisk and fresh and ready to go eight.

Good news on the message box: The phone company would provide the numbers, names and addresses of Aubrey Whittaker's outgoing and incoming calls for the week leading up to her murder. Give them until Monday afternoon.

Gary Brice at the *Journal* had "some things for you," please call back at her convenience.

Mike had left two more messages for her to call him as soon as she could.

Evan had left another message about wanting to talk. Merci noted the lack of a wiseguy tone in O'Brien's voice. It made an impression on her because he rarely said anything without it.

O'Brien was down in the lab, using a magnifier and an ultraviolet light to examine a white sheet of paper with a black shoeprint on it. The purple of the ultraviolet played off his face, gave him the look of a low-budget alien.

"What have you got there?" she asked, pulling up a stool next to him.

"To me it looks suspiciously like the shoeprint from Aubrey Whittaker's kitchen."

So much for Evan's serious message.

"Why the black light?"

He looked at her. A very small grin. "No reason whatsoever. A reason is what I was *searching* for."

"And that passes for science down here?"

"Lady Dick, I wanted to see what the ink would do in the UV, if it might bring up something we can't see without it. It didn't, but here, have a look anyway."

Evan was mid-twenties, lean and wiry, with a freckled face that often seemed amused. Red-brown hair and a button nose. Single. Drew women without knowing it, Merci had noticed. Sometimes she saw a solemnity come over his bright green eyes, like there was something serious that occupied his thoughts between amusements. She knew little about his personal life and was happy to keep it that way. He was the most thorough, organized and intelligent CSI she'd ever worked with.

She thought enough of O'Brien to write a letter of recommendation to Personnel earlier in the year, endorsing him as a candidate for deputy. Three other deputies had written in his favor also. Evan had been typically wry about his chances of acceptance, describing himself as a three-to-one underdog because of a mild epileptic condition. It was easily controlled by medication, but a condition nonetheless. "They won't give a spaz a gun," he'd told her. "Even though *you* might. Besides, they need good Igors down here in the lab. Pay us less, work us harder."

Merci assumed Evan would get in because, as a working CSI, he was conspicuously well qualified. He was young and fit. And it didn't hurt that his father had been a deputy in good standing—just as Clark's standing had helped her, and Pat McNally's standing had helped Mike. But the hiring committee had passed on Evan, just as Evan had predicted they would.

Merci had been typically pissed off about that because she believed in him. And because the higher he went the more important an ally he could become.

It bothered O'Brien considerably less. A bunch of them went out for beers the night of the announcement, with Lynda Coiner nursing a similar rejection due to poor uncorrected eyesight. Coiner ended up crying on Mike McNally's shoulder. Mike had been good with her, doting on her like one of his bloodhounds. O'Brien had laughed and cracked acid-wise all night and had driven Coiner home. Merci believed the rejection had hurt him because he'd never once said anything else about it, a reaction typical of the human male, and a quality she admired.

"All I see is a shoeprint, Evan."

"That's all it is. End of experiment."

He clicked off the UV lamp and rolled back on his stool.

"What's up, Evan?"

He shook his head and she saw the humor leave his face. He took a deep breath, let it out slow. "There's some evidence missing. Evidence from the Whittaker scene."

"Explain."

His look was sharp but his voice was calm. "It might have been misplaced around here. We're busy, it happens. It might have gotten thrown out. That happens, too. We're not perfect. I've looked at every inch of this lab. So has Lynda. It's gone."

Merci waited, met his now humorless green eyes. "What was it?"

"Fibers from the kitchen floor. Prints from the kitchen cabinets. A friendship card from the bedroom dresser we kept for a handwriting sample. We got forty-nine items of evidence out of that apartment. We've got forty-four of them here. Two fibers, two print cards and one handwriting sample—vaporized."

Merci thought it through. It wasn't the first time that evidence had gone missing. It always showed up somewhere. That, or the collection logs were the problem, dicks and techs and criminalists and CSIs and coroner's investigators and DA investigators and autopsy hacks all pitching in to produce an occasional overlap, duplication or omission. It was a wonder that it didn't happen more often.

More to the point, was the missing card one of the several sent by Mike?

"Well, Evan. It'll either show or it won't."

"It's the won't part I don't like."

He looked hard at her, then stood up and took off his lab coat. He pulled a sport jacket off the hanger and slipped it on.

"You're going to have to ask me a question, Sergeant Rayborn. Because I don't say things like I need to say to you right now, unless I have to."

"I'll do that then."

"All right. Look, I'm not supposed to know that Mike McNally's prints were all over Whittaker's apartment. But I know *everything* that goes on in this lab. I haven't said one word to anyone, except to you—right now. I won't. That's not the problem. The fact of Mike McNally's prints isn't the problem. It's his problem. It's yours. I just work here."

He waited then, eyeing her with something that looked like anger.

It took her a moment, but she got it. She understood the question she needed to ask. "Mike been hovering around down here again?"

O'Brien nodded yes, put his hands out and up as if trying to stop something coming at him—her words, she figured—then turned and went out.

• • •

Ten minutes later Merci was walking through the parking structure with a sharp alertness and a dull anxiety inside. The wind whistled in and bounced off the concrete at her.

Parking structures were on her to-fear list now, anything to do with cars, because that's where the Purse Snatcher had gotten her—in her own car, her own county-issue detective's Impala. She still dreamed of things that jumped from backseats. She walked up next to the car, used a flashlight to check the backseat, opened the door, then looked into the backseat again. Okay. All right. Don't be stupid.

She drove surface streets to the UCI Medical Center. It wasn't far out of her way home. The wind swayed and shook the streetlights.

The last thing she wanted to do was to be a bother to anyone, but she wanted Zamorra and Janine to know she cared enough to at least come by.

In the gift shop she bought a small, overpriced flower arrangement. She also bought a card and wrote a cheerful, get-well message inside.

She checked with the desk and got directions to the neuro ward. The neuro-ward nurse gave her the room number and pointed her down a hall.

Merci heard it before she got to the right room—low, muffled moans rising to high-pitched screams that sounded miles away. She wondered if they built hospital walls and doors thick just for that reason.

She stopped outside Janine Zamorra's room. The door

was shut. Merci felt a cold weight falling in her stomach, like an anchor racing down through dark water. Her arms and legs went heavy. It was more a wail than a scream. A woman's. More in terror than in pain. In helplessness. Like she was seeing something horrible coming but couldn't get away from it.

The nurse came up behind her so quietly Merci's first thought was of the nine.

"I can take the flowers," she said.

Janine Zamorra had gone silent. Merci could hear a man's voice, low and soothing, no words.

Merci looked at the nurse's face and saw nothing but shame and fear tucked under a facade of authority.

"I'll make sure she gets them."

Then another low moan, gaining intensity as it became a wail. Like an animal makes, Merci thought. An animal caught by other animals.

"What's going on in there?"

"She's stable. You should go."

The nurse held out one hand for the vase, and the other she clamped firmly on Merci's arm. She was a small woman, but strong, and she began to pull.

Upon being touched, Merci Rayborn's instincts were not violent but they contained the possibility of violence. And not for the first time in her life she realized the hideous insufficiency of such urges, the absolute certainty that the nine or a baton or a chokehold or a set of sharp plastic cuffs would do nothing at all to relieve Janine Zamorra's terror. Merci, who had once believed she had the answer to almost everything, realized again, to the embarrassment of her soul, that she had the answer to almost nothing.

And certainly not to this.

She handed the nurse the flowers and walked out. Janine's moan was on the rise as the neuro-ward doors swung shut behind Merci and sealed it off.

• • •

Mike's truck was in her driveway when she got home. Inside, she found him sitting in the living room with Clark, watching the TV. Tim, Jr., was on his lap.

Her son studied her like he always did when she came home, a wide-eyed stare that seemed to gather so much. Then Tim slid off Mike's lap and waddled toward her, his mouth a big smile, nonsense syllables bubbling out. She knelt down and he crashed into her and she gathered him up in her arms. He smelled sweet and good like always and she could see the flames from the fireplace reflected in his bright gray eyes. Clark had put him in a fuzzy red jumpsuit with white plastic soles on the feet. Merci loved jumpsuits that warmed his whole perfect body, wished she could buy a few in her size.

She nodded at Mike and her dad, then carried Tim into her bedroom where she could say nonsense syllables back at him, and get herself changed. This was one of her favorite parts of the day: home to The Men, change out of her trousers and boots, get the H&K off her shoulder and the backup .32 off her calf, blubber back and forth with her son. It was a time when her heart felt huge but light. But tonight it just felt big and heavy.

When she came back out Clark was in the kitchen and Mike was still in front of the television. His face was thick from yesterday's Scotch.

"Can we talk, Merci?"

"Let's go out back."

She got big down jackets for her and Tim, matching ones she'd found in a mail-order catalogue, with black and yellow panels and hoods if you needed them. She bought matching everythings, which Merci knew was silly but did anyway—something to do with uniforms, colors, them and us.

They walked out onto the patio. The security system went on and blanched the yard in a cold white light. The cats eyed them.

"Can I start by begging you to forgive me for what I did yesterday?"

"I can do that, but it'll take some time. You *threw* me, Mike. And you betrayed me."

Silence then. She glanced at him and saw the breath vapor coming from his nose. Mike's shoulders were slumped down into his sheriff windbreaker, his blond forelock hung down like the tail of a submissive dog.

"I should never have drank all that liquor."

"There's some other things you shouldn't have done, too."

"I know I was wrong."

She looked out at the windbreak along the orange grove. The tall eucalyptus trees hissed and heaved back and forth, the leaves flashing silver facets in the moonlight. She knelt down and watched Tim stare at the big trees, with something like awe on his face. Above the treeline the stars twinkled and a jagged moonlit cloud slid by.

Mike knelt in front of her. "If I could take a big black marker and draw a line across things, I'd do it. And I'd take everything that happened before yesterday, cut it off and throw it away. Merci, I've been trying awful hard lately to keep things contained. Keep things alive. I . . . this is not . . . this is the hardest thing I've ever said in my life, but I'm not happy without you. I want you. I want a life with you and Tim and Danny. I want to get us a big house with plenty of room for everyone. I want to work hard, I need that, but when I come home I want you to be there. I'll give you all the time and space you need. You could do anything you want. You could work. You could maybe have a baby with me, if you wanted one. I'll be okay either way. I'm thirty-eight now, and my career is solid. *Was* solid. And I know who I am and what I want. I want you. Because I love you."

He pulled something out of his windbreaker pocket and set it on her knee. Gray, rounded edges, a thin metal seam around the middle. Tim, lured as always by small objects, tried to take it. But Merci's hand reached it first and she could feel the velvet against her cold fingers.

"I know you can't answer now. But you can think about it. I just want you to think about it."

She looked at him. The wind ruffled his hair and he smiled.

"How afraid were you?" she asked. "How afraid that Aubrey might do it? I read your letters and cards. You know what I'm talking about."

In the cold light she saw his face go red.

"Um . . . worried. Yeah. I thought she might try to . . . expose me. When she started talking about that I realized I didn't really know her all that well. I didn't know what she would do. I realized that everything I'd done could be turned against me, make me look real bad."

Merci studied his puffy face, his tired eyes.

"Did you love her?"

"I never touched her. Except for those handshakes I told you about and one or two hugs. I never—"

"But did you *love* her, Mike?"

"I thought I was falling in love. And that's when I knew I had to end it."

She let the words hang. Even in the wind they stayed right there in front of her, solid as boulders, impervious to the elements.

"How were you going to end it?"

"When I walked out after dinner that night I knew it was over. I'd come right up to the edge and looked in. I wasn't going to go there. Never. I'd learned what I needed to know."

"And what was that, Mike?"

"It's not something I'm proud of."

"What was it you needed to know?"

"That someone would find me, um, lovable, I guess. That was all. It was a question I had between me and me, Merci. Not me and you. Not anybody else."

So you go to a prostitute to get your answer, she thought.

She handed the box back to him. She picked up Tim and stood.

Mike stayed down where he was. "I knew you wouldn't take it, and that's okay. I've had it for six months, but the time never seemed right. It sure isn't right now. But I wanted you to know where I stand. More important than that, though, more important than anything right now, is I want you to know how sorry I am for yesterday. Just know that. I'll keep the ring while you think. It'll be there."

He stood and kissed her on the cheek. Her face was so cold she could barely feel it.

Tim grabbed Mike's face and Mike smiled. In the harsh security light he looked like someone she barely knew, an exhausted man-boy with a smile cold as the stars.

Mike put an arm around Merci and Tim, hugging them gently. Then she felt the fingers of his other hand against the inside of her thigh.

"Let's go get warm together. I can hold you and you can hold me. It's been an awful long time. Maybe we can remember who we are."

"I know who I am."

He released her.

"I'm not going to lose you, Merci. They can strip me down to nothing and you can never look at me again, but I won't lose you. You're in here forever. I'm not letting you out."

He made a gun of his hand, and aimed it at his heart.

Chapter Fifteen

Merci rented a skiff in the Dana Point harbor early the next morning, Saturday, and guided the belching little outboard through the breakwater and into the bottomless sway of the Pacific. Her stomach went soft inside when she hit the open sea.

She bore south. The morning was cold and clear and she could see the great sandstone cliffs where the cattle hides had been thrown down to the trading vessels just a hundred short years ago. A cold sweat slicked her brow.

The bow of the little skiff took the swell hard and she felt the bench slamming up under her as she upped the throttle and sped south. She measured her velocity against the oncoming swell and it seemed considerable; she measured it against the breakwater rocks and it seemed almost no velocity at all.

While the engine screamed, an assembly of voices quarreled inside her head.

Mike is a good man, but you misunderstand him.

Mike is weak and capable of error.

You should help him.

You should suspect him.

You should abandon him.

You should love him.

Merci looked out at the towering white clouds to the west, saw the gulls circling over a kelp bed. The bench knocked against her butt and she tried to get more speed, but the little two-cycle was tapped out and she could smell the oil burning with the gas.

She almost gagged on the fumes, almost gagged on the nausea rising and falling in her gut.

She hugged the shore as best she could, staying a swimmable distance from the beach. She did not like the ocean, never had. It was untrustworthy and prone to violence. Nature's felon, she thought.

She had almost lost Tim, Jr., to it. Not to mention herself. For reasons that had nothing to do with her own will, it had rejected them and given them back their lives.

But Hess had loved this ocean and Merci told herself that Hess had some influence out here, that some residual goodwill had surely rubbed off on her from him. As a lover of Hess.

She thought of him and wondered why memory had to be a tribulation.

She squinted to the south and saw the San Clemente Pier and knew she was just a mile or two from 23 Wave

Street, from that tiny patch of ocean that held the key to Aubrey Whittaker's murder.

Half an hour later she was directly offshore of the Wave Street apartments. She tried to eyeball where that bullet had gone, assuming it had flown in a straight line from the gun, through Aubrey Whittaker's shocked heart, through the thin pane of the sliding glass door and into the infinite sea.

She looked down at the water around the bobbing boat: indigo blue with silver facets that flashed like mirrors, countless variations, never the same arrangement twice.

She realized that what she was hoping to find was roughly one-half inch square, maybe mushroomed out a little, but about that size. It would have sunk to the bottom, wherever that was.

She looked at her beach bag, which had slid off the aft bench and now lay soaked by spray and spill against the hull. Through the mesh she could see the two red adjustable swim fins, the pink mask and clear snorkel.

She touched the bag with the toe of her shoe. She hunched down deeper into her sweater against the cold day and told herself that she could suit up, don the mask and fins and make the dive. Make a hundred of them today. Make a hundred tomorrow and a hundred every day after that until the close of the age and she would never find the bullet. She would never even reach the bottom.

This truth went against every grain in her, against her belief that hard work paid off, her sense of hope itself.

Mike loved the girl.

Mike thought he loved her.

You can trust him with your life.

He can't be trusted with anything.

She sat for a long while, looking down into the shifting water, telling herself that miracles only come to the well positioned. And that was what she was.

She looked back toward 23 Wave Street. She looked west to Catalina, visible as a low hump above the distant horizon line. A late morning wind came up and she could feel it rattling through her joints.

Pulling the little outboard to life she carved a turn back the way she had come.

• • •

Two hours later she stood in Aubrey Whittaker's bedroom, contemplating herself in the mirrored closet door. The red leather dress fit tightly. Merci knew she was a slightly heavier woman than Aubrey. Slightly shorter.

Slightly not as beautiful, she thought.

She turned. The golden buckles caught the light. The leather smelled good, cool against her skin, a little stiff maybe, but leather formed to you, right?

She held up her hair with one hand. Then the other. She put both hands on her hips and released the left one out to one side. Turned again. But no matter what she did Merci saw nothing attractive before her, nothing alluring or seductive or sexual. She looked like a big woman in a little dress with tears on her face.

What had gone wrong?

She knew that whatever it was, it was at the center of what Mike had done, or not done.

Yes, because you are the key to him.

No, Mike is what Mike does.

You needed to love him, take those things out of him. They spoiled and festered and erupted.

I am not the mother of menace. I have a heart. A big one.

Big and cold. Big and cold.

Chapter Sixteen

Sunrise, Monday morning, the last stars fading into a pale sky while Merci parked her car up the road from Mike's house, behind a tree where he wouldn't notice it. Oak branches vanished when she turned off the headlights. She killed the engine, felt her nerves bristle, then settle.

She dangled an arm into the space behind the backseat, moving it around in the cool, comforting emptiness. She watched the smoke rise from chimneys up and down Modjeska Canyon, and she tried to banish the voice that told her she was wrong to be doing this.

She'd spent the last forty-eight hours listening to that voice. She'd argued with it, agreed with it, disputed with it, screamed back at it. Now, decided, all she could do was tell it to shut up and leave her alone.

At 7:02 she saw his van roll out of the driveway and down the road. Mike started work at quarter of eight, and Mike would rather be dead than late.

You're betraying him so you can know him?

You're investigating him to prove him innocent?

Ten minutes later she drove over, parked in front of the house and let herself in as the dogs commenced barking.

The house smelled of wood smoke and coffee like it always did. The fire was tamped down, just a glow behind the glass of the stove front. The animals in the pictures looked at her. The telephone desk was well organized, as all of Mike's things were organized. One message light on the machine, so she played it.

Mike, this's your old man, you there or—

The kitchen was neat, dishes washed, the empty Scotch bottle in the recycle bin.

She put her head into Danny's room, then into the spare bedroom, then went down the narrow hallway and into Mike's bedroom.

Familiar smells: aftershave, deodorant, the humid bouquet of after-shower man. The room was large and dark, with the only window opening to a steep hillside that blocked the sun at almost every hour of the day. She turned on two lamps.

His bed was unmade. There was a desk along one wall—just an overturned door set upon file cabinets—with a computer and a printer. The cables went through the doorknob hole and down to the wall. Bloodhound pictures, bloodhound calendars, bloodhound books. A Navajo blanket hung from an adjacent wall, above Mike's framed collection of arrowheads. The other wall had a bookcase and shelves for photographs, valued fossils and seashells, little sayings from the Bible that Mike's mother had written by hand on colored paper and set in small, standing frames.

> A good wife who can find?
> She is far more precious than jewels.
> The heart of her husband trusts in her,
> And he will have no lack of gain.

Dear Lord, Merci thought, *maybe You should just strike me dead right now and get it over with. The voice inside me would agree with You. Damn me. Damn me.*

But He didn't, and Merci turned to doing what she did best.

It took her less than a minute to find the black sweater in the dresser. The date-night sweater. It was tight on him, with a crew neck, and he wore it when he wanted to look good. It showed off his blond hair and fair skin and hard muscles.

. . . black wool and Orlon mix, definitely not from her dress, possibly a sweater or outergarment of some kind . . .

She read the label: 65 percent lambswool, 35 percent Orlon. Clean, folded, no blood.

She told herself it meant nothing, fundamentally nothing at all—except that he had wanted to look his best for Aubrey. A little fury rippled inside.

It meant little more than the beige carpet in the bedrooms of this house. The beige carpet she was standing on.

Betray him because you care for him? Or because he's humiliated you?

The closet was old and the runners were bad and she had to lean into it to get it to slide open. At the far end, jammed up against the side, were the things she left there: robe, a clean pair of jeans, a blouse, a light jacket.

She knelt down and looked at the shoes. Mike was a shoe guy—probably twenty pair in all. Size twelve. She began pulling them out one at a time and looking at the tread patterns. Nothing like Evan O'Brien's print. In the far corner, behind a long duster she found a dusty old duffel containing a worn pair of moccasins, two tennis shoes caked in mud, and a pair of chukka-style boots.

The tread pattern on the chukkas was like the one on the lab print. There was a dark, viscous buildup along one of the comma-shaped lugs that pointed toward the back. There was more trapped in the central circle of the right boot heel.

She cursed him. And she cursed herself. And she cursed God, too, as the creator of all things.

She put the shoes back into the duffel and put the duffel back behind the duster. She stood and leaned into the door to get it closed again.

She told herself there was an explanation. There was an explanation. There had to be some explanation.

Sweating now, heart pounding fast and hard, she went through his dresser, his bookshelves, his file cabinets, his desk drawers. If he wrote Aubrey Whittaker, she might have written back. Her affections. Her love. Her threats.

She found the little box he'd offered her the night before, safe under his white athletic socks. She opened it. A plain gold solitaire setting with a diamond, big as a pencil eraser and much more beautiful. She closed it quickly, hoping this might make her feel less loathsome. It didn't. She imagined a stain starting on her heart, spreading out to the end of the universe and beyond.

Easy. Easy now. There are explanations.

She found the little bundle under the bed, in the gun safe containing the .357 Magnum Mike kept there for home protection. He'd made her memorize the combination in case she needed it when he wasn't there: *4-4-5-7.* Over and over he'd made her repeat it, *4-4-5-7, 4-4-5-7,* and now she used it to find his love letters from the whore.

Her heart was thumping too hard and her brain was swimming with too much fury and guilt and hurt to read them. She just slapped them open and scanned: . . . *sooo cool of you to write . . . how outrageous for a cop to say those things to a girl like me . . . I've felt those emotions toward you, too . . . agree that friendship is one of God's sneaky little ways of . . . good man you are . . . be all right to meet you for coffee or a walk on the . . . pretty huge dif-*

ferences in the ways we live our . . . fondly, truly, respectfully yours, yours, yours, yours . . . A. W., Aubrey, A. Whittaker, WYW (you flatter me!) . . .

Damn me, she said. Then said it again. The whore was in love with him. Slow now. Go slow and learn what there is to know.

She checked the postmarks and dates. The most recent was a typewritten letter dated December 4.

Dear Mike, Dark Cloud, Detective-man, Major Dude,

I keep thinking about you all the time, no matter what I'm doing or who I'm doing it to! It's like having a friend with me all the time, glad you're not really there, though, a girl needs privacy sometimes, right? Now, I agree with you totally that I need a better way to make a living. Way down at the bottom of myself, the part of me that hates me tells me to keep doing what I do, but I know I shouldn't. It's just so . . . damned easy. And it also helps remind me what pigs men are, but you know, I wish that wasn't true. Now that I know you, I'm thinking maybe it's not.

But you know something? I wonder when you'll do the cool thing and give me what I deserve. I've given and given to you—never charged you a dime, ha, ha—but when are you going to give something back? I get the fact you're ashamed of me. I'm just a whore. I understand you can't be seen with me, what would your mommy think? I even understand you have another chick in your life. But Mike, if she makes you happy then why are you so miserable all the damn time? I make you happy. I can see it on your D.C. face! I think it's time for you to admit what I really am and admit what you've done. Time to offer something back. Time to service your debt! I don't ask for much. I get that no one can know about me, especially the people you work with, but I wonder if that might be the best thing that could happen to you—to have them know what you think of me, what you do with me, what we are. Maybe telling them would be the best thing I could do for you. So how can I change if you won't let me? Will I always just be Aubrey the professional joint copper to you? Hey man, I'm thinking of going private!

I hope we have a thousand hot nights to figure all this out!

Aubrey

P.S. I saw a painting in a book today—*Into the World Came a Soul Named Ida.* It was the grossest painting I've ever seen—a woman who's gotta be a hooker, just eaten alive by decay, a putrid, sad ruined body all fucked up by time and men. You're ready for maggots to jump outta the thing. It made me cry, and it made me think of what I never want to be. And to think you called me a Wise Young Woman. Sometimes I could just die, but who'd make the payments on my Caddy? Help! Help! Mr. Big Strong Policeman!

Merci bundled the letters back up and returned them to the pistol case. Shut the top and heard the lock click shut. Sat there for a minute on Mike's unmade bed and listened to a car heading down the road away from the house.

What a strange feeling. Surprise. Shock. It was like seeing herself in the world for the first time. Like realizing she wasn't who she thought she was, never had been. She had never felt so utterly fooled since the morning she got into her car and felt the hands of the monster she was looking for lock over her face. Was there no end to her stupidity? It seemed limitless.

She told herself there had to be an explanation.

And she remembered what he had said: *I bought a silencer. I had dinner with her then iced her. Arrest me.*

Explain that, Deputy.

• • •

The garage was actually a small barn, with two pads for cars, a big workroom, and a storage area upstairs.

Merci stood by the big workbench, looked at the toolboxes and cabinets, the yard tools hanging neatly from brackets in the pegboard walls, the canisters of gasoline and motor oil, the big bags of dog food that Polly, Molly and Dolly went through like water, the old freezer.

She could see her breath, the dew in the corners of the windows, the spiderwebs in the holly bush outside still beaded with moisture.

On one far end of the workbench were Mike's reloading tools. She pulled away the plastic covers. Mike reloaded .45s for his Colts, .357s for his Smith, 20-gauge shotshells for his Remington and .30-'06 loads for his rifle. Merci looked at the red Meac reloader. There was an open coffee can of .45 brass beside it, and the primers still stacked in the long tube looked like .45s to her.

She wished she could know which of these shells had been fired through Mike's Colt. She could take one, the lab could run it against the empty that Lynda Coiner found in Aubrey Whittaker's flower vase, and all this foolishness would be over.

Over, one way or another.

She remembered that the .45 used on Aubrey would have to fire a subsonic round for the silencer to work. Heavy bullet, light powder. She found the bullets in a green cardboard box: 255-grain Hornadys, roundnosed, jacketed. The powder canister on the Meac had a grains setting on the neck, which she wrote down in her blue notebook. She had no idea if Mike was making up heavy loads, light ones, or something in-between. Timmerman, out at the sheriff's range, would know.

The other end of the bench had a belt-driven grinder and a bandsaw bolted in, a row of big clamps screwed into the bench top, more toolboxes on top. Two small fly-tying vices were fastened near the corner. Mike's fishing rods were hung horizontally on the pegboard, neatly organized from shortest to longest. There were three reel boxes, three more tackle boxes, then all the flyfishing containers. She pulled them out one by one and looked through them.

The old pine box caught her eye, because it used to be in the bedroom. Mike had made it in woodshop, seventh grade, and the workmanship had survived the years. He'd stuck a decal on the lid before varnishing it, a blue-and-white oval that read *Hooked Up!* with the silhouette of a fisherman holding a dramatically bowed rod below the words. She knew it was where he kept his dry and wet flies, his nymphs and terrestrials, many of them handmade, all of them collected over two decades of enthusiasm for the sport. Now, it rested at the back of the bench, between two big plastic tackle boxes. One of Mike's fishnets lay on top, almost hiding it from sight. It was the *Hooked Up!* decal that she noticed through the black mesh.

Something about the box and the decal brought a lump to her throat, brought all of her shame and guilt boiling up, let the voice inside her start haranguing again: *You sneaking, distrustful, guilt-loving, dirt-hungry bitch, leave him alone while you have the chance . . .*

But she reached over and worked out the pine box anyway, centering it on the bench in front of her. The top tray held some of Mike's fly boxes and wallets—two aluminum, two leather, two plastic. She pulled it out and set it down on the bench, where it rested unevenly on the wood.

Below were the larger boxes, each bristling inside with flies. She remembered him showing her all these flies and naming them: mosquitoes and caddis, midges and buggers, blue duns and black gnats, Quill Gordons and Lt. Cahills, Royal Wulffs and Royal Trudes.

More than she could remember, plus designs of his own. Mike had actually named one for her—Blue Merci—because she was mourning the loss of Hess and unhappy every waking hour. Mike had caught a "more than satisfactory" German brown trout with it up on the Walker that month. He considered it lucky.

She liked the Lt. Cahill the best because it sounded like a cop.

Put them back, get out of here, forget you ever did what you're doing . . .

She did put them back. She put the tray back on top. And that was when she noticed the small bundle of cloth taped to the bottom of it, the reason it hadn't sat flush on the bench.

She held it up and looked: white cotton rolled tight, held with duct tape. The size of a film canister, maybe, but longer. Mike had fastened it to the bottom of the tray with an elastic band and four thumbtacks.

The tacks were hard to pry from the heavily varnished wood. She got two off one end and the bundle dropped into her palm. The tape rasped off. The white cotton unfurled quickly and something heavy and cold dropped to the bench. She recognized the packaging—a pair of underpants she had allowed Mike to keep some months ago after a night in bed that particularly pleased him. Against her better judgment. She'd felt strange letting him have them, like it was evidence, something nobody should see but her. He promised nobody would.

But it was nothing compared to what was inside. She stared down at the heavy cylinder on the bench top, a welded contraption with small holes all over it and something that looked like steel wool packed down beneath the holes. The inside was smooth, with more, bigger holes. One end was flat, with an opening in the middle about the size a .45 would need. The other was welded to a rectangular fitting lined with gasket material. There was a heavy band locked down by a screw so you could loosen and tighten it. There were light black burns at the exit end.

She looked at it in all its squat ugliness, its low purpose, its unaccountability. An object made of steel, fashioned by hand to do a job. No more.

She knew there was an explanation, even if it was the one she'd never wanted.

Merci's hands were shaking as she wrapped it and put it back, but the voice inside her was silent.

• • •

On her way out of Mike's house, Merci was forced to speak with Mrs. Heath, the next door neighbor. She was a rosy faced, overly sociable woman whom Merci found kind but intrusive. She loved living near a detective. She had an envelope in one hand, a dog leash in the other. Reggie, her Yorkie, bounced up and down at Merci's ankles like something powered by fresh batteries.

Merci realized what a problem this was, but she was still shaking from what she found in the barn, and she couldn't think a clear way out of it.

"I got some of Mike's mail," Mrs. Heath said, holding out the envelope. "I was just going to drop it in the box."

"I'll do that." The box was on the porch railing, protruding out where the postman could fill it without getting out of his little truck.

Mrs. Heath studied her, then the house. "Mike's not home?"

"Just left."

Merci watched her to see if she'd look for her car, nowhere in sight. She didn't. If Mrs. Heath had seen her walk up to the house, it was over. Either way, the chances of this getting back to Mike were now running about eighty-twenty.

"I'm always running late on Mondays," Merci offered.

"Beautiful, after the storm," said Mrs. Heath. The Yorkie stopped bouncing, sat and stared at Merci.

"It was a whopper, wasn't it?" Her mind was racing to

find a white lie to cover herself, but Merci was never good at thinking on her feet unless it was police business. She hit on something far-fetched, but it might play into Mrs. Heath's romantic enthusiasms.

"Mrs. Heath, can you help me keep a secret from Mike? His birthday's coming up in a few weeks, and I came back here to hide a couple of things around the house while he's gone. Little surprises."

"Like an Easter egg hunt?"

"Exactly. Some things for Danny, too."

"That's sweet. I won't say a thing."

"For a few weeks, anyway."

"You got it, dearie."

"Well, I'll put that letter in."

Mrs. Heath looked puzzled. "How come you parked so far down the street?"

Merci blushed, then ran interference with a smile. "Oh, he'd notice the tire tracks on the drive. You know how those detectives are."

"I do know. I should have thought of that."

If you ask about the footprints I'll have to shoot you, thought Merci.

"Won't he notice your footprints?"

Merci looked back at the drive. She wasn't heavy enough to leave good prints in the packed, graded dirt, but the rough outlines were there.

Mrs. Heath was looking, too. "How about this, Detective Rayborn? I'll walk up to the door, stepping where you did. I'll leave the letter in the box. That way, he'll be looking at my footprints, not yours. And Reggie's, too. If Mike asks, you can evade the truth without lying. They're not yours."

Fuck, Merci thought, this is getting to be an Agatha Christie novel. She faked what she could of patience and good cheer.

"Good thinking, Sergeant Heath!"

She watched the old woman deliver the letter, watched Reggie jump around while his mistress opened the rusty old mailbox door, watched Mrs. Heath return, carefully choosing her steps.

"Our little secret," she said. "We'll tell Mike about it *after* his birthday."

Merci smiled, waved and headed down the road toward her car. Mike's birthday wasn't for five weeks, but who knew, he might be in jail by then.

• • •

Before going in to headquarters, Merci went to the Sheriff's Firing Range in Anaheim. She talked briefly with the Weapons Instructor, said she was thinking about going to a .45 instead of her nine, wanted more stopping power.

Timmerman told her that stopping power and knockdown power were subjective and mysterious, some experts saying they were more related to velocity than to bullet mass. Others disagreed. With relish, he broke down Einstein's $E = MC^2$ into layman's terms for her, then argued its relevancy to shooting someone.

He himself drew his opinions from LaGarde's research for the classic *Gunshot Injuries,* in which suspended cadavers swayed very little when shot by .38-caliber guns, but oscillated dramatically when shot by a .45. This, he explained, is why LaGarde had recommended the .45 as the American Armed Services sidearm—in 1904.

"Remember," he said, "what stops a charging animal isn't the momentum of the bullet, it's the kinetic energy of the bullet on the *functioning* of the living body."

"I'll remember."

"There's also velocity, caliber, shape of the bullet point, its frangibility and penetration. Lots of factors."

Merci nodded along like she was interested, then checked out a Colt .45 to carry and test fire for a couple of weeks. He was kind enough to loan her a shoulder rig and a hip holster, too, and he threw in some wadcutter ammo to use on the range.

Chapter Seventeen

Mel Glandis reclined his big torso against the back of his chair and nodded at her. His office was every bit as bland and bureaucratic as Glandis himself, but it was a welcome calm in the storm that Mike McNally had caused.

Merci couldn't think straight about Mike right now. But she could make herself think straight about this.

"How come nobody cared about Patti Bailey? You're asking *me*?" A laugh from the assistant sheriff.

"Maybe back then you guys thought it was funny a woman got shot and you couldn't find the creep who did it. It isn't funny now."

Glandis straightened, his face going from amused to bovine. "Hell, I didn't mean it that way. What I meant was I was a fourth-year guy. Out of the power loop."

Merci knew Glandis well enough to understand that winning was what interested him: power and politics, vengeance and reward, who had what on whom, who could step on you, crush you, help you. A pack animal. As a lifelong disciple of Chuck Brighton, Glandis had had the early good luck to attach himself to a winner.

"That's why I asked you," said Merci. "You weren't the establishment around here—yet."

He smiled, taking this as the compliment she knew he would. He got up, moved across the floor on his small, dancer's feet, closed the door.

"Yeah. What you have to understand is nobody cared about any of the caseload that year. Everything here was in upheaval. The old sheriff, Bill Owen, he was in tight with the head of the County Board of Supervisors—that was Meeks. Ralph Meeks. And Meeks was getting heat for a kickback scheme from developers. You know the old story, the pols make the rules and throw the business to their friends, the friends aim some of it back. Someone gets in trouble and the fingers start pointing. Big stink in the press. About the same time Meeks was getting investigated by the Grand Jury, Bill Owen got down real low. You know, real low, real quiet, like he was looking out of a foxhole. Expecting fire."

"Was he on Meeks's payroll?"

"Nothing that obvious. Nothing you could prove. They were friends. Meeks got favors, Bill got favors. You know, friends."

"Then what was Owen's problem, besides being Meeks's friend?"

"Politics. Some of the deputies didn't like his ideas. You gotta remember, this was a real political time. Not like now. There was a clique of John Birchers in the department, and they really couldn't stand him. They thought everybody who wasn't a Bircher was a communist, and that included Owen, because he wasn't conservative enough for them. Wasn't tough enough on crime. That was part of the communist conspiracy, you know—let America rot from the inside out, let the criminals get the streets, like they did in Watts. Bumper stickers back then said *No Watts in Orange County.* Owen, he wouldn't issue concealed carry permits to anybody with a right-wing slant. So, when Owen tried to stay low on the Meeks scandal, the Birchers turned up the heat. They had him grilling on both sides."

"Who were they?"

Glandis gave her an odd look then, something guarded in his usually readable face. "There were a lot of them. Beck Rainer was the ringleader. The Birchers thought he'd make a good sheriff someday. There was a big, funny guy named Bob Vale, one of the lieutenants. There was Ed Springfield, Dave Boone, Bob Emmer. I think Roy Thornton, too, and his partner, Rymers. There was Pat McNally—Mike's old man. A bunch of the traffic guys on motorcycles—North and Morrison and Wilberforce. Your dad had something to do with them for a while, if I remember right."

Merci thought again of that Birch Society rally so many

years ago, set up to support the local police. She tried to relate it to the body of a prostitute dumped near the corner of Myford and Fourth.

"Where's Bailey come in?"

A wry expression from Glandis then, like little Merci would never learn.

"Well, Merci, I don't *know* exactly where she comes in. I'm just setting the stage for you. What I'm saying is, there's all this shit coming down at Owen and there's the Birchers agitating him from the inside, so this place is like a . . . like a cauldron. Everybody's worried. They're paranoid. And in an atmosphere like that, it's no wonder nobody really cared about a dead hooker in an orange grove."

Merci tried to draw a line again, the same one she'd tried to draw between Patti Bailey, Jesse Acuna and the cops he claimed beat him.

"Any of those men hang out at the De Anza Hotel in Santa Ana?"

Glandis nodded approvingly. "We all did. It was a great place, until the hookers ran it over."

"Ralph Meeks and Bill Owen?"

Glandis smiled. "They were big men back then. You wouldn't find them at a place like the De Anza. That was for us little guys. No."

He leaned forward then and looked at her, lacing his fingers like he was getting ready to pray.

"How about a change of topic, Merci?"

"Shoot."

"I'm going to be blunt and candid here for a minute. I want you to be the same."

She watched and waited.

"You think Brighton's a good sheriff?"

She thought for a moment, not about the question, but about why Glandis was asking it.

"Yes."

He nodded. "I always did, too. He always put the department first. Now, though, I wonder when he steps down if he's going to leave us with somebody good or somebody not-so-good. You've heard what that idiot Abelera wants to do—run this place like a Fortune-Five-Hundred company. Privatize half the work we do. I hope Brighton doesn't endorse *him*."

"Me, too."

"What do you think of Nelson Neal, as sheriff, I mean."

Here we go again, thought Merci. She told him the same thing about Nelson she'd told Brighton—not inspirational.

"Craig Braga?"

"He'd be good."

"Mel Glandis?"

She hesitated, looking for some hint of humor in Glandis's placid eyes. There wasn't any, and she understood what he was after.

"I'd be happy to work for you, if you got the nod from Brighton."

"What if I didn't?"

"You'd be a good sheriff, Mel. I didn't think you were angling that way."

But why not, she asked herself. Glandis was a rider of winning horses. He'd gotten where he was with loyal devotion to Brighton. Now he was worried his god was going to overlook him. In fact, she could think of worse people than Mel Glandis running the department. In his own clunky way he managed to get the job done, keep people working together.

"I'm just testing the waters," he said quietly. "I've asked a few deputies, people I respect. I don't want to make a fool out of myself. Don't want to upset the apple cart around here. But if there's a gap I can fill, if I can help the department, then I'll do it."

"What does Brighton think? Of you following him?"

Glandis smiled and shrugged. "You know Chuck. He likes to talk about retirement but he hates the idea of doing it. He's been on the verge of retirement for half a decade. I don't blame him. You want to hang on, do what you can do. But you know, there comes a time for fresh ideas, younger blood. That's just the way it works. We're all like boxers, we all want to fight one more time. That's when we get hurt. He's seventy-two years old. I'm fifty-eight. I think I can contribute. Anyway, thanks for being honest with me."

Fourteen years ago, as a first-year deputy working the jail, Merci had picked fifty-eight as the age she wanted to become sheriff. She considered it a lucky number for no reason. She didn't know if Glandis was usurping her good luck, or perhaps, in some way she was yet to understand, adding to it.

She disliked her superstitions but could never get rid of them.

"I don't lie very well." Just ask Mrs. Heath, she thought.

"Me neither. But I take care of the people who take care of me. Remember that. I will, when it comes time to pick a sharp detective to run homicide."

"That's good to know."

Glandis sighed. "So, what was Mike doing at the hooker's house that night?"

"Having dinner."

He slowly shook his head. "This can only end bad or worse. I'll help you on it if I can."

"How?"

"I have absolutely no idea."

"I don't, either. Maybe you could keep it to yourself, for a start."

"I will. I promise. Half the department knows anyway. By tomorrow, the other half. It gets out, Mike's dead. We'll all suffer if it does."

Merci felt her pulse speed up, the quick heat in her neck and ears. "It's like a bunch of little old biddies around here. It's all yap, yap, yap."

"It's the nature of the organizational beast."

"Chickenshit's what I call it."

"You've got a way with the language, Sergeant."

• • •

Back at her desk Merci tried to concentrate on the CSI reports on the Aubrey Whittaker scene. She was hoping something would pop, something would stand up and call attention to itself, something would take her mind off what she'd found at Mike's place.

But she couldn't take her mind off it, the way she couldn't let creeps get away with things. It just wasn't in her nature.

So she asked herself the same questions over and over, and came up with the same answers.

What possible motive could Mike have for keeping around a silencer and bloody boots he'd used in a murder? *None whatsoever.*

Was it just a device he'd made, or perhaps purchased, never used on Aubrey Whittaker at all? Was that quail or deer blood on the chukkas? An injured bloodhound? *Possibly.*

What if someone had planted it all there as part of a frame? *Who? And how did they get their hands on my goddamned underpants?*

It occurred to her again to simply confront him. Let him explain. That's what adults did, right? But if he had killed, he would destroy evidence. Maybe worse.

If he had not, his firearm would vindicate him, thanks to the precious brass from 23 Wave Street. She'd never have to reveal herself as the distrustful, prying, bitter bitch that she was. Reveal how furious she was at him.

The key was Mike's Colt. For him and for her.

One of the cadets brought around the afternoon mail. Merci got her monthly copy of the FBI *Law Enforcement Bulletin,* a pitch from a credit-card company, and a white envelope with her name written in a very simple, childlike hand. No return address, and the postmark was Santa Ana. The stamp pictured a top hat in stars and stripes. There was something hard inside, on the bottom, something that had creased the paper around it.

She opened it carefully, using her pocketknife. The one sheet of white paper read:

For P. B.—
23974 Tyler #355
Riverside, CA 92503

There was a key taped to the bottom of the sheet.

The writing was the same as on the envelope. It looked like a righty had done it left-handed, or the reverse.

For P. B.

Merci rolled back in her chair, spun around and looked around the detective's pen as if she'd get an explanation if she scowled hard enough. Dickinson was at his desk, lost in paper. Arbaugh had his feet up while he talked on the phone. Two uniforms sat with Metz, drinking coffee.

For Patti Bailey?

What in the hell is going on?

• • •

Zamorra walked in at quarter to three. His face was pale and his whiskers were dark but, as always, his black suit and white shirt looked crisp. No lipstick on the collar this time, she noted.

He nodded at her, sat. "I just dusted the hell out of Aubrey Whittaker's kitchen. Down low, where all the action was."

He swiveled his chair and held up the fingerprint cards.

"Coiner or O'Brien can—"

"No. I'll run them myself."

"Why?"

"I don't trust them. I don't trust anybody. Not lab techs, not brain surgeons, not God almighty on His tin throne in heaven. I'll have to trust me."

And I thought *I* got pissed off, thought Merci. "Fine. Run them yourself."

He looked away. "Sorry I'm so goddamned gone all the time. How do you like having an invisible partner?"

"I understand."

"The flowers were nice. She always liked, uh, whatever they were."

She felt shallow and inconsiderate. She felt worse than that for Paul, but what was it—sympathy, sorrow, fury?

"Mums," she said. "Take a walk with me, will you?"

They headed out of the Sheriff's Building on the south side, past the Forensic Sciences Building and the jail. The day was bright, soaked and scrubbed by the storm, with a chill in the air and a cap of snow out on Saddleback peak.

They got coffee from a vendor. Merci scorched her lips. She watched Paul drink his without even a wince. Merci was a fast walker but Zamorra kept getting up ahead.

"Look, partner," he said, turning. "I'm just so damned sorry I haven't been here. It's my job, it's the second most important thing in my life, but I can't be here."

"Paul, I *understand*."

"Yeah, well *I* don't."

They walked past a row of big magnolias with leaves green and waxy in the breeze. Zamorra crumpled his cup and dropped it in a trash bin. Merci still hadn't taken a full sip.

"What happened to her, Paul?"

"They put in the radiation and chemo seeds. Supposed to kill the tumor, spare the good brain cells. But the tumor is near the motor center—the part of your brain that tells you how to move your body. Well, she walked into the hospital at seven in the morning for the procedure. By seven that night she was in her room, losing . . . losing . . . *herself.* First her toes went, then her feet and ankles. Then her calves and knees. Then her thighs and her hips."

Zamorra stopped and looked back. When she caught up to him she saw the tears welling in his eyes, and the tremendous distance he seemed to be looking through.

"The movement just went away, one inch at a time. All she could do is watch and try to move and scream. Scream like nothing I've ever heard. And those fucking doctors, they came by to tell us, yeah, the pellets are turning you into a paraplegic, too late to do anything now, guess we missed the spot or maybe used too big a charge. Sorry, honey, but you'll never walk again. The thing that really rattles them is, was the radiation too strong, or the chemical too strong? That's what they're really worried about. I almost actually killed one of them, but I didn't want Janine to see it. Had his temple all lined up. Didn't want to lose my job. It wouldn't have mattered. Nothing fucking matters now, nothing you fucking do."

Merci said nothing.

"And you know what, Merci? I want to be here. I love this job. It matters. The last place in the world I want to be is in some hospital room watching my wife get paralyzed one inch at a time. I sat there watching her go and I just wanted to fly away, man, grow wings and just jump off the fifth floor neuro ward and never come back. She sees that in my face and it breaks her heart. It breaks her heart to be doing that to me."

They walked in silence. Merci's duty boots were quiet on the sidewalk, Zamorra's hard-soled brogues clicked with a martial sharpness.

"It breaks her heart to lose herself. She's got a bunch of wigs—all different styles and colors. She's got a new wardrobe. She's always got her face made up and her lipstick on and perfume dabbed on her wrists. She's fighting every step of the way. She's saying, 'you can kill my body but you can't kill me.' It's so graceful. So absolutely, beautifully hopelessly graceful."

Merci was unexpectedly relieved to know that the lipstick on Zamorra's shirt collar had been Janine's. The lipstick had become important to her, for reasons she had not allowed herself to think about.

"She knows you love her, Paul. That's what she's got to hang on to now."

"Fly away, fly away," he muttered. "That's what I'm good for. When this is over, I'll do it."

It seemed to her a witless invasion to ask, *What will you do?* They headed up Civic Center Drive, then down Flower. The sun was already lowering and Merci felt the night's cold creeping across the city. A string of Christmas lights went on around one of the bail bonds offices, Merci wondering what the point of such a cheery veneer was. Did it get you more business?

She came close to telling Paul what she'd found at Mike's, but she didn't. What she'd done wasn't just illegal, what she found wasn't just inadmissible. It was a betrayal of trust, pure and simple, and she'd done it willingly and she'd do it again. That didn't mean Paul had to know. She believed in the right to keep and bear secrets.

She'd already decided what to do about it. She had the gun from the range. All she had to do now was call Mike and make the arrangement. This time tomorrow she would know for sure if Mike's .45 had done what she thought it did. She'd never wanted so badly to be proven a fool, but she could hardly talk herself into believing there was even a chance of that.

So why burden Zamorra with it?

"Do you remember the Jesse Acuna beating?" she asked.

"People from the *barrio* remember it. I was ten. Why?"

"Patti Bailey told her sister she knew who did it."

"Customer?"

"That's the assumption."

"Acuna said it was cops."

"That's right, and Bailey lived in a room at the old De Anza—popular with law enforcement and certain ladies of the night."

Zamorra looked at her, a frown on his face. Somehow, it was a lighter expression than she'd seen on him in the last half hour. Something to think about except his wife, she thought, a distraction.

"When I was a kid, everybody assumed the cops did it. The *barrio* was smaller back then. When a Mexican got beat up we figured it was because he was a Mexican. The cops were either indifferent or they hated us. Take your pick. We weren't supposed to be doing anything but picking fruit or washing dishes."

"What was your take on it?"

"I thought Jesse Acuna was probably right. It wasn't until I started studying for the Sheriff Academy exam that I realized the obvious."

"Which was?"

He shrugged and looked at her again. Some wicked amusement showed through his pain. "The issue was his land, right?"

"A hundred acres between two big parcels."

"Well, who ended up with it, Merci?"

"Orange Coast Capital. For 4.2 mil."

"What did they do with it?"

"Turned it into housing tracts."

"Not all of it. They donated thirteen acres to the county, and the county turned it into a new facility."

"What kind?"

"It's ours. You're walking on Acuna's old orange farm every time you step inside the South County Sheriff Substation."

Merci felt the cool surprise of truth inside her. Acuna to Orange Coast Capital to Meeks to Owen, she thought: thirteen of the choicest acres in the county. 1969. And a dead hooker near the corner of Myford and Fourth who said she knew the truth.

• • •

She said good-bye to her partner on the building steps, then walked around the block again. The day was fading with a whimper, night closing strong, and she wished that God was prouder of the light He had created. Was it only there to separate the darkness? She tried to look on herself like God would, from way up there, trying to view herself as one of many human beings faced with tough questions and no good answers.

Looking down on herself she saw a woman looking for the truth. She knew the value of truth because she'd been taught to believe in it. It had occurred to her more than once that the truth was often dismal and sad. Look at Janine Zamorra. But at least the truth came with an ending, like a case that was finally solved. While lies seemed to go on forever, unsolved and fertile, breeding more and more lies to choke the world.

• • •

She went to the Vice Detail and found Mike at his desk, on the phone. His eyes lit up when he saw her, his face colored. Within a minute he'd hung up and waved her over. He held out the extra chair for her like a maître d', but Merci didn't sit.

It was hard to get the words out, but she managed.

"How about dinner at your place tonight?" she asked. "We can talk."

"You got it. I'll get steaks for us, kid stuff for Tim, Jr."

"No Tim, Jr. Just us."

Mike smiled. They agreed on seven.

He walked her out of the pen. In a quiet place along the

hallway he asked her if she'd been thinking about what they talked about last night. She said she had, but nothing more.

He smiled and took her hands, squeezing gently. "Bring your overnight things if you'd like. We can build a fire and keep the cold away. I'm so sorry for everything. I've missed you so damn much."

"I'll be going home. But that doesn't mean we can't have a fire."

He nodded and smiled again. It reminded her of Tim, Jr.'s, smile—it was all in the moment, irrespective of history or consequence.

"That's okay, too. See you then."

• • •

She left headquarters just before five, drove to the Newport Beach office of Dr. Joan Cash. Cash was a psychiatrist and a friend, in that order. They'd roomed together in college, Cash having seen Merci's "roommate wanted" posting on a Cal State Fullerton bulletin board.

Years later Merci had helped get Cash onto the county's subcontractor's list because Cash could hypnotize subjects so adroitly. Merci thought of it as a gift. She had actually let Cash experiment on her—just once—back in their undergraduate days, using all her might to keep from being put under. She'd chewed the inside of her cheek while Joan asked her to picture a lake in the mountains; she'd bitten the end of her tongue when Joan asked her to imagine clouds. One second she was tasting blood and the next she was talking in a dreamy but lucid hypnotic state, fully aware of herself but astonishingly relaxed and disinterested in saying anything but the truth. The things that came to her mind!

The friendship had grown distant over the years, as all of Merci's friendships had.

Once inside the consultation room, they hugged rather formally, smiled at each other, then hugged again harder.

"Thanks, on the short notice," said Merci.

"Just doing the billing. How are you?"

"I'm fine. This is about my partner."

Dr. Cash looked at her askance. Merci knew that Cash was displeased with her as a patient. For one thing, Merci's reluctant participation in her own Critical Incident Stress Management program made things difficult. Dr. Cash had told her as much. Cash—and a few fellow deputies with the boldness to say so—thought that Merci must be carrying an unbearable psychological load, given her use of deadly force, the death of her partner, the death of her mother and the birth of her son, all within a few short months.

But Merci believed that suffering and aloneness were part of the law enforcer's life. She believed there was more to life than lifting the scab. She believed they could take their defusings and debriefings and Eye Movement Desensitization and Reprocessing and stick them where the sun don't shine.

The nightmares would end; the stains in her soul would fade. If she had to awaken a hundred more times deep in the black morning with her legs beginning to cramp from chasing Colesceau through dream bamboo, then that was what she would do.

"Sit. Tell me about him."

Merci explained the basics of Paul Zamorra's hopeless predicament. Cash, as a physician acquainted with the glioblastoma, concurred that the situation was indeed hopeless, in the medical sense. She'd heard of the radiation/chemical implants, said she'd heard of bad complications.

"You think he might kill himself?" Cash asked her.

Merci nodded.

"Most suicides will communicate their intentions—verbally or nonverbally. Has he done that?"

"Yes. Said he wants to just fly away when all this is over. 'This,' being Janine's life."

Merci looked at the doctor, well aware that the suicide rate among cops is roughly three times the national average, that more cops lose their lives to suicide than to homicide.

Merci continued, "He didn't say a word about his wife to me, until a few days ago. Now, he's brought her up three different times. I think he wants to talk."

"Then he's ripe for a QPR intervention, and he wants you to do it."

Cash had presented a Sheriff Department lecture on suicide and QPR—Questioning, Persuading, Referring—just six months earlier, which Merci and forty-eight other deputies had attended. Merci had told herself she had no specific reason for being there other than to bolster her friend's attendance numbers. The upshot of the QPR intervention was you listened, then talked the potential suicide into getting professional help, fast. Cash had cited new studies showing that the hot phase of a suicide crisis was relatively short—three weeks.

"I'm afraid that if I suggest a shrink, he might take his toys and play somewhere else."

"I'm the somewhere else."

Merci considered.

"He thought this experimental treatment was going to save Janine. He told me that. It reminded me of your lecture—the part about predictions."

"Well, yes. Male suicides tend to make dire predictions. You know, something like 'the sun won't rise tomorrow' or 'they'll find me in some field someday.' But this hope about the new treatment . . . I can see where you're going with that."

"Everything seemed to be riding on it."

"And now it's failed."

Merci nodded, looked out the window at the completed fall of darkness. She disliked the winter months, when the light was gone by five and the nights seemed to last forever.

"Your partner may start looking for a place to do it. It's just like a homicide—he'll need means, motive and opportunity. With cops, it's almost always guns. You need to take the next step, Merci. You need to ask him the question. Be blunt about it if you have to: *Are you thinking of killing yourself?*"

"I know," she said quietly.

"Merci, is he absentee any more than you'd expect, given the situation?"

"He's gone a lot. I get the feeling he won't do anything while she's alive."

"You may be right, but you're the Gatekeeper, Merci—the first finder. You're the one who can aim him out of this. We've got great statistics on QPR success. It works. But it takes the first finder to make it work. You're it. Question him. Get him to me. That's my professional recommendation."

On her way to the door, Merci stopped and hugged the doctor again.

"Thank you."

"You've done the right thing here, Merci. I wish the care you took of yourself were as thoughtful and kind as the care you take of your partner."

"But I'm not suicidal, Joan. Come on. I'm fine."

"Being not suicidal and being fine are two very different things. Make an appointment and tell me about how fine you are then, will you? Bring Tim. I'd love to see him again."

"I'm not going to go through with that EMDR, with you or anyone else. I don't trust any initials but SD, P.D. or FBI."

They smiled, laughed.

"Look, girl, we don't have to do Eye Movement Desensitization if you don't want to. But the EMDR results have been fantastically good in situations very similar to yours."

Merci opened the door. "But that's me, Joan—fantastically good in every way."

"I love you, friend. Let me help you if I can. You've certainly helped me."

Chapter Eighteen

Tim was sitting on her father's lap at the dining-room table when Merci walked in. Clark's wedding album was open in front of them, just out of reach of Tim's greedy hands. Tim shrieked when he saw her, struggled to get free.

Merci could see the soft pain on Clark's face as he looked up at her. Merci kissed his cheek, then lifted Tim away. The Man was getting heavy. She glanced down at the album: a black and white shot of Clark and Marcella next to a giant wedding cake. They looked very young and very happy. Every couple of months Clark got the album out, got dreamy and quiet, took a walk or a drive, went to bed early.

"No dinner for me tonight," she said. "I'll be going over to Mike's."

She looked at her watch. The idea of seven o'clock sank through her heart like a boulder through mud.

"You work out your problems last night?"

"Just the usual disagreements, Dad. We're fine."

"He's a good guy."

"I can still disagree with him, can't I?"

He smiled a little, flipped the album page over.

Merci showered while Tim pouted at her from behind the mesh of his playpen. He hated confinement and held her fully responsible, but it was either that or he'd wander off, crack his head on something, swallow a toy, knock over the TV or—Tim's favorite—play with the electrical outlets. He was exceptionally hazardous. And he was talking a lot now—long sentences of nonsense syllables mixed with words, all of which he seemed to think she understood. *Wablum, bob-wop, mom-mom-mom, wob-lalla, mum-mum-mum, goy, goy, goy . . .*

She said them back to him from behind the clear glass shower door, and he seemed to understand them just fine. What exactly was she telling him? Shaving her legs, she hoped it was something helpful.

She loved the way Tim made her feel like she was an infant, too: carefree, opinionless, plugged directly into the moment, only one modifier necessary—*mine, mine, mine.* In Tim's world there was no seven o'clock date with a man you had once loved and were now reluctant even to look at.

In the mirror she saw herself, a tall, naked, big-boned, dark-haired woman chattering away like a mockingbird.

She carried on the conversation while she dried off, put on her makeup, got dressed. She made sure the clip was full, then put the borrowed Colt .45 in her purse, careful to turn her back to keep Tim from seeing it. Anything he saw, he'd try to get into.

Half an hour later she was back in the kitchen with a glass of wine, Tim up in the highchair, Clark fiddling with a soup he'd been making for the last three days.

"Back in '69, Dad, did you think there was something wrong with the Bailey case?" she asked.

Clark exhaled and turned. "I was burg-theft, Merci."

"You were a good investigator. You heard things."

"I never heard anything like that."

Clark had never talked much about his days on duty. He wasn't a raconteur, wasn't nostalgic, didn't think anybody was really interested. She knew for a fact that Clark could make a good story boring.

Merci had adopted some of her father's fundamental beliefs about being a cop years before she thought about becoming one: You did the job, you shut up about it, there was them and us, loose lips sink ships.

But she hadn't gotten her other beliefs about being a cop from Clark at all. She'd never understood where she did get them, certainly not from her rather beautiful, rather insecure, rather treacherous mother. Where she differed from Clark was: You kicked ass to the fullest lawful degree every day of your life, and that's how you kept criminals from taking over the planet. You were part of the balance of power, not just an employee in a bureaucracy. What you did made a difference, a damned large one. You were right and you were good, and you had a privilege to believe it and a responsibility to act it.

"Then what did you hear?"

"I heard Thornton say the body was moved. He talked too much, in my opinion."

"Thornton told me nobody cared about a dead whore. Glandis told me it was because nobody trusted anybody else in the department back then. Everybody worried about whether the next guy was a communist or not."

"That was one rotten year, Merci. But it really wasn't comical, or that simple."

"No. I know."

Merci watched Tim try to get the safety spoon to his mouth with a load of mashed potatoes on it. He stared at it so hard his eyes crossed. He started kicking. The potatoes were already on the bib, the high-chair tray, his face, his hair, his fists. Mouth open, Tim pushed the spoon into his chin, dropped it, pushed it around the tray top before getting it again. Still kicking. She wiped him off with a damp washcloth for the third time in five minutes.

"Were you for Bill Owen, or against?"

Clark turned and looked at her, then came over and sat down. "Against. Owen had been sheriff for twenty-two years. He was old. I thought we needed a man more hands-on. Someone who would clean things up a little, get a shine on the department. See, we had lots of undeveloped, open land back in those days. We were kind of a rural force. But the county was growing and we needed an organizer, someone to bring us up to speed. We didn't have a crime lab. We didn't have a morgue. We didn't have a substation down in south county. Bill, he just liked to sit back and watch things happen."

"What about him being tight with Meeks?"

"Meeks was powerful, dishonest. Development money ran the county government—everybody knew it. I tried to keep that out of my thinking, so far as the department was concerned. I didn't care who the sheriff's friends were."

Merci thought about this. It was pure Clark to remain neutral.

"Were you a Bircher?"

Clark sighed and turned a page in the wedding book. "Real briefly. About a year. But those guys threw too much heat, not enough light."

"Did Owen know you were against him?"

"Probably. But I was just a burg-theft investigator. I hardly ever talked to Bill Owen."

"So who were the guys *really* against Owen then? The deputies who wanted him out?"

Clark held up the book to Merci. He smiled, pointing to the picture of Marcella on a beach in Mexico. It was an Acapulco honeymoon. She looked like a Bond girl—big hair, big boobs, big sunglasses, little bikini.

"I asked you a question, Dad."

"Beck Rainer was the most obvious. He was popular, a good lieutenant, the point man. Ed Vale spoke his piece.

Then, a whole lot of rank-and-file guys—North, Wilberforce—guys like that. Jim O'Brien was a pretty outspoken young deputy then, a gung-ho Bircher. Funny as a rubber crutch. Tough as nails."

"Evan's father?"

"Yeah. Strange. Of all the men I worked with back then, the last one I'd pick as a suicide was Jim O'Brien. You never know who's going to crack."

"Where was Pat McNally on the Bill Owen debate?"

Clark nodded. "Pat was quiet. He wasn't an Owen supporter, but he didn't flaunt it."

"It was sudden when Owen stepped down, wasn't it?"

Clark shut the wedding album and shrugged. "Surprised everyone. I guess he'd just had enough. Merci, can I ask you where you're going with all this? There's no connect between department politics and Patti Bailey that I can see. The case got lost in the shuffle. Lots of them did. Don't swing for the fence every time."

Merci felt her neck go hot. She wiped Tim's face again. He smiled and grabbed for the dish.

"Look, Dad. Someone murdered Patti Bailey, cleaned it up real slick. Thornton takes the case, a good young dick, but he can't come up with anything. It looks to him like the body was moved. Thornton says there was no pressure for an arrest. Not from Owen in sixty-nine, not from Vance Putnam, who replaced him. Not from his partner, Rymers, who ran Homicide Detail and made the assignments. Thornton says nobody cared about a dead whore in sixty-nine. Glandis tells me the same thing. All right. But my question is *why not? Why* didn't anybody care? These men aren't incompetents. They're not animals. So *why don't they care?* Then you say the case got lost in the shuffle. Well, Dad, I appreciate that, but I want to know . . . *what shuffle?* They were busy. We're always busy. They didn't know when the sheriff was going to step down. Well, *we* don't know when Brighton's going to step down, but we don't lose the Aubrey Whittaker case in the goddamned alleged *shuffle.* The next and obvious question is: What if someone profited from her murder? Those are legit questions, if you ask me. Do you think that's swinging for the fence?"

Clark nodded amiably, smiled. "Yeah, I do. But carry it through, Merci. Maybe you're right and I'm wrong. What I'm saying is, solve the crime, not the world."

Her father's gentle tone turned Merci's anger to shame. Her resolve deflated to the flat dread that was Mike McNally and seven o'clock. She looked at her watch. She loved her father without reservation but his evenhandedness and rationality could embalm her passions in a second. In her mother's words: *He puts my heart to sleep sometimes.*

"I got a letter today," she said. "All it said was 'For P. B.'—Patti Bailey, I assume. There was a key in it, apparently to a storage area out in Riverside."

That got his attention. He stared at her evenly, but she could sense the wheels turning inside him. "Oh? That's damned strange."

"I'll say. Someone helping. Someone interfering. Someone being cute. I'll know more tomorrow."

"Then someone has an interest in your solving the case. Or in your not solving it. Be careful, Merci. What looks like help might not be."

"It's one more reason to kick butt, Dad. I'm going to solve the Bailey case if it kills me." Merci heard herself say this, ranking it among the top five stupidest things she'd said in her life.

"I don't mean that."

Her father reached out and put a cool, dry hand on Merci's heated face. "I know you don't. Tim knows you don't, too. Hey, say hi to Mike for me, will you?"

• • •

She got Zamorra at home. His voice was flat and unemotional, like he was reading off a script.

"Those prints I got out of Whittaker's kitchen, they didn't match up with any of the others we lifted. They're not hers. They're not Mike's. But they didn't score hits on AFIS or CAL-ID, not with the parameters I used. So he's not a printed criminal, and he's not law enforcement. Maybe it's Man Friend Number Two, like our neighbor friend heard. Maybe it's Man Friend Number Three—someone we haven't even considered yet. Whoever he is, he tore the drawers out and wrecked the runners the night she died."

Merci tried to reconcile the new prints with what she'd

found in Mike's barn. It was like trying to get two magnets to latch up when you had them turned wrong.

"What if it was earlier?"

"Meaning what?"

"If the prints were left earlier they could be from a tradesman—a guy fixing the drawers, a plumber, a house-cleaner she hired off the books for fifty bucks every other week."

"A guy she hired to yank out the drawers, wreck the runners?"

"No. Okay. No. I'm just trying to simplify, here."

"Merci, they popped real quick with the fingerprint dust. They're fresh. There was a struggle in the kitchen, and it wasn't Aubrey Whittaker."

It just wouldn't track, no matter how she tried to line things up. "What about Moladan?"

"I checked. But how about that little church boy, the one who bought the forty-five for home protection?"

"Lance Spartas."

"I'll shake him down tomorrow. He'll be glad to leave me a good set of prints."

"Shouldn't be hard, he's scared to death of being found out."

A long pause.

"Paul, the reason I called was to see how you're holding up."

"Fine." The same emotionless tone.

"Janine?"

"Ruined from the waist down. Both sides. No chance of it ever coming back."

"Fuck," she said, quietly.

But Zamorra said nothing. What did she expect him to do, make her feel better?

"What can I do for her, Paul?"

"There's not one thing on earth."

"What about you?"

"Shoot me in the head. I'll be fine."

This was her cue. She closed her eyes and jumped: "You thinking of doing that yourself, Paul?"

"I won't leave her. Ever."

"But when she's gone? She'll be gone someday."

"I'll deal with someday when it gets here."

"I want you to talk to a friend of mine. She's a doctor."

"That's funny."

"I'm serious. A good doctor."

Zamorra was silent for a few seconds. "I appreciate it, but no. The answer is a definite no."

"You know, Paul, maybe a few days off would—"

"If I don't get back to work soon, I'm *going* to shoot myself in the head. Look, I'm going to be back there just as soon as I can. Day after tomorrow, Janine's coming home, so I won't be in the next couple. I've got to arrange for in-home nursing, get one of those hospital beds with the motors in them, get her set up with a wheelchair and a portable john. I'll make the time to lean on Spartas, but that's probably it."

Merci tried to imagine what Paul Zamorra was feeling right now but she couldn't do it. At least with Hess it had been fast. It was never a matter of watching him die one inch at a time.

"I'm with you, Paul."

"Thanks. But you don't want to be anywhere near me."

"Don't tell me what I want. There's an end to this, you know. It'll be over someday."

Silence.

"Yeah, I know. I look forward to that day. I feel like scum for saying that, but it's true."

"You don't have years with her, Paul. But you've got days. You've got hours. Those hours are yours."

"I don't want them."

"Someday, you will. Talk to my friend. Just talk. Just once. It's absolutely confidential. She's a terrific person."

"I'm not in the mood for terrific people."

"I'm going to give you her business number now. Take your pen and write it down, Paul."

"Merci—"

"Just take the goddamned number, Paul. Write it down."

She waited a beat, digging the address book from her purse, then read it off to him. She asked him to repeat it and he did, his voice flat and uninflected, like a digitized operator giving you the number.

Chapter Nineteen

Merci drove out Modjeska Canyon through the leafless, quivering oaks, her hand tight on the wheel and her eyes fixed on the stripe that seemed to lap out of infinity at her. Black sky, black earth, black road.

She shivered, notched the heater up a level, took a deep breath. Alone in all this darkness, she felt trapped in a steel box, cut off from The Men, from her partner, from everybody and everything. She pictured a small boat vanishing into a black horizon and she was the only person on it. No, Janine Zamorra was on it, too, sitting in a wheelchair with blankets over her legs.

She told herself she was doing this for Mike. The same hopeless optimism that had let her secretly inspect his home now let her believe that she was giving Mike another chance. She quashed the dissenting voice inside her and she trembled because she knew she could be wrong. She'd been wrong before, profoundly.

It had cost everybody something, Hess his life.

For you, Mike, because I want to trust you. I want to believe in you. I want to know you.

He was wearing his favorite black sweater when he opened the door. When he hugged her she smelled a new scent on him, something clean and alpine. She'd forgotten how strong his arms were.

"You're cold, Merci."

Her fingertips were numb. Mike guided her inside and had her sit by the fire.

"It's good to see you," she said.

It wasn't untrue. She was afraid at what he might have done. But she wasn't afraid of *him.* No matter what he'd done, part of him would be a man who had treated her well, probably better than she deserved.

"*God,* it's good to see you. Red or white?"

"Red."

"Take your coat?"

"Not now."

The room was cold so she stayed by the fire, still wrapped in the coat. A minute later Mike came back with the wine. Lit by the orange flames in the firebox, Mike's face seemed to glow. She could see from the downiness of his hair that he'd just washed and dried it. After a shave Mike's cheeks flushed, and they were flushed now. Merci suddenly felt light-headed, like she was tipping over backward, slowly, but didn't have legs to stop herself. Just like Janine Zamorra didn't.

He touched her glass with his.

Upright again. "Mike, you said a lot of this was my fault. I think it was, too."

"Merci—"

"*No.* Let me finish. I'm going to tell you what I see. It's necessary. You need to see it, too."

He looked at her, said nothing.

"You know, you ran into a pretty tough girl when you met me. I look normal from the outside, but inside, I'm just . . . very hard sometimes. On me. And on the people I'm trying to love."

Mike had sat down on the same couch, but with plenty of distance between them, just the way she liked it.

"I've been in a haze since Hess died. You know that. I can work okay. I can raise my boy okay. But I can't get out of it. It's like this fog that just won't lift. And for the last two years plus, Mike, every time I look at you I say, now there's a good guy, nice looking and kind, and look how much he loves you. But I haven't loved you back. Not with all of me, or even a big part of me. I just haven't been present."

He spoke quietly. "I know that. I knew it was part of the deal."

What she wanted to say was, explain the silencer in your tackle box. And the letters in your pistol case, and the boots in your closet. And the missing friendship card and your presence in the crime lab. But if they were evidence of what she thought they were, Mike would destroy them and she would be guilty of not only treachery but unforgivable foolishness.

"I can't wash myself, Mike. I can't get clean. I can't start over."

He nodded, moved a little closer. "But you can't blame yourself forever, Merci. That's all I've ever tried to tell you. You got to put it all in a box and throw the box away."

A tackle box? she wondered. And where would Hess go? Hess. He was right in the middle of all of it. She couldn't throw him out, like an old pair of shoes, or a noisy tenant. It angered her that Hess was more a part of her sadness than of her joy, but she had not designed the circuitry of her own heart. She did not understand it, and she could not repair or replace it.

"I know that, but I can't shut up my own conscience. The voice is too strong. I might not hear it for a few days, then it comes roaring out at me. Right in the middle of breakfast. Or driving down the road. Or in a dream. Or when I look at you and tell myself I should love you."

She willed herself to see him as blameless. He sat there, scrubbed and decent, young and strong, forelock down and eyes alive, dressed and scented up for her, earnestly trying to win her heart the best way he knew. For what, the hundredth time?

Merci realized that this might be the last time she'd be able to see him like this. She felt a sweet movement in her heart right then, a movement that made her fingers warm and her eyes moist.

Then it was gone. Letters. Boots. Tackle box.

"I'll sell the ring, if it's too much pressure," he said.

"I need to use the head."

She gathered up her purse and went into Mike's bedroom, where the full bath was. In the mirror she looked yellow. She could feel her heart hitting her ribs. She bent over the toilet and vomited. Then she ran some hot water and washed her hands. She got her toothbrush from the drawer and loaded on the paste.

Back in the bedroom she listened, heard nothing. She looked at his bed, made up neatly now, pillows fluffed, bedspread taut. She imagined herself in there with him, locked up and sweating, chasing down that elusive release that came far less often than she wished. Muscles quivering, breath hot and fast. For just a minute or two, you were really free, gone, new.

What a perfect time to torture yourself with that image, she thought. She understood by now that the conscience is eager to betray.

Then she moved quietly back to the bathroom, where Mike often hung his shoulder rig on the robe hook. She pushed the door in and followed. Coughing to mask the sound, she carefully popped the holster snap and slid out his Colt .45, then slipped it into her coat. She pulled the range gun from her purse, put it in the rig. Left the snap off. Then she hung her coat.

She flushed the toilet again, washed her hands again.

Mike was standing by the fire.

"You okay?" he asked.

"I feel sick."

"I'll make some herbal tea."

"I hate herbal tea."

"It settles the stomach."

"Just some water."

Mike hopped to, brought her a glass with ice and a lemon slice on top.

"There's a bug going around the department," he said.

"Maybe that's what I've got."

• • •

Dinner lasted for several thousand years. Merci guided the talk toward Tim, Jr., and Danny. Mike almost always followed her conversational lead and rarely took it himself. He listened to her with an intensity that she originally had thought was a tool for getting her into bed. He could chatter like a jaybird about sports or hunting with his friends but Merci cared about neither. Tonight he was quiet, attentive, aglow in the candlelight. He looked good in the black sweater. She pictured him pushing his silenced Colt into Aubrey Whittaker's chest and pulling the trigger. She could picture his body okay, but his face was just fog.

She believed, but she did not believe.

She helped him clear and rinse the dishes. Mike slid the dish towel over the oven handle.

"Please come to bed with me now," he said.

"Okay."

• • •

It was over fast so they started in again. Merci surrendered to the wrongness of it all, she clutched it like a boozer his bottle, a suicide his gun. Beyond the wrongness she found something that had to be love because nothing else could possibly exist there. Love of what they once had. Love of Mike, the boy and the man. Love of love. Her climaxes were powerful implosions that seemed less of muscle and nerve than of bone. During them she was vertiginous and free and she wished they could go on for hours, leaving her exhausted and purged and molecularly rearranged into a completely different person—a good-natured blonde, perhaps, or a fundamentalist, a savant, a pilot. Her jugular throbbed and her ears roared.

When it was over they lay in the darkness breathing hard. She had done what she wanted to do. For just a few minutes she had loved and believed in him. She had given him everything she had, even the benefit of her doubt. She had testified to the innocence she had helped him lose. Offered proof of a trust she wanted so badly to feel.

And now, while Mike dozed beside her, she came back to herself with an awesome regret.

She looked up at the ceiling, knowing that whatever had been between them was over now. She would never look at him the same way, for better or for worse. There was betrayal and maybe murder. There was before Aubrey, and after. One thing had just ended; another was just beginning; and there was a fat black line dividing the two.

She got up, collected the condoms she had brought, went to the bathroom and dosed herself with the aerosol spermicide from her purse. Then she showered and dressed.

"Stay tonight," he whispered in the dark.

"No."

"I love you, Merci Rayborn."

She brushed away his hair and kissed his forehead. "I'll see you tomorrow."

Five miles down Modjeska Canyon Merci pulled onto a wide shoulder and parked the Impala. The moon was high and cast a silver light on the hillsides.

She took the .45 from her purse and aimed at the man in that moon, trying to keep him atop the sights. She couldn't hold it still.

Then it jumped in her hands and the noise hit her ears with a sharp crack. She collected the brass with a flashlight and a tissue. Then she emptied the clip and reloaded it. First she put in three shells from the new box she'd bought at the range. The top four cartridges were Mike's. She wiped down the gun with a rag from the trunk.

Five minutes later she let herself back into Mike's house. Nothing looked different. Even with the bloodhounds howling, Mike was a world-class sleeper once he was down.

She walked down the hallway to the bedroom and peeked in. He was over on his side now, facing the wall, curled up like a child, which was how he liked to do those deep first hours. She stepped in and closed the door half way. The room went deeper into shadow. No movement from Mike.

"Back forever?" he whispered, words slurring.

"You warmed me up so much I forgot my coat," she said. She went to the bathroom, left the lights off. She got the coat off the robe hook and put it on. Then she eased the range gun from the holster and slid it into her pocket.

"That was really nice, Merci."

"It was."

She replaced Mike's Colt. No snap.

She went over and touched Mike's cheek. Her hands were shaking again and she wanted to ask him to forgive her but she would not have forgiven him for this, and she knew it.

He was breathing heavy and deep, his hands balled into fists up near his chin. It reminded her of Tim. The sleep of a child, the sleep of the innocent.

• • •

She woke Gilliam up at home, 12:27 A.M., and told him what she needed.

"No case number, no NIBIN, no DrugFire, no IBIS, no

Brasscatcher. Nobody sees it, nobody touches it, nobody knows about it but you. Not Coiner, not O'Brien, nobody. *You and you only.*"

He understood completely. He asked no questions. He'd have what she needed by the start of the workday.

He gave her directions to his house and Merci wrote them down in her blue notebook, using the swing-out lamp above the radio for light, guiding the big car down Modjeska Canyon with her left hand at twelve o'clock, just like her father used to do.

She tried to concentrate on the road, but she had trouble thinking. Trouble knowing what to feel. Trouble believing that today was Tuesday, barely a week since she'd seen Aubrey Whittaker for the first time. Last Wednesday morning she'd argued with Mike about a movie date she wanted to break. And now, a few short days later, she was gathering evidence to determine whether or not Mike McNally was a killer. Her hand was locked on the wheel and her jaw clamped tight and her eyes weren't seeing well.

Too much, she thought. Too fast, too strange, too bad.

• • •

At home she checked on Tim, tucked the blankets up a little tighter, made sure his mittens were still on. He didn't budge. She turned up the heater.

Clark's door was closed. Dreaming of Marcella, thought Merci, of all they'd had and all they'd said good-bye to. Sometimes it crushed her to think that she, Merci, was the best of what her father had left. Or maybe Tim was. She wished he'd find someone new to love again, but he didn't socialize much except for the poker games on Wednesdays. She wondered if he considered himself alone.

She poured a huge Scotch, thought of Hess as she always did when she poured a huge Scotch, and took another shower. She lathered and rinsed her hair, then did it again. She scrubbed once with shower gel, once with soap. She stood under the hot powerful water and wished everything that felt unclean inside her could just run off and go down the drain like all the unclean things outside her. When she got out her eyes were red and she looked like hell.

She put her little .32 in her robe pocket and went back out to the living room. For a while she sat in her father's recliner, a butt-sprung old chair that was comfortable and worn. The old house creaked and her heart jumped. She hated her fear. She wondered if a modern, creakless home would be better for her, but that meant neighbors you'd have to see, no orange groves for protection, nothing between them and us.

I'll sell the ring, if it's too much pressure.

She sipped down some Scotch and wondered if life was sad like this for everybody. She hated her sadness like she hated her fear but she couldn't figure a way around it. The trouble was, everywhere she aimed an optimistic thought it ricocheted and came back at her head: She thought of a man she had loved and he was gone; she thought of her own mother and she was gone; she thought of Clark and he was alone; she thought of Mike and he was hiding silencers in his barn and good Jesus in heaven, even if he *hadn't* shot Aubrey Whittaker, what in hell was going on in that brain of his? Paul. Janine. It seemed like the only point of light in the whole miserable universe was Tim, Jr., so radiantly and perfectly happy. But what about five years from now? she thought. What's he going to be then, one of those kids who brings a gun to school and shoots everybody? How much time does he have before life wrecks him? What an awful thing to think. She hated herself for thinking it, for poisoning even her son's unlived future with her own fear and sadness. She wished she could crawl out of her skin. Become new. Become improved. Trade all the fear and sadness and become quiet, content, efficient and occasionally chipper. How long since she'd actually smiled without irony? How long since she'd laughed without bitterness? It felt like a million years. Was this too much to ask? And yet, if she had a choice she wouldn't choose this. It wasn't her nature to feel this way. She hadn't had a single miserable day in her whole life until what happened to Hess. Since then, that's all she'd had. Like something in the air, like something you couldn't get off you.

She considered Joan Cash's Eye Movement Desensitization and Reprocessing procedure, much promoted by the FBI in its Critical Incident Stress Management Program. But all she could think of with regard to EMDR was the opening scene of that horrible college movie where the razor slices the eyeball. It made her queasy.

So she told herself she was just feeling sorry for herself, that she only felt this way because she *chose* to feel this way. She reminded herself that she was captain of her own ship. That she was responsible for her own feelings. That the world you saw was the world you wanted to see. And all that other *crap* everyone was always trying to tell you. She wondered if she should give herself over to Jesus, but she couldn't respect a God that loved her unconditionally. It made her suspicious of Him. Those were some of the same reasons she couldn't marry Mike, so was she equating God with Mike now? What did *that* say about her? Fuck, it was just a goddamned mess.

She drank down most of the Scotch, hoping it would dull her sadness. Thirty seconds later, it did. Made her dizzy, too, in a good way. She could see why people lived on the stuff.

She dumped the rest down the drain and went in to check Tim again. There he was, perfection in a crib, the whole potential of the race contained in one individual thirty pound unit.

All she could do was shake her head and smile.

• • •

Later that morning—Merci had no idea what time—she dreamed that she was asleep in her bed, dreaming.

She heard something beside the bed. She woke and

reached under the bed frame for her H&K. When her hand found the butt of the gun, it froze. Hess stood across the room looking at her, his hands folded before him like he was standing in a reception line.

It's okay, he said, then he turned his back to her and vanished.

She jumped out of the bed before she even knew she was jumping. She landed hard on the floor. She looked at the wall through which Hess had traveled but it was simply the wall. Sweat ran down into her eyes and she could feel that she was soaked in it, her gown damp, palms slick, her hairline cooling.

She heard her father's footsteps on the hardwood hall, felt the air in the room change when the door flew open, and the next thing she knew she was stunned by light and he was lifting her off the floor and back into the bed.

"Bad dream," he said. His voice was soft, like he'd been dreaming, too, like he was talking down a five-year-old. "Just a bad dream, honey."

"Yeah. Hess."

"Hess. That's okay. He's fine, you know. Now you settle in. Settle in, girl. Just a bad dream."

"Good dream."

"That's right. That's it. There you are. A good dream.

Chapter Twenty

The address in the "For P. B." letter turned out to be Inland Storage in Riverside. Merci stopped at the gate and punched in the entry code. The old guy in the office gave her a long hard stare so she gave him one back. She drove around, following the numbers to 355. It was a maze. The doors were faded orange, some of the padlocks brown with rust. The early morning sun hung over the roofline, shot into her face like a spotlight.

She parked across from the unit, looked at the letter again. *For P. B.* It surprised her to think she was not the only person who gave a damn about Patti Bailey. She took her kit from the trunk and got back behind the wheel. She worked on a pair of fresh latex gloves, then brushed the key with black fingerprint dust. She found exactly what she expected to find, nothing.

She pulled the key off the letter, examined the dopple of glue and the little platform of paper stuck to it. Back in the crime lab she could fume the letter, envelope and stamp with cyanoacrylate, but something told her she'd be wasting her time. It was a newly cut key, a generic blank, no ID from a cutter or shop.

It slid easily into the padlock and the bolt jumped open. Merci worked it from the latch, then slid the catch into place. The big aluminum door shuddered as she pulled up on the handle, hooked her boot under the bottom and gave it a heave. Dust and rust showered down when the door slammed up. The sun shot in and held the cobwebs with light. Merci watched the motes swirl, sneezed twice.

Half a dozen pasteboard boxes. A bike with flat, white-wall tires. A yellow couch along the far wall. A stack of newspapers. A 70s era quad stereo with eight-track tape player, all four speakers. Bootleg tapes stacked on top, labels faded and peeling: Jefferson Airplane, Fifth Dimension, The Doors. Two metal file cabinets, a credenza. A Regulator clock hung on the left wall, two lamp stands without shades. A mattress and box spring leaned against the right wall, wrapped in plastic that had long since cracked and peeled. Two chests of drawers. A refrigerator that looked thirty years old. That was about it. Lots of space, not much stuff.

She sneezed again, then again, then stepped back into the sunlight for some fresh air. When she squinted back into the unit from a distance it looked like a diorama of a college student's room, or a bachelor's apartment from three decades ago. All it needed was lava lamps and one of those astrological sex position calendars that she had first seen, and been frankly mystified by, at a head shop when she was twelve.

For P. B.?

Says who?

Merci went back in, waving the air in front of her face. She noted the dusty-sweet smell of paperbacks and old boxes. There was mouse crap on the floor, and a mousetrap with part of a small gray skeleton in it. No cheese. She tapped the sofa with her hand and watched the dust puff up. She took a newspaper off the top of the stack and checked the date: February 11, 1970.

The file cabinets were empty. So were the credenza and dressers. When she opened the refrigerator the top half of the thick old gasket peeled away and hung in front of her. The freezer was an EAZY DE-frost, and Merci was surprised that even thirty years ago manufacturers misspelled names to get the attention of buyers.

The bike was a Schwinn. The mattress was from Sears. The quad system—her girlfriend Melanie had owned one—was by Pioneer.

The first box she looked in was filled with dishes. She lugged it off the stack and set it aside. The next had a few paperbacks, some loose pens and pencils, an old desk lamp with the cord wrapped around the base. There was an orange peace sign glued to the shade. The third box contained winter gear—gloves and mittens, fur-lined ladies' snow boots, a couple of plastic raincoats that remained tightly folded when she picked them up. Mice had made a nest in one of the boots. Shreds of newspaper and bits of cardboard fell to the ground when she turned it over and shook it.

The box at the bottom of the first stack was filled with hardcover books: *I Was Castro's Prisoner; Five Days to Oblivion; East Minus West Equals Zero; Witness; The Blue Book.* She opened the last one, a spiral-bound volume, and scanned the title page. It was the John Birch Society handbook, written by Robert Welch. Merci thought she remembered some of the titles from the bookshelf in her girlhood home. Clark and Marcella had had hundreds of books, but these seemed familiar. The mice had gnawed the cover of *Tail of the Paper Tiger.*

Another box: pots and pans. Another: typing paper and old Smith-Corona ribbons, carbon paper, envelopes yellowed with age, a heavy crank pencil sharpener, some rulers and a circular slide rule, and a stack of leaflets held together with a thick rubber band that crumbled away when she picked them up. The pamphlets had red and white covers: *Communism, Hypnotism and the Beatles*. She looked through one. The author seemed to be saying that the primitive jungle rhythms used in some Beatles songs could induce a hypnotic state in listeners, and that communist messages could be easily absorbed when someone was in such a state. There were other stacks: *Fluoride and Moscow; Disarmament and Surrender; The Obligations of the Informed American.*

The box on the bottom was the only one sealed with

tape. Merci noted that it was relatively new tape—it didn't crack or peel when she tried to get it off. She used her penknife, then folded open the flaps. On top was a thick stack of yellowed newspapers from late 1969. The black-and-white photography and the print and layout style made them look even older than they were.

Under the papers was a manila folder, and in the folder was an inexpensive date book for 1969 and an audiocassette. The cassette wasn't labeled. It was inside a locking plastic bag that Merci was almost certain was not made in 1969. The date book was jammed with names and numbers, shorthand, nicknames, code names, more numbers.

It reminded her of Aubrey Whittaker's. Merci looked through the first few pages, hoping to find the owner's name and address. None.

Under the folder was a black plastic garbage bag containing something light. Merci lifted it out and set it on the floor. She untied the loose knot—no cracking of the plastic—and looked in. A garment. Using both hands she carefully removed it and set it atop the bag. It was a blue satin dress, small, blasted with blood. There were two rips in the middle front, two more in the middle back. Still in the garbage bag were two shoes, which Merci pulled out one at a time: blue velveteen heels, high and petite. More blood, ancient and almost black.

Patti Bailey, she thought. Black book, cassette tape, and the last clothes she wore in her life.

The box held one more black plastic bag. Inside was a

smaller one, one of the locking freezer bags of the type that Merci herself occasionally used to freeze extra food. Sealed up in the freezer bag she found a Reuger .38 Special with a two-inch barrel and two loose casings. The blue steel was lightly rusted.

The evidence, she thought, the evidence that Thornton never found. More specifically, perhaps, the evidence that Thornton *should have found.*

The rest of the box contained another thick stack of old newspapers. Taped to these was a sheet of white paper. Big, marking-pen lettering, like the childish writing on the letter that had led her to this storage container, read:

MERCI—THOUGHT YOU MIGHT WANT TO
GET UP TO SPEED ON YOUR UNSOLVED.

She stepped back out to the dazzling sunlight. The breeze coming off the desert was cold. She got her crime-scene kit from the trunk, filled out a Field Evidence Sheet, photographed what she had found, sketched the scene in her own rudimentary manner, then packaged it back up and loaded it into the Impala. She figured the note and the key would have to be good enough to establish a permitted search. If a judge ruled against her, she'd lose the evidence as admissible. But if she didn't take it now, she was running the risk of losing it altogether. It had been hidden for thirty-two years and it could get hidden for thirty-two more. She tagged it all with the Patti Bailey case number from 1969: H38-069.

• • •

The manager of Inland Storage was Carl Zulch. His hair was white and cropped short, his skin was pale. His eyes were dark brown, rimmed with a thin circle of blue. She guessed him to be in his mid-seventies.

She badged him and Zulch insisted on writing down her ID number. She told him she needed to know who paid the rent on 355 and Zulch told her that was impossible—he'd need a court order.

"I've got better," she said. "Permission to search."

"Prove it."

She gave him a very hard stare, which Zulch returned. She went to the car, got the letter, put the key back in the envelope and set it on the counter.

Zulch read it. "Who's P. B.?"

"A woman who was murdered in 1969."

"Here?"

"No. Orange County. Who pays the rent here, Mr. Zulch?"

"Still impossible to say for sure," he said. "Because this is all I get for that unit. I get it every month. Every month for the last five years."

He shuffled through a drawer, came out with a stack of envelopes and pulled away the rubber band. It took him a while to find what he was looking for. He handed it across the counter to her.

The envelope was addressed in typewritten print, no return address, a no-lick stamp. Inside Merci found a twenty, a ten and two ones.

"Thirty-two a month," said Zulch. "Never late. Never a check. Never a note. It isn't the only space rented out like that. People have secrets. I keep them."

"Who do you call if it burns down? Who do you write to when the rent goes up?"

"We don't raise the rents once you're in."

"Don't tell me it's fire and earthquake proof, too."

Zulch had already raised a pale finger in anticipation. He used it to ply an old Rolodex, then he pinched out a card and set in on the counter.

The card was dated at the top. It said Bob Cartwright, followed by an address, phone number and signature.

"He opened the account five years ago, like it says."

"Is it used often?"

"No. I make the rounds in my golf cart sometimes, see if everything's all right. Never seen the renter."

"I'm taking the envelope and the money. I'll get you thirty-two bucks to cover it."

• • •

Merci hadn't even coded her way out of the complex when she placed a call to the renter of 355 on her cell phone. A woman answered. She'd never heard of Bob Cartwright.

She'd gotten this telephone number from Pac Bell when she bought the house eight years ago. She told Merci she never made purchases over the phone and to take her off the list if this was a telemarketing outfit.

Merci said she would.

Next she called headquarters and had one of the desk sergeants check the cross-referenced directory. The address used by Bob Cartwright didn't exist.

She had just hit the "end" button when the phone rang. The reception was bad but she recognized James Gilliam's even, unhurried voice.

"The casing from Whittaker's and the casing you gave me were fired by the same gun."

"How sure are you?"

"As sure as I can get. The extraction marks were identical, the firing marks identical. Perfect match, every land and groove lined up. Textbook."

"Could you say that in court?"

"Depends how you got the second case."

"You know that's not what I mean."

"I can't get a better match than those two cases. Same gun. No doubt whatsoever. No real room for dispute, no matter what firearms expert they brought in. It's a lock. I'm going to ask you one question now. Did that casing come from where I think it did?"

"Yeah."

"This could get bad."

"It's already bad. I'm not sure what to do."

"You have to talk to Brighton."

"Shit. Then what? What am I going to do?"

"Whatever he tells you to."

Merci listened to the static. She couldn't think it through right now. Her heart was pounding too hard and her brain felt foggy.

"Remember, Merci, the casings don't prove he killed her. We can only assume the found shell held the bullet that killed her. But we can't prove it without the bullet and the bullet's in the ocean. If there was corroborating evidence, then the casing is more damaging. Very damaging. Say, if those prints in the kitchen were made by shoes like his. Or say, some of the fibers matched up to clothes that were his. Things like that are what add up to a conviction. You know that. It's all complicated by the fact that he was there for dinner."

Merci couldn't talk. It was the first time in her life she found herself unable to speak. Finally, the words rushed out.

"What if he didn't do it? What if there's an explanation I'm not seeing?"

"Then there's still the question of how brass fired by his gun got into Aubrey Whittaker's apartment. He didn't leave it in the vase as a hostess gift."

"That isn't funny."

"I'm not trying to be."

"He's one of us, James. One of *us*."

There was a silence before Gilliam spoke again. "Whoever killed Aubrey Whittaker is definitely not one of us. Maybe he used to be. Whoever killed her should be arrested and charged."

Merci knew this but she hadn't really imagined it happening until now. Sergeant Michael McNally, arrested for the murder of Aubrey Whittaker. It sounded like a headline from some bogus souvenir newspaper.

"James, I'm bringing in evidence in the Patti Bailey murder."

"That would be thirty-two years old."

"I've got a gun and a letter envelope I want to Super Glue the living daylights out of. There's a dress, too. Four bullet holes in it and blood all over."

"The DNA possibilities should be interesting. We'll do what we can."

"I feel like things are getting worse by the second."

"I can offer proof of that. Zamorra busted in here yesterday with some fingerprint cards he'd taken himself. Wouldn't let anybody see them. Ran them against the prints your people collected in the apartment. Today, he tried to pull the same stunt so I kicked him out. I've documented it. I may have a talk with Brighton myself. If nothing else he's broken the protocol for chain of evidence. This isn't a serve-yourself forensics lab, for Zamorra or you-know-who or anybody else."

Merci caught the subtle emphasis on "your people," and the not-so-subtle suggestion that she should keep her partner from running amok in Gilliam's temple of science.

“He thought they botched the kitchen.”

“Then they should have been asked to go back and unbotch it.”

What was she supposed to do now, offer apologies for her partner?

“James, the walls are closing in.”

“They are. And it’s going to affect the whole department. For a long time. Be careful what you do, Merci. I ran the comparison myself, so nobody here knows anything about it. Nothing.”

Chapter Twenty-one

She met Colin Byrne in the UCI Library. He was wearing a shiny suit with a thin necktie, a fedora of gray felt. He looked even more slender and more preposterous than before. "It's my Marlowe garb," he said.

"No bullet holes in the tie."

"That was a little much."

He'd put together a thick notebook for her, everything and anything relating to bad cops in Orange County, 1965–1975. The clips were arranged chronologically, but he had cross-referenced them and had created a handy index of names and events in the back.

"A lot of that came from the smaller papers, some from law-enforcement publications. There was quite a bit of overlap between the cops and the Birch Society," he said. "So I went into archives, got the *American Opinion* newsletters and assembled this for you."

He handed her a binder, thick with the monthly Birch

Society newsletters. Behind those were a fat collection of *JBS Chapter 231* newsletters, which appeared to be hand-typed.

"There was lots on Jesse Acuna, and the De Anza Hotel, but I knew you had some of that stuff. I went light on it. There are some interesting names in there."

Merci collected the binders. "I really appreciate this, Mr. Byrne."

"You're very welcome."

• • •

She watched O'Brien set up the fuming chamber—a ten-gallon aquarium. It was brand-new. He wiped it out thoroughly with glass cleaner and paper towels, then set two shallow dessert dishes of water in two corners. He suspended the rusty .38 Special and the brass casings from wires connected to a plastic lid. He propped the storage payment envelope upright on the bottom, with two sides leaning against the glass. He reached in and squeezed the glue drops onto the bottom, distributing them evenly around the container for even evaporation. He counted each one out loud.

"Thirty-five drops," he said. "You can go forty, but I don't want to overdevelop anything. I can add later if I have to."

He sealed the top with tinfoil, pressing it along the sides of the tank. Then he put on another layer and secured it with masking tape.

"We'll cook it and watch it. The cyanoacrylate esters will polymerize when they hit the moisture and amino acids in the print residue. With older prints, the residue is going to be dry, so I don't want to accelerate it with heat. I put in two humidity sources instead of the usual one. My guess is eight hours. We might get something in less. We probably won't get anything at all—the body salts in fingerprints have rusted out the finish by now, ruined the prints. I've never fumed a piece of evidence that's this old."

O'Brien pointed at the case number on Merci's evidence sheet. "Never thought I'd work a case with sixty-nine on it. I was *born* in seventy."

"Sixty-five for me," she mumbled. The cyanoacrylate fumes had already made the tank glass pale.

"What's with the brass Gilliam was working on this morning? From across the room, it looked like a forty-five."

She stared hard at O'Brien, then ran her finger across her throat.

He retracted his head into his shoulders a little, a turtle with no shell. "I shall remain in ignorance. And happily so, for you, my lady, my queen, my god."

"Perfect. I'll be back."

• • •

Three o'clock sharp. Merci circled headquarters in her white Chevy, saw nobody at the corner of Flower and Civic Center, so she made the loop again. She could see the odd white of the sky far off in the north—a new storm, loaded with rain, supposed to hit by morning.

The second time around she saw him and pulled over. Wrapped in an overcoat against the chilly afternoon, Chuck Brighton bent his tall frame into her passenger's seat and shut his door. It took him a long time to get in.

"The last time I did this, some guy from the tax collector's office wanted to tell me the county had just gone bankrupt."

"What did you say to that?"

"I asked him why in hell he didn't tell me before it happened. Said he saw it coming but couldn't be sure. Not a believer in the proactive stance."

"My news isn't much better."

"I suspected that. Get away from here," he said. "I know half the people on these sidewalks. The other half I've thrown in jail."

She got out to Fourth Street, made a left. She passed the *carniceria,* the *zapateria,* the pawn shops and the bail bondsmen, the shop with wedding dresses racked out front, the Mexican music store. There were Christmas lights and tinsel in the windows, nativities and Santas with sleighs, *Feliz Navidad* and Merry Christmas painted on the glass in bright colors. She watched the street numbers.

Two blocks down the buildings were bigger, set back from the street, fronted by lawns or small parking lots.

"That's the old De Anza," she said. It was a big red-brick building with neat white awnings and trim. A wooden sign out front announced: GRECO, GRAFF AND REYES—ATTORNEYS AT LAW.

"First whores, then lawyers. You wonder what's next."

"You ever go there, back in the bad old days?"

Brighton smiled and shook his head. "All I did was work. My idea of fun was to drive the family up to Bridgeport, camp out and do some fishing. They made me sheriff at forty-two. That's too young. I didn't know how to do it, so I did twice as much as I had to."

"The Bailey case led me there. Her sister said Patti knew who beat up the farmer. The farmer said it was cops. The papers said cops were hanging out with girls at the De Anza. I figured if I could put Bailey there I might get a lead."

"Have you?"

"Not from the De Anza. But a concerned citizen sent me the key to a storage area in Riverside."

She explained what she'd found, and how she'd found it.

"I think it's the gun used to kill Bailey. It's being fumed right now in the lab."

Brighton grunted. "Gilliam told me. I can't figure who'd lead you out there. Send you the key. Somebody involved in her killing? Somebody covering somebody? What's in it for anybody, thirty-two years after the fact?"

"What's in it for me is a dead woman and the truth."

"Apparently you're not alone. Gilliam says the chances of lifting prints that old are small."

"It's worth a try."

"Absolutely."

Brighton watched the city going past the windows of Merci's Impala.

"So, why did you drag me out here?" he asked finally. "I don't think we drove out here to talk about a rusted gun, or Patti Bailey."

She spilled it all: the brass at Whittaker's, the missing friendship card and Mike's meddlesome presence in the lab, the letters and suggestions of blackmail, the chukka boots and sweater, the silencer, the switch at Mike's—no details about that—the three shots she took at the man in the moon, Gilliam's match on the casings.

She knew it was all just a storm of circumstance right now, except for the casings. The match pointed at Mike and only Mike.

"Sir . . . I'm just not sure what to do."

Brighton was staring at her. She kept her eyes on the road and waited. She waited a long time.

"Let me talk to Clay," he said quietly. "Right now, don't do anything. Don't say anything, either."

The name Clayton Brenkus made her heart sink. The old man ran the district attorney's office with a sharp tongue and an iron fist. His assistant prosecutors revered or hated him; his conviction rate was high. The old joke about him getting reelected term after term was that people were afraid to vote against him. The idea of setting him loose on

Mike somehow surprised her. She hadn't thought it through that far.

"I keep trying to figure what I'm not seeing," she said. "I keep looking for the out. For Mike. For all of us."

"That's Clay's business. He's been our DA for twenty years because he knows which cases he can win and which ones are losers."

"What did I miss, boss? What's right in front of me that I'm not seeing?"

"I don't know, Merci. Maybe you just did your job and caught a killer."

She made a U-turn and headed back up Fourth Street, past the De Anza again.

Brighton looked out at the building. "I don't remember Bailey being part of that place."

"The word is, she lived there but didn't work there."

"Maybe the whore-cop-farmer scenario is too neat," he said. "You take one side of it out and the triangle collapses."

"What's the side that won't hold?"

"Well, I never heard of Bailey linked to law enforcement. And what if Acuna had it wrong to begin with? He got threatened by guys who reminded him of policemen. He got beaten up by guys in masks. So that makes them cops? That's two weak sides, if you ask me. Thornton didn't get anywhere with Bailey and cops."

"But the cop rumor was a year after Bailey. The case was cold by then."

"Do you want to argue details or do you want to solve the crime?"

"Solve the crime."

"Then consider the possibility that you're wasting your time. Consider the possibility Patti Bailey didn't know squat about Jesse Acuna."

"I will consider. And I apologize, sir. I'm still arguing about those things with myself."

Brighton studied her, then went silent for a long while. She turned onto Flower, heading in.

"Who have you talked to about the Bailey case, except for Thornton?"

"Her sister. Glandis. My dad, a little."

"Did Mel ask if you thought he'd make a good sheriff?"

"Yes."

"And did he ask you if I was too old and worn out to be effective anymore?"

"No." Not in those words, she thought.

Brighton smiled. Nothing happy in it, she saw, like it was mostly to himself.

Overload, thought Merci: He's heard too much to process in ten minutes. Too much bad news, such as learning that one of his best investigators is staring down the barrel of Penal Code 187 for shooting a prostitute who was blackmailing him.

"You talk to Mike's dad about this?"

"Which? Mike or Bailey?"

"Either one."

"No," she said, realizing that if she wanted to pick Big Pat's memories of the Bailey murder, she'd better do it soon.

The sheriff stared out the window, hunched in the overcoat, and for the first time in her career Merci saw Brighton as old. She could feel his weakness and this made her feel both sorrow and excitement.

She looked out to the darkening northern sky and wondered what this said about her. She thought about nomadic male lions who fight their way into a pride and promptly eat the cubs and mate the females to establish their own bloodline.

"Aubrey Whittaker's father called my office this morning," said Brighton. His voice was flat and disembodied. "Saw her picture on the news. Her real name was Gail White, grew up in Bakersfield, ran away from home when she was sixteen. Hadn't talked to her for three years."

"How was he?"

"Concerned about her bank accounts."

"One of those." It had always amazed and angered her how many relatives of murder victims were mostly interested in the victim's estate.

"He's going to claim the body, make the arrangements. I've got his number for you, for whatever it's worth."

She looked out at the courthouse building, saw the lawyers heading in and out. A bail bondsman she knew hustled down the sidewalk, cupping a smoke in one hand, the other hand jammed in his coat pocket.

"I hope there's some kind of legitimate explanation for this," Brighton said. "For Mike. For you. For my department. For my own sorry hide. Stop. I'll walk it from here."

• • •

She pulled over beside the old courthouse and called Big Pat McNally. He wasn't home, but she didn't think he would be. More likely, by this time of day he'd be at Cancun Restaurant, down on First Street.

Like Clark, he was retired; unlike Clark, Pat McNally liked to get out and raise a little hell.

It was still early enough to park close to the restaurant. She guided in the Chevy, looked for Pat McNally's black Cadillac. It was taking up two spots out in the corner of the lot.

Pat himself was taking up a stool by the margarita blender, chatting up a pretty young thing who looked at Merci approaching and scuttled away like she'd been slapped.

"Didn't mean to ruin your moment," she said.

Big Pat lumbered off the stool and hugged her. His arms were huge and freckled and his neck seemed thick as a power pole. His hair was graying red, and he had the most gentle blue eyes Merci had ever seen. Crooked smile, quick laugh, good guy.

"You rescued me from temptation. It's the only thing I can't resist."

She sat down next to him, got coffee. She wondered if

she'd ever do such a thing again, the way things were stacking up against his son. She stared straight ahead.

He put his hand on her forearm, gave it a squeeze. "How you doin', Merci? Everything okay?"

She nodded and looked at him but she let her eyes betray her.

"What is it? That son of mine?"

"No. Mike's great." She tried to make it convincing. It occurred to her for the first time that she might ruin Big Pat along with his son. It seemed like every hour she had to recalculate the size of her betrayal.

His clear blue eyes roved over her face. He took a drink of his beer. "Lemme guess. He's asked you for the twentieth time to marry him, and you wish he'd stop."

"No, Pat. Really, it's not Mike."

"What then?"

"Patti Bailey."

He reeled back in an exaggerated gesture, like he was taking one on the chin. "All the miserable unsolveds and you got that one? Mikey told me."

"Can you tell me anything?"

"Well, Detective, that was a long time ago."

"I'm getting interference from the outside. Maybe it's help. I don't know what it is."

"You'll have to explain that one."

She did—the letter, the key, the storage unit, the gun and casings, the blood-riddled dress.

Pat looked at her slack-faced, like she was telling him a

whopper he just couldn't believe. She watched him choke down his surprise, try to make something good out of it.

"What else was in the box?"

"Newspapers from sixty-nine. That's it."

That wasn't it, because she had Patti Bailey's little black book and the unlabeled cassette tape in the trunk of her car. But she wasn't going to give those up until she looked at them. No lab, no Brighton, no McNally, no nobody.

"Well, you got solid physical evidence now. That's more than Thornton ever found. It's a start. But somebody's messin' with you, Merci. Somebody wants you to have this stuff. There's something in it for him. So ride it out as far as you can."

He leaned in close to her, his big red face right up close to hers. "But be careful. Anyone with enough balls to lead a cop around like that is dangerous. Patti Bailey was murdered. Thirty years or thirty minutes ago—it ain't some fuckin' game."

"Pat, it's like they're . . . inside of me. Watching everything I do. Moving me around like a chess piece. Like they're in the backseat of my goddamned car."

Big Pat sat back, observed a moment of silence for what Merci had gone through with the Purse Snatcher. Something about Pat reminded her of Hess, the way he wore his scars, the sharp sadness in eyes that had seen a lot, the same graceful refusal to become bitter. The difference was Pat had a life outside of work; Hess had never found one. He'd been close to finding one.

"The gun and the dress, they're safe in the lab now? Nobody can mess with them?"

She nodded. Safe as the lab can be, with detectives running all over it, stuff disappearing, Gilliam ready to put it off limits to everybody but his own staff.

Big Pat thought about this. She couldn't tell what. A cell phone rang and Merci got her purse, but it wasn't her phone. Pat's hand went to his ear.

"Yo. Hey, Bright. Yeah. Um-hm. You got it."

Got what, she wondered.

He set the tiny phone on the bar. He looked down at his beer, took it off the napkin, then looked at the sweat ring in the middle of the paper.

"Merci, it isn't easy doin' what you do. Lemme think about the Bailey case, see what I can remember after all these years. You watch yourself. You don't know what's going on and that isn't good. It's always when you're stepping easy on the ice, it breaks and in you go. Stay light, girl. Heads up."

He set out a couple of bills for the waitress, collected his phone and smokes and got off the stool. He hugged her again.

"Sorry," he said. "Boss barks, I still jump."

Chapter Twenty-two

After dinner she took Tim into her room and set him up with a stuffed gorilla to play with. The animal was almost as big as he was. Tim liked to sit the ape on the floor, then creep around back and sneak up on him, either kiss him or slug him.

Merci put the unlabeled cassette into her old boombox. She put a new blank in the second deck, hit the dub button and sat down on the floor with her back against the bed. She looked through the black book as she listened.

MAN: "Whazzat?"
WOMAN: "Zwhat?"
MAN: "Clickin' sound."
WOMAN: "My bubble gum." Chewing sounds.
MAN: "Chew a lot of that flavor, don't you?"
WOMAN: "Just yours, honey."
MAN: "I'm a lucky guy."

Woman: "I don't panic, it's organic. And it goes down smooth."

Man: "Want another drink?"

Woman: "Yeah, and how about another hit, honey?"

Man: "I'm still damned stoned."

Woman: "Poor Ralphie-Honey. Not used to that."

Man: "Like I got hit by a train."

Woman: "Like that farmer you were talking about."

Man: "That ain't funny."

Woman: "You said at least it got his attention."

Pause. Tape hiss. Covers rustling?

Man: "Know somethin', Patti Dear?"

Woman: "Tell me, honey."

Man: "For a fuckin' whore you sure got big ears."

Woman: "I'm horny, honey, not deaf. You say something and I listen to you. Everybody's talking about him. It's in the papers. You said it got his attention. I believe you."

Man, snide laughter: "Attention. Yeah, it got that."

Ice clinking in a glass. A match flares. Deep inhale.

Woman, smoke-choked: "You know who conked him?"

Man: "I told you I did. How come if you listen so well you gotta ask a dumbfuck question like that?"

Woman: "Because I wanna know, Meeksie. I'm interested. I care. Man, this dope is really good."

MAN: "You're stoned. I'm not telling you anything. You'd forget it by tomorrow anyway."

WOMAN, giggling: "I know you know. You're that kind of guy."

MAN: "Come here. Make yourself useful."

WOMAN, giggling still: "I'm just kidding, honey. I don't care what you know and what you don't."

MAN: "I don't just know the shit around this county, Patti. I make it happen. I'm the shit king."

WOMAN: "Groovy."

MAN: "Ought to have you banged on the head. Maybe you'd work more and talk less."

WOMAN: "I'm going to take care of you, Ralphie."

MAN: "What year?"

WOMAN: "This one. Good old nineteen sixty-nine. Mmmm."

MAN: "Oh, yeah. Oh, yeah, yeah."

The sounds of sex.

Merci hit the pause button and thought: Patti Bailey and Supervisor Ralph Meeks. So, Bailey's sister had it right, Patti had moved to a higher-end clientele after her biker days. And Meeks knew who had Acuna beaten, or claimed to Bailey that he did. He even implied he was behind it. Was he confessing a truth, or trying to impress her with a lie?

Merci looked over at Tim. She didn't like him hearing this kind of thing. He was chewing the gorilla's hand, paying her and the voices no apparent attention whatsoever.

She fast-forwarded through the heavy breathing, thought of the *Clockwork Orange* scene where they do it fast to the William Tell March. But on Patti Bailey's tape it didn't seem funny, it just seemed disgusting.

Woman: "This is Patti Jo Bailey about to tape-record William Owen of the Orange County Sheriff Department. He's the sheriff. I'll try to get him to say his name so you'll believe me, but that's not going to be easy. I got to be cool. He's not a drunk like Ralph Meeks. I'm going to try on Meeksie again, but I couldn't ask him more about that farmer without making him mad and suspicious. He made it sound the first time like he was responsible for the farmer getting almost murdered, losing his eye, getting all those stitches and his teeth knocked out. When I get everything on tape I can get, I'm going to play it for them and start spending all my new money. Far out. I'm turning this on as soon as he knocks, so there might be some sex and sex talk. Bill won't say much, and he's always in a hurry, but his voice should be enough for proof of what he's doing. Oh, yeah, this is July twenty-fifth, nineteen sixty-niner. The first entry on this tape, Meeks, was July ninth."

Tape hiss. Off.

Knocking on door.

WOMAN: "Who's there?"

MAN: "Jerry."

WOMAN: "Jerry who?"

MAN: "Open the fuckin' door, Patti."

Door opens.

WOMAN: "Hey, sweetie. 'Mon in."

MAN: "Hello."

Door closes.

WOMAN, flirtatiously: "You don't look like a Jerry to me."

MAN: "Not everybody looks like their dog, either."

WOMAN: "I'd say maybe a . . . say, a Bill Owen."

MAN: "Bullshit. Never heard of him."

WOMAN: "I'm just playing with you, sweetie. Just 'cause you're the big bad sheriff doesn't mean you got to be soooo uptight. Go with the flow. What's this, our fifth or sixth date?"

MAN: "Sheriff? You must be loaded. Beats me what date this is."

WOMAN: "Want a drink?"

MAN: "No time."

WOMAN: "What'll it be then?"

MAN: "The usual."

WOMAN, flirtatiously: "And what could that be?"

MAN: "Go sit on the bed. Just do it."

WOMAN: "There's the little matter of money."

A shuffling sound, the faint crackle of paper.

It didn't matter. Merci had her connection between law enforcement and Patti Bailey—Sheriff Bill Owen. And since Owen was tight with Meeks, and Meeks implied he'd arranged to have Jesse Acuna beaten, it didn't take a genius to do the addition: Owen.

Enter Patti Bailey. Party girl with big ears. When Bailey played her tape she made herself extremely dangerous. They had to pay up, or shut her up before the damage was done. Owen again? It was the simplest explanation.

That much made sense. But the second layer of mystery didn't. Who took the evidence after the murder? Who stored it? Why had they kept that evidence for thirty-two years?

Most important, who spilled the beans right into her own lap?

She looked over at Tim, now piling pillows on top of the gorilla. She thought that for an eighteen-month-old, he was purposeful and intelligent in his work. He looked over and smiled, a long string of drool hanging from his chin. He shrieked and went for another pillow.

Merci turned the tape player back on.

Car noise.

WOMAN: ". . . some of the best stuff I've ever had. I guess you got the pick of the good stuff."

MAN: "There's a lot of it around."

WOMAN: "Ever think of selling it?"

MAN: "It's just for favors. For friends."

WOMAN: "Whore friends like me. So, who is this guy?"

MAN: "Just a friend."

WOMAN: "Got lots of green, like the others?"

MAN: "Plenty of green."

WOMAN: "You don't seem real relaxed tonight. Something the matter?"

MAN: "I'm fine. I'm just tired. Double shift yesterday, make some extra. Don't light that thing in here."

WOMAN: "Then where am I gonna light it?"

MAN: "We'll pull over."

WOMAN: "Nothing but an orange grove. Where are we, anyway?"

MAN: "Myford and Fourth."

WOMAN: "Myford and Fourth. What's a Myford? Something to do with oranges?"

MAN: "Was a guy's name. Killed himself with a shotgun and a rifle, something like that. Shot himself three times. That was a long time ago."

WOMAN: "Far out. Doesn't sound like a suicide to me."

MAN: "There was a lot of talk about it."

Car noise stops.

MAN: "Let's take a walk. You can light the joint."

WOMAN: "I'm good at lighting joints. You interested in a real good light?"

MAN: "I'm always interested."

WOMAN: "I love it when you are, honey."

MAN: "I love you, too."

WOMAN: "I'm just a party girl to you guys."

MAN: "Who says I can't love a party girl?"

WOMAN: "Your own way, I guess."

Static. Sounds like the mike is rubbing against something, maybe being moved. Car doors open and shut. Footsteps on gravel, then footsteps on dirt—a road perhaps.

WOMAN: "Dark tonight."

MAN: "Moon's small. Just coming out."

Footsteps.

WOMAN: "Walking to China?"

MAN: "There's a cable spool out here we can sit on."

WOMAN: "You bring your other girlfriends here?"

MAN: "Only you."

More footsteps. A thud, then no footsteps. A rustling sound up near the mike.

WOMAN: "I'm lighting up."

MAN: "Do what you want."

A match flares, then puffing sounds.

WOMAN, smoke-choked, holding it in: ". . . Just . . . expands."

Coughing, more puffing.

WOMAN: "Blows my hair back."

A minute goes by. No conversation, just the sound of the woman smoking, and footsteps.

WOMAN: "Trippy, the way the moon shines on the water in that ditch? Lookit that. It looks like God's pouring melted silver into the ditch. Men shouldn't walk on God's moon."

MAN: "Nice. Here's that cable spool."

WOMAN: "Far out! It's like a giant spool for thread!"

MAN: "Sort of."

WOMAN: "You're kind of down tonight, baby. What's wrong? You ought to take a hit of this, just try to get in the groove. Go with it."

MAN: "I'm fine. This is all I need."

The sound of liquid in a bottle.

MAN: "Ah."

WOMAN puffs.

WOMAN, holding in smoke, letting it out: "Isn't it boss when it's hot enough to just walk around like this, no coat or nothing? Summer's great. I feel like going down to the beach and laying in the sun for a week. Except I gotta work. Business is better when it's hot, gets all you guys hot and horny, makes you pay up and get off with good old Patti. Boy, this dirt here's so soft. I got my toes in it. Look. It's warm feeling, not like you'd think dirt is gonna be at all. Mother Earth."

MAN: "Uh-huh."

Sound of movement.

WOMAN: "Come on, dance with me."

Sound of liquid against glass. A man's sigh.

WOMAN: "You like me, don't you?"

MAN: "You know I like you."

WOMAN: "Gonna leave your wife for me?"

MAN: "Can't do that."

WOMAN: "So, you're lovin' us both."

MAN: "I guess that's what I'm doing."

WOMAN: "She know?"

MAN: "She don't know anything 'cept how to scream and fight."

WOMAN: "So, where's this new john?"

MAN: "He'll be here."

WOMAN: "What's he do? Is he one of those big important guys?"

MAN: "No. He's a regular guy."

WOMAN: "How come we gotta meet in an orange grove? He get off doing it outdoors?"

MAN: "Yeah, that's what he said."

WOMAN: "I'm charging him triple what I charge you. I already told you that."

MAN: "Fine, Patti. You charge him what you want."

The woman hums a tune. It sounds like she's dancing, moving around.

WOMAN: "I think I was reincarnated as me. Before, I was a whale way down in the deep. Next, I'm gonna be a butterfly."

MAN: "They only live for a couple of weeks."

Woman: "So, then I'll get to be a lion. Or maybe an eagle or a hummingbird."

Man: "Can you see the man in the moon?"

Woman: "Lemme see now."

The woman's voice is fainter. Like the microphone is farther away, or perhaps she has turned around.

Woman: "Oh, yeah. There he is. Can't figure if he's happy or sad tonight. I think he changes moods. How do you know it's not a woman, though? Maybe I could get reincarnated as the first woman in the moon."

Man grunts. The sound of liquid on glass. Again. Then a shuffling sound. Footsteps. A pause. Then a loud blast, quickly followed by another.

Man, quietly: "Oh, God. Oh, my God."

Distant sounds. Grunting. Footsteps. Something being dragged. A man sobbing. Footsteps. Quiet.

Merci sat there for a long minute, listening to the tape hiss. Tim turned to her with an odd look on his face.

"It's okay," she said quietly. "It's okay, little man. I'm sorry. I shouldn't have done that to you."

She clicked off the player, picked up Tim and walked him into the living room. She looked out at the brightly lit yard and the dark grove beyond the fence. Just a few miles from here, she thought. Myford and Fourth. A hot night in early August, 1969.

She sat in the rocker, sang a quiet song to him. A few minutes later he went heavy and limp in her arms and she carried him into his room. She put him in the crib, raised the bars, turned on the monitor.

For a long while she stood and watched him, his arms thrown back, his mittens on against the drafts of the old house. She decided at that moment that she wouldn't lead him into her kind of life. Until now she'd always figured he could choose someday. Now it seemed to her that the best thing she could do for him was to keep him from doing what she did, from listening to things like he'd just heard when he was no longer too innocent to understand them. Anything, she thought, be anything but a cop.

• • •

Back in her bedroom she played the end of the tape again. Then she turned to the last page of Patti Bailey's black book and found the entry for August third.

4SV/6CM/7DL/8:30FD/11KQ

It must have been KQ at eleven, she thought: too light to see the man in the moon at eight-thirty. Not dark enough to hide the parked car, to make them invisible walking into the grove at Myford and Fourth.

KQ.

KQ, with dope he gives away. KQ, with a new "friend." KQ, whose other friends have plenty of money. KQ, married and messing around with Patti Bailey on the side. KQ, with a .38 Special on him, and his date unsuspecting.

Or maybe she was used to the gun, because he was a cop. Thus, the free dope, the weapon, the double shifts at work. And the trust. Bailey trusts him. Friend of Bill Owens and Ralph Meeks?

Merci played the end of the tape once more and tried to picture it, to see things that weren't right in front of her, as Hess had tried to teach her. She closed her eyes and imagined Patti Bailey standing on the dirt road along the dark trees, her back to KQ on the cable spool, looking out at the man in the moon, at the water in the culvert that looked to her like silver being poured. She saw KQ set down his bottle, lift himself off the rough wood of the cable spool, walk over to Patti and shoot her in the back. Twice, fast. Then KQ sobbing, pulling off her clothes and dragging the woman away.

The tape ran another ten minutes. Nothing but the quiet of the orange trees on a hot summer night. It clicked off.

• • •

Mike called at ten. "Hi, Merci. Sorry it's late, but I miss you."

"Nice to hear you."

"Really? Don't answer that. Last night was special to me. Sounds weird to say thanks, but thanks."

"It sounds weird to say you're welcome, so I won't. I . . . yes. It was special to me, too."

"What are you doing?"

She said she was reading over the Bailey case file. "I asked your dad about it today."

"Any help?"

"He's trying."

"It's a wonder he can remember anything, with all the beer he drinks."

"He's pretty sharp still."

Mike was quiet for a beat. "You feel like going away for a week? Just drop everything, cash in the vacation time? Carver in vice, he's got a line on a condo on Maui. We could leave, like Friday or something. Just forget everything. Stay warm, get a tan, maybe go fishing."

"I can't do that. You know I can't."

"Bring Tim."

"It's not that. I've just got a full plate at work."

More silence. "How's the Whittaker case coming?"

"It's coming."

"Am I still one of your suspects?"

"No. You weren't a suspect, Mike."

"Even when I said I did it?"

Merci said nothing.

"You might not believe this, but somehow I'm going to make this all up to you."

"It's not me you owe."

"Who then?"

"I have no idea, Mike. Aubrey Whittaker maybe."

Mike went quiet again. When he spoke his voice was so low she could hardly hear him.

"I owe somebody. I messed up. I shouldn't have done what I did. It makes everything bad. It stains everything. All I had was my reputation. Now it's gone. Shot to hell. I don't know how to get that stain off me."

"You were falling in love. It happens."

She wanted to give him a chance to confirm it. Even after everything that she'd found, it still mattered if he had betrayed her in his heart, whether he'd taken the woman to bed or not. Whether he'd murdered her or not. How petty, she thought, but it was too late to recall her statement.

"No, I wasn't. I'm in love with you. But I just . . . I swear, Merci, I just thought I could . . . change her. Make her different. Help her get out of what she was. That's what I wanted."

"She's out."

"Yeah. Okay. Look, Merci, I'm thinking I'll take that Maui trip anyway. Alone. I'm going to fly out on Friday. I just got to get away for a few days. Everybody in the department seems to know I had dinner with that girl."

"Do what you need to do, Mike."

"I'll let you know. Merci, please believe in me. I'm worth it. I'm going to make you see I'm worth it. It's just kind of hard to see right now."

• • •

Evan O'Brien called at 10:40.

"No dice on the .38 Special, Merci—too old, too dry, too rusted. Nothing off the Inland Storage envelope. Those no-lick stamps are great, people bear down and presto. But yours was clean. I can try an iodine fume. Then ninhydrin or silver nitrate. I wouldn't put the chances at real good."

"What about the envelope itself?"

"I actually did think of that. Clean, Lady Dick."

"Thanks for trying."

"It's my job, pain in the ass that it is sometimes. You're lucky you left when you did today. Zamorra blasts in here this afternoon and practically punches out Gilliam. It's about the evidence from the Whittaker scene, but I wasn't clear on exactly *what* evidence. Then Brighton storms in here later and lectures Gilliam behind closed doors for twenty minutes. I could see them—both really pissed off. Then Gilliam comes out and says the lab is now off limits to anyone who doesn't work in it. Off limits specifically to Mike McNally, Paul Zamorra and Merci Rayborn. We're setting up a sign-in, sign-out sheet by the door, just like it's a crime scene."

The anger shot up through her. "What the hell did I do to get on that list?"

"Don't ask me, but Zamorra glared and Brighton spoke and Gilliam clamped down. I'm calling you from home right now—I didn't want to use the lab line to call one of my own detectives. Shit, a bunch of paranoid old farts, if you ask me. I go upstairs later to run something by the arson guys, I see Brighton's got Pat McNally in his office. It's like the old boy's club around there. Soon as you make sheriff, I hope you've got the good sense to put me in charge of the lab."

"I'll see what I can do."

"Glandis pulse you on his move for Brighton's job?"

"Yeah."

"Me, too. I told him I thought he'd be great. It's not my fault he's stupid enough to believe me."

Merci was surprised to hear a woman giggle quietly in the background.

"Gotta go," said O'Brien.

"I guess you do."

She hung up and wondered what Brighton could possibly be telling Big Pat. Or not telling him. She would like to have been a fly on the wall for that one.

• • •

Brighton called at 11:05. He told her they were going to bring Mike to room 348 of the Newport Marriott the next morning at eight o'clock sharp. They'd have a closed-circuit video camera set up. He told her to be there at six so they could set her up in 350, next door.

"I don't think you should be the one to question him at this point," said Brighton. "I don't think he should see you. There's no need for that right now. Later, Merci, we might need you for that. Leave Zamorra out. You can bring him up to speed later."

"I agree. I understand."

"But I want you to direct us. Clay Brenkus and one of his assistants are going to depose you, first off. That'll give them the rough outline to follow—what he said, how you found what you found. Clay and I are going to sit in, let Mike know this is the real thing. I'll have a couple of deputies, men I trust, just in case Mike gets belligerent. We'll give him every chance to explain himself. Every chance, Merci. We'll have two DA investigators in position out at Mike's place, ready to go as soon as he gives us permission to search."

"What if he doesn't? He's got no reason to let us waltz in there and search his home."

"Then we'll arrest him. That, based on his confession to you, the hair and fiber evidence from the Whittaker scene, and the fact that he was with her an hour before she died. We can do a warrantless search on the emergency exception—that's assuming he'll destroy the evidence. I think that's a reasonable assumption, and so does Clay. The forty-five was in plain view, so we're covered there. We'll book it, shoot it and get our own casing. Even if we have to get phone warrants we can do that in less than a day."

She couldn't talk at first. She felt like she was in a bullet train in a tunnel, darkness smearing past the windows, no chance for clarity or perspective. It was Tuesday, exactly one week since the murder of Aubrey Whittaker. One *week.* Now they were going to question Mike McNally in connection with that homicide.

"I can't believe this is happening," she said quietly.

"It's only started to happen. Strap yourself in, young lady. It's going to be a long, rough ride."

Chapter Twenty-three

She woke up suddenly in the dark, rain roaring down on the house, Tim's cries coming through the monitor she'd turned up full blast because she slept like the dead. Her first thought was that some tremendous disaster had just befallen him, and she headed to his room fast, throwing on all the lights on the way.

The darkness seemed to reach for her and this scared her, and she hated the darkness for it. Her heart was pounding hard by the time she got to her son. He looked up at her with wide blue eyes filled with tears, his legs kicking, and she understood that the storm had scared him, that was all, just a baby's fear of a storm.

She carried him back to her room. Good God, she thought: Wouldn't it be great to be assured and confident and a little bit mean again, like she was before Hess? Before the Purse Snatcher? Before it was such an ordeal to get to your baby in a rainstorm?

She brought him to bed with her. He stopped crying almost instantly, then fell asleep against her chest while Merci stroked his small soft head and listened to the rain splattering onto the patio. She looked back to the doorway and realized she'd left every light on, including the one in her bedroom.

She rolled over, wrapped the pillow over her head and thought.

We'll be giving him every chance to explain himself.

And what explanation was there? That he'd hidden a silencer in his tackle box, but decided not to use it?

That it must be someone else's, planted there to frame him?

She could almost believe that. Almost. But it didn't account for his chukka boots with the blood on them, or the letters Aubrey had written him implying that she thought exposing him would be a good thing. It didn't explain the evidence—a card handwritten by him—gone missing from the crime lab. It didn't explain the fact that he'd had dinner in her apartment and allegedly left less than an hour before she was murdered. It didn't explain the underwear Merci had let him have, against her better instincts, later used to conceal a silencer.

She pictured the scene again. She saw Mike leaving Aubrey Whittaker's place, his blond hair bouncing as he takes the steps. She saw him coming back up a few minutes later—he looks tighter, more purposeful. She saw him standing in the porch light, knocking. She saw Aubrey at the door, peering through the peephole and opening the door to the guy who'd just left . . .

• • •

She got up and delivered sleeping Tim back to his crib, then dressed. It was just after 5 A.M. The world was still dark as she guided her Impala down the rut-riddled dirt road that led away from her house, her right hand absently feeling around in the space behind her seat—a habit by now. The rain boiled in the puddles, and in her brights it looked like acid frothing up, a witches' brew, something that would put your eyes out. She'd only slept four hours, and her head felt pressured, her eyeballs tight, her body heavy and inefficient.

Mike, I'm so goddamned sorry.

• • •

The head of hotel security, Ronald, met her in the lobby and took her up to room 350. They made the elevator ride in silence, Merci assuming that Ronald didn't think much of lady detectives.

Brighton let them in. Clay Brenkus shook her hand firmly and said, "It took a lot of balls for you to do this, young lady. Congratulations and good luck."

"I hope we have more than luck, Mr. Brenkus."

"It's Clay, and all we're doing is getting the truth. It isn't your truth or mine. It's McNally's. He did it or he didn't. We're going to find out which."

Guy Pitt, one of the assistant DAs Merci had worked

with, got her coffee and a croissant from a tray. "I'm going to depose you," he said quietly. "Marion here is going to swear you in, do the recording. Okay?"

Merci nodded. It felt just like a dream but she couldn't wake up. The rain washed down the windows in gallons.

A thin and lusterless woman rose from one of the couches and extended her hand. "I'm ready to start when you are, Guy."

"Merci, it's going to be me and Clay, two of our investigators, the sheriff and two of his men. I'll ask the questions. Remember, Mike confessed to you—about the shooting and about having a silencer in his possession. I'm still going to frame them in a way to make what you did seem reasonable and necessary, given the emergency exception rule under *Mincey versus Arizona.* All that means is, if you hadn't made a warrantless search, the evidence would have been destroyed. This is sworn testimony, but you're not in court. Relax, tell the truth, and if you don't understand something, just ask."

"Yeah."

"All right?"

"Yeah, Guy, I'm all right."

"When we're done, everyone's going into the room next door to interview Mike. You'll be able to hear and see from in here—we've got a camera set up next door, a closed-circuit monitor over there by the couch. If we have to, we'll shuttle some people back and forth, get some direction from you, clarify something. But we don't want you in there. We don't want him to know you're here, or what you did. Nothing about that yet."

Brighton walked her over toward the couch, a heavy arm around her shoulder. "You did the right thing."

"Then how come everybody has to keep telling me?"

"Easy does it."

• • •

The deposition took almost an hour. It was the usual thing with lawyers—too many questions, then more questions.

> *And the flyfishing tackle box that you described, what was the purpose of that box so far as you knew?*
>
> *It held flyfishing tackle.*
>
> *Was it used exclusively for flyfishing or for other kinds of fishing, so far as you knew?*
>
> *Just flyfishing.*
>
> *You say it was the only handmade box on the workbench?*
>
> *Only one I saw.*
>
> *And you say you had knowledge that it was handmade by Mr. McNally?*
>
> *Yes.*
>
> *And was the box in plain view, on the workbench of the workshop where Mr. McNally lives?*

There was a net over it. But I could see the box through the mesh. It wasn't hidden from view. It was obscured, slightly.

Or, questions she'd rather they never asked, but they did anyway.

Sergeant Rayborn, how could you be certain the undergarment—the undergarment surrounding the sound suppressor you found in the flyfishing tackle box—belonged to you?

Because I gave it to him.

When she was finished Merci went into the bathroom, washed her face in hot water, used one of the fat luxurious terry washcloths to scrub out all the whatever it was that seemed to be roiling out from inside her like poison. She threw the wet cloth into the corner just for spite, then felt bad, picked it up, rinsed it, squeezed it damp and hung it carefully over the shower rod, got angry for feeling bad then threw it back in the corner again.

• • •

Sitting down on the couch in room 348, Mike McNally had an expression like Hess used to have when he came out of a radiation treatment—stunned but undefeated.

His face was pale. He sat on his hands. He stared at the camera for a long beat, then studied someone across the room from him with a nervous disdain, like a rattlesnake looking up at a shovel.

"You're videotaping this?" he asked.

"Yes," said Brighton brusquely. "You don't mind?"

"What's this about, sir?" Mike sat forward, leaning toward the coffee table in front of him.

"Aubrey Whittaker, Tuesday night, last week."

Mike looked around. Merci could see part of Brighton's shoulder and the back of his head as he faced his vice detective. She could see Brenkus in profile, at the top of the screen. Between them were the two DA investigators. The two deputies Brighton had mentioned were off camera.

"Look, Mike," said Brighton. His voice was low, unhurried, confidential. "You had dinner with Aubrey Whittaker last week. She was murdered shortly after you left. I want you to tell me about that night. Everything about it. Your reason for accepting such an invite. Your feelings about the girl. Your state of mind when you got there. Heck, tell me about the dessert, too. I just want to know what happened. I want to know everything that happened. Because frankly, Mike, we've got some evidence collected that looks incriminating to us. This is your chance to spill it, come clean, get the record straight. We can be done with this and out of here in a couple of hours if you just tell us the truth. We can all go back to work, get on with things. That's what we'd all like most."

Merci watched Mike's expression go from alertness to

surprise to disbelief to embarrassment to anger. Mike wasn't subtle. Mike wasn't devious. Mike was obvious, his face an honest reflection of his heart. It was like watching a chameleon change colors.

"You think I killed her."

It wasn't a question.

"We don't think anything," said Brenkus. "All we're after is the truth, Mike."

"Oh," he said with sarcasm. "All right."

Mike sat back for a moment, then forward again. Merci could see his eyes get that distant look, then refocus, leading him back to the present. He nodded, as if sealing a deal with himself. He took a deep breath.

"I'm going to stand up," he said. "I'm going to walk to that window, look out. Any of you dumb monkeys got a problem with that?"

Brenkus looked to Brighton, Brighton to McNally, then glanced off to his left. Shadows in the room moved. Mike stood and walked toward the window, offscreen.

Everyone stood. The two plainclothes deputies followed him, trying to seem casual, unsure of how much urgency to show.

Merci looked out the window: rain slanting down through the dark morning sky.

Mike came back to the couch, but he didn't sit. "Well then, here's the truth: I won't answer a single one of your questions until I've got a lawyer."

Nobody spoke for a moment. Clay Brenkus shook his head and sighed.

"That's the hard way, Mike," said Brighton. "We'll need to go downtown for that."

"Let's go."

Mike had his forty-five out before Merci knew what he was doing. His arm straightened and the barrel lined up with Brighton. Bodies in motion then, and curses from unseen men in the room, shadows moving quick. Pitt jumped out of camera. Brenkus rolled off his seat. Brighton froze.

Mike spun the automatic around his finger, stopped it barrel up, his fingers out, then set it on the coffee table.

"May God forgive you assholes."

Then he looked straight at the monitor, which meant he looked straight at Merci. She'd never seen cold rage on his face before, but she saw it now. She didn't know he could look this way.

"You stupid woman," he said. "I can't believe you did this, you stupid, gutless bitch."

• • •

Brighton came in after they led Mike out. His face looked gray, ten years older than he'd looked the day before.

"With regards to the rest of this day at headquarters," he said to Merci, "miss it."

"I will."

His hard eyes bored into her. "I don't know what to say,

Merci. I don't know how this is going to play out. I just know that when the press finds out we've arrested our own vice cop in the Whittaker murder, it's going to be worse than a circus. Stay low. I'll take the heat."

She nodded. "I've got some interviews set up. The Bailey case."

"Do what you need to do. Look, I had a talk with Paul Zamorra yesterday. I think he's on the verge of hurting somebody, probably himself. I offered him a week off to get his wife settled, but he wouldn't take it. I think he should take it. I want you to encourage him in that direction. I don't want to force a leave on him, but I will."

"I understand, sir."

Brighton held up his hand. It was trembling. "Mike could have shot me a minute ago. It's just catching up with me. Maybe I *am* too old for this job. Maybe I should get out while I've still got an ass to sit on."

Chapter Twenty-four

Ralph Meeks answered his door wearing sheepskin boots that Merci thought made him look like a Sherpa.

"You're soakin' wet, honey."

"It's been raining six hours straight."

He was a short, skinny man, his legs lost in the baggy slacks he tucked into the boots. Bright little eyes, hair like steel wool. He wore a turtleneck under a bulky sweater with reindeer trailing across the yoke and chest.

Standing in the doorway, he rotated a large cigar and blew the smoke away from her. "Well, come in. At least you're good looking. What, six feet?"

"Five-eleven," she said, stepping into the towering entryway.

"I'm five-seven. I'm also seventy-nine years old. They make 'em bigger now. D cup?"

Her mouth parted in disbelief. Ralph Meeks cackled. "Just playin' with ya. My wife was flat as a window, so it doesn't really matter to me."

"Play some other way, Mr. Meeks, I'm here to—"

"I know, I know. To find out about who killed Patti Bailey and all those other current events. Now you walk down this shiny floor here *eleven* steps, turn left when you get to the room that smells like burning wood. Where it smells like burning wood, there's fire. Go in and sit by that fire. I'll get you some hot chocolate."

"No, thank you, I—"

"It's already made, you're gettin' it. Go, march, lady—I don't have all day."

She counted ten steps while she took in what she could see of the house: marble entryway with a big chandelier up high, a living room with white carpet and a view of the storm-blasted beach just a few yards away, a library with shelves twelve feet high and rolling ladders to get to them with.

Her eleventh step brought her to the study: huge fireplace with a raging fire, a leather recliner and couch arranged in front of the fire but not too close, an immense mahogany desk to her right, an entire wall of old oak file cabinets. It was all illuminated by recessed lights and storm glow from a large skylight cut in the vaulted ceiling above. The fire roared quietly like a river, and the rain slammed down on the skylight glass.

Meeks padded back in with a couple mugs of hot something, handed her one.

"Nice aroma, isn't it? It's orange wood, only kind I burn. Gotta get it from Riverside County now."

Merci nodded, looking at the little man.

"Like my house?"

"Looks fine to me."

"Nixon's place was just a hundred yards north of here. We used to party with him there, if you could call it partying. He was a crook, no doubt, but he didn't know how to have fun. Kind of the worst of both worlds."

"Did you help him get elected?"

"We threw some votes his way. Wasn't hard in Orange County."

"I thought the Birchers were after you."

"Sergeant, there's conservative Republicans, then there's Birchers. I was a registered *democrat* when I came here after the war, but I'd changed my colors by the election of fifty-two."

"How come?"

"Used to be the only game in town, the republicans. Hell, the local Republican Party chairman started out as a democrat. Switched when he realized there was only one real side here. Now we got that Mexican democrat woman in the Congress, so it's all changed. Politics are boring. Let's talk about hookers and murder and pretty ladies getting shot in the back. Sit—take the sofa over here. If it gets too hot you can take off your clothes." Meeks cackled again. "Come on, show some humor."

"You're not quite disgusting, Mr. Meeks. But you're close."

"I'm harmless."

She sat down and got out her blue notebook and her tape recorder. She turned it on, set it on the sofa toward him. "Get within a five-foot radius of me, Mr. Meeks, and I'll bash you over the head with my pistol."

He looked at her. "I'd *love* that."

Merci thought: The same way you loved it when Patti Bailey took out Big Ralphie?

"Look, Mr. Meeks, I've got some business to take care of here. You said you'd help me with it. I'm going to tape this conversation and make some notes if you don't mind."

"Wait, lady—I party with Richard Nixon and you think I'm gonna let you tape me? I don't talk to tapes. You want a tape, you can arrest me."

Meeks hovered next to the leather recliner. Merci saw that he was bent and stiff. He looked at his cigar, then at her. "Come on, lady. Can that thing and I'll help you. I'm good to my word."

Merci clicked off the tape recorder. But she already had part of what she wanted. Part of the bravado had already blown out of him. So she decided to hit him hard, see if he'd let her get right to the heart of things.

"How'd you meet Bailey?"

Meeks was still standing in front of the recliner. He seemed to consider her question as he sat. She watched him do it the old man way: position feet, turn, brace with free hand, bend legs and lower butt, stiffen as the weight shifts, keep the back straight, there. When he was finished he looked at her. His face was sharp and beveled by the firelight. His eyes were orange dots. He took an ash-tray from the stand beside the chair and brought it to his lap.

"I met her at a party."

"Who introduced you?"

"We introduced ourselves, you know, like regular people. In the kitchen. I was makin' a bourbon; she was looking for a light. She had a marijuana cigarette, so I gave her my matches. I told her to go outside and smoke that shit. It was a felony back then, possession. I went out there with my drink and we got to talking."

"Make a date?"

"Naw. I didn't do that kinda thing. I was married."

"You never made a date with her?"

"I just said I didn't."

"See her again after that?"

"Other parties. I wouldn't even remember her, if she didn't get murdered. You know how it is."

"That's the first lie you've told me, Mr. Meeks."

Merci stood and walked over to the fire. She could only get six feet away before the heat stopped her. She looked back at Meeks. He looked small in the big recliner, reindeer dancing across his sweater like it was Christmas morning or something. He blew a big plume of smoke.

"What do you want, lady?"

"Listen."

She went back to the recorder, pulled out the blank tape and put in her dub of Patti Bailey's.

She played the section with Meeks on it. He listened without moving, just cigar smoke rising around him.

"I've got her date book, too. Interesting listening, interesting reading. You were seeing her once a week or so. You'd drink. She'd smoke dope. You'd do your thing."

"I'm still listenin'."

"Good. This is the score here. I can take you downtown right now and book you on suspicion of assault with intent to kill Jesse Acuna. I can add conspiracy and probably make it stick. If the court won't convict you, the media will. I can make copies of that tape and hand them out to the press people, along with your home phone number. I can make the last few years of your life miserable, *Meeksie*. Or you can help me."

A silence while the fire roared, then he said: "I don't know who killed her. I had nothing to do with that. The papers said bikers were suspected, and I believed it. She had all kinds of rotten friends, guys you wouldn't mop vomit with. You gotta understand, lady, I was a supervisor, a politician. I liked the girls, yeah, I admit that. I mistreated my wife, and she never mistreated me that way. I even might have caused somebody to beat up that old guy, because I hated what he was doing to this county—I thought it was wrong. So I bad-mouthed him and maybe some young guys got wrong ideas. I'm not saying either way. But I *never* raised a finger against that Bailey whore, *ever.* Even when she threatened me with that tape, the same way you're threatening me with it now."

"What did you do?"

"I paid up, kept my mouth shut and hoped to Christ she'd keep hers that way. Then she was dead. I didn't cry any tears, either. I felt like I'd just been let out of death row."

"How much did you pay her?"

"Five grand. Nothing. She wanted fifteen, and I was good for that, but I wanted to buy some time."

"For what?"

"What do you think? Time is what she was selling me, silent time, so I wanted to finance it over as many months as I could. Like a car you can't really afford."

Merci tried to establish the timeline leading up to Bailey's murder in August. "That was when?"

"June. July."

"But in December, you stepped down from the Board of Supervisors. Resigned your elected office."

He shrugged. "That's two different things—the girl and the job. Not related. I quit because the Grand Jury was throwing rocks at me, the press was all over my ass, my own district was talking recall. The last thing I needed was some whore kicking dirt in my face, but she never did that, you know. In that way, I was clean. Bailey had been dead for four months when I quit. It wasn't her, it was all the other stuff."

"Kickbacks from Orange Coast Capital."

"People can call anything a kickback. I had friends. I helped them, yeah. They helped me, yeah. I'd get the board to approve a parcel for development. Because I believe in development, I believe in people, I believe we got a right to be here so why not be comfortable? Why not have a house and a supermarket and a filling station and a fuckin' fast-food place on every corner? What's wrong with that? What are you going to do instead—just leave it to the ground squirrels and cactus? So, something would get developed. The guys who made all the dough would take me skiing for a week, or we'd go down to Mexico for some marlin fishing. Now you tell me—that a kickback or just the way the world works?"

"It's a kickback."

Meeks blew a cloud of smoke, coughed. "Then I should have stepped down. I did the right thing."

"How did you meet Bailey? Skip the bourbon story."

He looked at her, then toward the fire. "Owen. They were friends."

"Where'd you meet with her?"

"Hotels. Different ones mostly."

"De Anza?"

"Too hot. Too lowlife. Naw, the old Grand in Anaheim, the Hotel Laguna. One up in Newport Beach, I forget the name."

"Who was 'KQ'?"

He looked at her, thought, shrugged. "Got no idea."

"Who else was she servicing?"

"About a thousand guys. Like I'd know?"

"Try."

Meeks puffed, tapped the cigar in the ashtray. "Some of the cops. Don't know names."

"Police or sheriff?"

"Deputies. Owen's guys. She talked a lot. She talked way too much."

"What did Owen do when she threatened him with the tape?"

"Same thing I did, far as I know. We didn't spend a lot of time comparing blackmail notes."

"Why not? Two powerful men. One little prostitute with big ideas."

Meeks was shaking his head. "The whole thing with blackmail and a whore is, you want to get away. Away from her and anybody associated with her. Me and Owen, we had to stand on our own feet. I didn't want to be around him if he fell. He didn't want to be around me if I did. That kind of thing puts a wall between you and everybody else. You just cover your own ass and hope your friends can, too."

"A month after you resigned, Owen did the same thing. You're going to tell me that wasn't connected to Bailey."

"The girl had been dead five months by then—what could it have to do with her? Owen had his own problems in the department. He wasn't young. The county was growing and he was running things the old way. The right-wingers wanted him out. Those guys had some sway back then. You look into that, you want to find out why Bill quit."

Merci looked up at the skylight. The rain was softer now, but it was still coming down.

Meeks coughed softly. "What are you going to do with that tape, that date book?"

"Leave them in Property, where they belong."

"That's good. You can hurt people with those things. Same way Bailey was trying to hurt people. I hope just because you're a cop and she was a whore you don't think it's any different."

"It's all the difference in the world."

"Explain that."

"Bailey fucked you for money because that was her job. But I'll fuck you for free, because that's mine."

Meeks laughed quietly. "Why do that? What do you want outta me?"

"I want to know who killed her. You know. I know that. So, if your memory gets any better, be sure to call. Until then, I'll do some legwork, put together assault and conspiracy charges based on that tape. Of course, how the tape got made is going to cause more trouble for you than what you say on it. That's your problem, not mine. You've got all my numbers on this card, and I'm putting this card into your hand in about five seconds."

She scrawled in her cell number on the back of a business card, walked over to Meeks and stood in his cloud of smoke. She gave it to him.

"I don't know who killed her, lady. How come you have

to show up in the twilight of my old age, and make my life miserable all over again?"

"You screwed a girl for money, you had an old farmer beaten so bad he was left half blind and toothless. That's wrong. It's illegal. And you have to pay for it."

"You simpleton. If I knew who killed the girl, don't you think I'd have told you by now?"

"You'll tell me, when the facts sink in. County lockup's a miserable place. We got three thousand beds for five thousand crooks. You might have to sleep on the floor. No smoking. You might even have to give your beach mansion here to your lawyers. Even if you got off, it would cost you. You'd have to burn scrap wood instead of the last orange trees in the state."

Chapter Twenty-five

She got a window booth at the Fisherman's Restaurant, out on the pier in San Clemente. It was less than five miles from Meeks's house, and she wanted somewhere warm and private to read Colin Byrne's "crooked cops" clips. See if they tracked with what Meeks had said.

She sat down and watched the Pacific surging just below her—black water, gray sky, white spume whipping off the swells and the damned rain pounding down again.

It gave her a queasy feeling to sit this close to the ocean that had once almost killed her and her son. That had been a stupid accident, really, absolutely her fault, something she'd never do again. She hadn't been sane those first few months after Tim was born. Somehow, the sea had forgiven her and offered her another chance.

Sitting over the ocean and watching it through glass was safe. It was confined. Or maybe *she* was. She told herself that being this close to it was like getting back on the horse that threw you. She looked down: The bullet that killed Aubrey Whittaker was out there somewhere, launched from the service automatic belonging to Mike McNally. A waitress brought her coffee and Merci stirred in plenty of milk and sugar.

Colin Byrne's research began with a few brief articles about street-level police corruption—excessive force, cops stealing impounded drugs and money, cops on the take from prostitution rings. A three-part investigative series on the cops and the De Anza Hotel pretty much fizzled out: Plenty of law enforcement officers admitted to going there to socialize but none, of course, knew anything about prostitution.

Byrne had followed a handful of other cops into the more interesting world of 1969 politics. He'd focused on a small group of law-enforcement officers—five Santa Ana P.D. and three sheriff's deputies—who were vocally right wing, in favor of organizing volunteer police departments in the neighborhoods, and openly critical of police and sheriff management.

The sheriff's deputies were familiar to her: Beck Rainer, Pat McNally, Art Rymers. The Santa Ana cops were just names; she'd never heard of them before.

She tracked all eight of the officers into the John Birch Society. They were all members. Most of them were members from the early sixties to the end of the decade but only a few of them were still active by 1972.

In the February 1967 JBS Chapter 231 newsletter, Beck Rainer wrote:

> In the face of the worldwide communist conspiracy, constant vigilance doesn't just make sense—it is mandatory if we are to maintain a free society. Part of Lenin's design to overthrow America is to accomplish it FROM THE INSIDE. Our schools, churches and neighborhoods must be kept as safe havens for learning, worship and lawful assembly. When they are corrupted by drug addicts who are forced to steal for their next fix, petty criminals with no respect for the law and "hippie" protesters who dance to every tune played back in Moscow, it is time for us to ACT. America will not fall like overripe fruit into the hands of communism if we are strong in the streets, strong in the schools, strong in the churches. I'm asking every one of you Society members to make an extra effort to inform your neighbors and your friends—those well-meaning men and women who are so susceptible to communist propaganda. Get them to your chapter meetings, show them some of the films that inspired you to join the Society, and most of all—GIVE THEM A COPY OF *THE BLUE BOOK.* Robert Welch's book is still the strongest weapon we have! Thank You!

• • •

Merci wondered how such a passage qualified Beck Rainer as a bad cop, aside from a little extra zeal.

The Los Angeles *Times* had printed several letters to the editor over the summer of 1969. They were complaints from citizens concerned about "squadrons" of "Nazi-like police motorcycles" parked on driveways in their neighborhoods, apparently during "Birch Society propaganda meetings."

A *Times* editorial warned of "vigilantism" and "misplaced patriotism" and said that "volunteer police departments are not the answer to crime and the perceived communist threat."

She followed Rainer's story in the papers: He accused Sheriff Bill Owen of "poor leadership" and "lax discipline" in a 1969 interview. He got himself on the ballot in the 1970 special election to elect a new sheriff after Owen's retirement in late 1969. But he failed to gain the support of Interim Sheriff Vance Putnam and couldn't sway the department rank and file, even though many Orange County conservatives stood behind him. He lost a narrow election to Chuck Brighton—Putnam's designated successor—in June of 1970. A disappointed Rainer vowed to run again. He was also one of sixty-five sworn deputies whose picture was supplied by Bill Owen for examination by Jesse Acuna. Merci scanned down the list, recognizing Rymers, Thornton and Pat McNally. Acuna had failed to identify any of them as the men in the white Mercedes, who had approached him that day with an offer for his property and a threat.

A small article printed in late 1978 profiled a successful private security company, Patriot Protective Services, run by ex-sheriff captain Beck Rainer. Rainer liked to employ law-enforcement and ex-law-enforcement officers in his company, "because they happen to know what they're doing." Merci looked at him in the picture: curly hair, a winning smile, hard eyes.

Colin Byrne had thoughtfully penciled in the current address and phone number for Patriot Protective.

Pat McNally was quoted often in the papers, and wrote often in the Birch Society newsletter. He was flamboyant and caustic. He called Supervisor Ralph Meeks a "lib with a checking account full of public money." He said Richard Nixon had "become a puppet of the communist conspiracy by sending American troops to die in Vietnam." He said, "Hanoi should be bombed level and if the Russians squeak, Moscow should be flattened next." McNally wrote a petition to allow members of volunteer police departments to carry firearms, running contrary to the opinions of Sheriff Bill Owen. Owen said he wouldn't endorse such a thing "no matter how many trigger-happy John Birchers signed it."

McNally wrote a long and passionate letter to the editor of the *Register*, saying that it was ludicrous for the Sheriff Department to supply personnel photographs of sworn deputies to a biased, angry and bitter old man who claimed, "without evidence and without reason, that he'd been baited and beaten by Mexican-hating cops."

McNally's last appearance in the file was a 1989 *Times* article looking back on the Jesse Acuna beating. McNally was a lieutenant by then, in administration. He said that the old passions of 1969 seemed "unwarranted" now, two decades later, and that "the world was just a different place back then. Cooler heads prevailed."

Cooler heads, thought Merci. Is that what they had? She turned to Byrne's index in the back and ran her finger down the list of players.

No KQ.

Jim O'Brien was listed, one page only.

Her heart sped up when she saw *Rayborn, Clark—pages 81, 88, 119.*

Her father was mentioned in the Birch Society Chapter 231 newsletter as a new member, recruited by O'Brien. The date was January 24, 1967. In a newsletter published six months later, Clark wrote an article about gun control, arguing that Hitler's first step in enslaving the Jews was to remove their right to keep and bear arms. "Big Government," he wrote, "would like to do the same to you. Without weapons, the citizen is helpless against the criminal as well as the political master."

The last reference to her father was from a community newspaper in Buena Park, where Clark made a commencement speech at the high school in 1970. The speech dealt with "our nation of laws" and called for the graduating seniors to "change our republic from within the law, not beyond it." The reporter said the address was stirring. Clark was booed and called a pig by some students.

Merci pictured her mild-mannered father up at the podium, trying to connect with three hundred teenagers who thought they had just become adults. It must have been hard for him to reveal his principles for people who just wanted to get out of the football stadium, get high and celebrate.

It wasn't until she got to the back of the Birch Society newsletters that Merci hit pay dirt. The May 1969 meeting of Chapter 231 was held in the home of Pat McNally, where American involvement in the United Nations was the topic of discussion. Among the member attendees listed were Clark Rayborn and Jim O'Brien. The speaker was Birch Society Section Leader Beck Rainer.

And among the eleven visiting guests was Patti Bailey.

• • •

Beck Rainer's Patriot Protective Services was headquartered in a quiet business park in the city of Orange. PPS had the third floor. There was a big reception room, some young guys filling out applications. A huge American flag was framed behind glass on one wall, along with some framed documents—Declaration of Independence, Preamble to the Constitution, Gettysburg Address, part of a speech by Teddy Roosevelt. And some big nature photographs with patriotic sayings under them—Grand Canyon, Half Dome, a stand of redwoods with sunlight spraying through.

Over the phone, Rainer had agreed to meet with Merci on short notice, and when she got there he was ready. He was a tall, slender man with big hands and arms a little too long for his sleeves. Corduroy pants, plaid shirt, an argyle pattern of wrinkles in the back of his neck. He stooped like a man used to stooping. He ambled down a quiet carpeted hallway and let Merci walk ahead of him into his office. No secretary, no receptionist. He had a bank of telephones on his desk and a big radio-dispatch console, like the ones they had at county.

"How's your dad?"

"Mom died about two years ago. He took it hard."

"Marcella was lovely. Too young for that."

"Fifty-six."

"My wife's healthy. I feel blessed."

There were framed posters of Porsches on the walls, and a few photographs of Rainer with Presidents Nixon, Ford, Reagan and Bush. A USC diploma. A John Birch Society award. More pictures: Rainer in uniform as a Trojan basketball player; Rainer in uniform as a sheriff's captain; Rainer with his wife and children; Rainer on horseback somewhere dark and green with pines a hundred feet high. Through a big window Merci could see that the rain had stopped. She looked out over the Orange County suburbs huddled beneath the gray sky, drenched and dripping, the colors rich and full.

"What kind of security do you do?"

"Every kind. Private residences—patrol, alarm systems, response. Some bodyguarding. Some industrial and plant work. The high-tech companies keep us busy. Lately, we've been getting a lot of the new guarded developments that are popping up all over. Everybody wants a guard gate and a courtesy patrol. We're up to three hundred employees."

"Still like to hire ex-cops?"

Rainer smiled, half pleasant, half carnivorous. "Sure, you interested?"

"Not yet."

"Some of it's interesting. The high-tech manufacturers have to be careful. Mostly employees ripping them off. The rest of it's pretty routine. That means we're doing our job, if it's routine."

Merci told him about drawing the Bailey unsolved, told him about the cassette recording and date book, about Bailey's evidence against Meeks on the Jesse Acuna beating, about Bailey's blackmail of Meeks and probably Owen, and who knew who else.

"Wow," he said flatly, "that takes me back. How'd you get the tape and date book?"

"I can't tell you."

He raised his eyebrows and nodded.

Merci continued. "And I can't figure out what Patti Bailey was doing at a JBS meeting three months before she was murdered."

"Now that's news to me. Which one?"

"May, sixty-nine. Pat McNally's house. You spoke about the United Nations. And Patti Bailey was a guest. I got that from the chapter newsletter. Chapter two thirty-one—the one with all the cops in it."

"Oh, I remember two thirty-one, all right. They'd meet and you'd have twenty black-and-white Harley Electra-Glides on the front lawn. Scared the daylights out of the neighbors, except the kids. They loved those big bikes. The teenagers thought we were pigs. But the kids still liked us."

Merci said nothing. She remembered—very dimly and dreamily—a suburban lawn filled with bright cop Harleys glistening in the evening sun. A JBS event? Probably. Her house? Pat McNally's? Who knew?

Rainer looked at her, gathering his thoughts. He sat upright now, the stoop gone, his eyes steady on her. "I'm surprised I don't remember meeting her. I got nervous before speeches, tended to block the world out while I got ready."

She searched for the chink in Rainer's calm armor, but she found none. No tic, no looking away or blinking, no brazen eye-lock. He looked like he was remembering.

"That's understandable. What I don't understand is what a hooker is doing at a Birch Society meeting to start with. That's a jarring combination if there ever was one."

"What's the old saying—politics and strange bedfellows?"

"There's no mention of murder in that saying."

"No. Or blackmail."

She waited for Rainer to take his nostalgia down a

notch, to come a little cleaner with her. She had the feeling she was being stroked. She hated being stroked.

"Let me try this, Mr. Rainer—I don't understand *how* Patti Bailey got there. She's in tight with Meeks and Owen. You right-wingers were banging hard on both those men. So, what's Bailey doing? Was she with the Birchers, keeping her eyes and ears open for Meeks and Owen? Or with Meeks and Owen, keeping her eyes open for you guys?"

Rainer sighed, then turned and looked out the window, then back at Merci. "Or with both, maybe? She was a prostitute, working for money."

"I know that. I was hoping you might be a little more specific, Mr. Rainer. I was hoping you'd skip the obvious generalities and tell me who the hell brought Patti Bailey to your speech that night. I'm working on a deadline here, and I'm about thirty-two years late."

He was nodding, like he knew her question in advance. "I don't know. I don't remember her. But I'll tell you that Pat McNally and Jim O'Brien were always good with the ladies. They were married guys, but they had reputations. Maybe neither one of them so much as laid eyes on her that night. Maybe she dressed decent and said she was a secretary worried about fluoride in the water. I don't know. But if there's a most likely candidate for who brought a hooker to a JBS meeting, it's one of them."

McNally or O'Brien, she thought. The happy conservatives, the family men, with a little stoned-out pleasure girl on the side.

Merci felt a little haunting go up her spine: father and son, Big Pat and Mike, both mixed up with prostitutes. And she'd been unsuspecting enough to waltz into Cancun Restaurant and ask Big Pat what he knew about the Bailey case.

Merci smiled and shook her head. Girl, she thought, sometimes the things you do surprise me.

But what if O'Brien and/or McNally had arranged for Patti to get to know the enemy—Meeks and Owen. Maybe got her to make a tape in case they said something interesting?

Flip it, she thought next: What if Owen aimed her at the bad boy Birchers of Chapter 231 to see what she could learn about *them*?

Or put both together, figure the common denominator is money, and you've got a hooker taking a little from both sides—like Rainer said. Any job that pays.

But someone put KQ onto her, KQ put two bullets through her body in an orange grove one evening and the whole circus came to an end.

Meeks and Owen quit.

O'Brien split for the desert and a better job. Twenty-five years later he killed himself. Were the seeds of his own destruction in him then? she wondered. Did they grow from what happened to Patti Bailey?

Pat McNally stayed where McNally was. Pat rose through the ranks, comfortably linked to Brighton. Who won? Who profited from Patti living, and who from her dying?

"I'm looking for a man with the initials KQ. Ring any bells?"

Rainer thought a minute. "No. Not many last names start with a Q."

Merci looked at the photographs of Rainer with all the Republican presidents since Kennedy.

"I read that your picture was one they gave to Jesse Acuna."

Rainer laughed. "In fact, it was. I was in *charge* of collecting those pictures."

"How did you choose which officers' pictures to give up and whose to not?"

"It was strictly volunteer," he said, smiling.

"Christ."

"The P.D.s all did it that way, too. There's no way the ACLU was going to bully us into giving up confidential personnel information. That's not the way it works."

"Goddamned commies, right?"

"Damn straight."

Merci looked out at the sky, the hills, the houses built on everything, the gas stations and boulevards, the schools and churches and stores. Cars, cars and more cars. Two point seven million people and growing, she thought.

Sometimes Orange County seemed like a little tank with a big school of fish in it, all hauling ass the same direction, nobody asking where they were going or why.

"How come you left the department? You were a captain. You were doing well for yourself."

"Brighton made my life miserable. He wasn't much on us right-wingers. He wanted to walk the middle of the road, please everybody he could to keep himself in office, be a moderate good guy. He thought the Society made the department look bad to the public, which was probably true. Our time had passed. By the time Nixon resigned, the conservative era was over. It was over for me, anyway. I figured I could get out from under his thumb, maybe run my own company. I'm glad I did. I make people feel safe. I keep the riffraff out of their neighborhoods. If somebody applies for work here and I think he's a bad apple, I don't hire him. We got good guys. I make a good living. I see the cops on the beat, or I see you, and I'm glad I'm not doing that anymore."

"How come? This looks boring."

"It is. But I'm alive and I don't have ulcers and I'm not drinking myself to sleep every night like a lot of the men I worked with. I'm not taking orders from some guy running his own popularity contest year after year. I can say what I think without getting transferred to Traffic. Brighton actually threatened me with that. I figured, if he wants to send me to Traffic because I thought Russian imperialists would like to eat this country alive, steal its wealth and drain its land like they drained their own, let him try. So I left the department. And I'm glad I did."

Rainer seemed to think about this, deciding whether or not he believed himself. "You look out that window, Sergeant Rayborn, what do you see?"

"Fish."

Rainer furrowed his brow, slowly nodded. "Not me. I see thousands of people sucking this country dry, people who can't even speak the language holding it up at gunpoint, drug-addled leeches living off the government, illiterate gang-bangers and pregnant twelve-year-olds breeding like rats, refugees from every failed third-rate democracy on earth feeding at the public trough. Everybody else is off at the malls or home watching TV. That's what I see, but everybody's got different eyes. I can respect that."

"Why don't you leave?"

"Thought about it a lot. But I hit my first baseball at a park two miles from here. I fell in love with my first girl at the high school around the corner. I buried my little brother here—he was killed by a sniper in Vietnam. So I intend to stick it out. It's mine as much as anybody's. I'm making a living. I'm one of the fish."

"You swim against the school, Mr. Rainer."

"You do, too. You're no-bullshit, on-target and generally pissed off about the world around you. It shows on your face. I admire that."

Rainer stood slowly and extended his hand. Merci stood and shook it.

"I hope you find out who killed that girl. Nobody's got a right to get away with that. You get tired of putting your life on the line every day for people who can't pronounce your name, come see me."

• • •

Sitting in her car in the PPS parking lot, Merci called the lab and asked for Evan O'Brien.

"I need to talk to you," she said.

"I need to talk to you," he answered.

"I'll pick you up in twenty. We'll pay respects to our dead."

"Why not Cancun, where all you gunslingers hang out?"

"I don't want them hearing what we talk about."

"Well, the dead don't blab."

Chapter Twenty-six

Sunlight slanted through the trees of Fairview Grove Memorial Park when they drove in. The headstones and earth were soaked dark, the pines glimmered with rainwater and sun, the grass was a brilliant, startling green. Merci thought it looked like a commercial. The graves of Hess and Jim O'Brien were both there, but far enough away you had to drive from one to the other.

Merci had run into Evan here one afternoon right after Hess was buried. Actually, Evan had recognized her Impala and had seen her standing by the grave. They'd visited here together only twice, Merci realizing after the first time that she preferred to be alone with Hess rather than sharing him with anybody.

Even a respectful co-mourner as Evan O'Brien—who to her surprise had checked his smart mouth at the entrance both times—was too much distraction when it came to Hess. She wanted to feel things about Hess, not explain him. And if what she felt was sad and disorganized and jagged with regret and longing, then so be it.

She figured O'Brien felt something comparable about his father. Or maybe he felt nothing like she did, but that wasn't the point. Remembrance wasn't tourism. Nobody listened in when you talked out here.

They stopped at Hess's place first. The headstone was simple black marble with white lettering, no chirping birds or sentimental quotes.

They stood for a long moment in the spongy grass. Then O'Brien broke the silence. "What's going on in my lab? Now it's off limits to anybody but Brighton and lab personnel. They took the sign-in sheet down. Gilliam's reassigning projects left and right, like he's shuffling the deck against a cheater. He's got us on a twenty-four standby but he won't say what we're standing by for. Must be something big, something that needs to be turned fast. Now, cut to the latest rumor: Mike McNally's been held in one of the interview rooms for the last six hours. I heard they brought him in this morning. I heard they haven't brought him out yet. Clay Brenkus has been seen. Guy Pitbull—his number one prosecutor—has been seen. High-dig defense attorney named Bob Rule has been seen. Brighton is shuffling around with a white face and Merci Rayborn is gone. There. Maybe you can fill in some gaps."

"They're questioning Mike for Aubrey Whittaker."

Evan shook his head and whistled quietly. "I knew it,

but I couldn't believe it. So, we're standing by for a warrant search."

Merci nodded.

"Shit," he whispered. "Mike."

"We tried something informal early this morning. Mike wouldn't budge without counsel."

"That makes him look bad."

"It's the right thing to do if he's guilty."

"Is he?"

"Hell, Evan, it sure looks that way."

Evan looked down at the grave. "What did you find?"

"Nothing."

"Somebody did. You've done an interview before a warrant search, you must know what's behind door number three. What did you find?"

"I can't tell you that now."

"Rumor is, they got a phone warrant about an hour ago."

"Then you'll see it before the end of the workday."

"If Gilliam lets me work in my own goddamned lab."

"That's his call."

Evan shook his head, toed the grass below him with his shoe. "I'd like to know what in hell Paul Zamorra found in Whittaker's place. Fingerprint cards, some fiber? It was hard to tell. If I got within twenty feet of him, he glared like I'd shot his dog."

"I'm not free to discuss that, Evan. I'm sorry. But I can tell you it looked like a struggle in Whittaker's kitchen. Remember? The drawers out, the runner bent up. Zamorra went after that angle. Trouble is, he came clean with Gilliam about what he'd found. That pissed Gilliam off. I don't know if it's even going to matter when they get done with Mike."

"It mattered enough to get the whole lab shut off. Hey, I don't mind that—less people in there the better. But when Gilliam starts watching *me* like I'm the next one to get thrown out, that worries me. If we missed something in the kitchen, then we missed something in the kitchen. Nobody's perfect, not even me. And poor Coiner, she's living on Tums and herbal tea. Now this rumor. She likes Mike. Thinks he walks on water. I guess you know that."

Merci looked at him, nodded. "Everybody likes Mike."

"I mean, nothing serious."

"Yeah."

"More like a schoolgirl crush," said Evan. "Hell, she's half his age."

Merci listened to the breeze shiver the big pines. Droplets burst off the boughs, diamonds in the sun.

"Evan did you try the iodine on the storage space envelope and stamp?"

"Gilliam took it over, personally. And he's not saying anything. Not to us anyway. I don't know what he's doing with it."

Merci felt the anger jet through her, like something hot shot into her veins. "Now I have to beg for help on a case unsolved for thirty-two years?"

"I'll find out what I can."

"I'll get Brighton to kick it out of him if I have to."

Evan looked at her and shook his head. He let out a sharp, dismissive little exhale. "Unless Brighton *ordered* him to take it over and keep a lid on it."

She looked at him and wondered. "Why?"

"How would I know?"

"Gilliam's tough enough to run his own lab without the sheriff standing over him."

"I agree. But if it's not about helping Gilliam steer clear of all you unscientific, gun-toting cowboys lurking around our sacred crime lab, then what *is* it about?"

Merci spoke before she thought. "It's about Bailey. Everything about Bailey stinks. An unsolved murder. An investigation that yielded less than it should have. And now, three decades later I've got some secret sonofabitch leading me straight to things Rymers and Thornton should have found. Now Brighton's square in the middle of it like some fat hen sitting on an egg."

"I don't think it's Bailey, or the evidence itself. I think it's Brighton making sure the crime lab stays under his fist."

"It was never under his fist."

"Gilliam would disagree," said Evan.

"Gilliam doesn't always see the big picture."

"Hmmm. I guess *I'd* disagree with that."

"Bailey," she said again.

Evan shrugged. "Thirty-two years is a long time. What I

heard was nobody cared about her then, so why should anybody care about her now?"

"That's what everybody says. Let's go over to your father's. Maybe he'll tell me what he remembers."

O'Brien smiled, something impish in his face. "Yeah. I'm sure Dad'll help you out all he can."

• • •

James and Margaret O'Brien's graves were under a big sycamore at the north end of the plots. The tree was naked now, but there were still some big brown leaves splayed out on the grass, big as dinner plates, pressed into the grass by the rain.

Evan reached down and swept a soggy leaf off the headstone. "I got the black granite, too, because the sun's not supposed to fade it as fast."

"That's what they say."

Merci read the inscription on the stone.

JAMES AND MARGARET O'BRIEN
DEATH CANNOT PART
ONE LOVE IN TWO HEARTS

"That's a good saying," Merci said.

"I made it up."

"Nice. What was it like back then, Evan? I mean, when you were growing up out in the desert?"

"I liked it. It was different. We had a swimming pool that collected scorpions all summer and stinkbugs all winter. Lots of land to roam around on. Room to run and think."

"What about your parents? Happy, pretty much?"

"Oh, *God*, no. Fights. Lots of fights. Mom going after Dad. Dad defending. Ever see two drunks fight?"

"No."

"Don't."

"Fights about what?"

He looked at her askance, then seemed to reach an agreement with himself. "Usually about the desert. How it was Dad's fault they were out there. She always said—yelled—that Dad got kicked out of a good job in a good place, then dragged her out to the desert, which she hated. The upshot was Dad was a coward for leaving. What he was afraid of, I don't know. Was she just busting his balls because she missed the beach? I don't know. Mom thought that if Dad had stood up for himself and been a real man, she wouldn't be stuck in that dustbucket town. She finally drank herself to death in seventy-six. Then Dad did what he did five years ago. The old house is mine now. That was part of his last will and testament. I figured I'd sell it, but I haven't. It's one of those things that remind me of them. How do you sell a house your parents killed themselves in? Doesn't seem altogether fitting."

Merci thought back to her conversations with Clark and

Thornton. "I thought Jim got a good job—pay raise, promotion."

"He did. He went straight to full sergeant. That wasn't good enough for her."

Merci heard the disdain in his voice.

Evan reached out and touched the stone again. "I took his side in most of those fights. I mean, just to myself. If I said anything, Mom would swat me around as hard as Dad, so I just kept quiet. I remember the first seizure I ever had. I was five, six years old. They were fighting and I had my hands up over my ears and I was screaming to myself. You know, screaming inside your head so nobody can hear you and you can't hear anybody? Mom and Dad were going at it out by the pool. Same old miserable argument about going back to a real life. Next thing I knew I was on my back looking up through a bunch of blood and they were kneeling over me. I thought one of them had hit me again. Turns out, I just spazzed and cut myself on the coffee table."

"That's a lot of pressure on a kid."

Evan shrugged. "Yeah, but you know, they loved me. I knew they loved me. They were kind of fucked up, all wrong for each other probably, but they loved me and I knew that. They really weren't such bad parents. I'm not repudiating them. I don't whine about that. They stood by me when it counted."

Merci thought about her next words, decided to let them out. "I'm told Jim had a reputation with the ladies."

Evan looked up at her, held her gaze, held it longer. His eyes got narrower and duller. "He was in the hospital room holding her hand when she died. I was holding the other one. He outlived her by almost twenty years and he never had a girlfriend or a date. Not one. Not one that I ever knew about. And I saw him a lot. We were close. We talked. Who said that about him?"

Not for the first time in her life Merci Rayborn wished she had just kept her mouth shut. Over the man's grave of all the goddamned places to open her stupid trap. She figured there was a special place in hell for people who never learned. Maybe she could run *that* department by the time she was fifty-eight.

"It doesn't matter, Evan."

"Yeah, well, it does to me. So tell your stoolie to go sit on a red-hot poker. And if he doesn't like that idea, tell him to come see me. I'll kick enough piss out of him to fill a bathtub."

"All right. I'll do that."

Evan stood and sighed. "Nobody sticks up for the dead. We got to do at least that much for them."

"At least."

She listened to the breeze in the trees again. Secrets in code, she thought, if you could just crack it you'd have the world boxed.

You got to put it all in a box and throw the box away.

Do you?

"Did your father ever talk about the Bailey case?" she asked.

He looked at her, a little surprised, then sighed quietly. "Not much. Dad didn't talk shop. Up to the day he died, he didn't talk shop."

"Was Patti Bailey part of those fights?"

"Somebody Bailey was mentioned. Yeah."

"Did he know her?"

"I can't remember. That whole story is vague, Merci. A long, *long* time ago. I mean, I've had a lot to think about since he did it. That was five years ago, almost. I think about him a lot, my mother a lot. I don't think for even one second about Patti Bailey. Know what I'm saying?"

She looked at him, studied the sharp Irish face that was so difficult to make serious. But it was serious now.

"Why did he do it, Evan?"

O'Brien raised his eyebrows and sighed. "Something ate him away. I don't know what it was. There was a big part of him I could never get to. I don't think anyone could."

This tracked with what Merci had learned about human beings through people like the Purse Snatcher: You could never know every part of one. Parts. Most of a person. But not all.

"I dream about him," he said. "All the time. In the dreams he's alive and healthy and we're doing things together. Things we never even did in real life. Fishing. Flying a plane. Playing catch with a baseball. I don't even like doing those things, but I dream about doing them with him."

• • •

She spent another half an hour back at Hess's grave, alone, standing in the damp turf with her coat collar pulled up against the cool breeze. Two years, three months, twenty-nine days. She thought of Hess and her heart ached; she thought of Mike and it ached in a different way; she thought of Aubrey Whittaker and Patti Bailey and it ached in still another. She felt like there were black vines growing inside her, trying to choke that heart once and for all. Her mother had always called it "your little wooden heart." No explanation. She thought of her mother, and then she thought of something her mother had told her once: When you're feeling blue, honey, do something nice for someone else.

It was one of the few things Marcella had ever told her that seemed to work. Merci had tried it.

Walking back toward her car she called Paul Zamorra on his cell phone. His voice was very quiet. She said she wanted to talk to him, face-to-face.

"Come on over," he said. "I'm at home, moving furniture."

He gave her the address.

• • •

Zamorra lived up in the Fullerton hills, above the suburbs, in a Spanish style home tucked back behind a long driveway. Merci parked and looked at the towering palm trees next to the garage, the courtyard with the fountain and benches around it, the big three-car garage with the doors swung open on Zamorra's work car, a late-model van and a bright red BMW convertible.

She opened the gate and walked into the courtyard: pots of flowers and plants placed artfully upon the pavers, the fountain trickling into itself, bromeliads latched to one wall and at least ten big bird-of-paradise plants in spectacular winter bloom. The bright orange-blue heads seemed to watch her as she went to the door.

Zamorra opened it before she knocked, let her in.

"Nice place," she said.

"Janine kept it up," he said. "Keeps it up."

Zamorra looked pale and hungry. He was shaven and dressed as usual—suit pants and white shirt—but the shirt was untucked and heavily marked with brown dirt.

"Did you come to tell me you've requested another partner?"

"Not really. I came to see if I could help. Do anything."

"Well, you can help me get this hospital bed set up."

Zamorra led her down an entryway, then past a living room with big windows that opened up to the backyard: pool, barbecue area, a lawn green as an emerald. To her left was the kitchen—about the size of Merci's whole house. What struck her was the silence. No music. No birds chirping. No traffic outside.

"This is quite a place, Paul."

"Janine's got money. In the family."

"It looks loved."

"We bought it cheap and remodeled. It was old enough to have asbestos in the ceilings so we had it torn out. I wondered if some of those slivers got into her brain somehow, started things growing. The doctor said probably not. I asked him what *did* start it growing, and he said bad luck."

"How is she?"

Zamorra didn't answer. He led Merci into a big suite at the far end of the house. The walls were white and the carpet was cream and the ceiling seemed twenty feet high. A sliding glass door opened outside to a trellised patio, a hot tub, and the swimming pool.

Merci saw the big mattress and box springs leaning against one of the walls. The stand with its rollers was propped up against them. Opposite, placed up next to a big wooden headboard, was a very narrow bed with metal railings and a heavy electrical cord running to the wall. There was a control pad with a cord, tied around one railing so it wouldn't slip down.

Zamorra pushed something on the control and the head of the bed began to rise. He stopped it and elevated the foot. Then he put them both back down. He watched the mattress move with a questioning intensity, and Merci wondered what he was seeing there.

"Great, isn't it?"

"It'll help her," said Merci.

"I figured I'd sleep in the big bed, since you can only solo in this contraption. I figured if she slept here, where she always slept, it would be good."

"Sure, make her feel like normal."

"Yeah, normal. Can you help me get the old stand over here?"

She balanced the big wobbly thing, followed him toward the glass door, then set it down. The box springs were easy, but the mattress weighed about a thousand pounds and didn't have any handles. She grunted it atop the springs and shoved it square with her knees.

Zamorra looked at the old bed with the same interrogatory expression he'd had for the new one.

"They cut her in half," he said. "The part of her that thinks and smiles still works."

Merci said nothing because what she imagined was not speakable.

She tried to take her mother's advice, tried to come up with something nice. Something helpful, fortifying, optimistic. For another of the few times in her life, Merci Rayborn could think of nothing to say.

"Look, Merci. I'm not going to dwell on this. I don't want your sympathy or your horror. I don't want you to even think about all this. It's our thing. We'll handle it. But you're my partner, and you need to know the score. That's the score."

"All right."

"I got the shrink's number. I'll call her when I'm ready

to call her. You did your part. The fact you gave it to me means something. Noted."

She nodded in agreement, a little pissed off that Zamorra could flatten her so easily with regard to Joan Cash's QPR counseling. But what was she supposed to do, argue with him while he rearranged the furniture for his dying wife? And when it came down to it, she behaved the same way when anyone mentioned EMDR to her. The difference was, she knew in her heart that she wasn't going to kill herself. But could she know the same about Zamorra?

"Merci, what in hell is going on with Mike McNally?"

• • •

They sat at a counter in the big kitchen. It was littered with unopened mail and newspapers. There was a bright red colander filled with oranges, and a blue one brimming with nuts still in their shells. The only thing that looked used was the coffee pot and a half-empty bottle of tequila over by the sink.

She told him about McNally—the boots with the blood, the letters and the silencer. She told him about the gun. She even implied how it was she managed to get that gun, fire it and replace it without him knowing. She told him every damned thing she could think of, even what the silencer was wrapped in, because she felt that since Paul had had to tell her his worst, she should tell him hers. It was a primitive and girlish feeling—like she'd had in the fifth grade with her best friend Melanie—but it had the same cathartic power now, maybe more.

"Mike's been at headquarters since this morning, getting the grill," she said. "I think, when it's over, they'll probably arrest him."

Zamorra listened without interrupting. Nothing about him looked surprised. "Gilliam matched the Whittaker shell and your shell to Mike's gun, one hundred percent, no doubt?"

She nodded.

"That still doesn't explain the kitchen. The struggle in the kitchen."

"No."

"I ran the prints I lifted from the kitchen—where the struggle took place. They're not on file. Remember the dustball I collected? I examined the fibers, but I don't know enough to say what they are. Some kind of clothing, I'd think. I'm going to get Gilliam to look at them for me. I don't get along with him, but he's the only one in that lab I trust anymore."

"Why not Coiner and O'Brien?"

Paul swept the counter in front of him with his palm. It looked like he was smoothing a sheet. His voice was quiet and flat, but she could hear his anger at the bottom of it.

"Coiner's sweet on Mike, okay? It's easy enough to notice. She lets him kick around that place like it's his sandbox. She's also the last one to see the handwriting sample—that friendship card—and three of the fingerprint cards that disappeared. O'Brien? He's got the little dog complex—we can't swear him as a deputy, so he overcompensates. He thinks he knows everything. He thinks he runs that place. But he gets into Aubrey Whittaker's kitchen where the signs of a struggle are clear as day, and what's he do? Nothing. No prints. No photographs in the original crime-scene reports. No mention of the bent runners, the drawers out. He's arrogant and sloppy, is what I'm saying. I'm not giving out my fingerprint cards to people who lose things, people who think they're too smart to learn. It's that simple."

She didn't say that she thought he was wrong. What bothered her more than Zamorra's distrust was what it said about Mike McNally.

"You don't think Mike did it."

"I think there's more to the story than who did it."

"Meaning what, Paul?"

Zamorra poured more coffee for each of them. "Two sets of footsteps on the stairs, according to the neighbor. Both of them within ten minutes of when she got shot. We can only account for one set, if it was Mike. A struggle in the kitchen, but who's there to struggle? Then, we get the evidence into the lab and it gets lost. Gilliam squawks to Brighton and together they throw everybody out. Everything we have points at Mike. But if Mike did it, a *cop* for Chrissakes, how come he left his prints everywhere and his brass in the flower vase? If you're going to cap somebody and get away with it, you don't sit down to dinner with them, leave, come back five minutes later and shoot them. That's the stupid way, that's the high-risk way. I'm not saying Mike didn't do it, but why would he do it like that? No, something's wrong. There's more than one guy involved, or more than one *person*, at least."

"Coiner? She found the brass, Paul. It's what led us to the gun, the gun to Mike."

"But she could still be trying to cover for him. Doing her job with one hand, undoing it with the other."

For a long moment neither spoke. Merci was trying to weigh the tonnage of Zamorra's implication—that she, Merci, was not only losing Mike to a prostitute, but that Mike had inspired Lynda Coiner to cover a murder. Mike McNally: killer, master manipulator. Merci Rayborn: idiot.

"This isn't about you," said Zamorra, apparently reading her mind.

It startled her. She stood and walked to the window, looked out at the rippling blue swimming pool, watched the palm fronds swaying high overhead against the fast white clouds.

"It's a flaw I've got, thinking everything on earth is about me."

"We've all got it. I feel worse for myself than I do for Janine sometimes."

She saw two black crows wheeling across the blue. When

the wind changed it caught them hard, their feathers flaring like someone had shot them. Even birds can't see a change in the wind, she thought.

She acknowledged for the first time just how damaging Mike's arrest was to her, to her plans and dreams, to her still-fragile psyche. On the inside she felt betrayed and belittled, like she didn't have a right to feel anything about anybody because she'd been so far off about a man she'd called her lover, like her heart was stupid and blind and unreliable.

From the outside, she just looked like a fool.

"I just realized how bad this arrest is for me," she said. "The fact that I believed in him, loved him, maybe. Trusted him, certainly. What terrible judgment. You can't trust a person like that very far. You can't have her running a detail or a section. Can you imagine someone with blind spots like mine, wanting to run the department someday?"

Zamorra looked at her. When he spoke next, it was with a gentleness she had rarely seen in him. "Think how bad you'll look if he's innocent."

"I haven't entertained that idea. I wouldn't have gone to Brighton with the evidence if I had. It went away when I found out Mike's gun fired the shell we found at Whittaker's."

Zamorra shook his head. "We'll never know *what* gun fired the bullet that killed her."

"That's cutting it pretty thin, Paul. Brass at the scene, fired from a gun carried exclusively by the accused. A silencer. Motive. Opportunity. Physical evidence a mile high. There's everything but a video. You think a jury's going to let him walk?"

"No. But I'm not talking about juries. I'm talking about who killed Aubrey Whittaker and who didn't."

"What are the options then? Mike's gun, but Mike didn't use it?"

"That's one. You borrowed it for an hour. Maybe someone else borrowed it for two hours. Or someone else shot her with a different weapon. Someone who was hoping the bullet would fly out the window, or was willing to dig it out of the plaster if it didn't. That would account for the ten minutes between the time our man knocked on the door and the time he left the apartment—he didn't find the hole in the glass right off. Or maybe this: Someone took the gun, just like you did, fired off a round in some private place, and took the empty with him."

"Then he put it in the flower vase in Aubrey Whittaker's apartment? Who?"

Zamorra was shaking his head but Merci couldn't tell if it was uncertainty or disgust. "Someone made a joke about that yesterday. I wasn't supposed to hear it. They said, maybe it was Merci Rayborn who killed the girl—she knew what Mike was up to with the whore."

She looked long and hard at Zamorra. "That's venom. Why would you pass it along?"

He didn't look away. "To let you know what you're up against. Because I'm on your side."

Merci answered her cell phone. It was Brighton.

"We arrested Mike half an hour ago," he said softly. "We'll have weapons charges, tampering, obstruction and murder. No announcement until tomorrow morning. Glandis and I will handle the press conference. You might want to be scarce around here. I'm giving the case to Wheeler and Teague. Work with them, Rayborn. We got the warrant, so I want you to help with the search."

Merci had trouble finding her voice. When she did, it was so weak she sounded like someone else. "I will."

"You did the right thing. And I know it was the hardest damned thing you've ever done in your life. Someday you'll be better off for this. Until then, *survive.* That's a direct order."

"Yes, sir."

When she hung up Zamorra was looking out the window. "We arrested him," he said.

"We did."

Chapter Twenty-seven

Merci waited until ten that night to go see Mike. She had to go through Brighton to get clearance into the protective block at the jail. He thought she was crazy, but she prevailed.

The jail was almost quiet that late, but she could see that security had been stepped up—two guards outside the protective block instead of the usual one. They let her through like she was a VIP, thanks to Brighton's call. Give them a day or two, she thought, until they find out how the case against Mike was made. Then see how hard the rank and file would land on her.

The suicide guard had his own chair and table set up in the hall. He was reading a paperback, chewing gum.

Mike was on his back on the cot, still in the street clothes she'd last seen him in, handcuffed, staring straight up. His head turned her way when she got to the bars.

There are thousands of expressions the human face can

register, but the one that Mike gave her now was unlike any she'd ever seen. Defeat and pride; alertness and resignation; fear and triumph. But most of all, disappointment.

"Mike."

He stared at her. "Hi."

"Hi."

She could hear the muted metallic shuffle of the jail around her, the slamming and clanging and the voices of men. It sounded like the soundtrack for hell, played from far away.

Mike lifted his feet, swung them off the cot and sat upright. No shoelaces. No belt. No tie. He held up his cuffed hands.

"I'd have to swallow my tongue."

"Don't."

"No. I'll need it to defend myself."

"Did you get Bob Rule?"

"He jumped at the chance. Innocent client. High profile. Or it will be, by noon tomorrow."

She looked at him, and she listened to his voice, and she understood his words, but she could think of nothing at all to say. She felt again like she was on the bullet train in a tunnel, everything just a blur of velocity.

He watched her, eyes heavy beneath the blond forelock, mouth frozen downward.

"I forbid you to ask me anything about Aubrey Whittaker, ever again."

"Agreed."

"You never agreed to anything before. I should go to jail more often. Why are you here? Just to gawk?"

"No. To . . . see you."

"It's curiosity, isn't it? You're looking for what you missed. For the one thing that would tell you I could do something like that. For the dead giveaway. You think, since you were so blind for so long, that now it must be visible."

"No. Just to see you."

"You've done that."

"And to see if there's . . . anything I can do to help you."

Mike smiled like a skull. *"Help me?"*

"Yes. There's Danny and Big Pat and—"

"Taken care of, woman. All taken care of. I am actually a man capable of taking care of my family. I even have dinner being delivered, because the slop they serve in here is so bad."

Merci felt a great flush of shame and sadness break over her face. She wanted to run and run and run some more, never come back, never have to look this man in the eye again.

"Okay. Then that's all, I guess."

He stood. She could see how red his hands were from the cuffs. He held them up beneath his chin to let the blood run down. He looked like he was praying.

"Wait. There is one thing you can do. Feed the dogs. I got everything covered for the next few days, but I forgot the dogs."

"I'd be . . . I mean, sure. I've got that. Long as you need it."

He looked at her. "Use your key. I'm sure you've got your warrant by now, so maybe you can combine it with your evidence search. Save yourself a trip."

"It's Wheeler's and Teague's now."

"No. This is ours, Merci. Yours and mine."

• • •

On her way through the parking lot Merci saw Lynda Coiner walking toward the jail entrance. She moved with purpose but not hurry, eyes straight ahead, her purse slung over her shoulder and a white paper bag in her hand.

• • •

Merci entered Mike's home in the blackness of Modjeska Canyon, just the glow of the porch light to guide her way.

Inside she smelled the familiar smells as she fumbled for the switch. The fire was out and the house was cold. She stood for a moment and pictured herself there with Tim, Jr., Mike and Danny, remembering clearly the happy gab of their little half-families rolled into one almost whole family and she inhaled deeply, dizzily, realizing how many things Mike had killed along with Aubrey Whittaker.

She got the kennel key from beneath a kitchen cabinet, where it hung on a hook beside the coffee mugs. Mike had kept the dog run locked since some neighborhood kids climbed the fence one day and let the dogs out to play.

Polly had wandered two miles down the canyon before someone found her and called.

Outside, the bloodhounds started yelping, and Merci swore there was something mournful in their voices but she knew she was eager for self-punishment and if it took personifying three dogs to beat herself even lower she would leap at the chance to do it.

"Hi, doggies," she said quietly. "Hi. Mike couldn't make it tonight so I'm going to be your server. My name is Merci."

She opened the gate to the run, then let Dolly, Molly and Polly out of their cages. Dolly and Molly shared a kennel space, but Polly, a true bitch, had to have her own. They grunted and knocked up against Merci's legs, looking up at her with what she believed were lugubrious expressions. She knelt and pet them, scratched behind their ears, ran her hand along their soft shiny coats.

She collected their bowls. The dogs—Mike always called them The Girls—followed her to the food bin, where she used an old dog food can to which Mike had soldered a handle to measure out the kibbles. She gave them each a little extra.

When she had lured them back into their cages with the full bowls, she closed the doors and swung the gate shut behind her. She locked it and took the key back inside. The whole time she felt this thick wet lump in the bottom of her throat, just waiting to burst out.

The great betrayer, she thought: Rayborn the treacherous, Rayborn the false, Rayborn and her thirty pieces of silver. Where, exactly, was that silver? It would not be found in the faces of the people she worked with. It wouldn't line her pocketbook, her smile or her soul. It's nowhere, she thought, because I didn't do it for money, I did it because it was right. *Right.* She was beginning to hate that word.

A few minutes later she was driving back down the dark canyon, her right hand dangling into the space behind the seat. The treetops were capped in silver light, branches bare and still. The stars were bright and there wasn't a cloud. The man in the moon looked down at her like she should be hung for treason, and she agreed, almost wholeheartedly.

She swung her arm back to the wheel and commanded herself to get her shit together. It was harder now to master her will, to make herself believe the things she wanted to believe, to force that will upon the world. It used to be easy, but she was younger then and more foolish.

She opened a window and felt the cold wind on her face. She held the steering wheel with one hand at twelve o'clock and punched the big V-8 up to eighty when she hit the interstate.

• • •

Clark was watching TV when she got home. He looked at her cautiously as she walked into the living room with a rather large Scotch on ice and sat down.

Earlier that evening, when she'd told her father about

Mike's arrest, Clark's face had gone pale. He'd quickly agreed to miss his poker night appearance to watch Tim, Jr., though they both acknowledged—without comment—how hard it would be for Clark to sit down at a card table with Big Pat.

Now, hours later, at least he had his color back.

"Jesus," she said quietly. She leaned forward, sipped the powerful drink, let some time pass. "I worked that case, Dad? You know, did all the usual things? Went by the book. Did what I do. And it led me straight to Mike. And no matter how hard I tried to bend things, see over the tops of them, it kept coming up Mike. I did something I shouldn't have done—I went to his place, used my key and did a search. I found threatening letters the girl had written him. I found bloody boots in his closet with the same sole print as her killer wore. I found a noise suppressor to fit a forty-five. I even fired some brass from his gun to compare against the crime-scene brass: match. I was looking for something that would point me away, tell me I was off. But I just . . . buried him."

"Mike buried Mike."

She drank again, sat back. "So now, we make our case and Mike makes his. We got the search warrant late today, so the judge covered my . . . overzealous police work. Nobody will have to know what a duplicitous bitch I am, if they don't already."

"Merci, your investigation led to an arrest. And who was being duplicitous?"

"Yeah, I know."

"Then don't forget it. This isn't the time for you to be pounding yourself down again, girl. This is the time for you to hold your head high and take your shots. You are going to take them. But you did what was right and you did what was hard. You could have hidden behind that badge and no one would have ever known the truth."

She nodded. Clark's words seemed to skip off her skin, like she was made of some ceramic that nothing could pierce.

"You know what I keep picturing? Me. Me, walking into work on the day when everybody's realized that I was the one who busted Mike McNally. I can't do it, Dad. I can't walk down that hall to the detective pen with everybody in the department hating my guts. How am I going to do my job anymore? How am I going to get to do the things I wanted to do?"

"You're going to find a way. That's what people do."

She looked at him steadily, understanding that his unconditional love was just like what she felt for Tim. It was a beautiful thing, maybe the most beautiful thing she'd witnessed on earth, but it could make fools of people and it often did.

"I'll find a way," she said quietly.

"I know you will."

"Listen to me, whining about me. The me expert. You know what I wish? I wish I could wrap up in a ball under the covers and could molt like a larvae, or a pupae, or whatever in hell those worms turn into. Then hatch out into an *angel*. An angel, but an angel with an H&K nine. And I could fly around catching the creeps and everything I did would be perfect. And I wouldn't have to walk into headquarters and look at two thousand sheriff's employees who think I betrayed them, who'd like to have my heart on a platter."

She wondered what Joan Cash would make of her little speech.

Clark chuckled. "An angel with a gun. No. You'd miss your son too much. And I'd miss *you*. I never wanted an angel, just a daughter."

"Yeah, well, you got one."

She stood, legs heavy, head aching, her heart beating slow and hard like it was doing so against its will.

Halfway across the room she stopped and looked back at her father. "You want to know what I kept thinking when I was finding that stuff in Mike's place? I kept thinking that there was still one good thing that could come of it."

"What?"

"I wouldn't have to marry him."

She couldn't read the expression on Clark's face. He stood, walked over and put his arms around her. He was a lean man, but tall, and even now his arms were strong.

She felt the tears burning her eyes but she didn't cry. She heard herself speak, tear-choked and snot-clogged, a voice she hated because it sounded weak and dependent and useless. "I wish I could stop the things that come into my head."

"They'll go away."

"Take me out and shoot me."

"Take you to bed. Come on, girl. It's been way too long a day."

• • •

She checked on Tim, made sure his cap was on, got the blankets up nice and snug. He was the most perfect living thing she had ever seen.

Then she went into her room and sat up in bed with the lights on, thinking. She could hear the creaks of the old house and the breeze outside. Twice, her father's phone rang, and twice she heard the almost imperceptible murmur of his voice. It was close to midnight.

She told herself that she had done the right thing. She wondered why the right thing had to feel so wrong. Then she slowly allowed herself to admit that her fall from grace within the department was going to be acceptable. She gathered this idea just one little bit at a time, like sweeping table crumbs into a palm, careful not to get too much all at once.

It doesn't matter, she thought, that you won't be running Homicide Detail by forty, or Crimes Against Persons by fifty, or be a viable candidate for sheriff by age fifty-eight—those were the dreams of a different woman. Maybe it would be better this way.

Maybe along with the disrespect she would get from the rank and file would come a little bit of freedom, too. Freedom for Tim, for herself, for whatever passions she might find outside of work. Her self-pity crept in, and she wondered why a big, strong woman like herself, so innately wired for the task of law-enforcement, had to fall victim to circumstance. Was it just bad luck? Would good luck follow?

Passions I might find outside of work.

She thought about that and admitted she had none, except Tim. She had no hobbies, no interests, no sports she played or art she loved; she had no real desire to travel, learn a new language or engage a culture other than her own. She watched movies for diversion, TV as a sedative, read books exclusively for facts, went to the big art shows up in L.A. because someone else always got the tickets.

She shook her head and smiled unhappily. Wasn't she just exactly like Hess in this way? Wasn't his single-mindedness and devotion to work what had first attracted her to him? She realized it was. And she also realized that, even back then, when she looked at the old warrior Hess she was looking at herself.

Admiring the great lonely hero she wanted to become. That was part of why she had loved him.

When she took the idea of work-as-life one step further,

Merci had to admit that there was something else about it that stole her heart: Work was something she could do alone. Sure, she would always have a partner. Sure, she would always be part of a team and a bureaucracy. But the essence of the work was individual effort, you against them. You against the whole world. You devised the broad strategies, made the mundane procedural calls as well as the split-second decisions that could—and often did—save a life or end one. It was impressive, really, the power that the world gave you when it issued you a badge and gun. It was all up to you.

As she sat there, Merci pictured herself sitting there: a dark-haired woman with a mirthless face and a half-empty glass of Scotch in her hand. Alone. This was always how she saw herself. Never connected to a department, a husband, a partner, a son, a father, a family. Just alone.

What exactly is it, she wondered, that makes you so special, so singled-out, so solitary and self-sustaining?

Nothing, she thought. Nothing at all.

After she had shot and killed the murderer Colesceau, Merci had felt her willpower depart. It had actually gone out of her, like breath. She had never told anyone. It was gone for several months, though she disguised the loss as best she could.

It came back slowly, piece by piece, and it was arranged differently than before. It was stiffer now. It was brittle and less tensile. It was afraid of new things. It was familiar but foreign, too, like a friend's face changed by surgery, like a twin you haven't seen for fifty years.

And Merci had understood since that day with Colesceau that you are not only what you make of yourself but what the world makes of you.

This world, the one you see around you right now. If there was an idea more humbling and frightening she had yet to think it.

Chapter Twenty-eight

Merci stood with Paul Zamorra in the back of the conference room while Sheriff Chuck Brighton, County of Orange, told the press and media that one of his own vice sergeants had been arrested for the murder of a prostitute.

Detectives Wheeler and Teague—one thin and one bulky—sat at a table behind the podium, trying to look bored.

Assistant Sheriff Melvin Glandis, taut with uniform, took over from Brighton to explain the investigation and field questions.

"Thank you," he said, stepping to the podium, though nobody had offered him one thing to be thankful for. Brighton stood aside but not back. Glandis nodded slightly, a man comfortable taking orders, his mouth set and grim.

Merci watched the camera lights blanch their faces, saw that every pit and wrinkle was highlighted by them, saw the sheen of sweat at Glandis's brow when he finished his brief summary of the investigation. Glandis sighed when a reporter asked how and when Sergeant Mike McNally became a suspect in the case.

"I'm not at liberty to discuss that at this time," Glandis said. "Next? Susanne?"

"Was Sergeant McNally involved with the woman?"

Glandis shook his head. "Sergeant McNally was part of a Vice Detail operation to curb outcall prostitution in the county."

"Then he knew Ms. Whittaker?"

"They had worked together on a limited basis, yes."

"Was there a personal relationship?"

"I'm not at liberty to discuss that at this time. Next? Dan?"

"Where is Sergeant McNally right now?"

"In the protective block at the county jail."

"Have you recovered the murder weapon, and if so, can you describe it?"

"We impounded a forty-five caliber Colt automatic belonging to Sergeant McNally. It is in our crime lab as we speak, undergoing a battery of firearms, toolmark and ballistic analyses. Next? Brice?"

"Did you find the silencer?"

"We have a warrant to search for such a device."

"McNally's property, or somewhere else?"

"I'm not at liberty to—"

"How's it look for special circumstances and a death penalty?"

Merci cringed at Brice's tone of voice, making light of

the idea of executing Mike McNally. She saw Glandis redden, too.

"What do you mean?" asked Glandis. "*How's it look?* This isn't a circus here, Brice, this is a man's life. And a woman's."

"The woman's life is over. So, special circumstances or not?"

"That isn't our decision. We made an arrest based on evidence. You can talk to the district attorney about that. Next? Bowman?"

"Mel, did he act alone?"

"We believe so."

"What was his motive?"

"We don't know yet. We're looking at a couple of possibilities."

"Do you have a witness?"

"I'm not at liberty . . ."

Merci saw Gary Brice turn in his seat and look back at her. He peered at her over the tops of his glasses, a gaze of pointed questioning of the fact that she and Zamorra weren't up there at the table instead of Wheeler and Teague. She shook her head slightly, looking away.

Brice was the only reporter who knew about her off-duty relationship with Mike—so far as she knew. Did reporters gossip like cops? Maybe not. Given the bigness of this breaking story, none of them had thought to ask why one team of detectives had started the investigation and another had taken it over. Gary Brice, she knew, was waiting to ask her in private.

Zamorra whispered in her ear, reading her mind again like it was easy, "Tell him it's none of his goddamned business. Or I will."

"I can do that," she murmured back.

"Meet me in the conference room when you get done with him. I've got something."

She nodded and headed out.

• • •

Brice caught up with her in the hall and Merci took him outside. She put on her sunglasses against the perfect afterstorm sunshine, walking fast with Brice beside her.

"I could have used a heads-up on this one," he said.

"We arrested him last night, Gary. Late."

"What gives—first it's your case and now it's not."

"Mike and I are friends, you know that. It's just a matter of common sense and procedure."

"Conflict of interest."

"You could call it that."

"So, how do I describe your relationship with Mike, in my paper?"

"Good friends, if you have to at all. The meat of this story isn't Mike and me. It's Mike."

"The meat of this story is how you caught him. Help me out here, Merci."

"I'm under a gag, Gary. As the case progresses, I'll be able to give you more."

"You haven't given me a damn thing. Come on, Sergeant—put yourself in my position. I've got a story. A sheriff's deputy arrested for the murder of a prostitute he was working with. I've got sheriff investigators—one of them the suspect's . . . friend—finding him out. *How?* What was your first break? How'd you even start *looking* at one of your own?"

She thought before she spoke. "The crime-scene evidence led us to suspect him. Interviews confirmed the suspicion. A search warrant turned up crucial evidence. There. Want me to write it for you?"

"What crime-scene evidence?"

"I can't be specific, Gary. We're trying to build a case right now. I don't want to hang him in the *Journal.* We want a fair trial."

"He was banging her, and she was going to blackmail him, right?"

She felt the anger jump into her face, fought the instinct to clutch the reporter's throat with both her hands and pinch his head off.

"I can't comment on that."

"I think you already have."

"What in the hell do you mean?"

"I thought you were tipping me that way."

Merci stopped and looked at him. "I just told you I can't comment on that."

"Well, can you explain this?"

Gary Brice reached into his coat pocket and pulled out a stapled collection of papers. He stepped forward, to her side, holding them firmly in both hands but out in front of her, so she could see them. He flipped slowly through the collection. There were eight pages in all. Each was a photocopy of a greeting card or letter—the ones between Mike and Aubrey Whittaker. Merci recognized some of them from Whittaker's apartment, others from Mike's home in Modjeska. One was the card that went missing from the lab almost one week ago. Reflexively, she reached out for them, but Brice snapped them away and folded them back into his pocket.

"Don't mess with my living," he said.

"When?" she asked quietly. "How?"

"U.S. mail, yesterday afternoon. They made about half sense then. Full sense now."

"Do you still have the—"

"Yeah, it's a standard legal size, no return address, a regular stamp. The handwriting is childish or wrong-handed. It came to my home. I've got it for you in the car if you want it. It's in a plastic bag that locks. D.C. stands for Dark Cloud—that's Mike. Aubrey or AW are self-explanatory. Right?"

Merci nodded but said nothing. She turned and started off around the parking lot, Brice beside her. The morning air was cool and she jammed her hands into her windbreaker. She tried to make her voice as convincing as possible, but even Merci could hear the emptiness of her promise.

"Gary, you sit on those for one week, and I'll make sure you get something better."

"There *is* nothing better. What I've gotten from you so far is the honor of sitting in a press conference with every other reporter in the county, watching Mel Glandis sweat peanut butter. Thanks. That was a real help."

She shook her head, stopped and turned. "I can impound those letters as evidence."

"I already copied them. I got copies of the copies. Come on."

She studied him, wished she had a fire hose to blow him out into the street. "All right. You've got the letters. You've got the front-page story for two weeks. And I'm going to ask you not to write it."

"Why?"

"Because you're obstructing justice. You're trying a man in the press. It's wrong and you shouldn't do it."

Brice laughed quickly. "It's my *job*."

"This is more important than your job."

"Wrong. This is what I have: Mike McNally, good cop, a single man, tries to help prostitute, prostitute does what prostitutes do—she tries to make a profit on it. Suggests blackmail. We can now factor in Merci Rayborn, a lady cop who was the staunch friend and lover of Mike. She heads the investigation for a while, then gets called off it when the arrows start pointing to her guy. That's a damned good story, and you know what? It's the *truth.* So don't tell me I'm a bottom feeder for wanting to tell the truth. There are people out there in this world—known as citizens—who've got a right to know. I happen to believe in that right. I happen to believe it's part of what makes this country great. I'm writing the story. I'm using file photos of you and Mike and Aubrey Whittaker. I just need two things from you."

She said nothing. Brice backed up a step. "One—tell me the whole thing, start to finish, in your own words. I'll use them and I won't change them. You can help me edit the copy to protect Mike, protect your case against him, whatever you want. I've never made an offer to let anybody edit my copy before, just to let you know."

"I won't do that and I never will."

"I understand. Two—how do you feel right now?"

"Oh, for Chrissakes, you're down to that level?"

"Believe it or not, it matters. *How does this make you feel?*"

"On the record or off?"

"Gimme both."

"On the record, Gary, it saddened me to see him arrested. Off the record—it broke my fucking heart."

He looked at her a little strangely then, like he was seeing some part of her for the first time. "How do you spell that modifier?"

She turned and started back. Brice caught up and walked along beside her, not speaking.

"Gary? I'll make you one last offer. You kill that story and I'll give you something better."

"What's better than this?"

"The truth."

"What's not true here? Name me one thing I've said that isn't the truth? *One thing!*"

She bit her lip and walked. She had no answer for that, other than the obvious.

"You're being used."

"But I'm enjoying it quite a bit."

"Something bad is going to come."

"Oh, and don't tell me—you don't want to see me get hurt."

"It's not that. I wish you were in a guillotine right now. I'd drop the blade."

"I might have to work that into my story."

"I tried, Gary. I tried to get through to you."

"Hey, don't give up on me. You've got my numbers."

At the steps to the Sheriff's Building entrance Merci could see a group of reporters around Mike's defense attorney, Bob Rule. He looked at her, then back to his group.

She broke in off the other direction, following Gary Brice to his car. The handwriting on Brice's envelope looked to her just like the writing on the envelope with the key inside. She guessed there'd be no prints.

One source, she thought: leading me to Bailey, and using the press to punish Mike.

• • •

Crisis mode in the Sheriff's Building. Merci could feel it when she walked in: grim looks, all business, and a tightness in the air that seemed to amplify sound while everybody tried to be quietly efficient. Brighton's door was closed. Glandis was locked to a telephone, sweat rings advanced from armpit to chest. The captains conferred around the desk of the undersheriff and the uniforms all seemed to have their chests out.

She found Zamorra in the conference room alone, slouched in a chair at the big table, a cup of coffee steaming in front of him. She shut the door behind her and sat across from him.

"Someone leaked to Brice at the *Journal,*" she said. "I think it's the same party who sent me the Bailey key. Brice now has copies of Mike's letters to Whittaker. Of Whittaker's letters back. He's going to run with the three-way romance gone bad—Mike, her and me."

"Get Brighton to call his publisher."

"I'll try. But it won't work. This is meat and potatoes for the *Journal.* It's a great goddamned story."

"Can you lean back? What do you have on Brice?"

"Nothing."

She sighed, then spoke very quietly. "Look, Paul. We're off the Whittaker case, right?"

"Right."

"But we've got some loose threads, right?"

Zamorra smiled just a little. "Loose threads are exactly what we have."

"So we can tie them up, our way of helping Wheeler and Teague, right? Our responsibility?"

"Absolutely."

"Okay. Good. Then what did you get?"

"Some kind of coat, maybe a heavy shirt, on the floor of Aubrey Whittaker's kitchen. Man's or woman's, they can't say. But they can say its got dark gray, purple and sea-green fibers in it. In the struggle, the garment got caught on the corner of the drawer. I pulled eight strands out of the wood. Found two more on the floor."

"Who's they?"

"Friends on the San Diego P.D. I ran the fibers down there Tuesday, got the call last night. I documented it all, everything. So the chain of evidence is tight."

Merci wondered how Zamorra had time for a three-hour drive to San Diego and back when he didn't have time for anything else. She banished that thought as suspicious and mean-spirited.

"Then I went through the Whittaker evidence list again—nothing like that in her wardrobe. I double-checked the dry cleaning you picked up—nothing there, either.

Now, how about Mike? Does he have a coat or shirt like that—gray background, with purple and green accents?"

She got out her blue notebook and made a note of her partner's findings. "No. Mike doesn't have anything like that. Not that I know of."

"I also sent down human hair—two samples I got from the kitchen floor. Dark and wavy. One is an inch long, the other an inch and a half. Whittaker's hair was blond. So is Mike's. I think our kitchen man left it when he fought, left his prints on the drawer runner and the floor, snagged his jacket or shirt."

"Moladan's got dark hair."

"No. CAL-ID's got him, but there was no hit on the prints."

"Lance Spartas?"

"I got him to volunteer a full set, right and left. No."

"Del Viggio?"

"His alibi washed with Molodan's girl, Cindy. It wasn't him. Okay, we know this guy was in her apartment that night. We know he's not a crook with a sheet because AFIS and CAL-ID would have them."

Merci spoke before she thought it through, and the words sounded strange when they came out. "What about a woman? Women wear sport coats. They leave fingerprints."

Zamorra looked across at her. "Coiner?"

"She paid Mike a visit in jail late last night. She brought him food. I'm just fishing now, Paul. It sounds wrong."

Zamorra went silent again. Then, "We know she likes him. Maybe we don't know how much. Or what she was getting back. Or not getting. But if you take it that way, you have to figure maybe they weren't struggling on the floor. Maybe they were getting it on ten feet from a fresh corpse. You factor in Coiner and you've got special circumstances. That's lying in wait and conspiracy. That's the death penalty."

Merci stood and walked once around the room. She could feel the strong, dark currents moving around inside.

"They . . . that wouldn't bend the drawer runners."

He said nothing, implying that maybe it would.

"Why would she give up the brass, Paul? Why not overlook it?"

"Because *someone* was going to find it. This way, it would take suspicion off of her."

"And put it on Mike."

Zamorra looked down at the table, then back to Merci. "Insurance, in case you and Mike came through all this intact."

"Did you include females in the CAL-ID search?"

"No. But I can do it that way, easy enough."

"Go ahead. It still doesn't make sense to me, Paul. The prints won't come up as Lynda's. And her hair is light brown."

Zamorra shrugged. "He wasn't alone in that apartment. Someone else was there. They did something in the kitchen. Mike knows. He wasn't alone. I'd bet my life on it."

• • •

Merci walked Gary Brice's envelope down to the lab just before ten that morning. A deputy she'd never seen before stopped her at the front desk, asked her to sign in and state reason for visit. She waited ten minutes for Gilliam to come out and get her. He closed his office door behind them and they sat.

"Sorry," he said. "We've got a full lockdown while we examine the evidence from Mike's place."

"What did they take in the search?"

"A homemade sound suppressor, one pair of chukka boots, his forty-five Colt and seven rounds of ammunition. Also some correspondence—cards and letters."

"I need to see them, the letters."

Gilliam frowned. "You're off the case, Merci. Why see the letters now?"

She told him what Gary Brice had received in the U.S. mail yesterday afternoon. She set the plastic bag with the legal-sized envelope in it on Gilliam's desk.

"If you've got the originals in evidence, I'll know they weren't just taken from Mike's place and copied to be sent to Brice. I'll know they were taken from Mike's place, copied and *returned* for us to find. Wheeler and Teague might want to know that."

Gilliam looked at her with something close to disbelief.

"James, Gary Brice is going to write his story. It's going

to be about a vice cop, a homicide investigator and a prostitute. I'd like to know who set us up for that."

"The originals are in the fuming chamber right now. Here, I'll take that."

Gilliam snagged the plastic bag a little impatiently, Merci thought. The pressure is making fools of us all, she thought.

• • •

Ten minutes later Merci knew what she wanted to know: Four of the cards and one of the letters collected from Mike's had been photocopied earlier, mailed to Brice, then returned to Mike's Modjeska Canyon home.

And there wasn't a trace of a fingerprint on any of them. Yet.

"Give it time," said Gilliam. "Six more hours, minimum. I'll set up the envelope to Brice right now."

Lynda Coiner, bent over a microscope, looked aside at Merci, then back to her instrument.

Evan O'Brien, scientifically clad in a white lab coat, stood beneath a bright overhead examination light, looking down at a small bundle wrapped in what Merci recognized as her own underwear.

He looked at her, then at the underwear, then back at her again. No expression. He shrugged.

One of the younger technicians walked past with a tray of vials filled with blood. He looked at Merci with controlled alarm, like she was a leper.

"Let us get on with our work," said Gilliam, taking her arm.

"Do I get to know the results on the storage payment envelope and stamp? The one I brought in with the gun? This is *Bailey* I'm talking about now, not Whittaker."

"Negative," he said. "No latents. Now, I imagine you want to get on your way to Aubrey Whittaker's apartment pretty quick. For Wheeler and Teague, of course."

He escorted her to the door. "Tell Zamorra we've got better facilities than San Diego P.D.," he said. "Tell Zamorra we're on his side here. We'd like to know whose side *he's* on."

"I'll tell him."

• • •

Merci stepped into the cold, bright apartment. Through the windows she could see the Pacific, brown with runoff. Her eyes went to the dark chalk outline on the carpet, Aubrey Whittaker's final silhouette.

Everything looked the same. She stepped around the chalk and went down the hall to the bedroom. Nothing looked disturbed. In the dresser she found the collection of notes and letters, recognizing two from the copies sent to Gary Brice—stolen from a sealed crime scene, copied, returned.

She stood on the front porch for a long moment, picturing what had happened for what seemed like the thousandth time. She wondered if Hess would have been proud of her. Then she excused herself from Hess and closed her eyes and tried to see what had happened that night, just over a week ago, Tuesday, December the eleventh.

She pictured Mike coming up the stairs. He's dressed in trousers and a sport coat and his black sweater, the one that shows his muscles and contrasts with his golden hair. He's purposeful but unhurried. His hands are empty but his coat is open. The forty-five is tucked into his left armpit, because the silencer makes it too long to fit in the holster. He stands in front of the door and wipes his right hand through his hair before he knocks. It's a quiet knock. The yellow porch light is on. Aubrey comes to the door, looks out. She sees it's Mike, wonders if he's left something. She opens the door. She smiles—half a greeting, half a question. Mike reaches under his coat and draws the gun, fires once and pushes her back into the room as she falls. She's dead before she hits. He walks around her, gets her under the arms and drags her a few feet further in—so he can shut the door. He shuts it. The look on his face is one of wild fear.

After that Merci saw nothing.

• • •

She opened her eyes, surprised to see Wheeler and Teague starting up the stairs, followed by Chuck Brighton.

Wheeler, the thin one, got there first. Teague lumbered up behind him, followed by Brighton, whose eyes were hidden behind dark aviator shades.

"Orange County Sheriff," said Wheeler.

"Prove it," said Merci.

Wheeler badged her with a sly grin and walked past her into the apartment.

Teague said hello and told her he wanted to talk later.

"Any time."

Then Brighton, who stopped and looked at her. She saw sky and clouds where his eyes should be. "Thought I'd see this for myself."

"Someone's been in here, messing with evidence. It's the second time this week, if I've got it figured right."

Brighton peeled off the glasses. He looked a hundred years old. "Gilliam showed me the letters. The ones to Gary Brice."

"They came from here—bedroom dresser, top right drawer. Whoever took them brought them back here for us to seize."

"Rayborn, what in the hell is going on?"

"Maybe Wheeler and Teague can find out. I've got some ideas, but they're not good ideas."

"No mas on this, Merci. No more involvement from you. When Bob Rule finds out about you and Mike—"

"I understand."

"So keep it clean. We've got a case to make."

"Yes, sir."

Brighton nodded. "Unbelievable zoo back at headquarters. You stay away from it if you can. Nobody's asking about you and Mike, for what that's worth. So far."

"They will, when Brice's article hits the paper."

"You and Zamorra take the murdered jogger and the chopped-up boy. Those will keep you busy."

Inwardly, Merci cringed at the words "chopped-up boy." She thought of a couple of things she'd like to say, but she didn't.

"I need deputy time cards for the Bailey case," she said.

"Time cards from thirty years ago? We wrote them by hand. I don't know if we keep them that far back."

"We do. They're in the records building, but you need to clear it."

He put the glasses back on, looked out toward Coast Highway, then back to her. "You still think we were the bad guys. Even back then."

"I'm just ruling us out."

"That's a weak argument. But from you, I'll accept it. Talk to Mel. He can authorize."

She took the cell phone from her belt, punched in the number and held it out to Brighton. "It's Records. Would you mind? They won't hustle it for Glandis or me."

Brighton looked at her from behind the dark glasses, then took the phone.

Chapter Twenty-nine

Merci saw the news crews and uplink vans set up outside the headquarters entrance, so she put her head down and accelerated. She was already halfway through them by the time they realized who she was. She brushed away the mikes and answered everything with the same three words: No damned comment. She lost them in the lobby, where a uniformed deputy clicked her through the personnel door and that was that.

The detective pen was almost empty now, midday, the dicks either in the field or out to lunch. The thought occurred to her that with one of their own arrested for murder, now was a good time not to be seen. And everybody was dying to talk to everybody else. Cancun would be a beehive of gossip right now, she thought.

The box of time cards was on her desk. It smelled of old paper and the corners were crumpled. She signed the Records Section slip on top and set the slip in her routing box.

She lugged the box into the empty conference room, then went back for the Bailey file and a fresh cup of coffee. A lieutenant passed her in the hallway. He raised his eyebrows and shrugged, but he said nothing.

Standing over the interview room table, Merci lifted out the time cards. They were organized by week. The assignment rosters were collected for each month, then stapled and put in manila folders.

To the left of the cards she set Patti Bailey's date book, opened to the last day of her life, August 4, 1969.

4SV/6CM/7DL/8:30FD/11KQ

One thing, she thought. Give me just one thing: the owner of the initials KQ. If he was a sheriff's deputy, he'll be in here.

It took her twenty minutes to strike out. She went through every time card filled out for the year and came up with no KQ. *No Anybody Q,* for that matter.

Code? It has to be.

She tried reversing them and looked through the time cards again.

No QK.

She tried using the letters before K and Q, thinking that Bailey might have just added one before she wrote.

The time cards again, but no JP.

She tried using the letters *after* K and Q, thinking that

Bailey might have just subtracted one letter before she wrote.

LR.

Back to the time cards. Bingo. She found a deputy Lee Ripley who happened to be working the night shift on August 4. She checked the assignment roster and discovered that Ripley had worked patrol that night. Interesting. She'd assumed a whore killer wouldn't be working the night he killed, but why? On patrol he'd have opportunity. He could have met her at eleven, just like her date book said. He was out, free, working without a partner like they used to in the old days.

Merci had never heard of him.

So she tried the code against days when Bailey met known subjects—Ralph Meeks and Bill Owen.

No RM. No BO. Wrong code.

Frustrated and not a little angry, she stood, walked around the table three times, then sat back down again. The coffee was hot and horrible but she drank it anyway.

She looked down at the calendared entries, trying to imagine a simple way to disguise the initials. Something a loaded hooker could remember and use without thinking about it too hard. Merci noted the rare letter Q repeated in the Owen date and the murder date, but the first initials weren't the same.

She walked around the table again three times in the opposite direction, on the vague notion that you always retraced your steps if you got lost. She sat down again, lost as ever. Vague indeed, she thought. She hooked her thumbs into her pants pockets, slumped back in the chair and looked down at the dizzying codes again.

And she began to admit that maybe this *wasn't* code at all, that maybe Meeks and Owens were off the books and KQ had nothing at all to do with the Sheriff Department.

But she tried reversing the initials, then adding and subtracting letters. Using this formula she got neither BO nor RM, and it was so difficult she was almost furious by the time she got the last combination scrambled.

Merci thought: What a bunch of shit. Then she took a deep breath and murmured the hackneyed phrase about when the going gets tough. . . .

So she tried subtracting *one* letter from the first initial and *two* letters from the last. One from the first, two from the second—easy to remember.

She liked what she saw. She checked it, then rechecked it.

Under this code, CQ became BO—Bill Owen, visited by Bailey at 3 P.M. on July 25. Confirmed by Bailey herself, in the tape recording she made.

The letters SO became RM—Ralph Meeks, visited by Bailey at 5 P.M. July 9. Confirmed by Bailey again, on the same tape.

The letters KQ became JO. And the Sheriff Department had employed a man with just those initials.

With her head clearing and her heart speeding up,

Merci opened the Bailey file and flipped through to the Coroner's Final Report. Bailey had died between 9 P.M. and one in the morning.

Next, she pulled the time cards for August 4, 1969. A total of ninety-three sworn Sheriff Department deputies worked that day: forty-one on day shift, twenty-nine on swing, twenty-three on night.

There he was.

Jim O'Brien had worked swing shift. He'd clocked in at five-ten and back out at one-sixteen the following morning.

Checking back to June and forward to September, Merci found that Jim O'Brien had worked day shifts every week except for one—the week that Bailey died.

It took her another two hours to do it, but she managed to trace the odd shift patterns of two other deputies on duty the night Bailey died. Partners Rayborn and McNally had pulled swing shifts that week also.

For the rest of the year in both directions, they had worked days.

A week of swings, and hell broke loose.

When the door opened she flinched. She turned, hoping nobody had seen her jerk like that.

Evan O'Brien stood there. "We're done with most of the McNally stuff. I can't tell you how it went, but I can smile."

He did. Then the smile disappeared. "You okay?"

"I'm fine," she said.

"I'll bet the press conference was a lot of fun."

"No."

"All right. I'll leave you alone. But Lynda and Gilliam and I are going to have a drink after work at Sal's. You're invited. Gilliam ordered me to tell you that."

Merci hesitated. Her thoughts flapped and hovered but they wouldn't land.

O'Brien waited, then spoke. "I'll drive us over if you want."

"No. But I do want to talk to you."

"Then come have a drink. We're just crime lab people, not lepers."

"I've got an errand to run. Will you come with me?"

He looked at her. "Sure. What's the errand?"

"I need to feed the dogs. At Mike's."

The look O'Brien gave her was like nothing she'd ever seen: It was hard to get such confusion out of a wiseass like Evan.

"I'll explain on the way there."

• • •

Merci gunned the Impala up Modjeska Canyon, tires chirping on the curves. The night was cold so she had the windbreaker buttoned all the way up and a pair of thin leather gloves on.

O'Brien wore a tan duster, his hands jammed deep into the pockets. He swayed when Merci took the turns and she realized he was small compared to the other men she'd driven in this car. Hess. Mike. Brighton. Clark.

"So, Sergeant, what did you want to talk about?"

"I think your father was with Patti Bailey the night she was killed."

O'Brien glanced across at her. "What do you mean, *with*? And how do you know?"

"As a customer. It's in her appointment book. Eleven that night. She died sometime between nine and one."

"A date and a murder are two different things."

"That's not what I said."

"It's what you meant."

She made a right turn, took it a little fast, saw O'Brien brace himself on the dash.

"Bailey made a tape," said Merci. "She had a county supervisor as a customer, she had Bill Owen, too—the old sheriff. She was going to blackmail them with it."

"Don't try to tell me my father is on that tape."

"She left the recorder running the night she was shot. There's a long conversation with the man who did it."

She saw O'Brien look at her again, then back to the road. Merci slowed as she approached Mike's turnoff.

"Well, okay, Merci. You've got a tape of a murder, and I've got a deceased father you think did it. What am I supposed to do? Raise him from the dead for a voice comparison?"

"Do you have his voice on tape? A video, maybe?"

"Of course I do. He was my father. But the voice on mine won't match the voice on yours. I can guarantee that."

"How?"

She pulled into Mike's driveway.

"Because he was a *good man*."

Merci pulled out the keys and looked at him.

"I'd appreciate a copy of that video, Evan."

He sighed and shook his head, then looked out at Mike's house. The dogs had started howling and again Merci thought she heard something plaintive in their voices.

"Looks like a miserable little place," he said, looking out the window.

"It's not that bad."

She still felt obliged to defend Mike, and she wondered why.

• • •

She let herself in and turned on the living-room lights. The house was even colder now. The fire had gone out and no one was there to start it up again.

"I didn't know he was a gun nut," said O'Brien, looking at the gun case by the kitchen.

"They're just guns, Evan. They don't make him a nut."

She went into the kitchen. Looking at the rinsed dishes in the rack, it felt like the old days with Mike. She would stand in this kitchen and assess the dinner damage and they would talk. She would wash and Mike would dry the pans, rack the dishes. Tim would be in his portable crib, or maybe on a blanket before he'd learned to crawl. The after-dinner part of the night was a good part, she thought now, when they yakked and cleaned things up and maybe had a drink.

Standing there now with a man close by reminded her of those past nights in a way that made her heart sink.

"I'll feed the dogs and we'll get out of here."

O'Brien looked at her with something like earnestness. "You know, Merci, just because a hooker's book says she was with a certain guy on a certain night, that doesn't mean she's telling the truth. What if he didn't show. What if she didn't? One thing that murdered people don't do too well is show up on time for appointments."

"I know. That's why I want the video."

"Then what? I mean, when the voices don't match, where do you go from there?"

A moment of silence, filled only with the jingle of big dogs against chain link.

"I don't know."

"Did you think that maybe he wanted to see Bailey for other reasons? Just because he was in her book doesn't make him a customer. Like, well, Mike and the Whittaker girl."

"Possible. The guy on the tape was a customer. There's no doubt about that."

She lugged the kibble bag out of the pantry, carried it to the kitchen slider and let O'Brien get the door for her. She hit the outdoor light and walked into the cold night.

Then the déjà vu tickled her again, as she looked down at the dogs and realized that she'd forgotten the key.

"Damn, I forgot the kennel key."

A wicked little chill ran up her back, because that was exactly what she'd said to Mike one night when she was feeding the dogs with him. *Those exact words.* She was standing then where she stood now, speaking in the same tone of voice. Mike had been standing where Evan now stood.

To be in Mike's home while he was in jail, asking another man to fetch the key, felt to her like a betrayal worse than anything she'd done so far. The dogs were holy, if you were Mike. Mike's dogs. It was like she'd rewritten history—erased Mike, wrote in someone else.

Damn, I forgot the kennel key. A moment later Mike was back with it. A moment later, O'Brien was back with it.

"You okay?" he asked, handing it to her.

"Perfect. I love doing this."

She let the dogs out of their runs and collected their bowls, let them follow her to the feeding table, where she measured out extra big portions. Dolly, Molly and Polly all tried to butt each other out of the way, knocking into Merci and almost buckling her knees.

She laughed and tried to push them away, knowing she wasn't strong enough to budge the hundred-pound dogs with her knees, but it reminded her of the scores of times she'd tried, the scores of times she'd looked down at their dolorous faces with the hanging ears and mournful eyes and seen that spark of play, and it made her laugh. Because the laughter felt so foreign, the causes of it seemed so long ago and ruined, it broke her heart to do all this again without Mike, with Mike in jail for murder, with Mike very likely never to do this again so long as he should live.

Dolly, Molly and Polly had no idea.

She felt something hot on her cheek, silently cursed her weakness, made sure her back was to O'Brien, whom she suddenly regretted bringing into Mike's home.

"You used to do this a lot," said Evan.

"Yeah."

"Did you love him?"

"I tried to."

"Well, these dogs love you."

"Yeah, that's right."

"Sometimes things are better when you remember them. You make them better than they were."

"I'm doing that right now."

O'Brien said nothing then, and Merci finished filling the bowls. She carried them one at a time into the correct kennels, using the sit and stay commands that the girls were so eager to obey whenever food was involved. She shut them in, waved O'Brien through the gate ahead of her and set the food bag back on the pantry floor.

O'Brien looked at her.

"Shit, lady. All I wanted to do was have a drink with someone I kind of like, and next thing I know, she's accusing my father of murder and making me feed her boyfriend's dogs."

"You're a sport. Thanks."

"Don't get sincere on me. I wouldn't know how to take it."

"Thanks anyway."

"But you still want my video of Dad?"

She nodded.

O'Brien smiled wryly, shaking his head. "Know what I think? I think I've been had. But being had by you isn't really so bad."

On their way back out of the canyon, he was silent. She glanced at him twice, and each time she found him gazing out the windshield at nothing, or maybe at everything. When he finally spoke, his voice was quiet and he still didn't look at her.

"You're not supposed to know this yet, but the chukka boots matched the prints in Whittaker's kitchen. The blood on them was Whittaker's blood. The toolmarks from the casing in the flower vase matched ones fired from the forty-five Wheeler and Teague brought in. And that thing wrapped up in female underwear was a homemade sound suppressor that fit nicely onto the Colt. It all lined up just right. It's a made case. Gilliam wanted to celebrate it tonight. He never liked McNally. He always liked you. I think he feels bad, pushing you out of the lab like he did."

• • •

Zamorra was the only one in the detective pen when Merci came back that night after dropping off O'Brien. It was almost eight.

He was cleanly shaven as always, dressed in a dark suit as always. He sat upright in his chair, both hands on the armrests, staring straight ahead. Merci could feel the emotion steaming off him, but she couldn't tell what it was: sadness, hatred, ecstasy, joy?

He said hello without looking at her, without even moving his lips, it seemed.

She sat down. "Janine?"

Zamorra said nothing, so Merci spun in her chair to face her desk, checked her routing bin to make sure the Records Section slip had been picked up, started to push the message button on her answering machine, then pulled her finger away and turned again to Zamorra.

"Paul, what is it?"

He seemed to snap out of his reverie. Then he looked at Merci like he'd just that moment become aware of her.

"I'm sorry," he said. "The uh . . . yes, Janine. The implants got infected. They're taking them out right now. Dangerous, because of the swelling."

"Go. Go be with her when she wakes up."

"She was in a coma when they took her away. They don't know if she'll come out or not."

"Go anyway."

He looked at her, dark eyes hungry and haunted and somehow hopeless. "Oh, I am. I just came here to see you. And to tell you I won't be around tomorrow."

"You could have called, Paul."

"I'm sorry. I want you to know that. I want you to know you've got a partner."

"I've got a partner who shouldn't be here right now."

"Look, San Diego still hasn't finished the CAL-ID run on the kitchen prints from Whittaker's. My man down there said he'd work it all night if he has to. I didn't give them any exclusionary parameters—they're looking male and female, every race and age, law-enforcement, the works. So it's—"

"It's going to take time, Paul. Let it take time."

He sighed, closed his eyes. "Last thing she said to me before she fell into the coma? 'I wish this was over, Paul. I wish this was all just over.' "

• • •

Mike was sitting on his cot, an uneaten tray of food in front of him. He looked up at Merci and held her gaze, then he lowered his stare back to the tray.

He hadn't shaved. His hair was dirty. The orange jail jumpsuit was a size too small, and his big muscled arms looked wrong in it.

"How are the girls?"

"Just fine. They know you're gone."

"I'd expect that. Dad's going to feed them starting tomorrow. You're done."

"Okay then."

He looked at her again, then stood. "Arraignment tomorrow. Bob Rule said expect Brenkus to ask two million bail. I think I'll be here a while."

"What do you need?"

Shaking his head he walked toward her, then stopped a yard away and crossed his arms. "Well, ten percent of two mil is two hundred grand. I need a father for Danny, someone to work my dogs, someone to keep the fire going at home. Which do you want?"

"I'm not your enemy."

"In that case, just stand there and look at me. Look at me right in the face, so I can look at you."

She did. Mike stared at her for at least a minute.

"Okay," he said. "I'm satisfied."

She said nothing.

"I couldn't decide if you were evil or not," he said. "And now I think I know. I had an interesting conversation with Mrs. Heath. And I found out you'd been in my home on Monday. Bob Rule spent two hours with her today."

She felt the blood rush to her face. "I was picking up my jacket."

"You didn't leave a jacket."

"I realized that when I couldn't find it."

Merci, an unpracticed liar, was surprised how convincing she sounded. Even to herself.

He smiled again, then walked back and sat on the thin mattress. "Sounds to me like a search without a warrant. You had no permission for entry. No legal right. I had every expectation of privacy there, and that's the legal issue. An illegal search voids the one they did yesterday. Everything they found can be suppressed."

"I didn't search. They found what they found, Mike. I'd spent time there with you. I was looking for a jacket. Come on."

"How'd they find that stuff so fast? *I* didn't even know where it was, so how did they? How did Wheeler and fat boy know where to look?"

Merci said nothing.

"No," he said. "I don't think you're evil. I think I've been framed and you've been used to do it."

"Who?"

Mike shook his head and exhaled sharply. "You're the crack investigator. You tell me."

Chapter Thirty

At home, Merci checked on her sleeping son, put his cap back on, tucked the blankets around him and stood there for a minute looking down at his face. She said a prayer for his well-being. Even though she believed that God only listened once in a while, it was worth a try. Clark was in the shower.

I didn't search.

There it was, a lie to the man she'd once loved and respected. But what was worse: following the evidence, as she had done, or washing her hands too early and turning the investigation over to Wheeler and Teague? Didn't she *owe* Mike that search?

Due process is what I owe him, she thought, same as anyone else.

He'd confessed to killing her. It was a sarcastic, angry, insincere confession, but he'd made it with no evidence against him. Nothing against him but the woman he was falling in love with found dead, and a betrayed lover asking him questions.

Because he knew I'd never believe it, she thought.

She got the Whittaker and Bailey files from the locked trunk of her car, set them on her bed. She turned up Tim's monitor all the way, so she could hear him breathing. She listened to the shower turn off in her father's bathroom, the clunk of the valve shutting and the grumble of the old pipes.

She sat crossed-legged on the floor, bowed her head into her hands and listened to the noisy collisions going on inside her brain: the evidence in Mike's home, his betrayal and her own. His claim that he was being framed and that she was being used. The unexplained struggle in the Whittaker kitchen. The violated crime scene, the distrust in the crime lab, the evidence lost or misplaced there. The letters sent to Gary Brice, the article that Brice would write.

She listened to Tim breathing in, Tim breathing out. Then, there was the Bailey case: Jim O'Brien meeting with Patti Bailey the night she died, him quitting the force a few months later, his eventual suicide. The note and key to the storage room, home to evidence damning Bill Owen, Ralph Meeks and Jim O'Brien. Evan, a colleague, protective of a father he might not have known very well at all. And the strange way that the cases had become connected through her, by a secret sender of keys and copied love letters.

Noise, noise, noise.

The phone in Clark's room rang. She listened to the murmur of his answer. Tim, Jr.'s breathing came through the amplifier, rhythmic and slow.

One thing at a time, she thought: one foot in front of the other. What *if* Mike had been framed? If that was true, then someone else had entered Aubrey Whittaker's apartment after Mike left, killed her, began setting up the evidence—the bullet casing, the bloody prints made with the chukka boots. The other evidence Mike had left himself. as dinner guest and admirer of Aubrey. And later—or maybe earlier—this framer would have to plant the silencer in the workshop. Where could you get a casing fired through Mike's Colt? How would you get his boots in order to bloody them?

Someone who knows his home.

Someone who shadowed him at the Sheriff's Firing Range, maybe, and picked up a casing after he'd shot?

She thought of Lynda Coiner. Had she visited Mike at home? How many times? Certainly a CSI was in a good position to frame a suspect, but *why*? Coiner liked him, she was doing little favors for him in jail. Cover for him, maybe—but not frame him. She could even believe Lynda Coiner having a secret passion for Mike. Merci could imagine them pursuing it together, without her knowledge. But was shy, professional Lynda Coiner capable of murdering Aubrey Whittaker?

Merci stood and walked to the window, looked out at the driveway bathed in the harsh glow of the security lights.

Evan O'Brien had almost as much opportunity as Lynda Coiner did, but what reason would he have to frame Mike?

Gilliam himself? What possible reason for ruining Mike and encouraging Merci to do the dirty work? Aside from his own longtime crush on her, none that she could see. Would he kill for that, frame for that? No.

Then, this: Aubrey Whittaker would not have opened her door for just anyone. There was no place to hide on the porch. The killer had stood there, bathed in the yellow porch light, easily visible through the peephole.

It was preposterous. Coiner and O'Brien were the CSIs. They had been at the crime scene with her, not long after Aubrey Whittaker had been murdered. Both of them had been at home when they got the call; both had shown up without hesitation. Gilliam was venerable, respected, professional.

Preposterous.

A framer would have to know that they were going to have dinner. A framer would have to know that they had written letters to each other, have to know where to find them. A framer would have to know when they were gone, when they were home, what they were planning, what they were doing. How could a framer know all that? He'd have to know them both very well. Watched them. Waited. Read their letters, listened in on their calls . . .

Merci heard Tim whimper, then say something in his sleep. Impressive, how sensitive the baby monitor was.

If you had a monitor for Mike and Aubrey you could learn everything you'd need to know to build a frame.

If you had a monitor for Mike and Aubrey . . .

She found the telephone company printout of calls made to and from Whittaker's apartment the last month. She added up the calls made to Mike's work and home numbers, and the calls received from them. Thirty-two in all. The total elapsed time was almost 330 minutes.

Plenty of time to listen, she thought. To hear them make their small talk and hatch their plans.

The idea hit her that Mike's team might have authorized a wiretap, but she could find nothing about one in the file she'd copied from vice. She called Kathy Hulet to confirm it: Mike himself had withdrawn the request for a Title 3 wiretap shortly after Whittaker had agreed to help them. So Whittaker's phone was clean—or was supposed to be.

Tim, Jr., sighed. So much louder than the actual sound, she thought.

Merci shook her head and went to her closet and felt the sudden cold dread wash down over her—the dread of darkness and cars, the dread of being alone and surprised, the dread of being *wrong about everything, just as she'd been wrong about the Purse Snatcher. And that had cost Hess his life.*

She dressed. Taking the baby monitor, she went into her father's room and gently shook him awake.

"I'm going out for a couple hours. Tim's asleep. I'm setting up the monitor in here."

"Where are you—?"

"Later. I'll be back, Dad."

She set the monitor on the floor beside his bed, the volume still set on high.

She checked the back of her car with a flashlight before opening the door. She had to get up close to the glass to see anything but reflection, and it gave her the usual fright to get this close to the glass. Okay. All right. She cranked the engine and pulled on the lights.

This one's for you, Mike.

• • •

Thirty minutes later she stood in front of the door to Aubrey Whittaker's apartment. The ocean air was damp and cold against her face. She closed her eyes for a moment and imagined the scene again. The visitor standing in the dull yellow porch light, the knock on the door. Aubrey looking out. Seeing someone for whom she's willing to open the door. She opens it. Her look of surprise. The muffled *wwhhpp* of the silenced gun as she falls and he follows her in, steps around her, drags her out of the way. . . .

Inside, Merci shut the door and looked out the peephole: an exaggerated yellow ellipse, Christmas lights twinkling in the great illusory distance. *She saw him. She recognized him. She knew him. She opened to the door to him.*

Merci hit the entryway light, then the kitchen lights, then the living-room lights. She looked through the blinds at the ocean, the black surge breaking into white on the beach, the lamps of a squid boat forming a tiny patch of light on the sea.

Back in the kitchen, Merci went to the little breakfast bar, lifted the cordless phone and listened. Still on. She played the messages on the recorder. There were three new ones since she'd last heard them: one a recorded sales pitch from an insurance agent; one from a dentist's receptionist, confirming a three o'clock appointment for the next day; one from Bobby at the Cadillac dealership with information about scheduled maintenance.

She turned over the receiver unit, saw nothing unusual. Then she knelt beside the bar and looked up. The sheetrock was visible where the tiles ended, an eighteen-inch overhang that ran for probably five feet. Nothing.

Another line?

In the bedroom, Merci pushed away the bed to find the phone jack. And she found what she was looking for, a small box with one tan line plugged into the phone jack, another one running down the wall to the floor, where it disappeared into the carpet. She pulled up the carpet and followed the line to the sliding glass door of the bedroom deck. It went outside through a very small, neat hole. Recently drilled she saw: There was still drywall dust on the plywood flooring.

On the deck outside, leaning over and using her flashlight, she could see the line as it traversed down the side of the building toward the alley.

A minute later she was in that alley, shaking a little in the cold December air as she traced the beam of her flashlight down the line. It disappeared behind a downspout that ran from the rain gutter to the ground. She knelt again. She trained the beam on the bottom of the spout. It made a ninety degree turn just before it hit a planter overflowing with big margarita daisies. Merci reached through the branches and put her fingers around the back of the spout. She felt around for just a second, then brought out the end of the tan line.

Two jacks.

For a tape recorder, she thought. A voice-activated tape recorder wired to the phone line. You could check it just by driving up and parking here in the alley. Take the tape. Put in a fresh one. Drive away. It would take less than one minute.

Merci shivered as a cold puff of wind blew a swirl of mist at her. A drop of water fell from the roof and ticked to the cement.

Aubrey, she thought, you were never quite alone.

She went around to the front of the building and climbed the stairs. She stood at the front door and imagined the scene again. This time, without Mike. She substituted a generic male, putting some nice clothes and a pleasant face on him to make her opening the door more likely.

Question: If a stranger had knocked on Aubrey's door, why had she opened it?

Because he had a good line? He'd have to, because Aubrey Whittaker would have been anything but gullible with regard to a man, late at night, knocking on the door of her home. But Alexander Coates, concerned neighbor who could differentiate between footsteps, hadn't heard any conversation at all.

No, she thought: Try again.

She went inside, shut the door and looked through the peephole.

Why?

Why did you open it?

She looked through the peephole again, and she thought of Hess and what he'd told her about seeing, and she knew.

She knew.

The light wasn't on. He'd unscrewed the bulb before he knocked. She'd seen only the shape of a man. Mike had just left after their dinner. She thought it was him, coming back for something he'd forgotten. She opened the door. Ten minutes later, after the struggle, on his way out, he screwed the light back in, so we'd assume she had recognized her caller.

Shivering again, her legs unsteady, she went back inside the apartment and turned off the porch light. Then she hustled down the stairs to her car and got her crime-scene kit from the trunk. She stood in front of Aubrey's door again and waited for the bulb to cool.

She pulled on a pair of fresh latex gloves and worked off the top of the light fixture. It was a glass hexagon with a peaked brass lid and a solid ball at the top. There was no screw to hold it; it had just been set in place. All she had to do was tilt it up, lift it by one corner, and set it into a paper evidence bag.

With the fixture lid out of the way, she reached up and in, finding the neck of the bulb, way down by the metal. Still warm. She held it firmly and twisted. Eight quarter-turns later it was loose and light in her hand, and she set it into another bag.

• • •

She called Zamorra from her car. The cell was patchy and he was hard to hear. Janine was still in the coma, she thought he said.

She told him what she'd found at Whittaker's, how perfectly it could fit into a frame. Maybe Mike was right. She didn't say it but she wondered if he could be innocent. *Innocent.* The idea moved around inside her like an immense blessing. A blessing as large as her willingness to feel it.

"But Merci, who put the nix on the Title 3 wiretap?"

"Mike did."

"That makes me wonder. He'd put a nix on it all right, if his private intercept was already installed."

"Think about what I found, Paul. Someone with a line into Whittaker's apartment could learn enough to frame Mike. And all he had to do was unscrew that bug light before he knocked. Easy. She'd think it was Mike, coming for something."

He was silent for a minute. The cell signal hissed and popped. "It's good to hope, Merci."

"I'm going to call you in one hour."

"I'll be here."

• • •

Back home she checked Tim and brought the monitor back from her dad's room. Clark didn't even stir.

She poured a tall Scotch on ice and walked the house in stocking feet as quietly as she could, listening to the creak of the floorboards and the groanings of the old furnace.

She called Zamorra but got a busy signal. Tried again and got another. Once more—still busy.

She thought about Mike.

She told herself not to think about Mike.

If he was guilty, her world would be torn apart—it already had been. But if he was *innocent,* her world would be torn apart in ways she hadn't yet even imagined.

Stop. Rest. Sleep.

Instead, she paced. Once around the house again, staring out the windows at the orange trees and the cold winter sky.

By midnight she was in bed, lights on, staring up at the ceiling and unable to sleep. She banished all thoughts of Mike, all thoughts of the Bailey case. She banished all the clatter of lies and half-truths and assumptions and contradictions. She thought of Tim Hess and Tim, Jr., and a pink house on a beach in Mexico. Little Tim was trying to catch sand crabs. Merci was standing a few yards away and when she looked past her son she could see his father on the porch in a hammock, reading a book. He looked up and waved.

And finally she fell backward into the black.

• • •

At 4 A.M. she awoke in a sour sweat. A disturbing dream. In it, she was standing in Mike's backyard, by the kennel gate, asking him for the key. Mike held a silenced .45 at his side, kind of hiding it, like he was ashamed to be seen with it. But Mike was not Mike, he was her father.

She sat up on the bed as the dream blended into recent memory.

The memory became a scene she could watch: She gets the dog food, she goes to the backyard and realizes she doesn't have the key.

Damn, I forgot the kennel key.

Something wrong then, but what was it?

She pictured Evan standing with her out by the kennels, the light shining down on his freckled face. He looked so small, huddled in the duster.

Wasn't that a gray sport coat he was wearing under it?

She checked her notebook entry after Zamorra's initial findings from the San Diego lab. *Dark gray, purple and sea-green fibers in it . . . in the struggle, the garment got caught on the corner of the drawer.*

She checked the Whittaker file and confirmed that identical fibers had gone missing from the lab, along with the fingerprint cards from the kitchen.

When she pictured Evan O'Brien standing in the light of Mike's backyard, helping her feed the dogs, she saw his dark gray sport coat under the duster. Green and purple accent fibers? She couldn't say. But was Evan wearing that coat the night they processed Whittaker's apartment?

No. She could remember him that night, just over a week ago, in his Sheriff Department windbreaker, jeans and athletic shoes. No sport coat on Evan.

But there were probably two million gray sport coats in Southern California.

She sat on the living-room couch and closed her eyes. Back to Mike's place again. The memory was still bothering her so she looked again.

She carries the bag of kibble from the pantry to the door. She hikes the bag onto one knee, using her free hand to work the slider. She steps into the cool canyon night. She goes toward the yapping dogs. She realizes she's forgotten the key.

Damn, I forgot the kennel key.

Mike comes back with the key.

Evan comes back with the key.

Something wrong, still, but what?

She asked herself why Evan O'Brien would kill Whittaker, and pin the murder on Mike? No matter how she turned the question, it didn't make sense. What profit was in it for him? What had Mike McNally ever done to Evan O'Brien?

It was five-thirty when her phone rang again.

"Merci, it's Zamorra. I'm still at the hospital, but I got the CAL-ID run from San Diego a couple of hours ago. I had to do some follow-up to make even half-sense of it. Ready?"

"Shoot, Paul."

"The prints in Whittaker's kitchen belong to Jim O'Brien. I had them run the cards again—same answer."

She said nothing.

"I talked to the San Bernardino Medical Examiner. O'Brien's suicide wasn't mysterious. The identification was easy and unquestioned. A routine case. He killed himself. But last week he was in Aubrey Whittaker's apartment."

Her thoughts were racing, but she slowed them down, tried to take them one at a time.

"Give me the case number on the suicide," she said quietly. "And the name of the first officer on scene."

• • •

It took her half an hour to track down Deputy Sean Carver of the San Bernardino Sheriff Department. His voice was young and a little slurred as he explained that he'd just gotten up for work.

He clearly remembered the Jim O'Brien scene. He'd met Jim a couple of times at Sheriff Department functions, and O'Brien struck him as a boozy old-timer just waiting out the days.

"He called us before he pulled the trigger," said Carver. "So I pretty much knew what I'd find. It was bad. They're all bad, I guess."

"No doubt in your mind it was suicide?"

"None. The coroner confirmed it. O'Brien had gunshot residue on his hand, prints all over the gun. Been drinking, too. Lots."

Mercy thought for a moment. "Nothing at all out of the ordinary? Nothing?"

Silence. Then a sigh.

"All right," he said.

"Okay," she agreed—to what she didn't know.

"One thing. It's been bothering me for five years."

"Unbother yourself with it."

"We got there just before the Coroner's Investigation Team and the Fire and Rescue people. O'Brien was dead—no doubt of that. We didn't disturb the scene or the body, except to see if he was still alive. Then I walked the house. Just a house. A house that wasn't used much. But in one of the bedrooms there was an envelope leaning up against the pillow. It was my first year on patrol. I was young. I didn't know if the envelope was related to the suicide or not. So I left it where it was. Didn't touch it. Went by the book. I told my partner about it, and he looked at it and said to tell the Watch Commander. I told the Watch Commander about it, I told the coroner's guys about it, I told the Homicide guys about it."

"You did right."

"Not quite. Because between the time I saw it and the M.E. did the medical autopsy three days later, the letter had goddamned disappeared. It either got tossed or lost or somebody took it or . . . who knows? When the Homicide hotshots got on scene they butted me out—I'd done my part. But I've always been ashamed of what I didn't do. I should have taken that damned envelope, waved it in the dicks' faces and made them read it. Maybe it didn't mean a thing. But maybe it did. It would have meant something to the person it was written to, that's for sure. Either way, I won't make that mistake again."

"Did you try to track it down?"

"Yeah. Taylor, one of the sergeants, got it as far as his desk. He never saw it again. Nobody did, that I could find. But I was the new kid—you know. If anybody had screwed up somehow, they weren't going to tell me about it."

Merci went with the obvious: "Anything written on it?"

"Yeah. 'To My Son.' That meant something to Taylor, too."

Merci's nerves rippled. "How so?"

"He talked to O'Brien's son two mornings after the suicide. At his desk. Taylor said he'd left the guy there alone while he got them coffees. For about one minute. He thought that was when the envelope got up and walked away."

"He'd made copies of it, though."

"He never opened it. Taylor wasn't sure what our authority was, just like I wasn't sure. The DA hadn't given him an answer yet. O'Brien was one of ours, so Taylor wanted to do right by him. If you find a note in the vicinity of the suicide, it's one thing. If you find a sealed letter marked for someone else in another part of the house, it's something else. A suicide scene is a crime scene. And you know how the search-and-seizure laws are always changing."

• • •

She called Zamorra, told him that Evan O'Brien was harboring a suicide letter and a videotape that might well prove Jim O'Brien killed Patti Bailey. And who knew, maybe it would also shed some light on how a dead man's fingerprints got into number 23 Wave Street.

"I'm going to bushwhack him outside his apartment in about half an hour," she said. "Get the goods."

"And if he won't turn them over?"

"I'll pinch his head and *make* him."

Chapter Thirty-one

O'Brien lived in a small apartment complex not far from headquarters, an uneasy neighborhood with graffiti on the walls and beer cans in the gutters. Merci had dropped him off here after SUDS sessions a couple of times. She remembered the number on his parking space because it was the age her mother had been when she died. She parked behind Evan's convertible coupe and shut off the engine.

Half an hour later he came around the corner into the parking area. His hair was still wet from the shower, he had a muffler loosely wrapped around his neck, a steaming mug in one hand and an old briefcase in the other. The duster again. She rolled down her window, watching two faint clouds of breath vanish in front of his nose.

He saw her, smiled and came over. "This my limo?"

"Kind of."

"Sorry, Sarge. I don't have that old birthday video after

all. I looked all over here. It must still be out at the old house."

"What about his suicide letter, Evan?"

His eyes widened and his mouth parted, but it took him a beat to get the words out.

"What?"

"The letter he wrote. Is that out at the old house, too?"

He looked hard at her, his face half puzzlement and half suspicion.

"Yeah, I think so . . . but—"

"Well, good, then. Get in. Put your briefcase in the trunk." She pulled the trunk release lever.

"Am I being abducted?"

"You might say so."

"Really?"

"Get in, Evan, it's cold out there. The door's open."

She saw the trunk door rise, heard the briefcase hit, watched the door slam shut. Then O'Brien came back around and climbed in, balancing the coffee. He looked at her, eyebrows up, his green eyes clear and penetrating and a little confused. He shut the door. "What gives, Merci?"

"Let's go get the tape and the letter."

"Right now?"

"Right now."

"You explain it to Gilliam then. I'm supposed to—"

"I will. What's the address?"

"Fourteen Rancho Verde. It's off Waterman, halfway up

the mountain. Sergeant Rayborn, maybe you should tell me what in hell we're doing."

She put the car into drive, eased out of the parking area.

"We're hoping to find out why your father's prints turned up in Aubrey Whittaker's apartment."

"That's not possible."

"Tell CAL-ID that."

"Dad's fingerprints?"

"So they say. We ran them twice to make sure."

O'Brien was quiet for a moment as they headed down the boulevard toward the freeway. She noted that the sport jacket under the duster was gray.

"All it can be is a mistake," he said. "He's dead. And they've got twenty-something million fingerprints to keep track of now."

She knew he was looking at her, but she didn't look back. He said nothing as she headed for the freeway.

"I've got to see the suicide note and run a voice comparison with the video. Evan, I think I can crack the Bailey case with them."

"That letter's not much of a read, Merci."

"I'm sorry, but I think it's worth it."

She called Zamorra, told him she was with Evan, gave him Jim O'Brien's address.

"I can't meet you there. I'll have to call in backup if you want it."

Merci felt the steady thumping of her heart, and the

warning that came with each beat. She knew something was wrong, and it made her alert and afraid.

She kept her voice as casual as she could. "That'd be fine."

"I'll do it right now. I can't leave here, Merci. I—"

"I know. How is she, Paul?"

"No change."

"Hang in there, partner."

"You, too."

Merci turned on the interior light, lowered the radio squelch, looked at Evan and Evan's coat. He was staring straight out the window, coffee cup at his lips. The traffic was already bunching up on the fifty-five, a column of white headlights behind her and red taillights ahead.

"Evan, is that the same sport coat you were wearing last night at Mike's?"

Gray. No green or purple accents. No accents at all, that she could see.

"Yeah, why?"

"I like it."

"Me, too. It was one of Dad's. So was this briefcase."

• • •

The house stood alone on the hillside, at the end of a long asphalt drive pocked by potholes filled with weeds. It was high desert here, still below the trees. A stiff wind came down off the mountain and Merci could feel it push hard against the Chevrolet like it wanted to fight. The last street sign she saw said Willow View and she wondered if Evan had fed her a fake address for Zamorra.

"What happened to Rancho Verde?"

"You're on it."

"One house on the whole street?"

"Yes, ma'am. It's a bunch of switchbacks, then you're in the driveway."

The house came into view as she came over the top of a steep rise. It was a low-slung mission-style home, with a clay roof and black wrought iron over the windows. Some of the tiles had slid onto the driveway, some of the window-panes were replaced by plywood. A bougainvillea that had once covered the porte cochere was long dead but still clinging to the stucco stanchion. The white walls were stained brown where rain had gathered and run down. The courtyard was filled with tumbleweeds quivering up against the garage doors like they were trying to get in. The fountain was blackened concrete filled with rainwater.

"Park anywhere you want," he said. "The sand's gonna blast your car no matter where you put it."

She pulled up under the carport and parked. She looked at Evan. He was facing away from her, toward the front door, which she saw was peeled and sun-blasted.

He turned to her with a glum expression. "I hate this place. It puts me in a bad mood."

"Thanks for having me over."

"If I remember right, it didn't really happen that way."

"Thanks anyway."

"Yeah, well, enjoy the smell of suicide. And forget whatever you think you know about my dad's prints at Whittaker's. Check the bloodstains in the living room if my word isn't good enough. Poe was right. You can't wash blood out no matter how hard you try."

She followed him to the door, waited while he worked a key in the lock. The tumbleweeds shivered against the garage doors. She heard the hard click of the dead bolt sliding into place. When she stepped inside she felt the crunch of sand between her duty boots and the stone floor.

"It's cold in here. Summer, it's a thousand degrees."

"Hard on the house paint."

"Hard on human skin."

Evan shut the door and ran the dead bolt in. Then he turned and looked at her. "You can see whatever you want to see in here. Just make it kind of chop-chop. I don't get anything out of being here, except sad."

"Let me see the suicide note."

"This way."

They walked down the entryway: kitchen on the left, counters covered with dust; dining room on the right, furniture covered with sheets. Straight ahead was a big living room with a fireplace to the left and sliding glass doors opening up to a backyard with a swimming pool. The floor was some kind of stone—slate, Merci guessed—with thick rows of grout connecting them. More sheets over the furniture. She could make out the shapes of two sofas, a couple of chairs. A big leather chair facing the fireplace was still uncovered.

Evan led her over, looked down at the floor. "You can see where the blood stained the rock," he said. "He was sitting in that chair when he did it. I left it there. The chair, I mean. I left the whole place the way it was. Could never figure out if cleaning it would be an insult to his memory or not, so I just left it."

"That's a tough call."

"You're stuck with what happened either way."

She noted the dark stains on the chair, some high up on the back, some on the seat.

"Head shot," said O'Brien. "The gun landed over there."

He pointed at the fireplace. Merci looked into the blackened pit, heard the wind shriek, watched a cloud of sand rise from behind the pool outside. She could feel the cold air coming down through the chimney. She went to the window and looked out. The pool was empty and bleached almost white. She could see big lines in the cavity where the gunite had cracked.

Evan walked across the room, still looking at the chair, like he was just seeing it for the first time. He stopped in the far corner, in front of a large TV. There were bookshelves filled with paperbacks and an entertainment cabinet with rows of videos, a stereo amp, speakers. He opened a drawer and looked in. She saw dust rise.

For a moment he stood there, neither moving nor speaking. Then he reached in and brought out a white envelope.

He stared at it. Then he came to her slowly, his shoes squeaking on the pavers, and handed her the letter. No eye contact.

"The letter. Taylor told me it was on my bed. I helped myself to it when I saw it on his desk, on the theory that it was addressed to me and not to some ham-faced slob named Taylor."

She opened it and pulled out the folded sheets: white typing paper, black ink, handwritten. The bright sunlight coming through the sliding glass door made it easy to read.

"Go ahead, Merci. Read it and weep."

December 18

Dear Son,

I'm done, I'm over, and I'm sorry to do this to you. I trust the coroner will get here well before you do, make it all presentable. I'll call them before I do it, make sure they've got a heads-up.

I want to get a few things straight, son. There was a time, a long time ago, when I killed a woman I thought was going to blackmail some people I knew. She was a prostitute, and I'd introduced them. I was keen on her myself because she was a real party girl, and your mother and I never got along much that way. The guys I'd hooked her up with—Bill Owen and a politician named Ralph Meeks—they were assholes.

They'd asked me to play the right-wing nut, infiltrate the Birch chapters, hang with the fascist Volunteer Police Department types, and report back to them on what was happening. The Birchers were Beck Rainer, Big Pat McNally and those guys. But it was funny. Because the right-wing nuts, the Birch guys, the Volunteer Police Department types, they were my types, too. I liked them and we got along. I subscribed to their ideas. Except with regards to loose women—I couldn't quite keep my hands off them. Always the professionals, though, I didn't mess around with anybody's wife. Anyway, Rainer and McNally and the right-wingers wanted me to keep an eye on Bill Owen and Ralph Meeks—it was their idea to get Patti Bailey, the prostitute, connected up with them. The tapes were their idea, too, although Patti was a bit of a conniver on her own.

So I was in the middle, spying on both sides, but I never gave Owen and Meeks anything really good. Corrupt old shits. They'd arranged to get Jesse Acuna beaten half to death, just to get his hundred acres. Tried to use me for that, but I refused. They bragged about it to Bailey, the arrogant fools. When Bailey threatened them with the tapes, they did just exactly what we thought they'd do: They sent one of their flunkies to tell me to shut her up and get the evidence. The flunky was Chuck Brighton—a real smoothie, a real kiss-ass. My so-called right-wing friends also thought that it was a good idea to shut her up. Surprised me. I said I wasn't going to kill a woman just to keep a couple of old pols safe in office. I said, are you guys crazy? And they said, it's for the good of the department, Jim. We've got to stick together. We can't have a hooker bringing down the sheriff and the head of the Board of Supervisors, even if we don't agree with them on everything. They said, don't worry, we'll collect all the evidence from the crime scene, we'll clean it up and no one will know—we just got to shut her up. I said I'm still not going to kill a girl just for that. Then they said, kill the hooker or we'll tell your wife what you've been doing with her the last few months—then you'll really wish Patti Bailey was dead. They meant it. I knew they'd do it. Some friends. They were guys I'd die for—and this is what they did for me. So I shut her up. It ruined me, son. It was evil and it was selfish and I spent twenty-seven years killing myself over and over for it. That's why today's such a great day—I'm finally doing it for real.

Anyway, my great friends, they didn't destroy the crime-scene evidence to save my sorry ass.

They kept the evidence and the tapes, turned it all over to goddamned Brighton. Brighton turned on his bosses then, used the tapes to get rid of Owen, make his own way to sheriff. I'm sure he got Owen to back him in the next election as part of not turning the tapes over to the newspapers and TV. McNally got a great promotion, tagging along on Brighton's coattails. So, it wasn't for the good of the department—it was to get Owen and Meeks out. Everybody got something out of it but me. Me? I was betrayed and guilty and wanted to die. I couldn't do anything because Brighton and Big Pat had the crime-scene stuff—they could use it against me any time they wanted. So I split for San Bernardino as soon as I could. Said good-bye to all those treacherous Orange County bastards. Best thing I ever did. Too late, though. Way too late to do any good.

I needed to get that off my chest. I feel better. Still not good enough to go on living this miserable life. I'm on to the next thing. You? You take care. Know I loved you. I was a rotten man and a rotten father, but nobody can accuse me of not loving my only son. I hope you get what you want out of life. Stay straight, be clean, and don't let your friends do to you what mine did to me. Look out for yourself, because nobody can do it for you. Don't mess with girls. Pick out a good one and stick with her. It's all the same in the end, so you may as well make someone a little happy if you can. I love you, Evan. Do not shed one tear for me. I'm happy now. I'm in the better place, wherever that is. I'll send you a postcard when I get a chance.

Love,
Dad

When she finished the letter she understood what had happened to Mike McNally. When she looked over at Evan, she understood just how close she had been to the truth.

He stood there, leaning against the entertainment cabinet, a big revolver in his hand.

"Dad's gun," he said. "I got it out of evidence when they were done. Put it right back here in the cabinet, where he always kept it."

"I understand," she said. "You should put that thing down, Evan."

"Dream on."

He lifted the barrel at her, made a soft clicking sound.

"Gotcha, girl."

"Come on, Evan."

"At first I didn't want you to see that letter. But the long ride out here gave me some time to think. I'm still in the driver's seat."

Merci stared at his face for any sign of O'Brien's mean

humor, any sign of his sarcasm. None. No humor, just a calm alertness. She tried to think of a way to lead him away from all this, let him off the hook.

"That letter's between you and your father. We'll keep it that way. Let's head out, get back to work."

"Now you come on. This is it, Lady Dick. Don't move either hand. Not one inch."

Her arms were at her sides. She still had the letter in her right hand. She dropped the sheets to the floor without looking down, then tilted her palms outward, spreading her fingers.

Evan tilted the revolver sideways like the TV cops, then righted it. The barrel was steady on her, no waver at all.

"It's better this way. I'm so goddamned proud of things, Merci. The way I led you into it, let you do the fun part. I'm tickled pink."

"You ruined Mike to get Big Pat back for what he did to your father. To get back at the whole department."

Evan shrugged, grinned. He was twenty feet away. She figured if she went for the H&K he might shoot her before she got her hand inside her coat. There was a sofa between them and that was all.

"But you left the mystery prints in Whittaker's kitchen. *Your* prints."

"I'll work around that. I knew Mike was working with one of the outcall girls, thought there might be an opportunity. I got her name and address off the wiretap request that was never filed. I got her picture from her sheet. Nice face. So I set up my own recorder on her phone and what do you know? Things developed. Pretty girl, horny guy, what do you expect? Waited outside the night they had dinner, went up and iced her. Planted the silencer and chukka boots when he was at work."

"I *knew* something was wrong at Mike's, but I couldn't nail it. You should never have known where the kennel key was. But you did, because you'd been inside."

O'Brien smiled. "No. I knew where it was before I ever picked the locks. Mike described it to Aubrey one night. He was talking about how knowing her made him question everything he did. Why he wore the clothes he wore. Why he shaved with a blue razor instead of a yellow one, why he kept the kennel key under the cabinet, why he always carried his wallet in his left pocket, why he combed his hair the way he did. She had him all shook up. The second I handed that key to you, I knew I'd made a mistake. I didn't know if you'd catch it or not."

The wind whistled against the windows, sent a spray of dust across the yard.

"Put down the gun. *Now.*"

"Merci, shut up. *Now.* You're taking your orders from me, babe. Get used to it."

He raised the revolver, steadied it with both hands, bringing the black of the barrel into line with her chest.

"Zamorra's off to the wrong address," he said. "It's on the other side of the county. San Bernardino County is the size of Delaware, in case you didn't know."

Keep him talking, she thought. Her heart was racing and her mind was jumping.

"What about the brass? How did you get brass from Mike's gun into Whittaker's flower vase?"

Evan smiled. "Mike went to the range twice a month. I followed him one day, watched some of the guys shoot, shot some targets myself. Picked up one of his empties along with my own. Easy. The hard part was lining up the shot so the bullet would go out the window and not stick in a wall stud. The lead wouldn't have matched the brass. I picked the lock on Whittaker's place one day, let myself in and figured it out. The picture windows gave me the idea. Figured I'd have to shoot her right there in the doorway, fast, on an up-angle, to get the bullet out into the ocean."

"You let Coiner find it. Nice."

"That was easy. She's a good CSI. The only thing that really went wrong was the struggle in the kitchen."

He smiled, laughed quickly, stopped smiling. "That had you and Zamorra pulling out your hair, didn't it?"

"There was no struggle," said Merci.

"So true."

"You had a seizure right there on the floor. Ripped up the drawers. Tore your coat, snagged one of your latex gloves. No blood, but you left your prints in places you didn't have time to clean up. You were dazed. You didn't know how much time had passed, how much noise you'd made. That's why there was a ten-minute gap between the time you went up and the time you came down. That's why you hesitated on the stairs. You were steadying yourself."

"Pretty much. I'm surprised you came up with Dad's prints from CAL-ID. You'd have to throw your parameters all the way back to deceased law enforcement to come up with them. Who'd ever think of that?"

"Zamorra."

"He's like a Gila monster: clamps onto something and won't let go 'til the sun goes down."

A grudging respect joined Merci's surprise and fear.

"You've been working on this for years."

"The hours fly when you're having a good time."

"You transposed your prints with your father's, after he killed himself. You were still working in Sacramento then, on the CAL-ID computer changeover. You couldn't just delete your own, somebody would realize a set was missing. So you traded yours for your father's. It got you out of the system. Just in case you ever left a print you wished you hadn't. Just in case you ever tore a glove. You knew those prints would be tough to find in the registry, attached to a dead man. Later, you got the job here in Orange County so you could do what you did. But you'd been thinking about it for almost two years."

"I was undecided, actually. But when the hiring committee passed on me for my minor medical condition, I figured fuck it, I'll stick the clowns were it hurts."

"You have."

O'Brien looked relaxed behind the gun. The barrel wasn't moving much at all. She could hear the wind howling behind her outside, could hear the sand hitting the windowpanes.

"I used to watch you and Mike in the living room at his place, Sergeant. There's a nice little clearing in the brush on the hillside behind the house. You can sit there and see right in the back window. I spent hours there. Remember the night you did him on the couch when *The Ten Commandments* was on?"

"Easter."

"You climaxed when Charlton Heston was coming down with the tablets. From the hillside, it looked like his hair turned white when he saw you having that big *O*. I started falling in love with you at that moment. Hated you, too. I still kind of love-hate you. I hate the way you smug bastards with the badges think you own the world. Nothing made me sicker than watching you and that big idiot McNally, walking around together like you owned the Sheriff Department, barging into my lab to tell me what to do. You don't deserve anything you have. I knew I was as good as you. Even when the personnel board turned me down for the epilepsy, I knew I was as good as you. And I proved it. I got Mike in jail for a murder he didn't commit. I got you to investigate him. I got Brighton's department looking like a bunch of whore killers and incompetents. I won. The little bastard who wasn't good enough to wear a badge beat all you arrogant suck-ups."

"You killed an innocent woman to get all that."

"She got what she deserved. So did Bailey. Whores ruin lives. Don't even bother me with that kind of thinking."

She watched his face for a tic or twitch, hoping the situation might breed a seizure. His eyes looked steady behind the barrel.

He smiled. "I took an extra Dilantin this morning. I'm steady as a pack mule right now."

"Why go to the trouble? Why not just take care of Big Pat and Brighton and be done with it?"

He shrugged, but the gun stayed trained on her. "Sure, I could have run over that drunkard Pat in a parking lot some night. I could have shot Brighton on one of his morning jogs. I thought about it. But, you know? That's too easy. I want them to watch their own ruin and not be able to stop it. I want Pat to watch his son rot. I want Brighton to watch his department fall apart because of the *shit* they pulled on Jim O'Brien. I want them to feel what Dad felt—ashamed and useless and betrayed. You know what my dad got for being a deputy, for being a friend to those guys? He got a drunk wife, a fucking epileptic son and his own bullet in his brain. That sucks. Death is too good for any of them. I wish you hadn't figured this out because now I've got to kill you and it kind of spoils things a little. On the other hand, I like the fact that someone knows. Makes it complete. It was delicious hating you, because really, to me, you're so beautiful—big and dark and proud and completely self-absorbed, completely full of yourself. You're two gallons of shit in a one-gallon bucket, Rayborn. I couldn't pass up using your undies when I found them in one of Mike's drawers. The whole show would have been great, watching you watch Mike go to prison. It would have eaten you alive. Better than cancer."

O'Brien smiled again and moved his feet apart just a little, into a more stable shooting stance. Merci's ears were roaring and she wondered if he could hear them.

Think. Anything. Keep him talking.

"How do you explain a dead detective in your dad's house?"

"Easy. You intercepted me on my way to work. True. Said you wanted me to supply the suicide note and videotape of dad. True again. I said the stuff was out here, so you said let's go. True. When we got here, I couldn't find the note. That will become true. But I showed you the suicide gun and you inspected it, must have assumed it was empty, and it went off. Sort of true. I administered CPR but it was too late. Then, just the obvious, I'll wipe the gun off before I put it in your hands. Then I'll help you shoot it through that window, but you'll be dead so it won't be difficult. I'll replace the spent cartridge so it looks like only one shell went off. I'll replace the glass with plywood so it matches half the other windows in here. Then I'll hit my hands with a double dose of solvent to get the gunshot residue off. After that it's my word against yours, but you won't have much to say. Accidents happen."

"Zamorra won't buy it."

"I'll handle Zamorra. He's so ditzed out right now, he probably *will* buy it."

"Your prints were in Whittaker's kitchen."

"Hey, babe, I'm a CSI. I *worked* that scene. Mistakes happen."

She dove behind the sofa, landing on her left side, hand already jammed under her coat. The room exploded with a roar and she felt something slam into her side. Two more booms then, the reports echoing through the room. Her leg seemed to burst into flames. She reached the nine over the couch top and fired twice but four loud detonations went off and the sheet over the couch puffed out and sprouted two holes. When the echoes died off she heard O'Brien curse, then footsteps fast away from her.

She labored to her knees with the H&K ready, saw O'Brien disappear into the kitchen, saw the smear of blood on the floor. She swung away her coat with one elbow, then reached down toward her bleeding holes. She poked her trigger finger in one and saw the tip come out the other. She almost fainted. The blood was already all over the place. There was a rip in her pants, down below the knee, but she couldn't tell if the bone was shattered or not. She stood and dragged herself toward the kitchen.

Blood on the floor and on the doorframe. The outside door swung open, banging in the wind. She steadied herself on the counter, got across the room to the door and looked out.

A pool house to her left, garages to her right, the whole

tableau dusted by the blowing sand. Eyes burning, the wind ripping at her face, a huge tumbleweed bouncing along and a few drops of blood leading up to the pool.

She took a deep breath, got the nine steady in both slippery hands and limped across the deck toward the pool. She looked in. No water, just a bunch of tumbleweeds trapped in the bottom. But she saw movement on the far wall, something rising up from the bottom, growing taller, the shadow of a man and all she could think of was jump out and turn midair and crank off three quick shots as she dropped straight down into an ocean of thorns.

She sank. She tried to stay upright but it was like treading broken glass. She got up against the near side and saw the gun barrel come over the lip of the deck, saw the hand behind it.

For a moment it seemed to watch her, one big black eye, then it moved right and left as if to locate her, and she was just about to roll to one side when the black eye dropped and skittered down the gunite and slid under the tumbleweeds.

She could feel her breath coming short and fast but she couldn't hear anything but the wind shrieking above her. O'Brien's hand was twitching rhythmically. She rolled away from it, toward the shallow end, fighting her way through the thorns and dust and finally got to the steps, trying to keep the sights of her gun on the facedown body of Evan O'Brien.

He lay outstretched on the deck with one hand dangling

in the empty air above the pool. She sat on the bottom step and leaned forward, resting the H&K on the deck, both hands still firm in spite of the blood and the sand and the thorns that had come off in her skin.

She got the sights lined up on O'Brien's side and held them there. She rested her arms on the deck and her weight on her arms. She panted. She listened to the wind howl. She looked down at the steps and they were heavy with blood and she felt light and painless and oddly content.

When she tried to stand she faltered and fell back down the poolside, boot toes scratching hopelessly for purchase, gun dropping from her hand.

Caught in the curve at the bottom, she looked forward and saw three things right in front of her face: one section of gunite and two bloody hands resting against it.

She wondered whose they were. Thorns everywhere, blood and sand. Must hurt.

She thought she heard sirens, but she thought she heard music, too.

Chapter Thirty-two

Her sense of time was all off: Minutes dragged to eternities while hours shot past like hummingbirds. In and out of the world, a world of uniforms and sharp voices, of sirens and tubes in her arms and mouth, of bright lights and hovering masks and finally a room that was quiet but active with the comings and goings of people she didn't know and, if she didn't just dream it, brief inquisitive appearances by her father and Paul Zamorra and Sheriff Chuck Brighton.

Cold. Sleep. Thirst. More cold. More sleep. More thirst.

Then more sirens and helicopter blades and the blustery roof of the UCI Medical Center where the Medi-Vac chopper circled to a stop and shook the needles in her veins. And another room hushed with activity, monitors everywhere, more faces she didn't know, more apparitional visitations by faces she did.

The first thing she noticed were her hands: swollen as if

by a thousand stings, small dark shards lodged deep in the red flesh. They hurt. The worst were the pads of her fingers, and around her nails. Moving either hand was like sticking it into a prickly pear cactus.

The next thing she noticed was her smell: not good. She pulled herself up from the bed, which set off an alarm, which brought two nurses skidding into the room. They strapped her down to the bed and gave her a whore's bath when she stopped crying and thrashing around.

Her lower torso was wrapped with gauze. Her right calf was wrapped with gauze. Her butt was wrapped in gauze then fitted loosely inside a large padded diaper. When her right hand began to boil with pus they added a sedative to her saline drip that made her feel like Joan Cash had hypnotized her. They pulled out the thorns. Then they left. She awakened some years later and held up her hands, mittened now in still more gauze but not throbbing like they were before.

She woke from a terrible dream in which she was shot up and filled with stickers, only to find it true. She screamed and strained against the bedstraps. A nurse added something else into her IV drip and the world got warm and fuzzy and humorous. Clark showed up with Tim. *The Men!*

She touched Tim with her white mittens then something like a soft hammer hit her. The next thing she knew she was sitting up in bed with a tray in front of her and a carton of orange juice with a straw steadied between the white bandaged clubs of her fingers.

Nobody was in the room but her father. He told her it was a whole day after he and Tim, Jr., had visited. Monday, the day before Christmas. He smiled and touched her forehead and told her everything was going to be just fine.

• • •

Medical news: gunshot to the right lower torso, flesh and muscle wound, lower rib chipped. Bone shards removed, remainder filed and shaped. Entrance and exit wounds sutured and stitched. Gunshot to right upper calf, no damage to bone or nerve, considerable localized destruction of flesh, replaced by tissue and skin graft from patient's posterior gluteal area. Minor flesh wounds on both hands and fingers caused by repeated contact with tumbleweeds—thorns removed and punctures cleaned.

Blood loss considerable, transfusions continuing, platelet and white cell levels below normal but rising.

Patient condition: fair.

Elapsed hospital time: four days and counting.

• • •

Afternoon, Christmas Day.

"O'Brien's dead," said Zamorra. His dark face wavered in and out of focus at the end of a cave. "You hit him three times—one in the arm, two in the chest."

"Wasted one," she heard herself croak. Her throat

burned and no amount of water seemed to bring any moisture to it. "Janine?"

"Let's talk about that later."

"The porch bulb and the fixture from Whittaker's are in my trunk."

"I'll get them."

"The suicide note. Get a copy from San Bernardino sheriffs, and get it back to me. Soon."

"Done. Merry Christmas."

"I'm sleepy."

"Rest."

"Get Brenkus."

• • •

That night came Clayton Brenkus, white-haired and stately. He sat. He questioned. His pen rolled across the paper in short bursts.

"He confessed?"

"Whittaker. The phone recorder. Planting evidence. His father killed Patti Bailey for his alleged friends. They betrayed him with it. Evan wanted restitution."

A long silence, a burst of pen on paper. "Last words are evidentiary and admissible."

"Get Mike out, for Chrissakes."

"For starters, yes. An appropriate Christmas present. Imagine the lawsuit we'll be up against."

"Imagine."

Pen on paper. Walls melting. Darkness filling in.

"I'm sleepy."

"Get some rest."

• • •

Morning.

". . . misses you all the time. So he lurches around your room trying to figure out where you are and I keep telling him but you know how that goes. He's eating tons, though, and sleeping a lot, so he's fine. When you get home we're going to spoil the heck out of you, we'll be your patient recovery team. Now look, try some more of these eggs. You've got to get your strength back or they'll never let you out of this place. You are *needed* at home, young lady. That's a direct order from Tim."

Clark leaning forward with a pile of yellow goop on a spoon, a pitying smile on his face.

"Kiss him for me."

"I have been. Gary Brice from the *Journal* has left twelve messages. I've talked to him three times. He said he's ready to collect payment for not running the articles on you and Mike. He said you'd know what he's talking about."

"I'm sleepy."

"Rest, honey."

• • •

Evening.

Brighton, tall and ancient, stood in the doorway with a bouquet.

"We're springing Mike soon."

"Um-hm."

"Gilliam and his people are going over everything O'Brien did the last week. All the evidence he handled, lost, tampered with, planted. *Everything.*"

"Lots."

"What can I do for you?"

"I'm sleepy."

"Get some rest."

He turned and walked away, then came back in, still holding the flowers. He set them on the floor because the little nightstand was already full of them.

• • •

Late night. Out the window she could see car lights creeping up and down Interstate 5, the gay domes of a theater complex in the distance. Rain rolled down the glass and smeared it all.

Merci walked around the floor, still tethered to the drip trolley, her right leg aching, her rib aching, her butt burning where the grafts had been taken. A nurse walked along beside her, talking about her children.

Gary Brice was waiting outside her room when she returned. "Merci," he said. "You look great for six days in two hospitals."

"I can't talk now, Gary."

"I know. I just want you to know that when you're ready, I am. You promised me the truth."

"You'll get it."

"O'Brien framed Mike, didn't he?"

"It's a long story. Later."

"Promise?"

"Promise."

"Exclusive?"

"All the way."

Zamorra came very late, shut the door and sat down by the window. In the harsh hospital light his eyes looked black and his skin looked gray. He was dressed in a dark suit as always, his white shirt collar pressed and his tie neatly knotted. The only thing his neatness did was reveal the exhaustion in his face.

"Janine," said Merci.

Zamorra nodded. "Let's just sit here a minute."

The minute seemed like an hour. It might have been. Merci opened her eyes, felt her head lagging to the side. The rain came down hard outside the window but she couldn't hear it over the hum of the heater, the muffled buzz of the hospital around her.

"What happened, Paul?"

"She went into a grand mal seizure Friday morning around eight. Not long after you told me you were going out to Jim O'Brien's old house with Evan. She died at nine forty-three."

Zamorra turned his eyes from her and looked out the window. His brow furrowed and his breath caught in his throat.

"That's why I . . . couldn't make it. I called the San Bernardino sheriffs with the address, told them there might be a deputy in trouble. Later, I realized that O'Brien might have given you the wrong address. So I got personnel here to dig out Jim O'Brien's address, called it in. By then, well, you were down and bleeding half to death. And your partner was just one building from where he is now."

"Paul."

His profile was clear against the black window but he still didn't look at her.

A nurse came in, checked the IV drip and the monitor, asked Merci if she wanted a pain med. Merci said no. The idea hit her that Zamorra needed it more than she did, but what drug on earth could repair a broken heart?

They sat for a while in the hourless time of the hospital.

"She had a nice voice," he said finally. "She sang to me sometimes. Broadway stuff, with lots of dramatics. Funny."

"What are you going to do, Paul?"

"The San Diego guys want me down there. Get a place with a little acreage, maybe."

"I mean now. Tonight."

"Nothing. Absolutely nothing."

"Promise me."

He turned her way. "If I was going to do that, I wouldn't be here right now. I'd crawl away and do it, like an old cat."

"Remember about the broken places healing up stronger than before."

"I know."

"You're young. Everything's going to change. Then change again."

Merci listened to the voices in the hall, the drone of the heater.

"I let you down, and I'm sorry," he said.

"I'll tell you something, Paul. I let my partner down once. It got him killed. There's nothing in the world that feels worse. I know that. You wish you could trade places, but you can't. And you won't forgive yourself for a long time. But you have to. We have to. It's the only way to keep going."

He looked at her. "You haven't? Yet?"

"I play it over all the time. This way and that. Try to change what I did, what I thought, what I believed. It can't be done. But look at me. I'm here. I made it. I'm alive. You don't have my life on your hands. So grieve for Janine. Grieve for yourself. But not for me. For whatever it's worth, Paul, I forgive you. Get over it. Go on."

And with those words she felt something break inside her, peel away and sink out of sight. Black water closed over it then a halo of ripples wobbled outward. She knew that Hess would have said the same to her. He would have forgiven her. He would have told her that the first person to forgive is not your enemy but yourself, that only the fool extends his suffering.

In that moment she loved Hess again, and she loved Paul Zamorra, and she loved Mike McNally and she even loved herself. For the first time in many months she believed she would be all right.

In the eye of her mind the last black ripple was gone now and something that could have been moonlight shone on the water.

"I can't go home tonight."

"Turn off the light. Sit back down. The nurse will bring you a blanket."

She woke up three times that night. The third, Zamorra was gone.

Chapter Thirty-three

A week later, on the second day of the New Year, Merci rented a little two-bedroom place on the sand at Ninth Street in Newport. It was cheap and smelled of pine cleanser and the ocean. There was old carpet, old furniture, old prints on the walls faded by the sun. Clark helped her and Tim move in, still trying to talk her out of it.

She had cut her hair short. She bought some baggy clothes that wouldn't hang up on her bandages. She rented the place as Gail White, trying to sweet-talk the old landlord into accepting cash in advance in lieu of proper ID. When he resisted she badged him and asked him to help her out goddamnit and he did. He showed up later that first afternoon with a bunch of carnations.

When Clark left she took Tim down to the waterline for a walk. She watched Tim waddle after the hunkered gulls. She watched the half-day boat put down anchor near a kelp bed. She passed a couple of kids smoking a joint by the lifeguard stand, glowered at them, then reminded herself who she was. Things that are not my problem for a hundred, she thought. She liked being "Gail." It was her way, off center as she often was, of showing respect.

She read the papers. She slept. She played with Tim. She watched the tube. She talked on the phone a little. She took more walks.

She attempted to call Paul Zamorra twice, as she'd been doing for the last week. No answer at home. No response to her messages. He'd taken a bereavement leave. Nobody in the department had any idea where he was. She made some inquiries with the San Diego SD but couldn't identify any of Zamorra's friends.

If I was going to do that I wouldn't be here right now. I'd crawl away and do it, like an old cat.

Merci also called Joan Cash at the close of each workday. No, Zamorra had not contacted her office with regard to counseling or anything else. Cash and Merci talked for almost an hour each time. They were long, wandering conversations that Cash without subtlety guided toward Merci's feelings about O'Brien, the Purse Snatcher, Hess.

Merci thought it was easier talking to Cash on the phone than it was face-to-face. She liked the idea of miles between them, even if their voices flew with the speed of electricity. Cash thought that Zamorra's "old cat" statement was a clear warning and, without saying so, suggested that Merci should prepare herself for anything.

Clark had saved for her all the newspaper articles relating to Mike's arrest, O'Brien's death, and the subsequent investigation of the framing of Mike.

She read them and saw that without Jim O'Brien's suicide letter there was no visible motive for Evan to have done what he did. Not even Gary Brice from the *Journal* could figure out why the CSI had gone to such lengths to make an innocent man suffer.

Brighton had acted mystified. Glandis had a lot of no comments. The rank and file expressed support for Mike, who refused to speak with the media. And Merci told none of them that she had the key to it all—a photocopy of Jim O'Brien's suicide letter—secured for her by Zamorra before his vanishing.

By the third day she was bored with Gail White, so she got Mel Glandis to come over after lunch.

• • •

He slumped his big body into the chair by the window in the living room, following her with his bovine eyes, face flushed and hands folded.

"My getting the Bailey case was no accident," she said. "You gave it to me for a reason. You knew something was wrong with it from the beginning, from way back in sixty-nine. You even had the evidence to prove it, but you didn't have the balls to try."

He smiled. "What are you talking about, Merci?"

"Evan said he wanted to get to the truth about Bailey.

When he asked you to help him dig it up, you jumped at the chance. You knew if you could cast a shadow on Brighton, you could muscle yourself into his office the same way he did. Evan mailed me the key to the storage area, but I think the storage unit was yours. Brighton and McNally had tried to hide that evidence, but you found out where it was. You took it. Kept it for a rainy day. Your little investment in the future. You just never had the nuts to use it, until Evan showed up. Dirty work's not your thing. All of which makes you more than the garden variety buttkisser I thought you were. It makes you an accomplice to murder."

His mouth dropped open, his face went redder. "Nothing you just said is true."

"Evan O'Brien said it was. Dying words, Mel. Admissible in court. He ratted out your fat ass."

Glandis stared at her. The part about Evan's admission was a lie, but she had no problem telling it because she figured that most of it had to be true.

"Mel, I don't think you knew Evan was going to murder Aubrey Whittaker. You wouldn't have the stomach for that. You just saw a way to open a can of worms, let the stink get onto Brighton. I'm going to let you take it from here. Tell me what happened and you'll walk back to your job. Lie to me and I'll have you arrested as a co-conspirator with O'Brien. I'll ruin you."

Glandis looked out the window. She guessed he'd roll over in less than thirty seconds. It took ten.

"Yeah, okay. I knew the Bailey case wasn't right, but I

didn't know *how.* I thought Brighton was covering something. McNally, too. I smelled Owen and Meeks in it, but I wasn't sure where. So I kept my eyes and ears open. I was partnered up with Rymers back in seventy-three and we got pretty tight. He got bills from Inland Storage in Riverside every month. Sent to him at headquarters. I wondered why. I heard him and Brighton saying something about the storage unit. I wondered. I saw Rymers get a key back from Big Pat one day. I wondered some more. So I took that key, went to Inland, had a look. They'd kept aside the evidence—the gun, Bailey's clothes, the tapes, her appointment book. Just in case Jim O'Brien's conscience got too heavy. Had the goods on Meeks and Owen. When O'Brien killed himself I knew they'd ditch the stuff, so I broke in and took it. Took everything in the unit, so they'd think it was a routine burg job. Rented my own little spot across town, stored it all."

"You think just like a rodent, Mel."

Glandis shrugged, as if the comment didn't bother him. Something in his face looked pleased.

"You must have drooled when Evan got hired, started talking about digging up the truth on Bailey."

"Yeah. When Brighton gave me the unsolveds to assign, you got Bailey. I wanted our best homicide investigator on it. I figured if anyone had the endurance to solve it, you did."

"I'm flattered."

Glandis lit up for a split second, looked like he believed her.

"But Merci, I didn't know what he was planning with Whittaker and Mike. I really didn't. After she died, I figured one of her johns, you know. Then when you found out all the stuff about Mike, I figured he got carried away with a girl who was going to blackmail him, so he shut her up. But Evan? No. I just knew the Bailey evidence would lead you toward Brighton, so I made sure you got it. That's all. If I'd have known what Evan was up to, I'd have . . ."

Merci watched him, heard the failure of his language.

"You'd have let Evan do it, Mel, then hoped he got caught. Because you want the department to fail. You want it to sink so you can rise to the top and rescue it."

He glanced at her, then down at the ancient green shag carpet. He was breathing deeply. He was looking at his small dancer's feet. Then he sat back and rolled his shoulders like a boxer, and looked straight at her.

"Don't you?" he asked. "Don't you want to rise to the top?"

"Damn right I do."

He smiled. "You know, Brighton would have to throw his weight behind me for sheriff if I handled this mess for him. If I could convince you to just forget about Bailey. Then, if I'm sheriff, you'll write your own ticket. Anything you want, Merci Rayborn. *Anything*."

She stared at him. "Get out of my sight, you craven rat."

"What are you gonna do?"

"Out of my sight."

Glandis stood. The sweat ran down his face, onto the collar of his shirt. "Don't crucify me. I didn't do anything wrong. I'm just a guy trying to get ahead, get what's mine."

She opened the door for him and when he was out, she slammed it. The little house shook and a picture fell off the wall. Tim started crying from his room.

One down, she thought, and one to go. She reached under the sofa and turned off the tape recorder, then went to get her son.

• • •

She carried Tim to the front gate of the Zamorra household in the Fullerton hills. The ornate wrought iron squeaked open at her touch. The courtyard fountain was still and the potted flowers were green and battered by the rain. She looked through a window and saw only the furniture inside. She rang the bell but no one answered.

No newspapers. No mail. The garage doors wouldn't budge.

She let herself through a side gate and followed the round stepping stones to the backyard. The swimming pool was covered with a pale blue tarp, leaves gathered in a brown puddle under the diving board.

She looked through the panes of a French door: the Zamorra master suite, complete with hospital bed in a fully upright position and a king mattress and springs on the floor beside it. The cut flowers in a vase bent down like they were looking for something on the bedstand.

Sometimes I wish I could just fly away.

Don't you do it, she thought. I can forgive anything but that.

• • •

Brighton got there in the early evening. He'd been reluctant to meet with her at her place, but she'd talked him into it over the phone. He stood and looked at the chair where Mel Glandis had sat just a few hours earlier. He didn't sit down. It was like his instincts told him not to, Merci thought, like he knew it wasn't a chair you got good news in.

Instead, Brighton knelt down and extended a big hand to Tim, who tried to pull off his wedding band.

"Cute boy," he said. "You're a cute boy, Tim, Jr. You look a little like Dad, a little like Mom. That's a good combination."

She set a copy of Jim O'Brien's suicide letter on the coffee table. Brighton looked up at her, rose and picked up the envelope.

"Have a seat while you read," she said.

"I'll stand." His eyes were wary in his lined, tired face. "I talked to Mike again today. He's doing okay. He'll be back to work in a week."

"I haven't talked to him."

"So he said. I think you might find him more forgiving than you believe. He understands what happened. He understands how Evan fooled us all."

"Me most of all."

"You. Me. Gilliam. All of us. It happens. If it didn't, we wouldn't have jobs."

"Some job, isn't it?"

Brighton pursed his lips and shrugged. "It beats selling shoes."

"Have you heard anything from Paul?"

"He signed out for a month. Something tells me he won't be coming back. Hot for San Diego sheriffs, I think. I'm not surprised he hasn't called you."

"Why is that?"

"It's his way. He doesn't complain. He doesn't explain. He just does what he does. When we hired him from Santa Ana P.D. we knew he was a little touchy."

He looked at her, then pulled the letter from the envelope. He read it slowly, looking up at her twice. Then he slid the letter back into the envelope.

"Interesting words," he said.

"And more of them, right here. Patti Bailey's."

She hit the play button on her tape recorder and turned up the volume.

MAN: "Whazzat?"

WOMAN: "Zwhat?"

MAN: "Clickin' sound."

WOMAN: "My bubble gum." Chewing sounds.

"It was actually the sound of Patti's tape recorder going on."

Brighton eyed her sharply. Merci held up the key that O'Brien had sent her, courtesy of Mel Glandis.

"Inland Storage, Riverside," she said. "That's where your box of Bailey evidence got to. After it disappeared from your unit at Security."

A look of bewilderment crossed his face. She saw that Brighton couldn't understand who had betrayed him. Because it was so much like what he himself had done to Bill Owen thirty-two years back. She wondered if schemers were most easily manipulated, if their cunning left a blind spot.

"Where'd you get that?"

"It doesn't matter right now. What I found in the box does."

"You tape-recording this?"

"I don't have to. You know what you're listening to right now. You've heard it. More than once, I'd guess. Bailey and Meeks. Bailey and Bill Owen. Bailey and Jim O'Brien. He shoots her in the back. You can hear her hit, hear him swear and cry. You put him up to it. You and Big Pat. Just like the letter says."

Brighton was nodding now, as if in agreement with

some minor point of order. "Jim O'Brien's dying words, thirty-two years after the fact, won't carry much weight in court."

"They'd carry a lot of weight on the front page of the *Times,* the *Register* or the *Journal.*"

"You won't do that."

"Why not?"

"You don't get it, do you?"

"It's all pretty much right here."

"No, Rayborn—the *consequences.* The consequences of you going to the media, or the Grand Jury, or whatever you're thinking."

"I understand that you'd be disgraced. Between the Bailey tape and O'Brien's letter, that's evidence of conspiracy to commit murder, blackmail, obstruction of justice."

"Sure. You could ruin me, but what would it do to *you*?"

"Nothing good."

"Then I don't understand. Why are you even thinking of this? It goes against your department. It goes against your superiors. It goes against your friends and supporters. You're going to bring down everybody around you. For what? Why?"

"For Patti Bailey. She's the one we were supposed to serve and protect. Remember?"

Brighton shook his head, looking down at Tim. Then he scooped up the boy and sat down by the window. He bounced Tim gently on his knee, his big weathered hands secure around Tim's soft middle.

The boy looked up at Merci and smiled, proud to be riding, proud to be on the lap of a big strong man.

"Let me set up a couple of scenarios for you, Merci. One: You expose all this to solve a thirty-two-year-old homicide case—fine. I'm deposed and Mel Glandis steps in as interim sheriff. Pat McNally goes down the drain. The men and women in the department look on you as a vulture—the detective who accused her own boyfriend of murder, the detective who dusted off an irrelevant case from three decades ago and made everyone suffer for her ideals. You'd be vapor. You'd be gone. They'd haze you right into the smog. So, you play the child and everyone gets hurt. Including you. Tim here—you'd be bringing him into a world that despises his mother. Nice. Great. Just how I'd want to raise my son."

Tim still bounced happily on Brighton's knee.

"Okay, here's scenario number two. You compromise with yourself, just a little. You know the truth about Bailey, you can let it out any time you want. It's not going away. O'Brien killed her—not me or Pat or anybody else. In your heart the case is solved, and there's no killer on the streets to do it again. Bailey's never coming back, no matter which way you play it. That's what you pay. Now, what do you get? You get whatever you want. Head of Homicide Detail, then Crimes Against Persons Section? Take it. A shot at my office a few years down the line? Take it. I'll back you with every ounce of my power and gratitude. You'd have a department that's with you instead of against you. You'd have a world that likes the sight of your face. You'd have a way to bring up this little guy with some advantages. And you can keep Clark out of it."

She felt the blood rise to her face, the quiet acceleration of her heartbeat. "What's to leave out?"

Brighton sighed, held Tim up for a face-to-face. "Tim, your grandfather paid for the storage of the Bailey evidence for ten years. Twenty-eight dollars a month, cash. He helped me, Tim. He helped an old friend stay above the bullshit that we all have to live with every day. That's what we cops do. Anyway, Tim, you can figure your old grandpa into the conspiracy, if that's what you want to do. He's part of it. It would come out and he'd suffer. But he did the right thing. He understood the difference between being a child, like you, and being a man."

Brighton looked at Merci, his eyes sharp and cold. "Jim killed that girl to protect himself and his friends. We covered it up for the good of the department, Sergeant. We covered it up to help get me where I needed to go. To help Frank Stills onto the Board of Supervisors. To keep the county clean. To make it a good place to live. To bring up kids like this one."

"Don't blame my son for your crimes, Brighton. That sickens me. It's all disposable with you, isn't it? Disposable law. Disposable friends. Disposable women. Who did Meeks and Owen get to beat up Jesse Acuna?"

"Some young L.A. cops. We learned of the arrangement through the tapes, used it to get a substation we needed badly. That was part of the deal when Stills stepped up and Meeks stepped down. What's it matter now?"

Brighton stood, Tim still between his hands. He held out the infant and Merci took him.

"Do the right thing for this little guy. He'll never thank you. He'll never know. But you will. Welcome to the world, Rayborn. Rough place. Every once in a while, you get a chance to do something good. Take it."

He touched Tim's cheek, looked at Merci without expression, then walked out.

Merci walked the little cottage with her heart pounding hard and a dark sleepiness hanging over her. She called Zamorra for the third time that day—just his message machine at home. She managed to get a home phone number for Janine's parents. They talked a while. They said Paul had spoken highly of her. They hadn't heard from or seen him since they buried their daughter. That was over a week ago. He'd looked terrible that day, eyes looking past everybody and everything for something they couldn't find. He said something about getting away for a while.

• • •

She got to Mike's place just before seven, sat in the car until she saw him open the front door. The dogs barked and bayed. The night was moonless and cold and the stars looked too far away to matter.

Mike stood in the doorway. The houselight behind him

seemed like the only light in Modjeska Canyon, the only light left in the world. Tim was in his car seat, head to the side and a little forward, shoulder straps secure, like a tiny parachutist on his way down.

She climbed out of the Impala, pain biting her side as she stood and walked up the stepping-stones toward the door. She stopped halfway.

"Hello, Mike," she said. It was cold enough that her breath condensed in the night air. She could see the faint clouds as she breathed.

"Hi, Merci."

She had already decided not to go in, but it hurt and angered her that he didn't ask her.

"I'm sorry for what I did. I made a bad call, a real bad one. I've never made a worse one. Well, maybe that's not true."

She heard her voice catch and she felt the hot tears running down her cheeks but she wouldn't crack. It was crucial that she not, for reasons she could not have explained.

"But I'm sorry Mike. I just . . . I just can't tell you how sorry I am to have put you through all that. I wish so bad there was a way to take it back, not do what I did."

His features were hard to make out with the light behind him. Maybe he wanted it that way.

"I accept your apology," he said quietly.

"And I . . . you know I really cared about you, Mike. I cared about you more than anybody but Tim, Jr., and Dad, but I was always just so . . . so . . . shitty at it. I couldn't get over Hess and I took it out on you and nothing made sense after a while. But you were a good friend and lover and I . . . I didn't ever intend to hurt you like I did."

"I know."

She wanted to tell him she loved him, but she knew she did not love him and had never loved him in the way that she had wanted to. They were the wrong words. They were words for a time that hadn't happened yet, and maybe would never happen.

"Forgive me."

Mike said nothing for a long minute. "All right."

"I mean genuinely forgive me? If I kneel down in front of you and look up and ask you to forgive me will you touch my head and forgive me?"

He seemed about to speak but didn't. She walked the rest of the way to the door and knelt down on the cold hard porch in front of him. The wound in her side jumped with pain and her leg felt hot and stiff. When she looked up she still couldn't see the expression on his face.

"Forgive me."

She watched the vapor come from his nose.

"You sold me cheap, Merci. The worst of it all is that after everything I am and everything I tried to be, you believed the worst about me. You believed I'd kill that girl."

"Forgive me for that, too."

He shut the door and locked it.

Then she heard the car pull in behind her, saw the face of the house bathed by headlights. She struggled up slowly, got her balance, turned and squinted. The lights went out and a door opened.

A moment later Lynda Coiner walked toward her.

"I'm sorry," Coiner said. Then she hustled past Merci like someone trying to get out of the rain. The door opened up to receive her, then shut again. Merci heard the dead bolt slide into place.

Chapter Thirty-four

Later that night she sat by the fire with her father, up close to get the warmth into her aching bones. Another storm front had swung down from the north and the rain came fast and hard against the roof.

Clark was stretched into his favorite recliner, his long body not quite comfortable in its contours, his hands folded across his lap and the flames flickering in his glasses.

It seemed like she had seen him in this position for as long as she could remember: sitting calmly by a fire while his wife fluttered around and made conversation that Clark only took a partial interest in. Answering quietly. Trying to dodge an argument. And if his black hair had thinned and grayed, and if his straight frame had bent and softened, he was still the same man entranced by the fire, intent upon it, as if the flames could offer him answers his life could not.

"Dad, did you know what the twenty-eight bucks a month was for?"

His attention turned from the fireplace to her, but he said nothing. Merci thought: Here I am, replacing my mother, trying to draw him into something he'd rather not talk about. Tough.

She continued. "I read Jim O'Brien's suicide letter to his son. He pretty much spelled it out. As an emissary of Bill Owen and Ralph Meeks, Brighton suggested that O'Brien shut up Patti Bailey for good. When that didn't work Brighton got Big Pat to threaten him, to say they'd rat out Jim to his wife if he wouldn't kill the girl. And that did work. But Brighton and Big Pat didn't destroy the crime-scene evidence to protect Jim, like they promised. They kept it and used it to make him threaten Owen and Meeks. Brighton had both of them on tape with her, talking about arranging the Acuna beating. That was probably enough. But O'Brien threatening to point a finger at them clinched the deal, sent them both into early retirement. Good for Brighton. Part of the deal was that he got Owen's nod as successor. Vance Putnam, the interim sheriff, was never a player."

"Go on."

"No, Dad. *You* go on. Help me out here. I just about got killed trying to solve this case, and you goddamned knew who did it all along. I'm more than just a little pissed off at you. If my ass wasn't important enough for you to save, then fine. But you came *that* close to letting Tim, Jr.'s, mother get killed, and that is most definitely not fucking fine. Am I clear?"

"Yes. Yes. I . . . was pretty sure that things had happened like you say. I never knew for sure. I understood the payment every month was connected to Bailey, to Owen and Meeks giving up, to Brighton ascending like he did. I paid it like I was asked to. But I never knew. I . . . distanced myself from Brighton and Pat after that. Went into admin. Tried to steer clear of everything. I knew there was blood on my hands, but I didn't know how much."

"You never wanted to know."

"No."

"You were brave enough to play the game, but not brave enough to collect your prize."

"You can look at it that way. Although there's another way to see it, too."

"Well, I'll tell you what was in that storage area you paid for. Bailey's dress and shoes. Bailey's tapes of Owen and Meeks. O'Brien's gun and the spent shells. All the things that you guys needed to cover up a murder and drive a man to suicide while you went about your lives. You. Big Pat. Brighton. Rymers was probably in on it, too, keeping his own partner in the cold. Glandis stole it all when Jim O'Brien killed himself. Thought he might need it someday. He got Evan to mail me a key."

Clark was looking at her again now. He sat up straight and moved his hands to the arms of the chair. "We never knew what happened to that box. And everything else. The whole place was cleaned out."

"Now you do. And you never told anyone what was in it."

"Oh, never."

"Not even me."

"No."

There was a long silence between them then, with only the sound of the rain pouring down outside.

"Okay, Dad—what's the other way I can see it? Conspiracy to cover a murder. Explain that in some other way, will you?"

"Well, daughter, I did it for you."

"I didn't *ask* you to."

Clark stood up and warmed his hands at the fire. His voice was soft.

"That's the whole point, don't you see? I was connected, Merci—through Brighton and Pat. They were friends. We were in it together, at the beginning. And once you've taken that first little step you can't go back. You can't unstep. For me, it was taking that evidence to the storage area. Rymers and I made the arrangements, took the box there, got keys made. I took over the payments after he died. I really *didn't* know what we were storing until I opened the box. Well, at that point, it was too late. I was in. Because what were my choices by then? Arrest Jim O'Brien for murder? With Brighton headed for sheriff, O'Brien headed for the desert and Big Pat still a man I called a friend? Then what? Get myself hazed out of the department, take a job as a security guard somewhere? Not with your mother and you depending on me. You were a kindergartner with a beautiful smile and a good mind and a whole future ahead of you, and I wasn't about to offer you anything but the best I had. No, it was too late to do the right thing. Too late."

She looked at him, slow and old by the fire, a lifetime of guilt carried on his slender frame.

"Now I've got that same choice to make," Merci said. "I can clear the Bailey case. That would mean taking down Brighton, Big Pat, you. Everybody. Or I can just leave it alone. If I lay down, Brighton paves my way—head of detail, head of section, whatever I want. He'd endorse me for sheriff at some point, if I wanted. It's everything I've dreamed of. If I don't, I'm ruined. And Tim along with me, I guess."

Clark looked back at her.

"What would you do if you were me?" she asked.

He thought for a long moment before he answered. "I already did it."

"If you could do it again."

"I'd have turned that evidence over to the DA instead of hiding it. I'd have done the right thing. Who knows? You'd probably be sitting here right now, just like you are, if I'd have done the right thing. But you're sitting here with a broken heart, because I didn't. See? I wanted to protect you. You were my greatest love, and my biggest . . . rationale. But all I accomplished was almost getting you killed thirty years later. Don't leave the Bailey case for Tim to solve."

She said nothing.

"And something else, daughter of mine. You'll make some real enemies if you go to the press, or the Grand Jury, or wherever you're thinking of going. Big enemies. But you'll make some friends, too. Everybody's going to respect your decision, whether they hate you for it or not. You can take that respect with you, if it comes to that. You won't be ruined. You'll just be . . . diverted for a while. You'll need to watch your back. Maybe this had to happen. Maybe it's all a way of getting you onto a better path."

"Which one? To where?"

"I've got no idea."

Merci stood and joined him closer to the fire. "I always thought that kind of optimism was just a handy crock of shit. Something people tell themselves to get by. Maybe it is. Maybe it isn't. But either way, what's the choice? It's worse to believe that life is just set up to make you miserable."

"Low percentage."

"But I never thought doing what's right could mess up so many people. My own father. My son."

"Doesn't make it less right."

"Right and wrong. Black and white. Yes and no. Them and us. That's why I became a cop to start with. So I'd know the answers right up front."

Clark set a hand on her shoulder. "Maybe you became a cop so you wouldn't have to ask the questions in the first place."

She looked up and studied his face. "There always was some of that in me. Yeah."

"Ask them. Here's your chance."

"Either way, I'm going to call Bailey's sister tomorrow. I'm going to tell her what she needs to know. It won't make her feel any better, but she thinks it will."

"You never know."

She looked at him. "That's the whole thing, Dad. Sometimes you *do* know. Sometimes you goddamned *do know*."

• • •

It was almost eleven when she called Gary Brice at home. She could hear a keyboard tapping as he answered.

"I've got a story for you," she said. "Six o'clock tomorrow morning, the snack stand at Fifteenth Street."

"I'll be early. Do I need sunscreen?"

"An umbrella maybe. And a tape recorder."

"I love you. I want to date you and have your baby and die for you."

She smiled, hung up on him.

Chapter Thirty-five

Two weeks later Merci Rayborn stepped off the witness stand in the Grand Jury room and followed the marshal out the door. She'd been on the stand for half a day and her legs were heavy and slow from sitting so long.

When she came through the double doors she saw the ocean of faces: press and TV and radio reporters gathered up close, an infantry of tan-clad deputies; Brighton and his entourage against one wall; Glandis and his against another; Mike and Big Pat McNally and a bunch of relatives she half-recognized off to her right; a bunch of the homicide guys off together in the back; and a whole lot of people she knew by face only, fellow deputies, lab personnel, support staff.

Every one of them was staring at her. She saw not one friendly gaze in that ocean of eyes.

There was a second's pause before the microphones were launched toward her, the video shooters crouched and fired, the reporters started yelling out questions all at once.

She lowered her head, held her purse up tight to her stomach and started through. She thought of Oswald in the Dallas P.D. basement, thought that a stout man in a hat would lunge out any second. She wondered what a bullet in the gut might feel like, moved the purse up closer to her heart.

. . . what led you to O'Brien any truth to the Bailey conspiracy how did you uncover evidence from thirty-two years ago why wasn't the suicide letter made public until recently have you talked to Sergeant McNally is it true Sheriff Chuck Brighton and your own father may have helped cover up the murder . . .

She looked up and over the heads and lights and microphones toward the stairway leading up to the lobby. The people on the stairway were frozen midway, looking down at her. There was sunlight coming through the windows up there but down here, surrounded by people, it was like being lost in a forest.

She made eight good steps before she stumbled and fell into a cameraman who backed off then kept shooting her on the floor while she gathered herself back up, her side shrieking in pain.

. . . your part in the biggest scandal the department has ever had did you have a love affair with O'Brien like you did with McNally will you quit the force now what future do you see with the department . . .

The stairway looked a hundred miles away. Merci felt a great rush of fury and sadness wash over her and her vision blurred and she felt herself pushing through the bodies but getting nowhere. She was aware of the tan uniforms around then, pressing in even harder. Shouting. Hard voices, angry voices.

They're going to shoot me, she thought. They're going to shoot me right here. She wanted to scream but she couldn't—she drew a breath but knew if she screamed they'd kill her on the spot.

Suddenly she understood what she had to do. She'd thought about it before, but the answer had always been no. But not now. Now it made sense, the only sense she could see. She got her badge holder from inside her coat and tried to drop it to the floor but she was crushed up so tight against the uniforms that it didn't fall. Instead, it wedged between her upraised arm and the chest of some deputy she'd never seen in her life and he looked her straight in the face with hate and backed away a half step and the black leather holder fell.

Then came a voice she'd heard before but couldn't place, so clear and furious, piercing through the shouting. "*Get back, get away, let me through goddamnit, let me through. . . .*"

She tried to take a step but couldn't. Her face was pushed into a tan, starched shirt. She could feel the great weight of the bodies around her, pushing her left, then right. She couldn't move forward even a step.

Then there was light. And space. She wondered if she was passing out but she had never passed out in her life and wasn't sure what it was like. She tripped and fell again and she looked for her badge on the floor but it was gone now and that was fine, her mind made up, this was over now, this was the end.

She made it to one knee. She heard shouting and curses, a fight of some kind, the *humpff* of contact. Her leg was killing her; it felt like she'd been shot in the side all over again. A strong hand fixed on her arm and yanked her up and she wondered if she was about to get punched. Someone fell in beside her and shoved her through the clot of bodies.

"Get back, get away goddamnit let us through. . . ."

Zamorra pushed her straight ahead. He was strong and rough and he pushed her like she was a weapon or a tool, something that couldn't be broken. He reached around her with his free hand and stuffed something into her inside coat pocket. "Think about that," he said. He pulled her up the stairs at a run and somehow she got her foot on each step and made it to the top.

The big lobby spread before her, bodies frozen, all eyes turned to her. She was breathing hard and she felt like an animal looking for a place to run.

The Men fell in beside her. She couldn't speak. Clark grim and Tim jabbering happily, jostled but firm in her father's arms. Tim reached out and she took him and she knew that in spite of having nothing, she had everything.

A bunch of uniforms closed in around her then, giving her space. Joe Casik was one of them. And some guys she didn't even know. Two patrolwomen. Plainclothes, too—both

Wheeler and Teague. Kathy Hulet from vice. Timmerman from the firing range. Gilliam, Ike Sumich and two more of the lab people. Some of the burg-theft investigators, a couple more from vice, a sour old lieutenant who hadn't said more than two sentences to her in ten years. Gary Brice, no tape recorder, no pen or notebook in sight, looking like he had no idea what to do but was ready to fight.

She started across the lobby floor toward the door. One of the video shooters circled around in front of her. He kept his distance and did his work. The next thing Merci knew she was outside the building and into a bright winter afternoon, sunlight breaking through enormous white clouds, a cold wind in her face.

T. Jefferson Parker returns with a moody, sexy, suspenseful novel about a scarred man, the father he idolized, and the secret he uncovers in

SILENT JOE

One

"Drive hard, Joe. Mary Ann's blue again, so I want to be home by ten."

This from the boss, Will. Will Trona, Orange County Supervisor, First District. Mary Ann is his wife.

"Yes, sir."

"Talk while you drive. Are you carrying?"

"The usual."

Will was on edge again. Lots of that lately. He sat down beside me like he usually did. Never in the backseat unless he was in conference. Only in the front, where he could watch the road and the gauges and me. He loved speed. Loved coming out of a turn with his head thrown back against the rest. He'd always ask me how I did it, go that fast into a turn and keep the car on the road.

And I always gave him the same answer: "Slow in, fast out," which is the first thing they teach you about curves in any driving school. A good car can do things most people think are impossible.

We headed down from Will's home in the Tustin hills. It was evening in the middle of June, the sun hanging in a pink haze of clouds and smog. Lots of new mansions up there, but Will's house wasn't one of them. Supervisors make a decent salary, plus some perks. Orange County is one of the most expensive places in the country. Will's place was a tear-down by the new standards of the neighborhood. Just old and plain, nothing wrong with it besides that.

In fact, it was a good house. More than good. I know because I grew up in it. Will's my father, kind of.

"First stop is the Front," he said, checking his watch. "Medina's finally peeking out the windows again."

He talked without looking at me. Leaned back his head, eyelids half down, but his eyes moving. He usually looked like he was disappointed with what he saw. Like he was judging it, trying to find a way to make it better. But there was also something affectionate in his expression. Pride of ownership.

Will reached down between his feet and snapped open his leather briefcase. He took out the black calendar, set the briefcase back on the floorboard, then started scribbling with a pen. He liked to talk while he wrote. Sometimes it was to himself, and sometimes it was to me. Growing up with him since I was five, working nights for him since I was sixteen, I've come to know when he's talking to me or talking to himself.

"Medina's getting a second chance. He registers five hundred illegal aliens to vote, they tell a *Times* reporter that they're illegals, but they're allowed to vote in a United States election. Allowed to, because Medina told them they could. And they all voted for me, because Medina told them to. Now, what am I supposed to do with that?"

I'd already thought about it. I checked the rearview as I answered. "Distance yourself. Five hundred votes isn't worth the scandal."

"That's shortsighted, Joe. Mean-spirited and stupid is what it is. I get the whole Latino vote thanks to Medina, and you think I should toss him overboard? Who taught you to treat your friends like that?"

Will's always teaching. Testing. Revising. Arguing it out. Saying things to see how they sound, to see if he believes them or not.

I've learned to see some things Will's way. Other things I'll never learn. Will Trona made me what I am, but even Will can only do so much. I'm less than half his age. I've got a long way to go.

But one thing Will taught me is to make up your mind fast and put the whole weight of your being behind that decision. Instantly. Later, if you have to change your mind, put all your weight behind *that* decision. Never be afraid to be wrong. Will hates only two things: indecision and stubbornness.

So I said, "You need the Latino vote to carry the First District, sir. You know that. And those votes won't go away. They love you."

Will shook his head and wrote again. He's a handsome

man, good build, strong in the neck and deep in the chest, with hands that got strong and dark working summers in construction, helping himself through school after Vietnam. Black hair combed back, gray on the sides, blue eyes. When he looks at you it's the same expression he gets in the car, head back a little, almost sleepy, but the eyes are alert. And if he smiles, the lines of his fifty-four years frame it in a way that convinces people that he knows and likes them. Most of the time, he does.

"Joe, pay attention to Medina tonight. Mouth shut, eyes open. You might actually learn something."

Mouth shut, eyes open. You might actually learn something.

One of Will's earliest lessons.

He closed the calendar and slid it back into the briefcase. Clicked it shut. Looked at his watch again. Then he leaned against the headrest and lowered his eyelids halfway and watched the white middle-class boulevard of Tustin become the *barrio* of Santa Ana.

"How was work today?"

"Quiet, sir."

"It's always quiet in there. Until there's a fight or a race riot."

"Yes."

By day, I'm a deputy for the Orange County Sheriff's Department. I work the Central Jail Complex, as do all new deputies. I've worked the jail four years now. Another year,

I'll qualify for reassignment to patrol and start becoming a real cop. I'm twenty-four years old.

I became a deputy because Will told me to. That's what he was, until he got elected supervisor. Will told me to become a deputy because he thought it would be good for me, and because he thought it would be useful for him to have a "kick-ass son" in the sheriff's department.

• • •

Down on Fourth Street, not far from the jail where I work, there's the Hispanic American Cultural Front. It's Jaime Medina's outfit. HACF does good things—distributes money and goods to the Hispanic poor, offers scholarships and stipends for needy students, expedites immigration, shelters families in crisis, all that.

But because of this misunderstanding about when Medina's almost-citizens could vote, the DA is considering closing down the place on charges of conspiracy and election fraud. They raided the HACF building last week for records. Front-page picture of guys in suits lugging cardboard boxes to a van.

Will shouldn't have been going there, with an investigation pending. And he's good friends with the DA, Philip Dent—one more reason to keep his nose clean while the investigation played out. But Will also represents Medina's district on the Board of Supervisors, a district you can't win without the Hispanic vote and Hispanic dollars. Another political pinch, one of the thousands in any supervisor's life. Sooner or later he'll have to take a stand, because, as Will taught me early on, politics is action.

"Joe, Jennifer is going to have something for us. While I'm talking to Jaime, put it in the trunk and lock it."

"Yes, sir."

I turned left off the boulevard, checking the mirrors again, looking out at the *zapateria* on one corner, the bridal store on the other with all the white-laced mannequins in the window. I studied the cars behind us, the people on the sidewalk. I was a little nervy myself that evening. Something in the air? Maybe. Maybe nothing that obvious. Even with the windows up and the air conditioner blowing you could hear the Mexican music jumping from the *discoteca.* A polka on mescaline. A dark-faced man in a white cowboy hat and boots stopped at the curb to let us turn, maybe recognizing Will Trona's car, maybe not, his face a walnut deadpan that had seen everything and was no longer impressed by any of it.

Then into a dirt parking lot in the shade of a huge pepper tree, facing the back door of the HACF headquarters. We stepped into the pleasant heat and Will, dressed in his usual trim dark suit and carrying his leather briefcase, led the way in.

The back doors were locked so Will rapped hard.

"Open up, Jaime! *La Migra!*"

The door cracked open, then swung all the way.

"As usual, you're not funny," said Jaime. He was a slender young man with stooped shoulders, tortoiseshell eyeglasses and khaki trousers that looked two sizes too big. "The racists raid me and you run away."

"So now I'm back. Let's do business. I'm in a hurry."

Medina turned and walked down the hall, Will following, then me.

They went into the office and Jaime shut the door behind them, acknowledging me for the first time with a hurried nod as the door shut. I'm used to being ignored, prefer it. With a face like mine, you don't want people paying attention to you. One of the first things Will taught me was that people were far less eager to gawk at me than I thought they were. He said that most people were afraid to even look. He was right. That was nineteen years ago, when he first took me into his home.

I went down the hall, through a set of saloon doors, and checked the work room. There were six stations: desk, phone, stacks of papers, and three chairs at each for clients. American flag on one wall, Mexican one on the other, travel posters, soccer posters, bullfight posters.

Quiet.

No clients since the raid.

No workers since the raid, except Jennifer, the assistant director under Jaime.

"Good evening, Miss Avila." I took off my hat.

"Mr. Trona. Good evening."

She came over, offered her hand and I shook it. She's a black-haired beauty, thirty, divorced with two. Smooth fingers. Wearing a man's white cotton shirt tucked into her jeans, small waist, nice straight shoulders, black boots. She changed to an apple-red lipstick a few months back, after a year of cinnamon brown.

"Will must be here."

"They're in Jaime's office."

She looked past me down the hall, just a reflexive glance, then walked back to her desk. Jennifer is taken with the boss. This is one of the many secrets I'm not supposed to know. The world is layered with them.

She said, "That thing for you is over by my chair."

"I'll get it, thank you."

It was a U.S. Open tennis bag, a big black one with a blazing yellow ball on it. Heavy. I carried it back out to the car and set it on the asphalt while I disarmed the alarm and opened the trunk. Then I set it in and spread a blanket over it, locked the trunk again, set the alarm.

Back inside I got a magazine from the lobby, then rolled a chair into the hallway and sat outside Jaime Medina's office.

Medina: *You've got to talk to Phil Dent, man. . . .*

Will: *I know him, Jaime. I don't own him.*

Medina: *Right . . . that's not your job, my . . . friend. . . .*

Jennifer walked past me, fresh with scent, and leaned into the office without knocking.

"Coffee, beer? Hi, Will."

"Coffee, please."

She whisked by me without a look, then back again a minute later with a couple of mugs in one hand and a carton of milk in the other.

She went into the office. Will muttered something and all three laughed. She came out and shut the door and looked at me like I'd just gotten there.

"Anything for you, Mr. Trona?"

"Nothing, thank you. I'm fine."

She walked past me and back to her station.

I spread the magazine across my knee but didn't look at it. My job is to watch and listen, not read. *Mouth shut, eyes open.*

I heard the traffic on the boulevard. I heard the air conditioner hum. I heard a car go by with a subwoofer that you could feel in your chest. I still felt a little wrong about things, but I didn't know why. Maybe it was just Will's mood rubbing off on me. I often catch myself adopting his feelings. Maybe because he adopted me as his son. I heard Jennifer dialing a telephone.

Medina: *There's all that tobacco settlement money, man . . . like a billion plus you're—*

Will: *That billion isn't mine, it's the county's, Jaime. I can't hand it over in a pillowcase. Didn't the ninety help?*

Jennifer: *Get Pearlita.*

Medina: *Every bit helps. But what am I going to do when it's gone? Sit and watch this place go straight to hell? We need the money for operations, Will. We need it for job training, for lawyers, for food, man, we need it for . . .*

Jennifer: *Okay, okay. Yeah, he's here right now.*

Medina: . . . *we can't even do anything when some poor pregnant Latina gets run over and killed a block from her apartment. We can't do anything when a Guatemalan kid gets shot to death by fascist Newport Beach cops. We're handcuffed, man, dead in the water.*

Will: *It's awful what happened, Jaime. I know it is.*

Medina: *Then help us find a way to help them, Will.*

I heard Jennifer put the phone back in its cradle. She turned my way but I didn't look up from the magazine.

Will: *You helped me find Savannah, so maybe Jack will take care of you. And the Reverend will put in a good word for you and the Front. I have already.*

Medina: *We need more than good words, Will.*

The office door opened. Medina, face pinched, led us down the hall and shook hands with both of us at the back door. Jennifer walked us outside, left the door open behind her.

Will gave me a nod. I went to the car, started the engine and hit the air conditioner. I could see them in the side mirror, Will in his dark suit and Jennifer in her jeans and boots and crisp white shirt, standing in the light of the open door. They talked for a while. Will set his briefcase on the asphalt.

Then he shook her hand like Will's shaken a million hands: an open-palmed reach and clinch, the left hand coming forward to enclose yours while he leans his head back in a posture of welcome and possession as he smiles at you.

"I love you," she said.

I couldn't hear anything over the air conditioner, but it was easy to read her apple-red lips.

Will reached into his pocket and handed her the money that I'd counted, rolled and rubber-banded for him, about the size of a half-smoked Churchill: just a couple of grand to help out some of her friends.

"I love you," he said back.

We drove out of Santa Ana and into Tustin. Will directed me to Tustin High School, had me pull up alongside the tennis courts. Not much tennis action by then, just two of the courts being used.

"Joe, fetch that tennis bag out of the trunk and take it over to the middle court. Leave it on the bench."

"Yes, sir."

When I got back we sat in silence for a minute or two. Will checked his watch.

"What's in the bag, Dad?"

"Silence."

"Is that an answer or an order, sir?"

"Reverend Daniel at the Grove," he said.

• • •

The Grove Club is never called the Grove Club by its members, just the Grove. It's hidden in the south county hills, off the 241 Toll Road, then up a winding private drive and past a gate staffed by two armed guards, usually moonlighting deputies. You can't see the Grove from any public road.

A canopy of enormous palm, sycamore and eucalyptus trees obscures aerial views. It has never been pictured in a newspaper or on the TV news.

I took the first few miles of the 241 at ninety miles an hour. The electronic marquee said "Take the Toll Road—Because Life is Too Short!" The marquee was the only light out there in miles and miles of dark hills. Just a couple other cars in sight.

Politically, Will fought all four of the toll roads because—although the public has to repair them, maintain them, and pay exorbitantly high tolls to drive on them—they're privately owned. The profits go into the pockets of the Toll Roads Agency. TRA sounds like a public outfit, but it's not—it's a consortium of extremely wealthy developers who are raising buildings along the toll roads before the asphalt is even dry. In south Orange County, you can watch half a city go up overnight.

There's more to the story. The TRA guys got the State Assembly to stop maintaining certain public highways in Orange County. The highways go unrepaired and unimproved through the year 2006, which guarantees customers for the toll roads because the unrepaired highways are dangerous and clotted with traffic six hours a day.

Anyway, Will lost that battle but was half glad that he did, because you can drive seriously fast on the spanking-new toll roads. We use them all the time, due to Will's hatred of traffic and love of speed.

Once I got past the first toll plaza I opened her up past

one-twenty and Will leaned over to get a good look at the speedometer, then sat back.

He chuckled. "Yeah, Joe."

Six months ago Will and his fellow supervisors voted themselves a car-allowance increase of two hundred percent, which allowed him to lease a BMW 750IL. The stock engine gets 330 horsepower out of 12 cylinders. It's a good car, fast but not quick, wakes up at sixty, stable at 160 mph, corners beautifully for a big sedan. Off the line it's not going to blow your hair back—a Saleen Cobra clobbered me at a traffic light last week

"Ah," he said quietly. "This feels good."

I pushed the throttle through the kick-down switch and the car hesitated for a fraction of a second, then barreled up to one-thirty-five, then one-forty. This model was built with a kill switch at 155 mph, but Will had me install a Dinan chip to override the governor. The chip also brought the horsepower up to 370. Will likes to listen to the muffled shriek of that engine under full acceleration, and so do I. When the German horses are running hard, nothing beats them for an honest ride.

"Son, sometimes I wish this road was ten thousand miles long. We could just drive for hours. Away from the Grub. I loathe the Grub."

Grub, for Grove Club—Will's contraction. He checked the time again.

"I know," I said.

Even though he loathes the Grub, the boss is a member

because he needs to be a member. As a man who isn't afraid to piss on the flames of free enterprise for the occasional good of the county, Will Trona is not Grove material.

But as a politician who votes himself a stupidly expensive car to be driven at criminal speeds on semi-work-related business, he becomes Grove material.

Obviously, as the supervisor of the powerful First District, he helps run the government, and the government can influence the business interests that dominate the Grove, so the Grove needs Will, too.

Will told me he pays two grand a month membership dues, all of which is covered by patrons. Dues for public servants are "nominal" because no honest one can afford the usual costs of membership. Most of the money goes into the Grove Trust, then into its Research & Action Committee, a nonprofit 527 Organization that operates free of both the FEC and the IRS.

Every year the trust coughs up several undisclosed millions for the causes and lobbies it thinks are vital to its interests. Its interests are profit and power. But they're interested in more than those things, too. Last year, for instance, the Grove Trust donated $60,000 to the Hillview Home for Children. That's enough for two mid-level salaried positions, for one year. I think highly of Hillview, and the struggle they go through for money. Hillview was where I spent most of the first five years of my life.

• • •

Two off-duty deputies logged us in and raised the gate. The Grove sat one mile in, tucked in a valley between the hills. It's an enclosed hacienda-style building, built around a large courtyard. The rounded archways of the colonnades are brick and adobe, wrapped by purple bougainvillea. The courtyard gardens and fountain are illuminated by recessed lights, and they glow from a distance like an emerald wrapped in tissue. The building itself is kept mostly dark on the outside.

I parked the car and followed Will to the entrance, where another off-duty cop wrote our names onto his sheet. He was about to ask me my name when I tipped back my hat to let him see who I was. I have notoriety because of this face. It's unmistakable. What happened to it was a big story when I was a baby.

Will led the way into the dining room, shook a few hands. I stood back, folding mine in front of me. An average night Grub: half the tables were couples, mostly older, lots of gray hair and diamonds set off by dinner jackets and dresses. Three major developers—one commercial and two residential. A building industry lobbyist who had formerly served as supervisor. Two assemblymen, a state senator, the lieutenant governor's top aide. A four-top of venture capitalists. A table of thirty-something guys made billionaires by the NASDAQ back in ninety-nine.

We went up the stairs to the lounge, which is a large room with an island bar, billiards tables and booths around the perimeter.

Will took his usual booth. I chose a cue and racked the table nearest the booth, where I could entertain myself and eavesdrop without making Will's guests nervous.

I glanced up at the third floor. I could see the wide burnished staircase and the closed door to one of the hospitality suites. A waiter knocked. Hush-hush stuff, up in those suites. Rich men and their dull secrets. I've spent time in all of them.

I got a good break, watched three balls clunk into their pockets.

The Reverend Daniel Alter, dapper and gray-haired, arrived exactly on time. He touched my arm on his way by, but didn't say anything. I watched him shake hands with Will, slide into the booth across from him, then draw the privacy curtain.

The Reverend Daniel runs an enormous "television ministry." The broadcasts originate in his multimillion-dollar "Chapel of Light" here in Orange County, and they go worldwide. You've probably seen him on TV. Daniel's sermons are upbeat and optimistic. On his show he sells Christian products—from compact discs and inspirational videos to Chapel of Light keychains that really light up. The money that floods in is tax-free and no one knows where it goes, not even Will Trona. That's what he tells me, anyway.

Reverend Daniel: *Here's this.*

Will: *Good-good.*

Reverend Daniel: *The bullpen is killing us.*

Will: *Then score more runs. I got the bag from Jaime.*

Reverend Daniel: *Do you have her?*

Will: *I know where she is. But I'm not so sure I trust those people with her.*

Reverend Daniel: *What could you mean by that?*

Will: *We'll see what.*

Reverend Daniel: *You've done a wonderful thing, Will. And Jack's done his part. It's all going to work out.*

A long pause then, while I banked the two ball across the felt and into a corner pocket.

Reverend Daniel: *I'm counting on you. Let God work this miracle for me through you.*

Will: *I don't think your God wants to do any miracles for you, Daniel. You've gotten about a thousand too many as it is.*

Reverend Daniel: *Don't be pissy, Will. I thought this was your kind of thing. Is everything set?*

Will: *It's been arranged, Dan. Don't worry.*

Reverend Daniel: *You know, Will, the Lord really does work in mysterious ways.*

Then the Reverend Daniel slid back the curtain and they both stepped out. Daniel glanced at the table, then looked at me with his half smile.

"I'd recommend the six," he said. "With plenty of follow."

Will clapped him on the shoulder and Reverend Daniel headed for the bar.

Will checked his watch.

"Let's go, Joe. We're picking up a package, making a delivery, then calling it quits. It's been a ball-buster of a day."

As we left the lounge, the Reverend sat at the bar next to a woman with shiny black hair and watched us go.

• • •

The fog rolled in as the night cooled, big swirls puffing in from the Pacific. Par for June. Down at the coast they call it June Gloom. When we got out of the hills and back into cell range, Will's phone went off.

He said, "Trona," then he listened a moment. "You got her, right?"

Listened again, then flipped the phone shut.

"Joe, we've got a package at seven thirty-three Lind Street, Anaheim. Flog this pompous piece of tin and get us over there. Boy, I'll be glad when this day's over."

"Yes, sir." I checked the mirrors, hit a hundred in less than ten seconds. "What's in this package, boss?"

"We're trying to do a good deed."

When we hit the Tustin city limits Will's phone rang again. He answered and listened. Then he said, "Things are lining up. I'll do what I can do, but I still can't turn coal into a diamond."

He flipped the phone shut, sighed.

We were almost into Anaheim when he dialed out.

"Looks like we'll be there on time," was all he said.

It was an apartment backing an alley in the ugly part of

Anaheim. Will told me to park in the alley. It was so narrow another car couldn't get by unless we moved. There was a row of carports to our left, and to our right a cinder-block wall wild with graffiti. Not a creature stirring, just the fog easing along.

"Be unfriendly," he said. Which is what he said if he thought there could be trouble, or if he just wanted me to intimidate people.

Will stood behind me as I knocked with my left hand, my right up under my coat lapel on the grip of one of the two forty-five Automatic Colt Pistols I usually carry.

"Yes? Who is it?"

"Open the door," I said.

The door cracked. A woman's face, fat, squinting until she saw my face, then her eyes opened wider.

I pushed past her and stepped inside. Her hands were empty and there was no movement behind her, just the sound of a TV.

She looked at my face, then I gave her a look at what was under my coat. Her eyes moved from the gun to my face, then back again. Trapped between two horror shows. She raised her hands slowly, deciding to look at the floor.

The apartment smelled of bacon and cigarettes. Bedsheets for curtains, carpet worn to the padding, padding worn to the plywood.

"I don' know anything about this, mister. They say come and watch a girl, I come and watch a girl. I don' know—"

Will, then: "Be calm, *señora*. She's okay, son. Where are they?"

She nodded toward the bedroom. "She here. He no here. Watching television."

"Stay put," I said to her. "What do I do, Boss?"

"Go get her."

The girl stood up from the floor when I walked in. She was small, blonde pale. Blue jeans and a Cirque du Soleil T-shirt, white sneakers. Twelve years old, maybe.

She studied my face. Children will do that sometimes, just stare. Often, they'll make a face, sometimes cry. Sometimes they run. I saw her eyes go afraid and her chin tremble.

"I'm Joe."

"I'm Savannah," she said very quietly.

Then she stepped forward and offered her small, quivering hand. I shook it. I pulled the brim of my hat down a little more, to help her.

"How do you do?" she asked.

"I'm not sure. Please come with me, though."

She slung a Pocahontas backpack over one shoulder and led the way out.

Going back down the stairs to the alley, I held the handle of my weapon. Will held the girl's hand.

I opened the passenger-side doors for them and waited while Will took her backpack off, strapped her in, adjusted the shoulder restraint for her small frame, showed her how the armrests tilted out of the seat back.

Of all the things that he is—husband, politician, agitator, manipulator, dreamer—I can forget that he is a father, too. An adoptive father, maybe the most generous fathers of all.

He had his hand on her shoulder, talking quietly, one foot dangling out the open door.

Headlights swerved toward us and I heard a car engine down the alley in front of me. No hurry, no threat, probably a renter heading for his carport.

"Sir, let's get going."

"I'm talking."

I heard another car coming up from behind, saw the headlight beams crawl up the shiny black trunk of the BMW.

I moved closer to the open rear door. "You should get in the car, Boss."

"I'm talking to Savannah."

I looked behind me, then ahead. Coming the same speed, no hurry, no brights. No problem?

Then both cars stopped. Eighty feet ahead, eighty feet behind. They vanished in a blanket of moving fog, then appeared again. I couldn't tell makes or models, had no chance at all on the plates.

"Possible trouble, sir."

"Where?"

"Everywhere."

I kicked Will's dangling foot in and slammed the door, got the remote pad out of my pocket.

Car doors opening. The shuffle of feet on asphalt.

In the fog-dulled wash of the headlights in front of me I saw three figures moving, growing larger. One tall, two shorter. Long coats, collars up, faces hard to see.

I threw open my door and pulled on the headlights, slammed the door closed behind me and locked everything with the remote.

I put my right hand under my jacket and on the butt of one forty-five. I turned and looked behind: two more coats emerging through the smoky headlights of their car. I put my left hand on the other ACP, which left me crossing my chest with both hands, like I was cold.

Then a deep, resonant voice from ahead, bouncing off the alley wall and the garages, hard to locate but easy to hear.

"Will! Ah, Will Trona! Let's talk."

Will was out of the car before I could stop him.

"Watch Savannah," he said. "I'll get rid of this dingleberry."

I shut the door on her and stepped after him, but he reeled and hissed straight into my face.

"I said watch the girl, Joe! So watch the girl!"

I stayed back with her but I watched him walk away, blanched white in the cross fire of the headlight beams.

The Tall One stepped forward. I couldn't see much of his face: couldn't even guess an age. His hands were in his coat pockets.

The two guys behind me had shaded to their left, putting me between them and our car, automatic weapons held close up to their coats, barrels down.

They didn't move.

They had us and I knew it and there wasn't one thing I could do right then except stand there and watch.

Will stopped about six feet short of the guy, put his hands on his hips and spread his feet a little.

Words floated back with the engine noise and exhaust. I unlocked the car doors with the remote, reached in and killed the interior lights.

"What's going on, Joe?" asked the girl. "I can't see."

"Say nothing. Absolutely nothing."

"Okay."

". . . hard man to catch up with, Will Trona. . . ."

There was a strange cadence to the voice, an almost cheerful lilt to the syllables. Just a little off, like a second language learned later in life.

Will: *"Who the hell are you?"*

". . . the girl in the car?"

Will: *"You with Alex?"*

"You're with Alex." Laughter. *"Little shit too scared to show his face, ah?"*

Then Will again: *"We had a deal. Get the hell out of here."*

"Now the deal is this."

The Tall One leaned forward and a sharp explosion cracked through the alley. Will dropped to his knees and bent over.

I yanked open the rear door, jumped in, unbuckled Savannah and shoved her all the way across the seat.

Looking through the windshield I saw the Tall One step forward. I pushed open the far door, climbed around Savannah, dragged her out of the car by one arm.

"What's happening? Is Will okay?"

"Shhh."

Pulling on the girl, I turned to see the shining end of the Tall One's hand pointed down at Will. Another hard crack, Will's head jerking once, smoke rising up against the fog and into the glare of the headlights.

"Savannah," I whispered. *"Get ready to run! Two honks is me. Two honks is me."*

I picked her up and dangled her over the cinder-block wall, then let go. I heard her land, then fast footsteps. The footsteps of the men behind me got louder.

I dropped to the pavement, drew one weapon and slid back into the rear seat of the dark car. The two behind me came fast, machine guns up. They were looking at the wall, where they'd last seen me.

When they got close enough I shot them both. The left one fell hard. The right one shuddered and stopped and unleashed a wild automatic burst that jerked the firing gun back into his own face. Then a clatter and a groan.

Staying low, I backed out and spilled again onto the pavement. On elbows and knees I wriggled to the front of the car, pressing in close to the body panel, gun out ahead of me.

Even in the headlights I only saw shapes: the Tall One, the two others walking slowly toward me. And Will on the ground. Distance off. Perspective off. Everything a pale haze.

Shit, what was that?

The deep voice again: *Go see.*

I pointed my .45 toward the voices, watched the fog beyond the sights.

I think there's two down, over by the car.

Go see!

I inched the sights to my left, tracking the voice.

Then footsteps came at me, two sets, close together. Shapes coalescing in the headlights.

I can't see a goddamned thing!

The footsteps stopped.

Shit . . . it's Nix and Luke. Wasted, man. I'm not going in there. . . .

The fog blew open, then closed again. Strange-looking men.

I heard the Tall One behind them, and his clear voice cutting through the fog.

Get back here. Now! Move!

The sound of men running, shapes illuminated in the wash of headlights.

Tall One: *Get over here.*

Nix and Luke are dead over there, man. . . .

I heard two sharp cracks, and two muffled thuds. Then

two more shots, as twin orange comets flashed down from the Tall One's hand.

A moment later the car reversed with a chirp of rubber and jumped backwards, the bright slash of the headlights sweeping the asphalt. I saw the two men down beyond Will, one of them moving, one not. When the car backed out of the alley and roared down the street on the other side of the cinder blocks I ran.

Will was huddled on his knees, forehead to the ground, arms around his middle. Blood on his head and his clothes and the asphalt. I put my hand on his back.

"Oops," he whispered.

"Quiet, Boss. You're all right."

I ran back to the car and brought it forward. I got Will into the passenger seat. He sat up okay. Wet and heavy. Smell of metal. Blood on my face where his head had rested when I dragged him in.

One of the men that the Tall One had shot was still moving as I guided the big car around him. I tore out to Lincoln Boulevard running the late-night signals, my palm slick on the horn, clumps of fog tearing past the windows.

"You're okay, Will. You're going to be okay."

His head was back on the rest and his eyes were open to the headliner. A dull light in those eyes. Shoulder and shirt and lap full of blood.

"Hang on, Dad. Please hang on. We're almost there."

"Mary Ann."

I hit a hundred southbound. The cars seemed to rocket backwards at us. Will's head rattled when I shot across the lane dividers. Then he leaned forward like he always did, to watch the gauges and me.

"Everyone."

"Everyone *what*, Dad?"

He coughed a red mess onto the windshield and hung forward against his shoulder strap. Taillights rushed by.

I fishtailed down the Chapman off-ramp, ran three reds and skidded into the UC Irvine Medical Center Emergency lot, smoking to a stop on the ambulance ramp.

Will was slumped against the door. When I ran around and opened the door he fell into my arms and I carried him up the ramp, understanding that he didn't need a doctor.

I slipped to my knees but kept him balanced because it was the only thing I could do for him and I wanted to do it well. Two ER guys were running a gurney down toward us.

• • •

Hell is waiting.

I paced the emergency waiting room and the walkways outside, making the calls that needed to be made—first to my mother, Mary Ann, then to brothers Junior and Glenn.

Those were the hardest calls I'd made in my life, no contest. I couldn't tell them that Will was going to die. I couldn't tell them he was going to live. I blubbered only that he'd been shot, choking out the words.

I drove the car off the emergency ramp and parked it in the lot. The interior was urgent with the smells of blood and leather and the ugly stink of human panic.

• • •

Twenty minutes later, an emergency-room doctor told me that we had lost Will.

Lost.

That word was a bullet through my heart. It told me that Will was gone now, and gone forever. It told me that I'd let down the person I loved most on this earth, that I'd failed my primary mission. And on its spiraling, smoking way through my heart and into the night, it told me I would find the people who did this to Will and I would deal with them.

I managed to call my mother and brothers again. To give them the bullet.

Too late, of course. They were already on their way to the hospital.

Against the protests of a doctor and two sheriff deputies, I got into Will's car and drove back to the Lind Street apartment.

Red lights, yellow tape, neighbors everywhere and three blankets with bodies under them. Anaheim PD was on scene. A patrolman marched at my car with a flashlight, waving me away.

I backed out and drove the dark streets and wide empty boulevards looking for the girl. I crawled along at ten miles an hour, honking twice, lightly, over and over. Up and down, going slow, brights on and all four windows down. Come out, come out wherever you are. The fog was still thick and sometimes I couldn't even see a block ahead. Every few minutes I'd pull over, stop, honk again and listen. Watch.

I finally got Mom on my cell phone and she sounded close to panic. She was at the hospital. They wouldn't let her see him. I did my best to keep her talking and settle her down, told her to call Reverend Alter, then turned my car around for UCI Medical Center just as an Anaheim PD cruiser pulled me over. Both officers were tight, fingering their sidearms as I badged them.

"What in hell are you doing here, Deputy?"

"Looking for a girl."

"Is that blood in the car?"

"Yes, it is."

"Step out, please, slowly. Hands away from your body, Mr. Trona."

Two

I spent the next three hours at the Anaheim PD with two homicide detectives—the tall pale one was Guy Alagna and the stocky dark one was Lucia Fuentes.

As soon as I told them about Savannah, Fuentes left the interview room and stayed away for half an hour. Alagna, whose nose hooked from his face like a sharp white beak, asked me for the third time if I could describe the tall gunman to him.

"Too dark," I said for the third time. "Too much fog. They were all wearing long coats."

I was getting weary. I was beginning to note all the things that had changed. Would change. The rest of my life without him alive. Ever. The world was brand-new to me, and I hated it.

"And those coats again, Joe. What did they look like?"

I described the long overcoats for the third time. I looked down at my hat, balanced on my knee.

"Color?"

"Night, Detective Alagna. Fog. No colors."

"Okay, all right."

Then he was silent for a long beat. I could feel his stare on my face. Sooner or later, most people have to gawk.

I drank bad coffee from a foam cup and looked at the two-way mirror, picturing the men in the June fog, Will approaching. June Gloom with the blade of murder hidden in it. I strained to catch a glimpse of the Tall One's face—just one feature, just one thing to go on. Nothing. Fog. Motion. Exhaust rising, voices. The insulting little pop of that handgun. And again.

Every few minutes a roar would start building in my ears, beginning low, like waves on a distant beach, then getting louder and louder until my head was two inches from a jet turbine. But it wasn't a jet, it was a voice, and the voice said only three words over and over, louder and louder: *you killed him you killed him you killed him you killed him you killed him you killed him you killed him* . . .

Please stop. Remember. Eyes open, mouth shut.

I'll get rid of this dingleberry.

How did Will know he was a dingleberry?

Will! Ah, Will Trona! Let's talk.

The deep and resonant voice replayed in my mind with a haunting clarity. I heard the odd lilt of the words, almost cheerful.

Did the shooter know him, or just pretend to?

. . . you with Alex?

"And you're sure they didn't take anything off him?" Alagna asked again.

"They took his life, sir."

In the corner of my eye I saw him studying me. Then I turned on him and he looked away. People are ashamed of themselves when I catch them staring, but not before I catch them.

"You know what I mean, Joe."

"Nothing that I saw, Detective."

"Back to the car again. They take anything from the car?"

"They never touched the car."

"Okay, all right. So, let me get this straight—the shooter called Will by name. And Will asked if the shooter was with Alex. And Will said a deal's a deal, or something like that, and the guy shot him in the gut?"

"The shooter said, 'Now the deal is this.' "

And then he asked again about the two men I'd shot, both dead on scene when the cops got there. I told him again, exactly what had happened. He wouldn't give me their names or anything else about them.

"So, you couldn't see well enough to describe the man who shot your father, but you could see well enough to drop two guys, moving, with two shots."

"Like I said, sir, they were close—twenty feet maybe."

"I guess you're a good shot."

"I'm a good shot."

Everything I told Alagna and Fuentes was correct, though I forgot a few things.

For example, I forgot to mention Will's briefcase. He rarely went anywhere without it, so it contained the outlines of his life. More than the outlines. It held his calendar and appointment books, his notes and letters, his drafts and reports, his to-do list, his doodles. Everything he might use in a day—from a tiny tape recorder to a toothbrush and paste—Will carried with him in that old leather case. I carried it with me into the interview room and set it beside me as if it were my own. No one questioned it.

And I didn't consider the tennis bag we'd picked up from the HACF to be Alagna's business, either.

I wasn't about to offer too much to a cop I didn't know, some paleface who had to ask three times what an overcoat looked like.

I also forgot to mention Will's gift to Jennifer Avila that evening, the two thousand dollars I'd counted and rolled. Likewise, their private words.

I forgot that I heard anything but hello and good-bye between Will, Jaime Medina and the Reverend Daniel Alter.

I forgot to recount Will's quick conversations on his cell phone, just minutes before he died. And I wondered how I could get a phone company log of those calls. A homicide investigator sure could, but a fourth-year deputy? It would take a while.

And I forgot to mention that Mary Ann, my adoptive mother, had been blue lately, and that Will was trying hard to get home by ten.

All of that was Will's business; none of it was Alagna's.

Lucia Fuentes barreled back into the room. "One of the shooters is hanging on. No ID on him, but he's alive."

Alagna looked at me. "Maybe he can fill in some of Mr. Trona's sizable gaps."

I nodded but said nothing. Instead I stared down at Will's briefcase, noting the drop of dried blood near the handle. I hoped Alagna wouldn't notice it. I didn't think he would.

"But I struck out on the girl," Fuentes continued. "Nothing at all on a missing twelve-year-old named Savannah. The National Center, the FBI, Sacramento—not even Joe's sheriffs here—nobody's looking for her. Maybe it's an alias."

Alagna stared at me. "I doubt her daddy lets her run around with fifty-year-old guys after dark."

"Maybe that's exactly what her daddy does," snapped Fuentes.

"Joe, you know if the supervisor was bent that way?"

I stared back at Alagna then, and a flush came to his waxy skin.

"Detective Alagna, he was a good man." I said. "And I'll pretend you didn't ask that stupid question."

"Big words from a fourth-year jailer."

"We can settle differences any way you'd like, sir."

"I don't settle."

"Come on, you assholes," said Füentes. "What's wrong with you, Guy?"

Alagna looked away, his ears turning red. It was quite a contrast with his white beak of a nose.

What was wrong with Guy was that he was afraid of me, and angry about it. Nothing in the world seems to make healthy, tough cops madder than a twenty-four-year-old monster who can't be intimidated.

I not only have a face that looks like something made in hell, but I'm tall and strong. I'm conversant with most weapons, and I've spent nearly my whole life learning how to defend myself—every method and school, every technique you can imagine—so that what happened when I was nine months old never happens again. I've promised myself that it will never happen again.

But my best weapon is that people sense I'm not afraid of anything. Maybe it's the scar tissue. My eyes. My voice. I really don't know.

In fact, there are two things I'm afraid of. One is my father, my real father, the one who did this to me when I was nine months old. His name is Thor Svendson and he's out there somewhere. If he ever appears again I'll be ready. I have five black belts, two regional Golden Gloves titles and a Sheriff Department Distinguished Marksman pin to prove I'm ready.

The other thing that terrified me—although I didn't know it until then—was living without Will. And of the two, life without Will was by far the worst.

So, with my ruined face and apparent fearlessness, most people are afraid of me. It's been true since I was very young. As I grew used to people fearing me, I tried to develop good manners, to strike some balance. I came to believe that they were mandatory for a man with a face like mine. I've worked almost as hard at having good manners as I have at mastering Ken-po, or the recoil nuances of the Colt .45 ACP.

"So Joe," said Lucia Fuentes. "Explain the girl to us. If your father wasn't that way, then what was he doing with her?"

"I'm not sure. He said he was trying to do a good deed."

They looked at each other.

Then the voice started building again inside me: *you killed him you killed him you killed him . . .*

I felt like I was in that fog again, the fog that rolled in the night before. Secret fog. Killer fog. I wished I could blow it all away, step from it into something clear and sunny and true. I couldn't do that, but I had a quiet spot I could go to. I can go there any time I want. So I went.

"I've told you what I know," I said, standing, hat in hand. "Call me anytime if I can help more. I'd like to know who the girl was, Detectives. I'd like to help her if I can. Pardon me, but I have to go to work now, or I'll be late."

Alagna looked at Fuentes like she should stop me.

Fuentes looked at me like someone missing her bus. When I walked out the sun was just starting to come up.

The reporters converged and I was happy to see them. I just gave them the basics, but I made sure they knew that a girl named Savannah was loose in the night. I described her exactly, right down to her clothing and backpack and good manners and fine straight hair. I even sketched her face on my notepad as best I could. It came out slightly better than nothing.

The reporters liked this: here was a chance to help find her, maybe do something good. They're the second most cynical people, after cops.

• • •

Sunrise in the county, and me alone in Will's car, the freeways jammed already, everybody acting like Will was still alive. What was wrong with these fools? And what was wrong with Alagna and Fuentes, letting me drive off in a car that was part of a homicide scene, instead of impounding it?

I got through to Mom on my cell phone again. Reverend Daniel Alter had met her at the hospital and she was now in the Chapel of Light sanctuary. She had taken a mild sedative. Her voice sounded light and insubstantial. One of the assistant ministers was going to take her home because she felt too woozy to drive. I told her I'd drive her home myself, but she insisted that I work, stay focused, stay useful. I told her I'd be over as soon as my shift was over.

In the sheriff's gym I showered, shaved and put on my uniform, then walked across the compound to my job.

• • •

Orange County Jail. Sixth largest in the nation. Three thousand inmates, three thousand orange jumpsuits. Seventy percent of them are felons. And a hundred jailers like me, mostly young guys, armed only with pepper spray, trying to keep order. Hundreds of new inmates come through the Intake-Release Center every day, a total of seventy thousand every year. Hundreds are released back into society, every day. In and out. In and out. We call it the Loop. The jail is an enormous rotating swirl, a storm system of defeat, fury, violence and boredom.

During the day, Men's Central is my world. It's a world of strict order and, usually, quiet compliance. Power and submission. Good guys green, bad guys orange. Hands in your pockets, eyes forward, shut up. Pull your pockets, show your socks. Them and us. It's also a world of shanks whittled from bed frames, clubs made of knotted T-shirts filled with bars of soap, of rotgut liquor made from leftover bits of fruit and bread smuggled in from the mess hall, of drugs and black tattoos and kites—notes—smuggled down from the shot-callers in Tank 29 of Module F, or from protective custody in Module J, to the low-security guys who can pass them along to friends and allies on the outside. It's a world of silence. It's a world of dimly lit guard stations, so the inmates can't watch us watching them. A world of racial gangs, of respect and vengeance, of endless lies and infinite bullshit.

I like it. I like my friends and coworkers, and the delicate predatory balance between us and the inmates. I like some of the inmates at times. Their scams are clever and they manage to get away with things that surprise me. But what I like most is the orderliness of things: the buzzers and bells and schedules and rules, the heavy keys, the food we eat in the staff dining room. These are institutional things, and as an institutional boy I came to rely on them. My four years at Hillview Home for Children brought those things into my blood in a way I can't get rid of.

• • •

That morning I was scheduled to work in Module J, which is set up for the protective custody of the particularly dangerous, the notorious, the well-known, for child molesters and sexual deviants who would upset the general population, sometimes even for law enforcement personnel doing time on the wrong side of the bars.

Mod J is set up in four sectors, with a total of one hundred and seventy inmates. It's one big circle, with our guard station in the center. Between the cells and the guard station are the day rooms, which have picnic-style benches and tables, and a TV. From the dimly lit confines of the station, we can look through the glass and see into every cell. In-cell cameras make every inmate visible on the station video console, and each cell is wired for sound.

It's very quiet in Module J, and the inmates are slightly more respectful of us than they are in the other mods. Maybe it's because of the seriousness of their crimes, or because many of them are on trial and facing very long, or perhaps capital, sentences. Whatever the reasons, the men in Mod J are a little less likely to amuse themselves with chatter about my face.

My first two years I rotated between the Men's Central modules and got my fill of "shitface," "acidhead," "Frankenstein," whatever. The names didn't get to me, though the repetition almost did. I never cracked, showed my anger or lost my manners. I just learned to withdraw into the quiet spot and view the inmates with the detached interest of a birdwatcher.

Happened to you?

Nothing, why?

'Cause you got shit all over your face, shitface!

You get the picture.

Of course, people behind bars are braver than most. You're protected from them, but they're protected from you, too. Even my most sincerely murderous stare often brings nothing but added volume: *OH, look at SHITface starin' at me NOW!* As a keeper, once you step through the heavy doors of the jail, you're not just working there, you're *in* it. Sometimes, you forget. Sometimes, it feels like you've been there forever and you're going to be there another forever. It's hard on a guy who tries to have good manners.

Then you take a deep breath and remember that you've got a shift and they've got a sentence. It's like coming out of a nightmare.

In the briefing room I signed in and sat down for roll call. After that, Sergeant Delano gave us the morning book: yesterday ten blacks and ten Latinos got into it in the mess hall. It was over quickly, didn't escalate, no time for us to get out the bats and hats—our batons and riot helmets. A few bruises, a few cuts. No weapons. As a result, we were 9–13—cleared and ready—to conduct a Module F cell search at 1300. We call a surprise search a shake. Deputy Smith had discovered a shank hidden in the sole of a shower sandal—sharpened and slid directly through the rubber. There were rumors of trouble upstate. They say that inmate violence trickles down from the max pens to the jails, and at first I thought it was myth. But after three years here, I can tell you that it's true, so rumors of trouble at Pelican Bay or Folsom or Cochran or San Quentin are always taken seriously. We took up a collection for a barbecue to celebrate our captain getting a promotion, then broke.

I checked out my radio and keys, then walked the tunnel down to Mod J. When I got to the guard station I glanced at the video monitors to check my prisoners. Everybody looked fine. Gary Sargola, the Ice-Box Killer, was asleep with one leg raised because he suffers phlebitis.

Dave Hauser, assistant district attorney turned drug dealer, was watching *Good Morning America*.

Dr. Chapin Fortnell, child psychiatrist awaiting trial on thirty-eight counts of molestation of six boys over the last ten years, sat upright and alert on his cot, writing something in crayon, the sharpest instrument we allow him since he tried to open a vein with a felt-tipped marker two months ago.

Serial rapist Frankie Dilsey, convicted of three forcibles and waiting sentencing for three more, was making faces in the steel mirror over his basin, drumming his long fingers on the rim, swaying his hips to a song playing only in his head.

Sammy Nguyen, a young Vietnamese gangster charged with killing a police officer during a traffic stop, lay on his bunk staring at a picture of his girlfriend that we had allowed him to tape to the ceiling. He glanced toward the video camera like he knew I was watching, smiled, turned back to his picture of Bernadette. He's a bright guy, Sammy. Quiet for the most part, fairly polite, has his code of honor and sticks with it. He's high up in the Vietnamese gang structure, probably has fifty guys under him.

Will and Sammy had a history. They'd only met once, about two months before, in the Bamboo 33 nightclub. Will had gone there to help some of his Vietnamese friends. It was the club's grand opening, and the owners wanted Will there to certify their importance, maybe get their pictures in the papers. Will had taken Mary Ann, driven them himself, and that's why I wasn't there.

The grand opening went fine, Will said, but this handsome hood named Sammy Nguyen and his girlfriend, Bernadette, kept approaching him with some chatter about opening a savings and loan in Little Saigon. Will said he'd get back to them and tried to steer away, but Sammy and Bernadette kept hanging around until Will took Mary Ann to another table.

Next thing he knew, this Sammy cat was staring blankly at him. The gangsters call it a mad-dog, and you're supposed to show respect by looking away.

Will knew the score. He was a deputy for twenty-plus years. So he mad-dogged Sammy back, digging down deep for the thoughts that let you keep a stare. He told me he thought about 'Nam and some friends of his who died there so jerks like Sammy could live here. But a lot of good people came here, too, and he wondered what that whole war was worth. Will said he kind of got lost in the thought and time passed. And the next he knew, Sammy had looked away. That meant Sammy still hadn't gotten his respect, and according to the rules of gangland, he was entitled to murder Will Trona in order to finally get some.

Punk shit, was what Will had called it. He forgot about him until the next day, when Sammy Nguyen was arrested for allegedly gunning down a Westminster cop named Dennis Franklin. The shooting had taken place just a couple of hours after Will and Sammy talked at Bamboo 33.

Will took it hard. He didn't know Franklin but he wondered if he'd talked to Sammy better that night, heard him out about the savings and loan idea, didn't mad-dog him, maybe the hood would have left Bamboo 33 in a hopeful mood rather than a murderous one.

All Franklin had done to Sammy was pull him over for speeding on Bolsa Avenue. Will and Mary Ann contributed fifty thousand dollars to a trust for Franklin's widow and their two-year-old. The papers loved that, and wanted to know why the Tronas had singled out Dennis Franklin's family. Will said because he was a good cop, didn't mention what had happened between him and Sammy Nguyen.

I left the guard station and walked to Sammy's cell. Dim lights, near silence, the hushed setting of a dream. The he-she's—men in various stages of gender reassignment—stared at me. Clarkson, a mass murderer of children, ignored me. I walked up behind the runner—a trusty—as he pushed Sammy's breakfast tray through the slot.

"Hello, Deputy Joe. Sorry about your father."

Jailhouse gossip travels at the speed of light.

"Thank you."

Sammy sat down with the tray across his knees, but he didn't look at the food. "I met him once, you know."

I looked at him but said nothing. He'd shared this information before.

"And he was insulting to me and Bernadette. I could have had him killed for his behavior that night and been within my rights."

"Yes, you told me that before. It's baby-like, Sammy, that kind of thinking."

Sammy thought about this for a moment. He took off his glasses and set them on his pillow.

"But I didn't. I had nothing to do with this."

I believed him, because we'd been opening Sammy's incoming and outgoing mail since his arrest. I knew he was directing gang business through Bernadette. She was his lieutenant as well as his woman, and he told her everything in those letters. Sammy was inside on a murder rap, all right, but he was up to his elbows in gun trafficking, fraud, home invasion and stolen goods. He'd never once mentioned Will, or the insult, in any of his letters. If he let a contract on Will, he'd have done it through the mail with his woman.

It amazes me that a guy as bright and suspicious as Sammy wouldn't think that his mail was being read.

"Did you see it happen?"

"Yes. Five men."

"That's a contract, Joe."

"That's what it looked like."

"Were you close?"

"The fog was bad. They all wore long coats, collars up. The leader was tall."

Suspicion spread across Sammy's wide, guileful face. I routinely lie to Sammy and the other inmates—some lies too big to be believed, others too small to even sound untrue. If the inmates get only the truth, they'll strip it off you like piranha. You need some bluff to keep them back. You need a rap. That's what they use on us and that's what they get from us.

So even when you tell them the truth, like I was doing, they assume you're lying. In jail, not even the truth sounds true.

"The Cobra Kings," said Sammy. "They wear long coats, dress good. Not predictable, Joe, because their blood is mixed. Vietnamese and American. Vietnamese and black American. Vietnamese and Mexican American. GI's fucky-fucky and out comes—what do the newspapers call them, 'children of the war'? Mutts. Everybody hates them. They grow up, they find each other, make a gang in Saigon. Everybody still hates them. So they come here, land of the free. All that."

"Friends of yours?"

He shook his head no.

"The shooter knew Will by name," I said. "But I don't think Will knew him."

He smiled a flash of straight white teeth.

"Your father, maybe he had some friends that aren't so good for him. That happens in politics. People help you, but they're not good for you."

"That's not exactly news."

The smile again, wrinkles at the corners of his eyes. "You see the shooter's face, Joe?"

"Hard to see."

At this, Sammy's face was all cynicism and doubt. "You heard him say your father's name, but you didn't see his face?"

"Fog," I said.

He studied me, guessing my levels of treachery. I was happy to let him do that. Something like victory crossed his face and I wanted him to have it.

"I heard three guys got stepped on. One still alive. You do that?"

I nodded. "Two."

"How did it feel?"

"Not bad. Compared to watching my father die."

"You ever kill before?"

"No."

"This is sad, Joe. A very sad development. Who shot the other two?"

"The Tall One tried to thin the witness list."

Sammy considered. "Bad leadership. Very cold. Very Cobra King. I'd guess it was the money, though, Joe—less people to split it with."

"There was a girl," I said.

"What girl?"

"Savannah."

"Did they step on her, too?"

"No. Do you know her?"

"I do not."

"Something on a girl named Savannah would help me, Sammy. Maybe in connection with someone named Alex. No last name on either."

Sammy registers emotions convincingly and clearly, like an actor. I've watched him during interviews and visitations and he's a master of surprise, outrage, innocence, threat. He loves exaggeration.

But when he wants to give nothing away his cunning face becomes depthless and mute as a daisy. You can't see anything at all behind it, no matter how hard you look. That's what he gave me.

Then Sammy's blank look broke into a frankly optimistic expression.

"You get my rat trap yet?"

"You can't have a rat trap."

"I've got a huge rat in here. He comes and goes whenever he wants. Through the ducts."

We do have our share of rats, mice and cockroaches. But I thought he wanted the trap for something else, though I'm not sure what. Sammy likes gadgets, tools. In a cell search last week we found a pair of canine nail clippers, brand-new, still in the package. They're the kind with the small sharp blade that slides through the oval hole, and the heavy curved handles for power. He could make a good shank out of them, but I don't think he had anything that lowly in mind. Sammy isn't just a punk—Will was wrong about that. He's something more intelligent and more dangerous, and far less predictable.

Like I said, we've got stops on all of Sammy Nguyen's mail, incoming and outgoing, so the clippers didn't come through the post office. Sammy might have got them from Frankie Dilsey, in the adjacent cell, or in the day room. Maybe in the exercise pen, which is on the roof of the building. Or maybe from one of the guards. He also might have gotten them from a visitor, or his lawyer, which could get him disbarred.

I stared into Sammy Nguyen's dark eyes as he stared

back into mine. His temper is well known. Not counting officer Dennis Franklin, our homicide detectives suspect Sammy Nguyen of personally carrying out eight murders. Seven are considered to be gangland business. The other was a young man they think was moving in on Bernadette Lee, shot three times in the face in a Garden Grove parking lot.

I thought of the shooter in the fog and wondered if Sammy could have let a contract on Will some other way than in a letter to Bernadette. Sammy got fifteen minutes a day on one of the Mod J pay phones—maybe he used that.

Then the voice inside my head again, just a taunting whisper: *you killed him you killed him you killed him* . . .

I could have stepped through the bars of the cell and forced the truth out of Sammy—if he had any truth in him. He was a clever man and a murderer, but he wouldn't stand a chance against me.

Whatever I got from him would be unconstitutional and not evidentiary, but a courtroom wouldn't be the point. I could arrange with the other deputies here so that no one would ever know what really happened in Sammy's cell, or why. Those things occur, though more rarely than you might think.

But inside my mind I climbed up and got to the quiet spot and I looked out of it and told myself that if I wasn't smart enough to figure out a guy like Sammy, then maybe I shouldn't be a deputy in the first place.

Like he'd been reading my thoughts, Sammy smiled

and opened his hands, palms up. "I'm sorry your father got shot, Joe. This girl, Savannah—maybe I can find something out. You get me that trap, I'll see what I can do."

• • •

In the briefing room I heated up one of the breakfast sandwiches I keep frozen in the refrigerator. While the microwave groaned I stared down at the floor. Tears fell from my eyes and I could feel them on my cheeks and on my big scar, where tears always feel cooler, and in my mind the fog started rolling in again, trying to choke off the noise.

I had had enough.

You killed him you killed him you . . .

Through the clamor, I tried to think. And this is what I came up with: I didn't think Sammy was behind what happened. I didn't think that Sammy knew this was going to go down. I think it surprised him as much as it did Will.

The real surprise was Savannah. I could tell by his empty look when I first asked about her that Sammy was hiding something. Something he didn't want to give me right away. Something that might be valuable to me.

I didn't get it. A sweet young girl sees terrible things, she runs away into the night, and a guy like Sammy Nguyen wants to parlay her into a new rat trap.

You tell me about human nature. I give up.